MORTAL COILS

MORTAL COILS

AN ORIGINAL NOVEL FROM THE BLACK BALLAD

CHRIS DURSTON

DEDICATION

To my daughter. I hope you pick a better career than "apprentice necromancer." I'll support you either way, of course.

And to Hannah, who encouraged me to think that maybe I could write this book after all, and then made sure I actually did.

TABLE OF CONTENTS

Prologue ix
Chapter 1 1
Chapter 2 10
Chapter 3 24
Chapter 4 29
Chapter 5 39
Chapter 6 46
Chapter 7 54
Chapter 8 63
Chapter 9 72
Chapter 10 83
Chapter 11 93
Chapter 12 99
Chapter 13 109
Chapter 14 117
Chapter 15 126
Chapter 16 139
Chapter 17 148
Chapter 18 158
Chapter 19 167
Chapter 20 179
Chapter 21 194
Chapter 22 208
Chapter 23 217
Chapter 24 238
Chapter 25 245
Chapter 26 258
Chapter 27 267
Chapter 28 282
Chapter 29 293
Chapter 30 299
Chapter 31 308

CHAPTER 32 316
CHAPTER 33 326
CHAPTER 34 336
CHAPTER 35 341
CHAPTER 36 354
CHAPTER 37 367
BOOK CLUB QUESTIONS 377
AUTHOR BIO 379

PROLOGUE

At the intersection of three wide, dusty roads that cut their way through dry, dead fields, an army of the dead gathered.

From her position atop the stone tower jutting into the sky behind the mass of flesh, Mara surveyed the scene. She had perhaps a thousand undead at her command, all currently milling around aimlessly while they waited for orders. She'd served with living soldiers in the past; it was hard to deny they made for better conversation, but equally irrefutable that they were far harder to manage. Ghouls didn't cause trouble in their downtime. Not for those who commanded them, anyway.

It just makes sense, she mused, watching her force shambling around in uncoordinated, meandering loops. *Most people who want an army have to pay soldiers, feed them, keep them happy. We just recycle bodies nobody's using. Whatever anyone might think of necromancy, they can't deny it's efficient.*

"A good force," said a smooth voice from behind her.

She didn't jump; she was used to it. She'd served him for a decade, after all.

Her master, Raskith, had carefully cultivated an appearance of charisma, even of appeal; his precisely youthful face with its dark hair and neat beard, his syrupy voice, and his dark, rich clothes were all chosen to elicit the impression of a deep, fruity wine. Those who spent any time at all in his presence quickly came to learn that the person Raskith presented to the world was little more than a pungent aroma masking the underlying scent of rot and mold.

Mara, meanwhile, opted for far simpler garb: unornamented black leather armor over unornamented black robes, her dark hair tied up in a practical bun. Her master had drilled into her the value of appearances, of outwardly displaying the characteristics one wanted others to see. Personally, she thought that wearing something so obviously functional and no-nonsense was a perfectly good way of living up to that philosophy.

Raskith stepped up beside her and ran a dry finger across the solid stone crenellations. "And this is a good position. You did well finding somewhere so close to our destination."

Mara gave the barest of nods in response. The tower's previous owners, the farming family who had kept the land verdant and bountiful for decades, shambled around somewhere in the throng of mindless bodies below. She raised her gaze from the army she and her master had raised to serve them and stared over the force at what lay beyond. A mile or so away, a second tower rose twice, three times the height of the one she occupied. Unlike the simple cylinder upon which Mara and Raskith had taken up their post, this taller tower was unmistakably designed as an outward reflection of the personality that had built it. It *had character*, although Mara would never have stooped so low as to use such a phrase herself: it was crooked in three different directions at once, its walls were a stuffed-together mishmash of bricks in different colors and sizes, and it had no fewer than four conical or half-spherical roofs tiled in shades of rainbow vomit.

She let her features slide into a sneer of disdain. *Raskith shows the world a charming face. A competent presence, if an affable one. This wizard shows ... an ostentatious buffoon. I know which side I'd rather be on.*

"Don't let his eccentricities fool you," Raskith murmured, his long hands slowly, casually gripping Mara's upper arms in what was perhaps meant to be affection. "Despite his choice of décor, Daroc is still one of the most powerful mages on the continent. He may be older now than when he single-handedly turned the tide of the Blightquell War, but wizards like him only grow stronger with age."

Mara knew all this, of course. There was a reason the quintessential image of a wizard was an elderly, cloaked figure with flowing white hair—and a flowing white beard if it were a man, which in Mara's view it far too often was, but perhaps the multitude of notable female wizards throughout history hadn't made for as dramatic paintings and statues as their hairy-chinned counterparts. Perhaps there was some causal link between beards and the magnificence of an artwork.

"Once we've defeated Daroc," Mara said, keeping her posture still under Raskith's touch, "I'll be a fully fledged necromancer. Yes?"

"If you can revive a corpse belonging to a mage of his power, you will have proven yourself," said Raskith. His breath was ripe and warm on her ear.

"Then the conditions of my apprenticeship will have been met."

Raskith's fingers flexed slightly, then retreated from her. "Say what you mean."

She turned to face him, willing her eyes to stay steady, not to flicker for the barest of moments. "My parents and my brother will no longer be yours to harm, should I fail," she said.

She felt her throat betray her, heard her clear tone falter for half a syllable. Raskith never missed the slightest sign of doubt.

"That was the agreement," he said, meeting her gaze coolly, evenly. "And I think you would have to agree it was effective motivation. To think one with your power could be born in such an irrelevant place to such irrelevant people... I simply had to claim you for my apprentice, and I had to provide the proper impetus for you to become who you were always meant to be."

"You haven't confirmed it."

Raskith stared at her a moment longer, then looked away with an amused exhalation. "I confirm it," he said. "Your family will be safe when your apprenticeship ends. From me, at least. But really, Mara, I had thought you were beyond such useless attachments."

She bowed her head. "I am, Lord Raskith," she said. "I only meant to ensure the ... legalities were resolved."

I don't care about them, she told herself. *About that. I don't. Just tying up all the loose ends. I'll find myself ensorcelled by a trickster spirit or something if I don't make a habit of ensuring all my contracts' terms are properly fulfilled.*

When he'd first taken her from her family, of course, she had cared very much, only submitting to his instruction for the sake of protecting them. Over time, though, she'd come to see the appeal of the power he offered. And, as all apprentices to masters of the dark arts did, she fully intended to one day use it to destroy him. He encouraged it, even.

"How very thorough of you." Raskith smiled widely, lips stretching and parting to show his gleaming white teeth. "I do like the sound of *Lord*, you know. Once we have what we came for, there will be none who can deny me that title."

"All will know your power," Mara intoned automatically. She made a mental note to herself: *When I'm as strong as he is, I will be at least fifty percent less prone to grandstanding and monologuing.*

If Raskith noticed the lack of enthusiasm, it was outweighed by his ego's pleasure at the words. "We destroy Daroc and collect his copy of the *Tome of the Beyond*," he purred, "and then we advance on the Seven Nations one by one. And you know what we do to each of them, don't you?"

Mara nodded. She had heard it a hundred times. But she knew her master wanted to be the one to utter the pithy slogan, so she obliged him. "Reduce the population; defile the holy places; leave the fields unable to bear food."

"Decimation, desecration, desolation," Raskith said, with a tone and a grin that reminded Mara of a nightcat stumbling across the fresh corpse of a juicy bird.

"There's something you haven't explained," Mara said, turning away from him to gaze out at Daroc's tower again.

"Oh?"

"If Daroc is so powerful, how do we plan to defeat him with only an army of weak ghouls?" Her master had tasked her with raising over half of the undead soldiers herself—a greater feat than any she had accomplished before, but still not enough to pose a real threat to an archmage like Daroc.

Behind her, a honey-smooth chuckle rumbled quietly in Raskith's throat. "Leave that to me, my apprentice."

She scoffed internally, careful not to show any outward reaction. *I won't be your apprentice forever*, she thought, aiming the mental sentiment in his direction. She was fairly certain he couldn't read her thoughts—if he could, she'd have been in a lot of trouble far sooner. *You won't always be able to talk down to me. To dismiss me. I might not be your equal now, and I might need you to become as strong as I want to be, but one day—*

He stepped beside her and placed a hand on her shoulder, interrupting her mental diatribe.

What was that about not monologuing?

It was, Mara had often reflected, truly impressive how much force he could exert over her body with such little pressure from his fingers. No magic. No flexing of physical muscles. Only pure command. "Now," he said, "why don't you give the order?"

Mara allowed herself one long, deep breath. Then she reached for the vial around her neck, the one that contained her necromantic focus: a petal from a peacebloom flower, the broken tip of a blade that had killed a dozen warriors, and a magically shrunken human skull, all suspended in a preserving liquid infused with powdered scythemaw teeth and the venom of a spithopper. The contradictory sensations of pure death—saturated with emptiness, alive with unlife, writhing with still-ness—flooded through her body as her fingers made contact with the little symbol of demise. A familiar shiver ran down to her toes.

Let's storm the tower.

Then she formed the energy into a notion, and shaped the notion into a command.

"*Advance.*"

Her army obeyed.

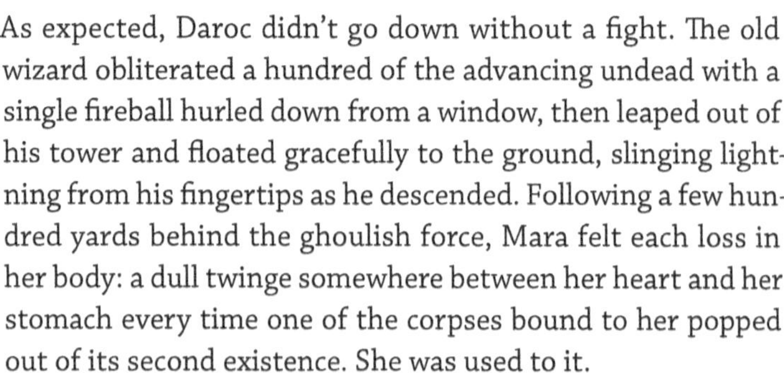

As expected, Daroc didn't go down without a fight. The old wizard obliterated a hundred of the advancing undead with a single fireball hurled down from a window, then leaped out of his tower and floated gracefully to the ground, slinging light-ning from his fingertips as he descended. Following a few hundred yards behind the ghoulish force, Mara felt each loss in her body: a dull twinge somewhere between her heart and her stomach every time one of the corpses bound to her popped out of its second existence. She was used to it.

She stared at the backs of the undead immediately in front of her: the two slowest, most shambling corpses, the ones Raskith had specifically exhumed for reasons he hadn't explained. Most of their force had been plucked from battlefields and revivified shortly after their first deaths, when the bodies were still not long divorced from the souls that had inhabited them. Even then, ghouls—or wraiths, or zombies, or whatever one wanted to call the most basic tier of ambulatory cadavers—struggled to move with anything close to the smoothness they had mustered in life. These dug-up shufflers had spent a long time in the ground, and it showed.

Beside her, the master necromancer pulled a few items from within his cloak—far more items than should possibly have been able to fit in its pockets, even as deep as they were. His dexterous hands crushed poisonous bulbs into dust, which a sweep of his fingers collected into a swirling orb; a little match struck itself against a blood-rusted dagger and set light to the dusty sphere; he sprinkled clippings of hair from long-dead heads into the mix. In a few moments, the master necromancer marched with a growing ball of purple-black flame before him. Tiny bones floated up from his pockets, arranging themselves into sigils and runes that spelled curses of destruction and devastation in a dozen dead languages; the flames leaped to them too, surrounding Raskith with a halo of burning, vicious words.

He's making a show of it, she thought. *There's no need for all the visuals, really. Just having the items nearby would be enough to fuel any spell he wanted to cast. But Raskith wouldn't be Raskith without a bit of theater.*

Mara, for her part, simply touched the obsidian ring on her left middle finger. Imbued with the inchoate power that pooled in graveyards, in once-holy places, in sites of accidents, the ring provided a reservoir of magical energy for her to withdraw and mold to her will. She formed a protective shield of viridian aura around herself, not bothering to shape any offensive spells yet. The ghouls before her, and her master beside her, would handle the offense.

Daroc sent spell after spell into the crowd; from her position at the back, Mara could see twice-dead bodies flying gracelessly through the air as they reached the line of fire.

"Master," she said.

"Hmm?"

"You don't expect the ghouls to overpower Daroc, do you?"

"Not at all," said Raskith. "The army is just an obfuscation, really. Everyone expects a necromancer to come with a battalion of faceless servants, which means they fail to look closer. But it was a wonderful demonstration of your power, so I consider it more than worthwhile."

Mara said no more.

When Daroc had laid waste to a full nine-tenths of the undead army, Raskith made his move. He rose into the air, his flaming enchantments wreathing him in power, and shot toward the old wizard. A burst of violet light streaked in his wake. Mara lost sight of him as he descended, the remaining ghouls concealing him from her view, but she could see and hear the signs of battle between two of the most powerful magic wielders of their age. Light crackled and screamed from the collision of the combatants in the shadow of the wizard's tower; more undead went soaring off unceremoniously, battered by the waves of power emanating from the clash.

What am I supposed to do? she wondered. *Stay back, or join the fray?*

She was spared from making the decision by an explosion of force, a dome of solid aura that burst from Daroc and Raskith and cleared the field of almost all the remaining ghouls. When the dust settled, Mara had a clear line of sight to her master and his opponent.

And Daroc had a clear line of sight to her.

With one hand, the old wizard deflected a blow from a flaming spear that appeared from the air to jab at him; with the other, he reached toward Mara and clenched his fist. Her shield failed almost immediately against his pure crushing strength. Daroc pulled her across the field toward him and extended one long finger, conjuring a thorned rope of stinging orange light that constricted around Mara's torso, pinning her arms behind her back and tying her legs together.

Oh, that's gonna scratch the armor. Not that I care about how it looks or anything.

She fell to her knees, unable to move, and stared at Daroc with as much dark rage as she could muster. Her eyes, the pale green of a stagnant pool beneath the moonlight, glimmered with what she hoped was a sinister glint.

That was too easy for him. I'm nowhere near his level in a direct fight between mages. Next time, I need to fight dirtier.

"An apprentice, Raskith?" the wizard rumbled. "I'm surprised."

In response, Raskith sent a barrage of burning bones toward Daroc, who simply stepped out of their path and thrust a palm upward. An enormous cylinder of dirt erupted from the ground like a great worm, intercepting the bones and swallowing them in its untidy maw before retreating into the earth.

"Or perhaps I shouldn't be surprised," Daroc mused, looking back at Mara. "I suppose your entire life has been about creating expendable servants."

"Is that so much worse," Raskith challenged, "than whatever you want to call the connections you form? You gain nothing from befriending those weaker than you. All you get is pain when they inevitably die." He besieged Daroc with more flurries of spells, all of which the old mage easily deflected or avoided.

"This isn't a debate," said Daroc. Then he launched an attack of his own: an array of steel bars rose out of the ground and surrounded Raskith in a cage before twisting inward, pressing and crushing.

"Oh, no," said Raskith, letting out a low laugh. Mara knew that laugh. She'd heard him practicing it a hundred times. "I have evidence. Look behind my apprentice."

Daroc's whole body shook with a raucous laugh. "The old *look over there*? Really, Raskith?" He shook his head in amusement. "You know full well that you can't defeat me," he said, turning toward Mara, "even if I look away from—"

He froze.

Raskith didn't hesitate to take advantage of the moment of distraction, blasting free from his cage and launching a barrage of obsidian spears that slammed into Daroc. The wizard stumbled, crying out in what sounded more like despair than pain to Mara; Raskith raised his hand as if grabbing an invisible throat, and a huge hand formed out of glowing bones, squeezing Daroc and forcing him to his knees.

"You see?" Raskith said, striding casually forward. "Proof. Connection is weakness."

Tears streamed from Daroc's eyes, soaking his beard. Mara, still bound by the magical rope, twisted her head to look behind her. The two slow corpses, the ones Raskith had made a point of raising from their graves, were the only remnant of their army. They'd been so ungainly, so languorous, that the destructive magic that had taken out the rest of the ghouls hadn't reached them. Only now had they caught up to the action.

Mara peered closely at their faces—the face of an elderly woman, and that of a man in perhaps his mid-thirties. Was that a hint of resemblance she could see between their features and Daroc's?

Oh, that's despicable, she mused, though she meant it as a compliment. *Effective though. If I ever want to be as powerful as Raskith, I need to be as ruthless as he is.*

The wizard's shoulders rose and fell heavily. Raskith flexed his fingers and the great osseous hand followed suit, crushing the old man's torso further.

"You," Daroc grunted, "are despicable."

"Thank you," said Raskith with a wide smile. His eyes flicked to Mara, kneeling there beside them. With the twitch of a finger, he dispelled Daroc's binding spell. Mara fell forward, her suddenly unrestrained limbs unfolding with a distinct lack of elegance.

She pushed herself to her feet, brushing off the dirt, and tried not to feel too embarrassed about falling over in front of two mages of such elevated status.

"Mara," said Raskith, "would you mind going inside the tower and fetching the *Tome of the Beyond* for me?"

She nodded and strode past them, deliberately not sparing a glance for the defeated wizard. It didn't take much searching: a thick volume immediately stood out to her from a shelf just behind the door, its leather cover a mélange of shades of black, white, and gray. Daroc hadn't thought he'd need to hide anything, she supposed. He'd assumed nobody would ever get this far.

She took the *Tome* and carried it out of the tower, holding it out to her master.

"My hands are somewhat occupied," he said in a performatively apologetic tone, giving her a look that might have been remonstrative or conspiratorial. "Why don't you open it?"

She couldn't prevent a momentary flicker of confusion from flitting across her features, but she didn't disobey. Of course she didn't.

Mara opened the *Tome of the Beyond*, holding the first page out for Raskith to see.

"Perfect," the necromancer susurrated.

"What do you plan to do with that?" Daroc demanded, his voice a harsh wheeze.

"I should have thought that would be obvious," Raskith said dismissively. He turned his attention to Mara. "This book," he told her, "is the key to transcending our powers. We necromancers can raise bodies to our service, but this... this is thanomancy, the knowledge to compel the souls of the dead."

Mara digested the information. There was supposed to be a clear divide between resurrection, the divine magic that restored the deceased to true life, and the necromantic power to call up corpses from the earth to serve their master's will.

If he's saying this book would allow him to perform a perverted resurrection—a true revival, but with body and soul both chained to his command... She couldn't begin to fathom the implications.

"Ahhh," Raskith said, snapping Mara out of her thoughts. The *Tome* was rapidly flipping its pages in her hands, presumably at Raskith's direction. "So there *is* a place between life and death. I thought as much."

He read a few more pages, then smiled.

"Well," he said to Daroc. "Thank you very kindly for your continued service."

The wizard's eyes widened. "No."

"Oh, don't worry," said Raskith. "I don't intend for the first soul I call back from beyond to be yours. I'm sure you're absolutely riddled with enchantments to prevent that sort of thing, and I've no intention of risking everything by biting off more than I can chew." He paused, and a familiar expression of satisfaction slid across his face. "Your body, however, will be wonderfully useful." With his free hand, the one that wasn't controlling the skeletal hand imprisoning Daroc, he gestured to Mara. "Finish him."

She blinked. "I... me?"

"Absolutely," said Raskith. His lips peeled apart in a grin. "Do the honor."

Mara swallowed and handed her master the *Tome of the Beyond*, then stepped in front of Daroc.

"You don't have a spell strong enough to kill me," the old mage spat. "But go ahead. Do his bidding. You're no less a slave than the corpses you pull out of their graves."

Mara sighed, knowing that the first sentence he'd said was true. She didn't think too hard about the last sentence.

Then she punched him in the face.

If Mara had learned one thing about fighting wizards—which she'd done a few times at Raskith's command, but never one as distinguished as Daroc—it was that they were fragile. They might bend the elements to their will, might be capable of hurling magics that could level buildings, but they invariably had glass jaws.

The old man's head snapped to the side. He stayed in his kneeling position, held there by Raskith's cadaverous grip.

"Good," said Raskith.

"You'll be next," said Daroc. His gaze turned to the two walking dead who still hobbled around behind Mara.

She hit him again. And again. On the third blow, a hollow crack ripped the air. Daroc's head spun farther than it should've.

The bony hand released him. The wizard's body fell to the dirt.

Ooh, that one felt good in my bones. Stupid squishy wizards. A juvenile insult, but it felt good. She expended so much energy on appearing stoic and passionless that thoughts like that were indulgences, little acts of rebellion.

Raskith's laughter saturated the air, filling Mara's ears with its fermented sweetness. "In another life," he said, "you would have been a wonderful warrior monk."

He's not wrong. In a straight fight, at least, I always was more of a puncher-who-can-do-necromancy than a necromancer-who-can-punch.

Mara wiped her knuckles, then turned to the two corpses that still wandered nearby. With a thought, she severed their connection to the living world. They dropped, instantly becoming undignified, clumsy heaps.

"Wasteful," her master said.

Mara looked away from the bodies, staring down at Daroc. The motion just so happened to hide her face from Raskith. Not that she needed to hide anything. Of course not. "We don't need them now."

It's inefficient, keeping them animated. That's all.

Raskith gave one casual sigh, then shrugged as if he couldn't care less. He stepped beside his apprentice. "Now then," he said. "Raise him."

Mara set to it.

The ritual for reviving a mage's body was only slightly more complicated than that for animating a common ghoul from any old corpse. The real factor that separated the two was not in the placement of runes and focus items, but in the demand on the necromancer's will and strength. It took more power, more directed resolve, to revivify a body in such a way that it retained some of the abilities it had had in life.

The fact that it was possible at all had led many to theorize that magical ability must be somehow physical, attached to biology, at least in part. Yet almost all magics in this world (for the existence of others was accepted by most scholars as indubitable) required some sort of external power source or symbolic item like her ring and vial. Nobody had quite worked out exactly how it all functioned.

None of that mattered much to Mara as she worked, placing various trinkets inside the lines and shapes she'd carefully scratched into the dirt with the tip of a cursed knife. It wasn't really relevant *why* a corpse could be reanimated to wield magic at its master's command, only that it could be done.

She stood and examined her work.

"That ought to do it," said Raskith approvingly. His approval was for the power it would bring him, she knew, not for her accomplishment—or, gods knew, for Mara herself. "Just one minor adjustment."

He waved his hand; Mara's lines edited themselves, changing the parameters of the ritual. She frowned.

"Master, I—"

"My dear Mara," said Raskith, his smile unfaltering. "My precious apprentice. Proving that you can conduct this ritual will earn you the title of necromancer. Until then, it would be awfully irresponsible of me to allow you to attempt binding a servant so powerful to *you* as its master. All sorts of harm could come to you, should things go awry."

Mara took a deep breath. There was some sense to what Raskith was saying—some merit to the notion that he was a safer candidate to command a potentially unruly wight than she—but then, there was always truth behind effective manipulation. "Of course," she made herself say.

There's nothing to gain from arguing here, she told herself, as she had hundreds of times before.

"Good," said her master. "Begin."

Mara gathered the aura of death in her soul, drawing from her ring and from the wizard's corpse that lay before her. And, she realized, from the *Tome of the Beyond*, which dripped with the stench of finality as if its pages were wet and saturated with death. She closed her eyes, condensed the ambient, nebulous magic into a pool of liquid, and poured it into the lines etched into the earth.

Now for the hard part.

Mara turned all her attention to maintaining her force of will, focusing her essence on the task at hand. She was used to the sensation by now: a stretching inside her, like her very soul was straining to reach out from itself and into the world beyond. Any slip of concentration could see that extending part of herself damaged in the recoil as it snapped back like over-stretched elastic—or, worse, severed entirely. It was unlikely to happen at her level of power, while the spells she cast only demanded her inner being to exert itself so far beyond the boundaries of natural physics, but a mage wielding magics of higher complexity could wreak all sorts of irreversible havoc on their souls if they weren't careful.

This was harder than the simple animations she was used to; that was clear immediately. Her power, trying to reach out from her self as it had done so many times before, stumbled. The sensation wasn't unlike reaching the top of a flight of stairs and raising a foot to clear a final imagined step; Mara's stomach twisted in a sharp jolt. She refocused and pushed, feeling as if she were trying to force a thick liquid through a small hole, or perhaps a strainer whose mesh was woven too tightly. Her power obeyed, a congealed flow at first, but she willed it to work. And it did, coursing quicker and smoother until her magic was sluicing through the ritual lines like a thunderous, rapid river.

Rekh, God of Death, in your name I commit this act of profanity against nature's order.

She grasped for the pool of magical power she could feel in the corpse, and she tethered it to the world of the living, weaving threads of magic in loose stitches between body and aura and space. Her strength became the strength of dead muscles, her will the will of lifeless tendons. Then, with a twist, she felt ownership over the body shift from Daroc's soul to hers, then to Raskith's. The stitches pulled tight. It was done.

Mara opened her eyes.

Her lines were glowing indigo-black, and Raskith was smiling. And Daroc's body was stirring.

"Wonderful," the master necromancer hissed. "Wonderful."

"It's done," said Mara, swaying slightly as her awareness returned to her exhausted body.

Raskith strode to her and patted her on the cheek as Daroc's corpse climbed to its feet. The wizard's hands gripped his over-rotated head and turned it back to face forward.

"You," said Raskith, "are now a fully-fledged practitioner of the necromantic arts."

Mara felt … something. Not the rush of pride she'd hoped for, nor the despair she'd dreaded might come against her will. Just *something*, a vague murmur of her gut. That was all she felt at the moment she'd worked toward for a decade.

"Here," said Raskith, handing her the *Tome of the Beyond*. "It's full of death aura. Use it to restore some of your strength."

Mara took it. "Yes, Lord Raskith."

Her master cast an appraising eye over Daroc's undead body. "A good raising," he said. "I can feel his strength. A mindless corpse, but one with magical power entirely at my command." He reached into his pockets with both hands, withdrawing two small items: a miniature dagger and what looked like a lock of hair tied in a white ribbon. The hair, Mara noticed through her tired haze, was the same sable as her own. "Thank you, Mara," he said. Then he brought his hands together, crushing the two objects in his palms.

Something snapped inside Mara. She felt it in her body, in her soul: an unnatural pop, an unclean tear. Her mind felt like a sack of wet flour, her body like a dead, half-butchered pig. The ground rushed up to meet her, or perhaps she fell to the ground. She couldn't tell the difference, and it didn't seem to matter much.

What did—what am I—what?

"A mature necromancer," Raskith murmured, staring down at his fallen apprentice. She could do nothing but stare up from where she'd fallen, unable to move a muscle—not even an eyeball. "Now *that* will be a formidable servant indeed."

Mara tried to speak, to grunt, to whimper. Nothing came out.

So this is how I die. I hoped it might be … grander.

"Do keep hold of the *Tome* until it's over," Raskith said, as if she could do anything else. "That connection to what lies beyond should ease your travel in both directions." He kneeled, his dark eyes boring into her. "Don't worry; I'll conduct sufficient trials first. I won't bring you back until I fully understand every detail of the power the *Tome* will give me. It would be such a shame for this not to go perfectly."

He gave a theatrical sigh. "It's never been done before, you know. To raise a necromancer not just as a mindless wight, but with their soul and their full power bound to their master's will… and a soul that will have seen the world beyond death?"

A true smile crept across his face—not the false presentation he usually adopted, but a sincere expression of satisfaction. If Mara's blood hadn't already been freezing, that smile would've stopped it. "I can hardly imagine how powerful you'll be."

Mara had wondered, in the years of her apprenticeship, what her final thoughts would be if Raskith ever killed her—though neither had ever openly acknowledged it, both had always known it was a distinct possibility. She'd imagined thoughts of rage, of vengeance, of despair, of terror, of resignation.

All she felt was a fuzzy disappointment.

Then she slipped into oblivion.

CHAPTER 1

Grass of night-mist gray and stalks of dragon-eye gold swayed under a rippling vortex sky. Flakes of ash fell in a constant, dry drizzle. There was stillness and there was motion; there was the certainty of eternal unchangingness, of eons folding into themselves with not a mote of dust out of the place it started in, and there was the audacious fact that nothing ever remains truly constant. The grass fields undulated despite the fact that there was no breeze; their leaves danced because they knew they ought to, because they remembered that grass ought to be blown by the wind.

In an unremarkable spot somewhere in the expanse, a place with absolutely nothing to distinguish it from the horizon-touching sameness in every direction, the grass began to cower. The soot-gray leaves leaned outward from a central point that none of them wanted to touch, straining to escape; in moments, a flattened circle ten feet wide had appeared amidst the otherwise featureless stretch of field.

Directly above the point from which the grass yearned to flee, a silvery-gold droplet of liquid light coalesced beneath the swirling sky and began to fall. Its descent cut a trail through the air behind it, like the shimmering stream left behind by a tear streaking down a dirty face. For miles around, faces turned to the light. Some turned away uncaring; some watched as it fell with expressions of rapture, or hope, or sorrow, or hunger. Its passing was noted in a grand city of gleaming marble, in a road lined with holy buildings, in a silent graveyard of stone faces.

Mara knew none of this as she fell. She was aware only of the dim knowledge that she, or something that remembered being her very well, still existed. That was ... not a surprise, exactly, but welcome. She felt rather than saw the warm golden glow that surrounded and suffused her, warming her bones with the freshly insecure knowledge that she was *alive*.

The teardrop of light touched down in the field. It sank into the grass, sloughing itself off from the human form inside it like water sliding off the sides of an umbrella.

And Mara opened her eyes.

I'm not dead.

She patted her own body, feeling the familiar clothes, the same musculature. An image flashed into her mind: Raskith standing above her as she lay on the ground. Dying.

No way am I not dead.

She flexed her fingers, suddenly more grateful than she had ever been to have muscles and tendons and nerves that allowed her to move her limbs and digits, and reached for the vial around her neck. With a thought, she cast her awareness out into her own body: a simple spell for examining a person's physical condition, which could be invaluable for healing. Or for other things.

Blood's still flowing, she realized, reveling in the steady pumping of her heart. *But I'm sure as shit not alive. Which makes this place...*

"Well, hello there," said a voice. It was quite obviously trying to sound grandiose and important, but its naturally reedy tones let it down somewhat.

Mara turned to the source of the voice, steeling herself for whatever she might see. Every instinct in her was screaming at her to get out of the open, to find somewhere she couldn't be attacked from any angle at any moment, but she held her composure.

"Greetings," she said neutrally, glancing down at her interlocutor. A figure in a dirty cloak stood before her, stout and solid. Their face was hidden in the depths of their hood, but two yellow glints gave the impression of eyes; smooth, elegant, ice-blue horns sprouted from beneath the cowl, their tips reaching just about to the height of Mara's shoulders.

The newcomer spread their arms wide; stubby porcine trotters, two-toed and hairy, appeared from within the wide sleeves. "Welcome to the Sunless Crossing."

Mara glanced at the sky above, an eddying pool of purples and grays and blacks. "Indicative name," she said.

The cloak swayed as the figure's shoulders jerked with their raucous guffawing. The laugh cut off as abruptly as it had started. "And what might yours be?"

"Where I come from," said Mara carefully, "it's considered rude to start up a conversation and not introduce yourself first." Names had power. That was a fundamental fact of the world. She wasn't about to give hers to the first stranger she met in a place about which she knew nothing whatsoever.

"Very well," said the stranger, straightening their posture and brushing down their grimy cloak as if it were the finest robes. Their voice took on a new tone, which Mara thought was intended to be deep and intimidating, but which came out as a barely comprehensible grumble. "You shall know me as the Master of Shadows."

"Shadows," Mara muttered. She looked at the sky again, then down at the grass that surrounded them. "I think you need a sun to have shadows."

"Impudence!" croaked the cloaked figure, gesticulating indignantly. "I am also called the Seeker of … ah, of Great Power, and the Wielder of Hero-Slaying Treasures!"

Mara frowned at them. "And what did you want from me, exactly?"

The stranger paused their irate pointing and hopping and hurriedly recovered their formal posture. "You, poor lost soul, are in the process of passing from the life you knew to the one that awaits you beyond."

"So I *am* dead," Mara said. The words tasted bitter, almost grainy in her mouth, like badly strained tea that had been left to stew for far too long. *There wasn't really any other possibility,* she thought, *but … having it confirmed still isn't exactly pleasant.*

"You are indeed," said the Master-Seeker of Great Shadow-Slaying Heroes almost jovially. "But fear not, for I am here, my child. Here to take you to the world that comes next." The hooded face stretched up toward her own. "All you have to do is accept me as your god, and I shall welcome you into my paradise."

Mara snorted. She couldn't help it. *This little cylinder of a thing wants me to worship it?*

"I already have a god," she said, turning away.

A meaty hand slapped against her arm. She turned her head slowly back toward the owner of the offending hand, channeling her old master's coldest, most intimidating stare.

"Did you just try to grab me?" she asked in a dangerous whisper. *Does he not know he's only got two fingers and they're practically stuck together?*

"I never *try* to do anything!" her assailant declared. "I struck you in precisely the manner I intended to!"

Mara bared her teeth. "This conversation is over." She called upon the aura of death in her ring, siphoning off just a drop of power and letting it flow through her, through the items in the vial around her neck, letting it shape into the most basic and useful magic any necromancer could wield. "This is a world of the dead, right?"

The cowled head nodded uncertainly.

"Well then," Mara said, gathering the spell in her hand, "I'm the worst possible person you could have picked on."

"And why might that be?"

"Because death bows to me."

She released the power, casting a magic she'd used hundreds of times in her life. The most important thing for any would-be master of the dead to be able to do, as Raskith had drilled into her for years, was severing the connection that tethered the undead body or spirit to the living world. Should a raised servant ever somehow pose any sort of danger to the necromancer, or show any sign of resisting their master's will, it was crucial to have a failsafe: a technique that could immediately end that particular undead's existence. It was as basic as spells could come, requiring only a tiny amount of magical power and no ritual or focus beyond the basic memento mori that any raiser of the dead worth their salt would have on their person at all times. She knew it as well as she knew how to speak. It had never failed her.

The spell fizzled out immediately.

The cloaked figure looked down at the purplish sparks sputtering pathetically in Mara's hand. "Did you just—?"

Before they could finish, she was already weaving another spell, a variant of the first. Most mundane folk assumed that instantly killing a creature would be more difficult than asserting dominance over them, but that wasn't true—certainly not for someone whose entire magical essence was bound toward the manipulation of death itself. That said, the hex that dismayed and dismissed the unliving, causing them to flee from the caster without doing them further harm, was only slightly more complicated, and one that any magic-wielder could learn without the stigma of associating with necromancy. Such insensible proprieties meant little to Mara, of course, but it was nevertheless useful to have another such tool when one spent so much time among the raised.

The spell hopped lugubriously from Mara's hand to the would-be god's torso. The cloaked head turned away from her as if remembering something was still in the oven.

Now walk away.

And turned right back to her again.

"What are you—are you trying to dominate my will or something? That's very impolite."

"Oh, shit."

With a grunting, snorting screech, the stranger leaped at Mara. The dense body smacked her full force in the stomach, driving her to the ground; callused toes and hard nails struck her in the chest, in the shoulders. Mara grabbed one of the horns and yanked with all her might, sending her assailant sailing off her with a confused squeal. Before the cloaked figure could regain its footing, Mara had already bolted upright and launched herself forward, delivering a solid punch right into the middle of the shadowed face.

The self-styled god fell back, their hood falling from their face. Mara caught a glimpse of a piggish jaw beneath a squat duck-like beak, furry, floppy ears, and glistening eyes set deep within the folds of a swollen forehead and cheeks, before they yelped and covered their face with their hands.

Just in time for a two-foot-tall man with a wild gray beard and four iridescent wings like a dragonfly's to fly in and slam both feet into their ear with a perfect double-footed dropkick.

The pig-duck-human-thing dropped like a sack of potatoes.

"I didn't wanna do that to ya," said the bearded man, skittering around in the air like a dragonfly, alternating between hovering and scooting around in sharp shapes. "You gotta stop doin' this, Orgrumm, or I'm gonna keep kickin' ya." His voice was gruff, rough, and completely at odds with the shimmering beauty of his wings.

Orgrumm groaned and lumbered off into the wide expanse of wheat. Clouds of ash puffed off the stalks as he disturbed them on his way. The winged man turned his attention to Mara.

"Well then. Sorry 'bout that."

"I didn't need saving," Mara said icily.

"Nah, sure ya didn't. But Orgrumm needed kickin', so..." He shrugged, the motion causing him to bob up and down in the air. Now that he had come to at least something more of a stop, rather than being a blurred missile, Mara could see him more clearly: a face whose narrow features and deep lines comfortably settled into one of the grumpiest expressions she'd ever seen, a cloak that rippled off his body like a gray mist, and thoroughly sturdy boots. His clothing opened across his torso—to make space for his wings, she thought—revealing wiry muscles beneath. He flicked his monumental beard over his shoulder and nodded in greeting. "Name's Irasca. Of the Ashen Shepherds."

Mara waited for further explanation as to what an Ashen Shepherd might be. Irasca offered none.

He wants me to ask, she thought. It was something Raskith did all the time: dangle information, then withhold it, forcing her to ask if she wanted to know. It was just another expression of his dominance over her, another way in which she was compelled to act according to his will. So, rather than give Irasca the pleasure of following the conversation he wanted to have, she pointed in the direction Orgrumm had gone.

"What sort of creature was that?" she asked.

A quiet rumble vibrated from Irasca's throat. "That," he said, folding his arms in midair, "is a desperate soul. A remnant

a' somethin', maybe once a god of some kind, but not no more."
He gave a disparaging sniff. "Far as species, not a clue. Let's call
'im a quork. Like quack pork."

Despite herself, Mara had to stifle a laugh at that one. *I've
been dead ten minutes and I've already had a pig-duck try to recruit
me to worship it and a ripped old fey with a hell of a kick on him say
"quack pork" to me. Death is weirder than I thought.*

"It—he—really used to be a god?" she asked, staring after
Orgrumm thoughtfully.

"Well, sorta, maybe. I dunno." Irasca kicked the air, an
ungraceful "good riddance" sort of punt. "Gods're weird. And
complicated." He looked her up and down, taking in the robes,
the leather armor, the coldly determined expression. "Lemme
guess. Your god'll be one of death and whatnot."

Should I deny that? Mara wondered. *We're all dead, so presumably people wouldn't look down on worshiping a god of death
as much as the living do...*

"Thought so," mumbled Irasca before she could answer,
peering closely at her face. "Marquis of the Final End? No,
wait," he chirped as she opened her mouth, "most livin' worlds
dunno too much about old Marky, do they? Prolly somethin'
more local, eh?"

"Something more local," Mara agreed.

"I should mention," said Irasca, stroking his veritable beard
with strong fingers, "you might wanna find a change of clothes
or somethin'. Not everyone here takes too kindly to those who
tried to control death while they were alive. Some of these
folks'll have had bad experiences on that front, what with
being dead and all."

She glanced down at her attire. "I'm that obvious?"

He gave her another appraising look, then waggled his
hand in a "so-so" gesture. "To some, most likely." Then he

turned and floated away, beckoning over his shoulder for her to follow. "C'mon, now. Got a tour to give ya."

She made to follow, stumbling as her foot caught on something. Bending down, she picked up the *Tome of the Beyond*, leaving a rectangular imprint in the grass. With the book tucked inside her robes, she walked after the fey man.

CHAPTER 2

All Mara could see at first was the swaying grass, stretching all the way to the horizon in every direction, and the purple-gray swirl that was the sky above. She was a tiny speck between two expansive planes. The sky above; the earth below; her in the middle. She felt almost divorced from her physicality, her mind picturing the scene in third person, situating her in the center of flat discs of which, no matter how far or fast she walked, she would always remain perfectly in the middle. It was strangely peaceful.

Irasca guided her; the fey man had some innate sense of their location and their destination, she guessed, to be able to pick out the way in a place so devoid of landmarks, of directionality. He flew ahead, hovering around the height of Mara's shoulder.

She said nothing, content to remain silent as they traversed the fields. Her fingers stretched out into the stalks of grass, letting them lightly tap her in turn. The soft smudge of ash caressed her fingertips.

An hour passed. Two, maybe three.

Warm light stained the horizon, bleeding into the sky like dye in water, a living heart within the cold, dead gray. Mara took an involuntary breath of awe as a wooden roof emerged into view, rising out of the swathes of grass.

For the first time since they'd started their journey, Irasca turned his head back toward her. "That's the Junction," he announced, a note of pride in his voice. "Welcome."

The Junction was a grand wooden lodge, its outer walls assembled from great logs of rich red-brown stacked atop one another. From the number of windows cut into its exterior and paned with ash-flecked glass, Mara guessed it must have had at least four, maybe five stories. Lanterns hung from its eaves, blazing with a welcoming orange light. Half-muffled conversations drifted out; snippets of songs escaped the windows. The scent of hot, fresh stew saturated the air, cutting through what Mara suddenly realized had been a nose-blockingly stuffy aroma of grass and cold, damp ash.

If I were still with Raskith and we'd come across a place like this, we'd already have killed everyone inside and turned it into a hive of ghouls.

"Most folks tend to say somethin' like, 'By the gods! What a beautiful and glorious sight!' right about now," said Irasca wryly.

Mara collected herself. Part of her genuinely couldn't help finding the Junction impressive, even endearing. Another part was busy running through scenarios, working out the best route by which it might be besieged and all its inhabitants brutally destroyed. After trudging through the great span of grass, though, most of her was just relieved at the notion of being somewhere warm, somewhere *inside*. "It's quite something," she said.

"That it is," Irasca agreed, nodding.

I guess that was a sufficiently thrilled response.

"Come on then," said the old man, his coruscating wings a blur as he floated toward the door.

Mara made to follow, then found her gaze flicking upward at a hint of movement from the roof.

"Don't worry about the gargoyles," said Irasca without looking back. "They're an alright bunch, mostly."

"Gargoyles," Mara repeated.

"Them's the ones. Don't tend to bother folks who don't bother them." Irasca approached the door, an unassuming entrance painted in a light gray that stood out from the darker tones around it. He slid a foot under the handle and hovered backward, pulling it open.

Mara blinked as she crossed the threshold after him, her eyes taking a moment to adjust to the light after hours in the sooty twilight. The smell of food fully took over her nostrils; the sounds of activity, of people talking and cleaning and cooking, filled her ears. Warmth embraced her.

Idyllic. I hate it.

She did her best to hide her disdain for the sheer hominess of the scene. People of varying sizes, shapes, and colors bustled back and forth from a door to her left, which from the smells and the crashing of pots she assumed was probably the kitchen. Straight ahead, soft chairs and couches were dotted around a spacious living room, where a fire blazed in the hearth. The walls were illuminated in mellow gold, rustic and welcoming. To her right, a set of wide stairs ascended to the next floor of the building. Each wooden step looked almost soft, as if it had been sanded to a blissful smoothness only that day.

Mara resisted the urge to sneer. The stream of people issuing from the kitchen with steaming bowls, the assortment of loungers enjoying the comfort of the living room... they were all far too comfortable. There was no sense of vigilance, no deterrent to threats. Even from a brief glance, she could tell their defenses were pudgy, unexercised. *This place wouldn't stand a chance against an attacker who had even half a sense of what they were doing.*

"C'mon," said Irasca, bobbing up the stairs. "I've got some explainin' to do, haven't I?"

Mara didn't follow. "In public," she said, folding her arms and setting her feet. "Not following you upstairs. You get it."

Irasca sighed and floated back down. "Not unfair." He jerked his thumb over his shoulder. "Go up, then up again, then in the third room on the left. Nobody's in there, you can lock it, whatever. There's fresh clothes, a bath. Bowl a' fruit, probably." He glided toward the kitchen. "When you're ready, come back down and we'll talk."

She frowned at him. "How do I know there's not someone waiting to ambush me up there?"

The two-foot-tall man rolled his eyes right back in his head, a remarkably childish expression on such an old face. But then, an old face and gray beard on a body with glimmering wings was something of a juxtaposition too. Irasca was full of contradictions, Mara supposed. "If I wanted to ambush you, d'you not think I'd have done it when you were all out alone in the open, disoriented, no idea where you were, fresh from falling out of the sky?"

"I fell out of the sky?"

"Also," he said, with a meaningful look at her, "I don't think I'd be missin' the mark if I reckoned you could see off most unwanted attention, would I?"

"Probably not," she admitted.

"Well then," said Irasca, and he waved in the direction of the stairs before floating off to the kitchen, apparently satisfied that that was the end of the conversation.

Mara watched him go, then sighed and trudged up the stairs.

A few minutes later, she returned to the lodge's ground floor in what she thought was a sufficiently inconspicuous outfit: simple, lightweight leather armor of the kind any non-threatening person looking to do any sort of traveling might wear to stave off the most basic of attacks, beneath which were a plain shirt and trousers (with pockets, she'd made sure) in greenish, breathable cotton. Her hair was tied in a plain bun. Across her shoulder was slung a satchel in which she'd stuffed her old clothes, the *Tome of the Beyond*, and the small number of coins that had been in her pocket when she died. Her ring and vial stayed on her person. She looked like a regular civilian of the sort most people wouldn't look twice at. Of the sort she and Raskith had murdered and raised a thousand times.

She had to admit, the Junction's facilities weren't half bad. The room to which Irasca had directed her was stocked with clothes in all sizes, fresh drinking water, and even a hot bath. The latter was a luxury she'd rarely been allowed, so she'd taken a brief dip almost out of spite for her old life and the man who had controlled it. Not without caution, of course: she'd ripped a strip of fabric from the bedsheet in the room to which Irasca had directed her and used it to weave a protective net across the door, imbuing it with a simple spell to keep people out. In the process of casting the spell, she'd realized that her ring was absolutely full to bursting with the aura of death. It made sense, she supposed, given that she was dead and—presumably—in a place of death.

"Well, don't you clean up a treat," said Irasca as she approached him where he sat in the living room, slouching on the arm of one of the chairs with his wings draped over the sides. She gave him a glare. "Too far, you're right," he said with surprising immediate humility, holding his hands up. "You look different, is all. Not in a bad way."

She sank into the chair opposite, not bothering with a response. As if on cue, a stout person with fat red cheeks rushed over and handed her a bowl of stew, zipped around the room, and passed steaming bowls to the other inhabitants, most of whom consisted of four—no, five—identical people all greeting each other like old friends, then went rushing off again. Mara narrowed her eyes threateningly in the direction of the room's other patrons, but none were paying attention.

"Right," Irasca said, nodding as if to himself. "First things first. Sorry about Orgrumm. That shouldn't've happened— you get the salesman types out by the Gray Vista, that's bad enough, but they're not meant to be in the fields. He must've got himself killed and dropped back in right as you showed up. Poor bastard's on his fifth or sixth go-round now, so he'll be unravellin' before long, anyway…"

He trailed off, staring at nothing in particular.

This is supposed to be an explanation?

Mara cleared her throat.

"Right, right." Irasca held up a finger for patience. "I should start at the beginning. Never quite got a spiel down for this."

"Sunless Crossing," she prompted. "That's what this place is called?"

He nodded.

"And it's … the afterlife?"

"Ah," he said, a smile rustling his beard. "Not quite. There's a lot of afterlives, see. Lot of gods, lot of planes of existence where the dead go t'rest. This place is … not quite one of 'em."

"A place between life and death," Mara guessed, remembering Raskith's words from the *Tome of the Beyond*.

Irasca snapped his fingers. "That's it exactly. Should put that on a sign or somethin'. The Sunless Crossing is where folks come whose bodies're dead—dead as can be, don't get me wrong; as far as *life*'s concerned, they're out of the picture—but who aren't ready to head off to their final restin' place just yet. Ruled by the Sovereign and Arbiter of the Godless Monarchy, populated by dead'uns and angelic'uns and all kindsa things of all kindsa strange and powerful natures."

Mara frowned, only half taking in Irasca's last sentence. She hadn't felt ready to die, exactly, but she didn't think she had any intentions of delaying her trip to whatever awaited her at the ultimate end. "What do you mean, people who aren't ready?"

"Well, that's a question," said Irasca, steepling his fingers. Mara began to get the impression he was enjoying his rambling storytelling. "Some of 'em don't yet have a god who'll take 'em—either they never worshiped one at all, or the one they prayed to doesn't like 'em enough. Some, not many, have something they want to do before they go. Some don't know who they are or what they want. But most're here because life might not be done with 'em yet."

Not done with them yet... She froze, her eyes involuntarily widening. Irasca noticed.

"Hit a bit of a note there? Stew's probably going cold, by the way."

Her mind raced. Raskith had killed her for the express purpose of bringing her back to the world of the living as his undead servant. If being in the Sunless Crossing, not in the afterlife of Rekh, meant that she was eligible for resurrection...

"How do I make sure I don't get brought back?" she demanded.

Irasca raised an eyebrow at her sudden interest. "Not interested in returning to the world of the living?"

She shook her head firmly. "Not the way *he*'d do it." Then, because she was in fact quite hungry, she ate a spoonful of stew. It was better than she'd expected. No meat, but whatever vegetables were in it were rich and hearty.

He gave a slow nod. "Right. I won't ask."

Mara actually felt a surge of appreciation toward the tetchy old fey for that.

"Look," he said, sitting up, "the Sunless Crossing exists for the most part because there needed to be a place for souls to wait to be resurrected. Probably, anyway. Dunno how it all started, but the long and short of it is that long as you're here, you're close enough to the world of life that someone up there can reach down here and tug you right back. Some gods make their resurrection magicks in such a way as they need consent, a willing soul, but a lot don't play nice like that, and necromancers sure as all hells don't. Far as I know, you get called back by somethin' what doesn't ask for permission, you can't just decide not to go. Only way to avoid it is … well, don't be in the Sunless Crossing. Find a way to move on quick."

Mara digested this—and the stew, which she'd finished faster than she'd expected while he spoke—then plopped her bowl on the floor, grabbed her satchel, opened it on her lap, and pulled out the *Tome of the Beyond*. "The person who wants to bring me back," she said, holding up the book, "he needs this to do it. I think. But if it came with me…"

"Ah," said Irasca, shaking his head. "No dice. You showed up here with whatever was on you when you died, but think about it. When people die, their stuff doesn't just disappear."

She let the book fall onto her leg, trying not to look too dismayed. "This is just a … copy?"

"Sorta," he said, shrugging. The movement caused his wings to shimmer in the lantern light. "It ain't the original thing. What it is, is sorta…" He sighed deeply. "Ah, I'm not that good at explainin' all this."

"You don't say."

"Long and short of it is," he said, plowing valiantly on, "everything here is made of … memory. Sorta. The things you brought with you, they're based on your memories of what those things were like when you had 'em in life. How well d'you know that book?"

"Not well."

He gestured with his chin. "Try openin' it."

She let the *Tome* fall open, its pages flipping past, and stopped it in a random spot. The page she'd landed on was full of something that looked like words, but mostly wasn't. It was an approximation of the alphabet she was familiar with, but not quite right: gibberish that looked as if it were pretending not to be gibberish. There were occasional legible words, mostly things like *death*, *wraith*, *conquest*, and similarly ominous things.

"I don't think this is what the original had in it," she said.

"Nah," said Irasca. "That'll be the book as you imagine it: full of some kinda writing that says something-or-other, and that's about the best impression the Crossing can do of the thing you remember."

"So ... he's still got the real one," Mara said, dropping the *Tome* on the floor.

"If he was near you when you died, he does."

Mara picked a spot on the wooden floor and glared at it. "He very much was."

"Ah." Irasca scratched his chin.

Mara found herself touching her own face. "And my body? I'm guessing this is... what, an imagined version of my body too?"

"Sorta," said the old fey. "It's how your soul remembers you lookin', the body your internalized identity says you oughta have or somethin' like that." He wagged a finger. "Don't go thinkin' you can just think yourself into bein' stronger or faster or different, though—memories don't quite work like that for us. There're stories about folks whose willpower was so strong they managed to persuade themselves not to remember needing to eat and sleep, or else they just came to some sorta understandin' about bein' dead and realized they didn't really have to be limited by what livin' folks could do. Seen it a couple times meself. Quite a thing."

Irasca stroked his beard, thinking for a moment. Mara waited for him to continue.

"They say," he continued after a moment, "there're some who found themselves arrivin' here in the bodies they felt they should've had too, if they felt it strong enough while they were alive. Like they could finally be who they were s'posed to be. Must've been nice for 'em."

He shook his head almost wistfully, then frowned as if trying to remember how many items were left on his Sunless Crossing Day One Induction checklist. "If you've got anything else on you, just so you know, it probably won't be a whole lotta use here. Coins?"

She nodded.

"Yeah, those're of no worth in the Crossing. We got folks from gods know how many different nations across all different worlds and planes and dimensions and that. Couldn't possibly keep track of it if we let everyone use their own currency."

Different worlds, Mara thought.

"This is a lot to take in," Irasca said, watching her carefully.

"It is," she agreed. "But I haven't got time—I can't let him bring me back. None of the rest of it matters to me. I just need to get out of here. And fast."

He nodded slowly. "Wouldn't be any strange thing if you needed some time just to … adjust to the new situation. Being dead and all that. A lotta new souls never really get past that bit."

"It's inconvenient," she said, not really thinking about what she was saying, "but I've got to work with it."

He said he was going to do tests first, she remembered. *Enough to make sure that when he was ready to raise me, he'd be certain nothing would go wrong. But that might not take him much time...*

"Does time pass at the same rate here as in the living world?" she asked abruptly.

His brow furrowed. "Probably thereabouts," he said. "Don't think anyone's ever properly measured. Bit difficult to do, really. Always seems to be changin'. Only thing what's consistent for sure is time always passes quicker here than outside. You spend a day here, it'll be less than a day for your folks back in the land of the living. Dunno how much less, but less."

"Doesn't matter," she said. "I've got no way of knowing how long I actually have, so ... I just have to..."

"You gotta move on," said Irasca solemnly. "Gotta go find that eternal end."

Which means persuading Rekh to let me in, Mara thought, and shivered. *Nobody really knows what Rekh's afterlife is like. Everyone who follows him is too busy disturbing the order of life and death to really imagine that they'll eventually die themselves. But there's no way any other god'll want me, not after what I've done.*

"Well," said Irasca, interrupting her thoughts, "best send you on your way so you can be done with it." He floated off the armchair and toward a large set of double doors, an expression of resigned sadness pulling at his eyes and mouth. "You can leave your stuff there. Someone'll take it to the Gilded Hills. Well, not the Hills exactly, them's for shiny things, but that general area at any rate."

She hesitated for just a moment, thinking about the old clothes in the satchel. The entire life they represented. Then she shook her head, scoffed at the thought of ever wearing the uniform of a necromancer again, and dropped the satchel on the chair and the *Tome* on the floor next to the empty stew bowl. Her ring stayed on her finger and her vial around her neck, hidden beneath her clothes. "You seem … unhappy."

"Oh, no." He turned his face toward her, trying and failing to smile. "It's a strange life, or … well, *life*, meetin' so many newcomers, introducin' 'em to the place, and then sendin' most of 'em straight off again."

"You could probably … find a new job."

He chuckled. "Ah, no. This is me. An Ashen Shepherd is what I am, and an Ashen Shepherd is what I'll be until it's finally time for me to go wherever I'm goin'." He floated backward into the door, extending a foot behind him to push it open. "Best of luck to ya."

Mara followed him out of the open door onto a porch illuminated with yet more lanterns, their light shining on clean wooden boards that led to steps coated in dusty ash. Beyond lay the fields of gray-gold grass, and beyond that…

"It's smaller," she said, turning to Irasca in confusion.

"Eh?"

"The field went straight to the horizon before," she said, pointing. "I couldn't see anything past the edge of the grass, but now…"

As she stared out of the Junction, the first thing she couldn't help but notice was the roiling storm, a constant churning darkness that crackled and swirled out in the distance, surrounding the fields in all directions.

"Ah, right," said Irasca, nodding. "The Ashen Fields are … a bit peculiar, size-wise. Not the most consistent." He pointed to the storm, shaking his head in warning. "That's the Storm of Broken Worlds. Dead gods. Bad news." He turned and made a wide sweeping gesture as if indicating everything else within the horizon of the cataclysm. "Then there's a buncha other places, but you can find 'em for yourself. Somewhere off in the Fields there's a big statue—Nyxia. Goddess who made the whole place. Quite a beautiful bit of art, if you fancy getting up all close. Makes a good waypoint, anyway."

Mara's eyes kept darting around the Storm of Broken Worlds, chasing its irregular forks of lightning and its whirling clouds. "Sometime, maybe," she murmured.

"Anyway," said Irasca, "I know the storm makes it look like you're seeing all there is to see, but there is more over the horizon. Storm's just that big you can see it from wher-ever—although not everyone sees it until they first enter the Junction, for some reason. But there's a lot more. Lotta folks start with Atonement Grove, over that-a-way. Quickest way into Nox Valar, and that's where you're gonna wanna go for... well, most things."

"What's Nox Valar?"

"You'll see," he said, smiling reminiscently. "There's a lot more I could tell about this place, if you wanted."

"I think I'm one of those people who learns best by going out and doing things themselves."

"I imagine you are," he said. Then he cleared his throat and gave her a meaningful look. "Y'know, I could come with you, if you liked. Part of my job to keep going with new souls a little while, show 'em to the first stops on their journey. If you want anyway."

Mara stared at Irasca. His posture was difficult to read—given that his whole body was suspended by wings in his upper back, he wasn't standing in a way she would've been familiar with—but his face looked earnest.

I think this really is just someone who wants to help. She sighed. *Easy way to get yourself killed. Only fools go out of their way for others.*

"I appreciate the offer," she told him, arranging her features into an expression of grateful fondness, "but I think I'm going to have to do this myself."

"Course," he said, a slight frown playing at his gnarled face. "If you feel that's best."

She made to step out into the fields, then turned back toward him. "Thank you," she said, finding that she did, in fact, mean it.

Irasca positively beamed, the frown disappearing like clouds vanishing to make way for pure sunlight. "You're welcome," he said. Then he hovered back into the Junction, his shimmering wings beating like a hummingbird's, and closed the door.

Alone, Mara turned to the fields and took a breath. Then she strode down the steps and out into the grass, leaving the warm light of the Junction behind.

CHAPTER 3

It was peculiarly freeing to have no real sense of what she was doing. No master directing her, no concrete objective to fulfill. Just the notion that her journey was her own, and that there was no right way to progress.

It was also, of course, boundlessly frustrating, given that she needed to complete whatever journey she had to undertake before Raskith could finish his own tasks. She wasn't sure why exactly she'd refused Irasca's offer of accompaniment; partly a long-honed instinct that she was better relying on none but herself, and perhaps partly a whisper of a sense that nobody else could truly show her the way to navigate her own death.

She headed in the direction the Ashen Shepherd's waggling finger had pointed when he'd mentioned Atonement Grove. It wasn't much to go on, but it was as good a starting place as any. She glanced back at the Junction; the stretch of grass through which she'd walked was cleaner than the rest, its ashy dusting now adorning the legs of her new clothes. The light from the Junction spread outward, saturating the area around itself with warmth; where it dissipated, the stalks shifted gradually from rich charcoal with hints of sparkling amber to a dull, sooty matte in the half-light. There were, she realized, pale patches of light meandering down from the vortex of clouds above, mingling with the flakes of ash as they fell.

Soon the Junction was far behind her, and a copse of trees loomed ahead. It was difficult to miss: egregiously gleaming in contrast to the field of wheat, with its muted gold beneath a suffocating layer of cinders the hue of hoary smoke, the trees bore fresh green leaves and bright red, pink, yellow, even some blue fruits.

Must be Atonement Grove. I should've asked why the name— if it's to do with being paid back for the things I've done in life, I'm in real trouble.

"Well-a-well-a-welcome," said a deep voice that crackled like the trunk of a winter-frosted tree breaking under its own weight.

Mara turned her head in the direction of the voice. A large figure was shrouded against the flickering Storm of Broken Worlds, arms folded, feet planted in the swaying grass.

"And you are?" she called.

"I'd be Gront," said the figure, taking a few steps toward her. *Shit, he's big.*

Gront must have been nearly twice her height and easily three times her bulk. His head had the graceful, feline bulk of a predator; short, dark fur covered his face, and two huge, tusk-like teeth stabbed up from his bottom jaw. He wore a nonde-script cloak that was perhaps too small—it clung to his form, doing little to conceal the fact that he was wearing heavy armor over his whole body.

"And who would you be then?" asked Gront. He stopped a few feet from her, his amber eyes staring down his muzzle.

"Just passing through," said Mara. She met his gaze and stood before him casually, maintaining her external composure as Raskith had taught her. Internally, she was gathering power from her ring, running it through the focusing items in her vial, letting it collect her intentions like a stream picking up detritus as it flowed.

Possessions work as I remember them, and I remember the power these things had.

"That's not who you *are*," said Gront, leaning down. Hot breath tickled her face. "Everyone's just passing through, some faster than others. But that's just what they're *doing*." He raised a hand—not much, just a few inches—and beckoned. In her peripheral vision, she saw three more shapes walking toward them.

The magical aura formed itself into a shape … and then Mara let it go, releasing the tension that held it together. It dissolved into her body, into the air, mingling with the rest of the death energy that drenched the Sunless Crossing.

The spell for deterring undead didn't work on Orgrumm, she reminded herself. Was it because he was a god, or whatever almost-god-thing Irasca said he was? If I try it on this guy and it doesn't work the first time, he'll pummel me into the ground.

"I'm just a newcomer," she said, still keeping her eyes fixed on his.

"Sure," he said. "All of us are at one point or another."

"Are you here to steal from me?" she asked, her voice perfectly steady.

"Steal from—" He drew himself up and laughed. It sounded like a boulder smashing through a hunk of ice. "Oh, no. No, no, no. I like to welcome newcomers, is all."

"But you're not an Ashen Shepherd."

He spat into the grass. "Bunch of do-gooders. No. I'm here to offer you a chance. See, I remember showing up here, all confused. I had nothing." The leonid nostrils flared. "That wasn't easy. So, well, I like to give new faces the opportunity to start with a little bit more than nothing."

"Opportunity?"

The great head gave a considered nod. "A bet. Contest of skill—you pick the game. Against me or any of my friends here. You win, we give you a Crossway Coin. A good one, too, not a useless one."

"I think you know I don't know what a Crossway Coin is," said Mara.

A rumbling chuckle reverberated from Gront's huge chest. "Trust me when I say they're just about the only kind of coin that comes in handy around here."

"Sounds too good to be true," she said, finally taking a good look around at the others. She turned her head slowly, deliberately, taking in each of the group in turn. Gront's *friends* included one diminutive, pointy-eared person she suspected might be a goblin, someone she was fairly certain was a half-orc with what looked like an oversized, serrated butcher's cleaver in each hand, and a blubbery biped that resembled nothing so much as a whale with feet. She turned her attention back to Gront, who was watching her patiently. "What do you get if I lose?"

"Well, anything you've got of value," said Gront. "Which, to be fair, for a lot of new faces isn't anything at all when they get here, 'specially when they find out there's no value to gold and jewels here. Now, if you were one of those new faces with nothing to wager, what I'd probably suggest is that you go off and gather a couple of Crossway Coins of your own the regular way, which is to say you join the back of the queue and get a near-worthless coin in return. Then you bet your low-value coins against our high-value ones, and we all have a good time." His cloak fluttered as he kneeled, bringing his face close to Mara's. "But I see that ring. And the chain around your neck. I'd be willing to bet they're more valuable than an end-of-the-line Crossway Coin."

"Only to me," Mara said. It was true: unless he was a trained necromancer or some other mage that could shape death aura, Gront wouldn't be able to use the magic in her ring—if he could get it on any of his massive fingers in the first place. As for her vial, not even Raskith could have used it. It was her own focus of power, and it would do nothing in any other hands.

Gront hummed deeply, the sound echoing out of his throat as if out of a cavern in a mountainside. "Well," he said, "I can't force you to play."

"It wouldn't go well for you if you tried," said Mara.

His eyes widened. Then he threw back his head and guffawed to the heavens. "I like you," he said, and Mara thought he genuinely meant it. He stood and waved to his compatriots. "Right," he called, "no luck this time. Out of here until the next one!" He turned to leave, his massive bulk shifting powerfully.

Mara blinked. "Wait. You're genuinely not going to attack me?"

The great head turned back toward her. "Would you prefer it if I did?"

"No," she said. "I just ... really thought you were going to."

"Well," he said, "that might be your problem."

Huh.

She watched him leave, beckoning his group after him with a huge paw.

There's got to be more to this, but I'm not going to look a gift thundersteed in the mouth.

Atonement Grove awaited.

CHAPTER 4

The thicket that was Atonement Grove bore fruit in abundance, Mara found: apples, plums, pomegranates, pears, lemons, other things that looked like no fruit she'd ever seen, all in what looked like perfect health and ripeness. The dappled canopy of leaves above protected the trees beneath from the falling ash; the bright colors, cooler and more alive than the lantern light of the Junction, blared in Mara's vision in stark contrast to the ever-present gray of the Sunless Crossing. A gentle, constant psithurism brushed her ears, a soft cushion beneath all other sounds. It was ... peaceful.

She found herself plucking a pear and taking a hefty bite, allowing the juices to flow down her chin. There was something celebratory about it, something life-affirming in this world of the dead.

I don't even really like pears, she thought, dropping the rest of the half-eaten fruit out of spite for the notion that she of all people should get to enjoy its sweetness.

There was a natural path through the trees—not a paved road, but a winding passage, one that seemed to open between the trunks of its own volition as she approached. She followed it until she came to a clearing, a round space between the trees.

Before her was a clear, still pond, its surface reflecting the verdant, shuffling canopy of leaves overhead.

She stood at the edge of the pool, wondering whether she was supposed to drink the water, or perhaps walk in and submerge herself.

Why does getting to the afterlife have to mean undertaking a personal journey, or whatever's supposed to be happening here? Those are for heroes, not … whatever I am. She exhaled heavily, casting an idle look around at the trees that surrounded the pool. No Shepherd appeared to guide her. *Well, I did tell Irasca I wanted to do this myself.*

She turned her gaze to the water. The image on its surface shifted and warped, and in moments she was staring at the peculiar vision of her own death, playing out as if she were watching it from above.

Mara let it unfold, grimacing in distaste.

I look pathetic. He made me look pathetic.

The vision faded. Her reflection stared back at her, clear and free of distortion. "What am I supposed to do here then?" she asked aloud.

"You don't know," said her reflection. "That's the problem."

Mara tilted her head. Her reflection followed suit.

"Well, this is unexpected," she said.

"Not really," said the Mara in the water. "You were half-expecting something like this. Face to face with your authentic self to face true judgment, or something along those lines."

Mara sat down by the edge of the pool, crossing her legs and resting her hands on the grass behind her. "You're honest, aren't you?"

"Completely, I'm afraid."

"Yeah." Mara clicked her tongue off the roof of her mouth, sighing. "That's what I was worried about."

"At least you don't need to worry about your family," said the reflection.

Mara glanced down, frowning at herself. "I wasn't."

"I know." The other her gave a small, sad smile that looked so sincere, so out of place on her features, that Mara spat right into her counterpart's face. Her visage distorted in the ripples, momentarily warping the smile into one of sinister cruelty. Then the water stilled, and she was wearing that same earnest, empathetic expression again. It was *hateful*. "But you've been thinking it's because you don't care. It's actually because you know Raskith can't hurt them."

Mara couldn't hide an instant of shock and relief passing across her face. She schooled her features in a moment, even more desperate to hide her thoughts from her reflection, from herself, than from others. "Because of the contract," she realized. "He swore on both our blood that he couldn't harm them once I was no longer an apprentice, couldn't even indirectly allow harm to come to them."

"You aren't an apprentice anymore," her reflection said.

Mara shifted, putting her back to the water and holding her knees. "So what are you saying then?" she asked. "That because I care a little bit, that makes me ... a good person? A necromancer with a heart of gold?"

"Oh, no," said the reflection from behind and below. "Your heart is a pulsating mass of black fungus and rot. You're a genuinely terrible person."

"Complete honesty," Mara muttered. The words didn't sting. She knew them to be true.

"Just because you have a little bit of residual interest in the people who raised you doesn't make up for everything you and Raskith did."

"I was going to defeat him, at least," Mara mused.

"You were going to do what *all* evil apprentices do and try to kill him so you could take his place as the most powerful master of darkness," her reflection corrected.

"Fair point."

"You swore yourself to Rekh," her own voice reminded her seriously. "To the service of the one who revels in all that abhors the natural order of the world. You can't just decide to be a good person now that you're dead."

Mara huffed. "Is that not how it works? I thought some gods were all about second chances."

"I think you have to undergo a sincere change. I don't think you can just decide to have a change of heart on something like the god you committed your life—well, your existence—to." A wistful sigh rose from the pool and drifted off into the trees, where it was lost in the gentle whispering of the leaves. "We don't have time for that. We need to move on, and fast. It's Rekh, whatever he has in store for us beyond the end, or eternity under Raskith's command."

"Thought as much," Mara muttered. She stood, brushing herself off, and glanced down at her reflection. "You know, if you're so honest and self-aware, I would've expected you to be more... I don't know, bitter. Or more obviously evil or something."

"There's not really any point when it's only myself I have to talk to," said the pool-Mara, shrugging. "I'm not *happy*, exactly, but... well, how Raskith always acted was just a mask. How you act now—and how you would've acted if you'd ever taken his place—all just more masks. I don't have any need for one."

"Must be nice." Mara crossed to the nearest tree, liberated a fat purple fig, and brought it back to the edge of the pool, where she dropped it on her reflection's face. "This was useless. Have fun being in a pond forever."

"You're well aware that's a misrepresentation of my existence," said the reflection, infuriatingly.

Mara walked away, sticking her middle finger up as she went.

It wasn't hard to find the way out of the Grove. She had a feeling that she could have picked any direction and walked in a straight line, leaving the pool in the center of the copse, and she'd have been out within a few minutes. The trees cleared, giving her an unfettered view of the Sunless Crossing once more.

"What in the f—?"

A grand, gleaming city dominated the Ashen Fields. Atop a wide, flat mesa in the middle of the plain, towers of clean white and black stretched up toward the sky. Mara couldn't tell how far it was from her, but she could see thick streams of water plunging off the sides of the mesa, white mist rising where it hit the ground. For there to be that much mist, that much force, the waterfalls must have been enormous, which meant the city itself must have been...

She shook her head, momentarily disoriented by the scale of it. There it still was when she looked back, gleaming starkly against the gray prairie.

Whatever it's made out of, someone's gone to a lot of trouble to enchant it to repel dirt, Mara thought, brushing a light dusting of ash out of her hair. It was, of course, instantly replaced by the ever-falling flakes. *This place wants you to be impressed.* And, she had to admit, it was working.

She took two deep breaths, then started walking. *Nowhere else to go. May as well check out the giant shining city that wasn't there before.*

She walked for an hour or two, the gleaming marble growing larger and larger as she drew nearer. Her legs suddenly felt lighter; she glanced down, realizing that she'd stepped out of the thick grass and onto a smooth road of what looked like packed dirt. There were grooves, she saw, as if the road were regularly traveled by something with wheels.

As she peered down, reveling in the sudden absence of resistance to every step, a noise caught her ear, bright and ringing. She realized for the first time that the ashfall wasn't entirely silent; the dry precipitation landed on the grass with the quietest of brushes. In such constant motion, the ashfall created an underlying rustle, barely noticeable unless you focused on it but creating a gentle muffling effect that dulled everything else ever so slightly. This new sound cut through that like a flaming sword through an iceworm.

She turned and saw its source: violently garish, obnoxiously colorful, a trail of carts rolled across the fields. Flags and banners and bunting and paper streamers and puppets, and the occasional burst of dyed fire that screamed bright against the dark landscape, a glaring burst of flamboyant light that made Mara's eyes twitch. She turned her head left and right, looking for somewhere to duck into, but there was nothing except the swaying grass.

I don't think I'm going to get along with these people.

And people there were; people of all natures. Some walked, some rode, some flew. One flitted as a stream of orange-and-blue smoke through the air; one became a ball of mud and disappeared into the earth before popping back out again; one was only visible as a head and shoulders gliding through the dirt, bobbing up and down as if swimming beneath the surface. Many were adorned in outfits that matched the garishness of the convoy itself, and many of those were dancing or tumbling or climbing on the carts, but a fair proportion kept themselves more reserved in dress and behavior.

And then there was the noise. The initial blare had come from a long-necked brass instrument wielded carelessly by an eight-foot-tall person with feathered wings that looked as if they were naturally white, but had had several buckets of multicolored paint thrown over them. Others followed, joyously screeching out on flutes or hammering drums or tearing at strings. Some of it could have been called music, perhaps, but none of the musicians seemed to have any interest in joining up their tunes with what the others were playing. Beneath the tones of the instruments swelled the cries and yaps of voices in song or conversation.

Mara half-expected to see a menagerie of animals traveling with the group, but—although she saw sapient people with features that reminded her of animals of every kind— there were none. *I'm guessing animals don't wind up in purgatory,* she mused.

"Ho, traveler!" a voice called, clear and resonant even above the cacophony. "A greeting from the Cavalcade of Strays!"

Mara raised one hand in the most unenthusiastic salutation she could muster. She took a couple of steps off the side of the road, getting out of the way of the train of bodies and carts.

At the head of the convoy, a lone figure broke free and skipped ahead to Mara. "You know," she said, "most people are more excited to see us."

"I don't know what I'm seeing," Mara said.

The woman gave a sharp bark of laughter. "Of course not," she said. "Who would?" She was tall and broad, her skin a lighter gray than the ash blanketing the surrounding span of leaves and stalks: an *alive* gray, somehow, augmented by streaks of pink and blue painted on her cheeks. "I'm Nozan. Need anything?"

Mara tilted her head to look past Nozan at the miscellany of hues. "What sort of anything?"

"Oh, you know. Things that are things. Things that do things. Things that thing things."

Mara tried to resist giving the woman a look of utter withering. She failed.

"Oh, you're one of those who's all serious all the time?" Nozan gave an exaggerated pout, slapping her hands on her thighs. "Come *ooon*. You're dead. What reason is there to be anything other than free and ridiculous?"

"I ... don't know how to respond to that."

Nozan patted her on the shoulder. Mara pushed the hand off. "When I was alive," said Nozan, "I had to spend my whole life beating people up with a bunch of other people who did nothing but beat people up. We were pretty good at it. Did a lot of beating. Captured a few towns. And now I'm dead, and I don't have to beat anyone up anymore, and it's *great*."

Mara nodded slowly. "Good for you," she said, returning Nozan's pat. The woman's upper arm—which Mara had to stretch up above her head to reach—was as firm as rock. "So, you're the leader of the... what did you call it?"

"Cavalcade of Strays," said Nozan. "And, well, I'm at the front today. We don't have a *leader*. We just sort of let life lead us where it will."

"Life?"

Nozan laughed again. The carts caught up to them, the din of the procession drowning out her merriment. "Alright, not *life* exactly. Although..." She made a wide, sweeping gesture with her arm, indicating the hubbub and the rabble. "Hard not to think of this as life, eh?"

Mara's gaze swept over the parade. It was hard to argue with that. Taking a more pragmatic view, since Nozan had suggested that the Cavalcade might have things to offer, she glanced at each of the carts as it rolled past. Some were laden with fireworks, some with food; in some were gleaming gems, in others a medley of bric-à-brac.

"So," said Nozan, "see anything you need?"

"I thought all the *things* went to the Gilded Hills," Mara said, still watching the Cavalcade proceed past.

"Oh, sure," said Nozan, nodding sagely. "Most do. Some don't. Some of the ones that do come out again."

Mara looked back at the larger woman. "I don't have anything to trade."

"Oh, everyone's got something," said Nozan. "But if you're not in need of anything, all is well and we'll be on our way. Unless... if you don't mind my saying so, because I mean this as the highest of compliments, you seem like a little bit of a stray yourself. Always room for more."

"Can't," said Mara. "I need to get out of this place, and fast."

The tall stray raised an eyebrow at that. "Oh? What, trying to get yourself resurrected faster?"

"The opposite."

"Ahh. You know, I might know someone who could help with that... Varun!" She waved a hand at one of the passing wanderers, a lean man in scratched half-plate armor with a pair of short, straight swords hanging from his back. He peeled off from the procession and headed toward them, nodding to Nozan.

"Yeah."

"Got one here who's looking to finish her journey before she gets called back, if I'm understanding right. That right?"

Her question was directed at Mara, but Mara didn't move.

She was frozen, staring at the face of the man before her. His skin was night-black with patches of stark white; his hair was blazing red.

"Hey," said Varun, frowning at Mara. "Do we know each other?"

"I don't think so," Mara managed to say.

But she knew that face.

It was the face of the first corpse she'd ever raised.

CHAPTER 5

Raskith strode through a burning village as if he had no cares in the world. His robes swished around his body with every step. Mara followed, unable to stop staring at the towering flames, the gushes of black smoke.

"What do we have to gain from this?" she asked.

Her master turned sharply and stopped in place; she almost walked into him.

"Do you question my methods?"

"No, Master." She bowed her head quickly, not yet hardened to the ways of the necromancer. Someday she would learn how to hide her thoughts from him; until then, she would hide her face and hope that would suffice. One day, of course, she would indeed stop hiding her face, but not because she had learned to pretend indifference to the suffering they caused. "I only wonder at the ... strategic value of this conquest."

"It is reasonable," Raskith declared, and Mara breathed a sigh of relief, "to want to understand tactics and strategy." He turned again and walked on; she scurried after. "Laying waste to a small village such as this," he said as he went, "serves two important ends. The first is that our power comes not only from our mastery over death, but from...?"

"Our reputation, Master."

"Precisely. Causing visible destruction, even to a place so incon-sequential as this…" He paused to wave a hand lazily in the direc-tion of a surviving villager, who had launched herself at him with an anguished wail. Her cry was cut short as her neck snapped; she collapsed and slid a few inches along the dusty ground, her hair, face, and clothes collecting dirt until her body came to a halt. She didn't move again. "It instills fear," Raskith lectured as if he had never been interrupted. "It makes people pay attention to us. It makes us feared. And fear makes people foolish."

He stopped beside the wreckage of a house. Trapped beneath a fallen, blackened panel of wood—what had been the door, Mara guessed—lay a man with marbled black-and-white skin, on his back, his eyes closed. Raskith extended a foot and nudged him in his mass of fire-red hair.

The man's eyes shot open, pupils rolling back in his head. He let out a cry of agony and rage that made the inside of Mara's ears feel as if they were about to shatter.

"Did you just raise him?" she asked.

"Oh, no," said Raskith. "No, this one is very much alive. That's just the sort of noise people make when they're in a lot of pain."

"Oh," said Mara.

The fallen man lifted his head, straining his neck to look at his own body. He beheld himself crushed beneath the wood, and he screamed again. His fingers clawed desperately at whatever debris they could reach, but to no avail.

Raskith sighed and flicked a hand. The man just about had time to look up at the two figures looming above him before a blade of condensed purple-black aura slammed itself through his forehead.

He fell silent.

"Now," drawled Raskith, a mere glance sending the heavy wood flying off the body, "let us carry this most valuable of resources somewhere a little quieter and explore the second purpose that causing such wanton havoc might serve." He left a pregnant pause of the kind that demanded the obvious question.

"What purpose, Master?"

His dark lips stretched themselves into an unctuous smile. "Why, the education of my apprentice, of course."

Mara fell back onto the grass, panting from the effort. It had taken her over an hour of painstaking mental exertion to create her first raising circle, not to mention the physical strain of hunching down and pressing her chalk into the soft earth until it left a solid impression. When she was stronger, she would be able to carve out lines with a mere thought, but doing things the hard way was part of earning the right to do them the powerful way.

In the center of the circle lay the corpse. Raskith had made her carry that on her back from the village to the nearby plain rather than simply move it with magic too.

"Well," said Raskith, lounging on a tree stump, "I think you're ready to take your first step into true necromancy, don't you?"

Mara nodded and crossed her legs, straightening her back, finding a posture in which she could close her eyes and focus on the task at hand. Her fingers found the vial around her neck, only recently completed with all the necessary items brought together. She'd felt a sense of real pride in her work and herself when she'd finished building her focus, then a vague twinge of guilt for feeling proud of something she'd accomplished in her apprenticeship to Raskith. But she suppressed the twinge. She wasn't yet perfect at it, but she would be.

She began the process as her master had taught her, diving into herself and finding the power of death, cycling it around herself, forming it. She called upon Rekh, the god of death, to guide her and let her serve him in the greatest way she could. She pushed her strength into the lifeless body.

When she opened her eyes twenty minutes later, sweat was dripping from her face. Her cheeks were flushed, her breathing ragged.

But it was done.

In the middle of the circle, the corpse clambered to its feet, ungainly and inelegant. Clouded white eyes stared out of the slack, gawking face.

"Well done, Mara," said Raskith, layering his tone with a fruity note of appreciation.

"Thank you, Master," she managed to say. She hauled herself to her feet, muscles trembling, and beheld her work.

The wraith, absent her instructions, simply stood there before her, hunched and swaying. Raskith had drilled hours upon hours of theoretical knowledge into her about the precise mechanism by which necromancy caused a body to animate, how the head tended to slump as the magic prioritized control over the joints necessary for locomotion, the changes the body's muscles underwent as they were primed for simple, primal physical movements. She remembered none of it as she stared into the dead face.

"Now then," said Raskith. "Order it to attack me."

She whipped her head around to stare at him. "What?"

He raised a dark eyebrow.

"I mean… Master, for what reason would I do such a thing?"

"Well," he said, standing up tall and brushing his robes clean of imaginary dirt, "raising is only the first part of mastery. If your wraith can do nothing but stand in one spot until it falls over, all your prowess over death allows you to accomplish very little."

She looked from her master to her new wraith and back again.

"You have the knowledge," said Raskith, investigating his fingernails with an air of absent calm. "I hope you're not worried your very first raising might actually hurt me."

"No, Master," she said, shaking her head. The thought had, in fact, occurred to her … in that his direction had prompted her to

wonder just how much stronger she would need to be before she could obliterate her master. "I only hope to serve well."

"Of course," he said dryly. "Now, order it to attack me."

Mara took a deep breath, reaching for her power. She could feel the wraith there, tethered to her, its presence lurking just outside the boundaries of her own spirit. A thin thread of death energy linked them together; she followed it, pushing her awareness into the corpse.

Her sense of self fizzed, instinctively afraid of inhabiting another body. The wraith's dead muscles pulsed; she felt it almost as if they were her own. Cold viscera filled the corpse. Mara was quietly grateful for the fact that her senses were outside her physical form; the sensation of wet, lifeless innards occupying the body she was in would have made it a struggle not to throw up the contents of her stomach.

She reached out to the wraith: to the physical parts that composed it, to the magic that gave it function. And she gave it a single, simple instruction.

Kill him.

It resisted for just a moment, some lingering will loath to bend to the will of another. But it wasn't enough.

Mara opened her eyes. The wraith took one hesitant step, then a second. By the third, it had broken into a full run, lurching and launching toward Raskith. The master necromancer raised a hand, fingers curling into a gesture of power.

The wraith fell over its own feet a good five yards from him. Its face slammed into the grass, momentum nearly carrying its rear end over the top. A second later, it had come to a halt, a jumbled pile of uncoordinated limbs at the mage's feet.

"A strong first attempt," said Raskith approvingly.

"Eh," said Varun, shrugging. "You just look kind of familiar."

"Got one of those faces," said Mara, trying very hard to keep her expression politely interested.

Thank you, Raskith, for teaching me to hide my feelings in high-pressure situations.

"Sure." Varun frowned at her a moment longer, then shook his head. "What was that about a journey? Couldn't hear you over the... well, all of it."

Despite herself, Mara snorted. This man, with his dented armor and his perpetual scowl, was as much at contrast with the Cavalcade of Strays as the Cavalcade itself was with the gray emptiness that surrounded it. He glanced at her, a flicker of amusement passing across his face.

"Ah, you explain," said Nozan, waving a hand at Mara. "I've got a Cavalcade to steer through the Crossing, you know. If one wheel gets bent, you can bet it'll all be my fault!" She darted off, flashing a final smile as she disappeared back toward the head of the procession.

Varun sighed and turned his attention to Mara. He was tall, she realized, taller than his hunched corpse had been. His irises were the same dappled monochrome as his skin, and they bore into her as he stared down. She averted her gaze, scratching the back of her neck in the hopes of looking simply awkward and uncertain.

"I, er, need to find a way into my afterlife," she said. "And fast."

She didn't look up to meet his eyes, but she could feel his gaze intensifying on the top of her head.

"And why would you need to do that?" he asked.

"Because someone's going to try to resurrect me," she said, forcing herself to look at him, "and I really, *really* don't want that to happen."

Varun regarded her intensely for a few moments. Then he let out a long sigh through his nostrils and shook his head, rubbing the bridge of his nose. "Right."

"What?"

"Nozan probably thinks this is funny," he muttered, then let out one more heavy sigh and put his hands on his hips. "Alright," he said. His tone was decisive, albeit with perhaps a note of reluctance. "I'll help you do what you need to do."

Mara narrowed her eyes. "Why?"

He shrugged. "I have my reasons. You've got yours."

Can't argue too much with that. If I force him to share, he's going to want me to return the favor.

She nodded and extended a hand, as she'd seen people do when agreeing to undertake an endeavor together. Varun looked at it for a moment, then reached out and clasped her wrist for a moment before letting go.

"So," she said, "what do I need to do first?"

"Nox Valar," he said, raising his chin toward the great city. "You can see it, right?"

She followed his gaze, letting the great marble sight dominate her field of view again. "As of about an hour ago."

"Good first step," said Varun. He threw one casual wave over his shoulder, then started walking toward the city.

Mara took one last glance at the Cavalcade of Strays as it continued to blare and shine on its way.

Thank all the gods spending time with that isn't a mandatory step on the route to the afterlife.

She followed Varun.

CHAPTER 6

"So," said Mara when the silence had stretched on too long, "the Cavalcade of Strays seems like a fun bunch."

Varun gave a quiet chuckle without looking at her. "Oh, they are, if that's the sort of thing you enjoy."

"Not you though?"

He thought about it. The grand cityscape loomed ever higher above them as they proceeded toward it. Mara kept thinking they must be nearly there, that it couldn't possibly be any bigger, and then it was still farther away than she thought and even bigger than her eyes had told her.

"It was a useful way to spend some time," he said eventually.

Mara glanced at his face. He was staring vaguely downward at a point a yard or two ahead of his feet as they trudged through the grass. *I don't want to prod too hard, but I'd rather not commit to spending time with someone I know nothing about…* "Useful in what way?"

"I want to become a god," he said, still staring at the grass before them.

Mara considered this. "Huh," she said eventually.

"Most people think that's kind of stupid."

"I don't think so," she said. "Doesn't everyone sort of want to become a god, in their own way?"

That stumped him for a second, and then he chuckled. "Maybe. I don't think people tend to invest in it quite the way I've done it though."

Come to think of it, did Raskith ever say he was going to try to ascend to godhood? Seems like the sort of thing he'd have done, but I can't remember him ever mentioning it.

"What's the plan?" she asked, genuinely curious. "Do you know what you need to do to make it happen?"

"Not exactly," said Varun, "but I do have a strategy of sorts."

Mara waited for him to continue. *I've got him talking now. He wants to tell me. I'll just let him.*

"See, different worlds have different concepts of godhood," said Varun after a moment. "On mine, we just saw gods as ... unreachable. These personifications of some concept or other, beings that had been dreamed up to be the ultimate representation of each part of existence. Ever present, never changing. Other worlds see them as more like regular mortals who have just transcended what it usually means to exist through amassing great power or something." He took a breath. Mara got the sense he enjoyed explaining, despite his projected air of aloofness. "Here, though, there are people who've had access to gods in ways most universes don't get. So the Crossing has a better understanding of what it means to be a god than most living worlds."

"Makes sense."

He glanced at her. "It does?"

She shrugged. "Well, yeah. Where we go after we die is one of the big things people are worried about, one of the big things they look for gods to answer. Here, we're halfway to finding out for ourselves exactly what happens to us for eternity."

"True," he conceded, and lapsed into silence.

Mara got the sense that he might have been irritated at the interruption, so she obliged him. "So what does it really mean? To be a god?"

"It's kind of complicated," he said, pausing.

He's just saying that so it seems more impressive when he launches into an explanation in three, two, one...

"The long and short of it," he began, right on cue, "is that there are these things that are ... not physically real, but real anyway. Most people call them domains. They're like the purest expression of a concept, or even the concept truly in itself, abstracted from imperfect examples. There'll never be, I don't know, a cloud that's the perfect, ideal representation of what it is to be all the clouds there'll ever be, but there's a domain of cloud somewhere—or maybe not somewhere, I don't know whether it makes sense to think of them as being located any-where—that takes everything it means to be a cloud and con-denses it into ... something."

"And these domains," Mara said, when she was sure she wasn't jumping in before his next sentence, "there's one for ... everything there is?"

"No idea." Varun shrugged. "Probably."

She turned the notion over in her mind. "So, what, each of these *domains* has a god?"

"Or gods," he said. "As I understand it, it's about faith—but not in the direction you might think. I've met a lot of people who thought gods were granted their power by the sheer fact that people believed in them, but it's not quite that simple. If the domain has sufficient faith in a person, or entity or what-ever, to recognize it as an exemplar of itself... well, then you have a god."

Mara frowned. "Well, that sounds as if gods can only be created by the domains themselves."

"Some are," he said. "The purest ones, I suppose, and often the oldest, are simply brought into existence by the domain understanding that some being like them must *be*. But other beings can make themselves known to a domain, shape themselves to be close to its nature, and if they're lucky, the domain might acknowledge them." A wry smile flashed across his face. "One way to do that, of course, is to murder one of the domain's existing champions, but that's a bit of a tall order."

"So your plan is to become a perfect representation of some concept or other in the hopes the domain'll decide you're suited to godhood," Mara summarized.

"That's about it."

"Do you have a particular domain in mind?"

He shook his head. "Nope."

She couldn't help throwing up her hands in exasperation. "Well then, how in all the hells do you expect to become a perfect representation of some concept or other without even knowing which one it is?"

"I don't have time to mold myself to a domain," said Varun. "It'd take … centuries."

"What's the rush?"

"I'm not that patient."

That's fair enough. At least he's honest about it.

"Instead," Varun continued, "I'm trying to become passingly familiar with as many different things as I possibly can. Step two is to hope I'm just naturally brilliant at one of them. Then I stick with that one, starting at an advanced level and saving all the time of working up from the basics."

Mara spent a while trying to work out whether that was an utterly ingenious plan or an atrociously foolish one, because it was definitely one or the other rather than falling somewhere in the middle. She just had no idea which.

"What have you tried so far?" she asked eventually, giving up on the attempt to categorize Varun's efforts as brilliant or nonsensical.

"Oh, a few things," he mused. "I just open myself to new experiences. Perhaps I should have tried to do that a little more while I was alive."

Before Raskith killed you and I animated your corpse, Mara couldn't help thinking.

She opened her mouth to ask something else, suddenly afraid that he would hear her thoughts unless she said something, anything, aloud, but he had come to a stop, staring upward. She followed his gaze, realizing they had finally reached the base of the mesa. Some distance along the side of the walls of the plateau, a raging torrent crashed down over the edge and into the Ashen Fields below.

Before them was a huge archway carved into the stone face of the cliff; the apex of the opening must have been sixty feet above the ground, and the wall itself extended far beyond that. Mara began to feel slightly dizzy, the cliff seeming to go up forever; before she tore her eyes away, she noticed that there were rows upon rows of what looked like statues peering vigilantly out from the walls.

"What are those?" she muttered, irrationally concerned that the statues might hear her.

"Oh, just the dead gargoyles," said Varun, almost cheerily. "They die, they turn to stone, they sit around and look all ominous. Come on; we've got a long way to go yet."

We have?!

He led her through the archway into a tunnel lit by hundreds of torches, their flames sputtering with different colors; she swept her gaze from side to side, wary of guards or traps or some other open or secret test to gain entrance. The outline of the arch had been shaped by tools or magic into hundreds of faces: people of all kinds, all natures, some humanoid and some less so, in varying states of joy or despair or wonder or fear.

"Those are supposed to represent all the people who pass through here," Varun explained, seeing her head turning. "Of course, what you see here probably doesn't come close to a tenth of the actual variety; people come in all kinds of bodies, especially when you factor in how many different worlds lead here."

Mara decided she wasn't keen on looking at rows upon rows of faces. The artwork wasn't bad; if anything, it was too good, too lifelike. Something about the reminder of just how many people went through the journey of death—and, no matter how small a proportion of the total, how many journeys she and Raskith had interrupted—made her stomach twist just a little.

I didn't actually trouble many of them, she reminded herself. *I put the bodies they weren't using anymore to work, but they wouldn't have known about that. Except the ones whose souls I did call back, but... well, can't do much about that now. Oh, and some of the ones I raised as wraiths, it was me who killed them in the first place. So ... I'm not a good person, but I knew that anyway. I'm fine with that. I am.*

She glanced over at Varun, trying not to see the image of his mindless, dead face.

"Come on," he said, starting up the tunnel. "Ascension Row awaits."

The gradient felt slight at first, but went on for long enough that Mara's legs began to burn.

I haven't even got real muscles anymore and they're still managing to hurt, Mara lamented internally, but she wasn't about to show any sign of weakness to Varun. She didn't actively mistrust the man, but it would take more than a conversation about his aspirations of godhood to make her properly comfortable that he wouldn't stab her if it would benefit him.

She frowned at the thought. *Come to think of it…*

"Hey," she said, trying not to sound out of breath, "what happens if we die while we're here? Do we just get … obliterated?" *That would actually be preferable to being bound to Raskith, and probably to entering Rekh's afterlife too…*

Varun glanced over his shoulder at her. "Briefly," he answered, "but you come back. You just fall from the sky again, like you did the first time. It's not without consequences though."

"Like what?"

He sighed, as if remembering something unpleasant. "You get two deaths here with no lasting ill effects," he said. "You just come back together and find yourself in the Ashen Fields the next morning. Starting from the third death, you start to … unravel. Maybe you forget something; maybe you become a little less real. Do it a few times, you'll be more like a ghost than a person."

"Have you died here?"

"Not yet. Came close a few times though."

The image of Varun breathing his last beneath the ruins of his house flitted through her mind. She shook it away.

They continued up the tunnel, which wound slowly around as it ascended.

More like a hall in a grand cathedral than a tunnel, Mara thought: the multitude of torches lighting the way gave the huge space an imposing resplendence, as did the stone columns dotted along its length. There was nothing to indicate how far they'd come, nor how far they had left to go.

Idly, she reached for the power in her ring. It was full to bursting with the aura of death, as befitted her surroundings.

Those spells didn't work on Orgrumm, she thought, *but maybe I could use magic on myself?*

She pulled a stream of magic from the ring and cycled it around her body in patterns of strength, focusing on her lungs and legs. When the power illuminated the full series of lines and curves required, she flashed her will into it, casting a spell of enhancement.

Her breathing calmed; the ache in her legs subsided. She picked up her pace, casually overtaking Varun.

"You've perked up," he observed.

"Are we nearly there?" she asked over her shoulder.

"I have no idea," he said. "Almost, probably?"

A moment later, the space before them began to lighten. The effect was mild, subtle; not the sudden radiance of the sun cutting through the darkness, but a gradual leak of pale half-light suffusing with the torches' flames.

"I guess we're there," Varun said, deadpan.

Mara let him catch up, and the two of them emerged from the subterrain. Above was the soft, endlessly revolving purple of the sunless sky. Before them was the edge of the cliff; past that, the expansive stretches of the Ashen Fields, until they terminated at the forbidding storm. She turned away from the edge, stepping around the tunnel's exit, and found herself ant-like beneath the enormous reaches of Nox Valar's towers and structures.

And between her and the city was Orgrumm.

CHAPTER 7

"**O**h, fuck *off*," said Mara, and punched Orgrumm in the face.

With an undignified squeal, the self-proclaimed god went flying. Mara shook out her knuckles; even with her arm and hand strengthened by the same spell that had empowered her legs up Ascension Row, hitting that hard left an ache. She'd certainly come off better than Orgrumm though.

"You could have just said no!" the duck-pig-man squawked, struggling to his feet and tripping over his robes. He dashed off toward the heights of the city, wailing.

Mara gave her shoulder a couple of good rotations in its socket, then turned to Varun. He was staring at her with an expression of curious amusement, one eyebrow cocked.

"That seemed disproportionate," he said.

She waved a hand at Orgrumm's retreating form dismissively. "Ran into him once before. He's no good. And besides, he reckons he's a god, so he should be able to take one good punch."

"Ah." Varun nodded, apparently satisfied. "Well, before you did that, I was about to say something along the lines of 'Welcome to the Gray Vista, don't listen to anyone who tries to get you to worship them here,' but I see you've learned that lesson already."

"What's the deal with that?" Mara asked. "Irasca—the Ashen Shepherd I met—said something about people trying to sell something, but … he wasn't the best at explaining."

Varun nodded again. "This is the only route into Nox Valar, which makes it something of a target for people looking for newcomers who might not know how things work. Some types try to take advantage of that—most are fraudsters just trying to cheat people out of their possessions or services, but some might well be divine in some capacity, just … old, or forgotten, or diminished, searching for anyone who'll pray to them just once and make them feel like a god again. But for anyone to lower themselves to that kind of approach is considered, ah, tacky."

They began to move purposefully toward the city. For the first time since arriving, Mara soon found herself among other people. They thronged by Nox Valar, coming, going, hurrying, talking, and going about whatever business dead people went about.

"So," said Varun, his voice a low murmur under the noise of the crowds, "that was quite a punch."

"I've had some practice."

"You really punched a man twenty feet with the strength of your muscles alone?"

Mara saw no reason to deny the implication. "I might have enhanced it a bit."

"I thought as much when we were coming up the tunnel," Varun said. "I'd have had you down as the lone-ranging fist-fighter type, but I'm assuming you have more up your sleeves than that."

How much do I give away here?

"How common is magic in the Crossing?" she asked.

"Oh, every other person's some sort of magic user," he said, navigating through the crowd with easy precision. "Only thing is—your Shepherd told you about the fact that people come here from different worlds, right?"

She nodded. "He didn't say much more than that. Just sort of dropped that on me and then went off on some tangent about something else."

"It takes a minute to get used to, but it starts to feel normal soon enough," said Varun. "Anyway, not all worlds work the same. There are different ... ways of using magic, different routes to gaining it, depending on which world you come from." He glanced at her hand. "I'd guess yours works pretty similarly to mine, actually. In my world, magic was pretty rare. Most people who used it had some kind of item that they stored power in—condensed it from their surroundings or something, I think—and usually some sort of ... focus—was that the word? A thing that helped them shape spells for whatever their purposes were. More complicated spells took rituals—you know, drawing big circles of runes, bringing other pre-pared items into the mix, that kind of thing."

"That's ... about it," Mara admitted. "Wait—similar to yours? You can use magic too?"

"I couldn't when I was alive," said Varun. "I don't know a whole lot about the theory behind it, but there are two main kinds of magic in most worlds, and that holds true here too. There's the magic people can learn and use through some power of their own, and there's the magic that comes from the gods."

Mara tried not to let her shock show. *He's been given power by a god? Mine isn't even divine in that way—Raskith and I always worked in the service of Rekh, but he didn't give us our magic. We used it in his name, but it came from us.*

"Speaking of the gods," Varun started, a note of hesitation in his voice, "your plan is to persuade one to let you into their final resting place before you're ... unwillingly resurrected?"

"Unless you know of any better way to avoid it," Mara said.

He shook his head, a strange expression crossing his face. "If you're in the Crossing, you can be pulled back," he said.

Mara made a *tsk* sound with her tongue. "Yeah, that's about what Irasca said too."

The odd look on Varun's face slid away, replaced by a sly smile. "Is Irasca the grumpy one with the wings?" He made a flapping motion with his hands.

"That's him."

"Ah. I liked him."

Mara gave a quiet laugh. "I don't think he was as grumpy as he wanted people to think. Seemed to actually care what happened to me. It was weird."

Varun frowned. "That's something of a sad thing to say."

Mara stopped talking.

The taller man guided her through Nox Valar without further conversation, occasionally pointing at something to tell her in brief what it was—or, to be more precise, its name, which was not always a particularly useful indicator of what it was.

"Crag Veil," he said, indicating a stone hall with expansive white walls concealing what lay beyond, an enormous black steel sword and shield adorning its exterior. "Whetstone Bluff, and the Arena Exemplar beyond that," was his comment with a nod in the general direction of what looked like an entire bustling district at whose purpose Mara could only guess. "Exora's Belfry," with a glance at a tower that jutted up cleanly above the rest of the city beneath.

She saw people of more kinds than she had ever dreamed could exist as they walked, catching only the barest glance of most of them. Occasionally, she would catch a glimpse of white gleaming through the crowd; craning her neck or leaning around the people surrounding her, she might spot a hint of plate armor.

"Who are the ones in white armor?" she asked in an undertone.

"Ah," said Varun. "That'll be the Nyxian Guard. Not that you would have been planning to, but you're best off not messing with them."

Mara turned her head as another of the Guard went past, this one bearing a great helmet that looked like the skull of some great horned beast.

Wait, she thought, looking closer at the texture of it, *that is a skull. And at least some of that plate's made of bone too. Intense.*

"They're quite formidable," said Varun, following her gaze. "Not to be trifled with. And yes, if you're wondering, they're wearing bone armor. Enchanted, of course: all the intimidation factor, none of the brittleness."

"They keep order here?"

"Something like that. And they take their duties very seriously." He swallowed, suddenly looking as if he were tasting something unpleasant. "They're not dead," he said.

Mara frowned at him until she thought the lines in her forehead would be creased permanently into her skin.

"It's possible to come here other than by dying," Varun explained when the amusement of watching her frown as hard as she could had worn off. "Few do, but it does happen through various routes for various reasons. The Nyxian Guard are all still numbered among the living."

He fell silent. Mara got the impression he was waiting to see whether she worked out the reason for herself. "Because," she began, "because..."

Oh, wait. I probably do know this one.

"Because it would be … inconvenient if one of the people responsible for keeping the peace were to be unexpectedly spirited out of the Crossing," she guessed. "You don't want your guard to be subject to possible resurrection at any moment."

"There you go," said Varun. "Look at them closely if you get the chance—it's hard to see, but there's something more … tangible about them. More vivid."

"Wait," said Mara, "if the living can come here, can we leave by the same paths? Go back to a living world without being resurrected?"

"It's a good thought, but nobody's made it work so far," said Varun. "Sometimes the dead can send a message out, if we can persuade one of the living to take it. Or a Pale Horseman, but…" He shuddered. "Less said about that, the better. Anyway, no, the short answer is that whatever the living do to traverse the boundaries between worlds, those roads are closed to the dead."

They walked on, but something was niggling at Mara.

"What happens if someone who's still alive dies here?" she asked. "Do they just come back here like we do?"

Varun scowled, the sour expression back on his face. "Utter obliteration," he said. "Just gone, body and spirit. Consumed by the Crossing, never to be seen in any life or afterlife again."

Mara whistled. "Harsh."

After what must have been two or three hours of traversing Nox Valar—during which time Varun pulled out a coin and manipulated it through a series of dexterous patterns repeatedly in his fingers, citing it as an appeal to the domain of precision and finesse, almost dropping it several times before genuinely dropping it and losing it in the footfall—they passed a colossal four-sided monolith of black and white. Each of the two sides Mara could see—and, she saw as her perspective changed, the third, so she assumed it was the same on all four—bore a straight, wide window of clear glass that ran from the center of the base right up to the tip. Within, she could see golden sand falling.

"We might end up going there," Varun said, seeing her curious gaze, "but there's something probably worth trying first. You have a god already, right?"

Mara tore her eyes from the pyramid. "What?"

"Well, your plan is to persuade a god to accept you into their afterlife, so I assume you have one in mind. One you followed when you were alive?"

"Oh," said Mara. "Yes. Er…"

I can't say Rekh. Even if most people here wouldn't have heard of him, Varun's from my world. He'll know what that name means.

"It's a god of rebirth," she said.

"Fitting."

"It's called … Raskith."

"Right," said Varun. "Then a temple to Raskith is what we're after." He gestured to what lay ahead, and Mara turned her face forward. There had been so much to see that she'd barely thought to wonder where their destination might be.

Before her was a road that stretched for perhaps a mile directly straight from her perspective before curving off as far as she could see in either direction.

It's a circle, she realized. *A circle a mile wide.*

On the other side of the road—in the middle of the circle— was a tree. Or not a tree. It looked like a tree, but it was so vast that Mara found it difficult to think of it as a tree rather than as some enormous entity that happened to be in the shape of a tree. Its trunk was entirely concealed by billowing curtains of white petals and entangling clouds of thin green leaves.

"That's the Etherwood," said Varun. "Quite a thing, right?"

"Quite a thing," Mara had to agree. She dragged her gaze down to the base of the tree and saw the still gleam of water beneath—a circular pond separated the Etherwood from the road. She thought she could see at least one narrow stream flowing away from the center, gently wandering outward.

That'll be where the waterfalls come from.

Looking down the road, she could see buildings lining the outer side. Temples, she thought: some bore images of deific figures, others grand icons. Some were humbler than others, but all had that mystique about them that suggested wisdom might be found within.

"That's the center of Nox Valar," Varun told her, gesturing toward the great tree. "And this," he spread his arms wide, indicating the road as it ran off in either direction, "is the Road to Eternity."

"Too many names," Mara groaned, rubbing her eyes.

"You don't have to remember them all," he said, putting a hand gently on her shoulder. At his touch, she reached reflexively for her power, ready to blast his hand right off his arm, but she held herself back. He steered her onto the road. "We're going to find a friend of mine," he announced, striding purposefully along the Road to Eternity as it curved gently around the Etherwood. "A priest—cleric—vicar? I don't know. Works at one of the temples—you might've noticed, the Road is essentially just a district of temples to... well, probably to as many gods as people have ever worshiped. Anyway, I think she might be able to help you."

"Thanks," Mara said.

He glanced down. "Yeah." He turned his gaze ahead again. The corner of his lip tweaked upward, almost but not quite a smile.

"What?"

"It's nothing," he said, looking as if he were trying not to break into a full-toothed grin. "I just... I think you and Iona are going to get along, that's all."

"Right," said Mara dubiously.

A short way around the Road to Eternity, Varun veered off the path and led Mara toward a square building that looked as if a child had assembled it out of multicolored bricks. Compared to most of the temples surrounding it, this one looked less like a holy place of worship and more like an architect deciding to give up on any semblance of cohesiveness and becoming an abstract artist instead.

A young woman emerged, beaming from ear to ear. She was short, all rounded edges, and her hair was a nut-brown nest of straggly strands atop her head. Deerish, large brown eyes gleamed in a turquoise-skinned face. Blue and silver robes swayed from her body, flared sleeves accentuating her movements.

"Varun!" she called, spreading her arms wide. Then she turned her attention to Mara. "And a newcomer! I am *absolutely delighted* to welcome you—ah, come here!"

She advanced, and Mara became keenly, intensely aware that she was about to be hugged.

Idon'twantitIdon'twantitIdon'twantit—

Warmth. Comfort. Unconditional sympathy and reassurance.

Hey, this actually isn't that bad.

CHAPTER 8

"**Y**ou don't hug well!" the cleric chirped, releasing Mara. Despite her words, her face still radiated joy.

"Um," said Mara, blinking as if coming out of a deep sleep. "Sorry. Not a lot of practice, I guess."

"We'll fix that." The young woman trotted over to Varun and embraced him too. Her head only came to his sternum, but his lower half disappeared amidst her robes. "I'm Iona," she said as she released the tall man.

"Mara."

Iona's already large eyes widened, glistening with emotion. "That," she said, "is an absolutely beautiful name." She balled up her hands and squeezed them in front of her face with a giddy squeal, as if the jubilation were simply too much for her.

Mara shot a glance at Varun. He looked as if he were trying not to laugh.

I don't know whether to be flattered or insulted at how excited he was to see the two of us meet. He must think I'm the complete opposite of this ... whatever this is. Which is true, but still.

"You're ... effervescent," Mara said dryly.

Iona's cherubic head bobbed up and down. "I'm one of the senior devotees of Aurethen," she declared with an air of absolute pride. "Our worship is all about being truly, completely ourselves, feeling every emotion in the purest, strongest way we can." She raised a finger, teacherly. "If I can express myself as ostentatiously as possible, I'm serving my god. It's wonderful!"

Mara blinked, then gave what she hoped was a polite nod of interest. "So it's literally your holy duty to be as exuberant as possible ... all the time."

"That's it exactly!" Iona declared. "I like her," she said to Varun.

Fucking hell.

"Knew you would," said Varun, grinning. "We're probably not staying, I'm afraid—Mara needs to move on. And quickly."

Iona frowned. "Move on? Into oblivion? But then she won't be able to feel all the emotions Aurethen gifted every conscious creature." Her bottom lip disappeared between her teeth, her brow knitting tighter than a chokesnake's constricting grasp. "She'll miss out on *everything*!" the cleric lamented.

"Well, yeah," said Mara, unaffected. "That's death."

Iona gave her one of the most furious glares she'd ever received. "I don't know whether I like her anymore," Iona told Varun.

This woman's blood pressure would be an absolute liability if she still had blood pressure. Wait, do we still have blood? If our bodies work as we remember them, do people with no knowledge of anatomy not have all the same organs?

"We've talked about this," Varun said, shaking Mara out of the rabbit hole she'd been inadvertently spelunking. "People have the right to go on to their eternal rest. You will at some point."

"Yeah," said Iona, folding her arms emphatically, "but Aurethen's afterlife is all about feeling everything all the time."

"Well," said Varun, "everyone can go to whichever afterlife they *strongly feel* is the one they want, right? And some of them will get to feel more things there, and some won't, and that's what they felt they wanted too."

Mara tilted her head at Varun, intrigued. *I can't tell whether this is a manipulative appeal to Iona's … idiosyncrasies, or whether it's just good logic.*

"Fine!" barked Iona, pouting spectacularly. She turned to Mara. "Can I interest you in joining the ranks of the devotees of Aurethen, where all are welcome and the only rule is that you have to completely, one hundred percent feel every authentic feeling all the time?"

That sounds worse than being Raskith's undead minion.

"I'm in a bit of a hurry," Mara said as politely as she could. "I don't think I'd have time to, er, fully embrace Aurethen and your teachings before... well, before time ran out."

"What's the rush?" Iona asked. Then she glanced at Varun. "Oh. *Ohhhh.* You sentimental thing. You've gone and taken on another one?"

Varun rolled his eyes. "Yeah. Something like that."

"Are you sure that's good for you? I don't want you getting hurt—but if you do, make sure to express it as vividly as possible, alright?"

The little cleric was talking to the much larger man as if she were his mother; he wore an expression of strained, barely maintained patience, like a teenager who knew things would only be worse if he didn't at least pretend to listen.

"Boop," said Varun after Iona had spent a solid few minutes expressing her vibrant concern for his wellbeing, and poked the tip of her nose.

She froze mid-sentence, staring in disbelief, then broke into the loudest laughter Mara had ever heard. "What was *that*?!" she gasped through peals of mirth.

He shrugged. "There might be a domain of comedic inter-ruption, right?"

"If you end up becoming a god of *comedy*, of all things," said Iona, wiping tears from her face, "we're all in terrible trouble." A look of sudden seriousness painted itself on her soft features. "Speaking of trouble, how can I help? I assume you've come here for some kind of assistance, not just to kill time and wait."

Varun wrapped an arm around her, protective and broth-erly, and walked with her toward her temple. Mara followed, close enough to hear the conversation but not so close as to insert herself into their existing dynamic.

"That is a very good assumption," said Varun. "Do you still have a list somewhere of all the temples on the Road to Eternity? Mara has a god already—what was the name again?" He directed the question over his shoulder to Mara.

"Raskith," said Mara, already regretting the choice. Not so much because she was afraid that Varun might recognize it—as far as she knew, only a few powerful people knew her master by name, with most who'd heard of him only knowing of *the master necromancer*—as because she hated that she now had to say his name.

"Huh," said Iona. "Doesn't ring a bell. We can look though. What kind of god?"

"Rebirth," Varun said.

Thank you, Varun. Might have taken me a second too long to remember what I'd said.

"Fun!" Iona declared, her next few steps a merry skip.

They entered the temple, which was just as haphazard on the inside as it was on the outside. It was as if several different buildings, each of which had been doused in one shocking shade of paint or another, had been sliced up and roughly stuck together. A couple of devotees milled around, one of whom appeared to be a tree with roughly humanoid limbs and a leafy beard; Iona bustled to the back. Varun watched her go, then turned to Mara.

"You're probably wondering why the temple looks so … unorthodox," he said.

Mara, who had been making no real effort to disguise her bewilderment as she took in the jumble of mismatched bits of architecture, blinked and nodded. "I feel like it's a reasonable thing to wonder."

He chuckled. "In essence, it's just that Aurethen's acolytes don't really have any … impulse control, you might say. If one of the temple's caretakers decided that they felt a strong urge to change the decor, they'd just do it. If anyone objected, they'd have the defense that they were just being particularly pious. Of course, they respect all those who held the temple before them too much to replace things entirely, so they just keep adding new bits, one brick or pillar or candelabra at a time."

"Aurethen's people seem like a liability," Mara murmured.

Varun raised an eyebrow. "They are, but that's what makes them interesting. And, trust me, they have their uses."

Uses? Is he admitting to…?

"Not that you should only spend time with people because you think they're useful, of course," he continued, "but believe me, being on the good side of someone like Iona can come in handy."

Ah. Not just a manipulator then. Genuinely cares. Shame. Works out well for me, though, having an altruist willing to assist me toward my goals.

"Nope!" Iona trumpeted, wandering back over. "Checked the list. Nothing about a Raskith." She turned her wide eyes to Mara inquisitively. "Unless it's got a silent W or anything?"

Mara shook her head.

"Ah, well. Some gods don't get much in the way of temples. Some actively don't want to be worshiped, although that does make getting into their afterlives a bit tricky. There's always the Marquis of the Final End, if you're willing to scooch over from rebirth to acceptance of death?"

"Can I have a look at the list?" Mara asked.

Iona's eyes narrowed, rendering them ... still unusually wide. "Why?"

She shrugged. "Just to see if there's anything on there that sounds close enough to my beliefs, I guess. Or if Raskith might be in there under any other name—I think people called him a few things, but I can't remember them all. Maybe if I just skim through though..."

Iona considered it, her lips scrunching to the side. "I mean, it's not secret information or anything—you could get all the names just by walking around the Road to Eternity and noting down every temple you went past. Why not?"

"Thanks," Mara said with a nod of acknowledgment. Iona guided her to a small room off the main space; in keeping with the haphazard design of the place, it felt almost like walking into another building entirely. Inside was a row of drawers and a small reading table, atop which was a small book with pages as thin as a fly's wings. It was open to around three-quarters of the way in.

"Have at it," said the priest with a wide smile, and left her to it.

Mara leaned over the table, peering at the book. It looked to be in alphabetical order: the Rs were showing, a small strip of paper lying between *Raquatan* and *Razel*.

It would've been very worrying if Iona had *found Raskith in here*, Mara thought, scanning down the page in search of her true god. *Huh. No Rekh either.*

She wondered what that meant: was Rekh only known to such a small number of people that a temple had never been worth building for them? If there were so many worlds, perhaps Rekh had only made himself apparent in hers, and of all the people in her world, there were surely few who would choose to follow him. Or perhaps exaltation of a god whose entire being revolved around subverting the natural course of death was frowned upon in the afterlife.

She flipped through the pages for a few minutes, looking for any monikers under which Rekh might be known. She found several interesting-sounding epithets, some of which were apparently the actual names of the gods and others just titles by which they were known. There was "Bringer of Not-Too-Many Bees, The (see also: Healer of Lesser and Fewer Bee-Stings, The)," "She Who Courts Nightmarish Absolution," "Bladesister, The," "One Exalted Above All Birds and Clouds, The," and something just called "Noneness."

Presumably, the one about bees comes from a world where bees are important, so people need a god to handle … bee-related issues, Mara mused. *The gods people worship tell you a lot about what's important to them. Raskith knew that well.*

A few of the entries were even neatly crossed out or amended with notes like "afterlife closed to newcomers," "presumed killed," "worship no longer in fashion," "opposing deity murdered all followers," that sort of thing. But nothing that sounded like it might have been Rekh.

Great. I have no idea what I need to do to appease the only god that's likely to have me.

Mara heaved a sigh and made to flip the book closed, but not before glancing at "Marquis of the Final End, The." The brief description outlined that worship of the Marquis was in essence the pure act of living a fulfilling life and accepting that it would one day come to an end.

"Bit late for that," she murmured.

There were a few other lines on the page: "Megarion the Pained," "Mindweavers, Father Of," "Mistress of Mutual

Exclusivity, Or Not, But Not Both," "Mnemoch, Lord of Forgetting." Just above the Marquis's entry was something called "Majin," whose note said simply: "DO NOT TRUST." In the nearby margin was a scribble in a different hand: "God? Or something else?"

Mara's gaze lingered on that one for a moment, and then she closed the book and headed back out. Iona and Varun were in animated conversation—the former more animated than the latter—but both turned toward her as she emerged.

"Nothing," she said in response to Varun's expectant look. He nodded, his face set.

"That's inconvenient," he said, "but not unmanageable."

"What about getting someone *else* to resurrect you?" Iona suggested.

Mara blinked at her. "That's an option?"

"I mean, we'd need to find a Pale Horseman and something to pay them with to carry a message to someone back in your living world, and probably also a big old diamond to send with them—if that's how resurrection works in your world, anyway—"

Mara shook her head. "That sounds … time-consuming." *And besides, there's nobody else. Other than my family, who probably don't even know whether I'm alive or dead, I don't know any other living people from my world, let alone ones who'd be willing to bring me back. That's … kind of sad, now I think about it.* "What I need to know," she mused aloud, "is how much time I have. Then I'd be able to work out what I could afford to try…"

"I was thinking exactly the same thing," said Varun.

Iona clapped her hands, her face lighting up. "Visit to the Keepers?"

Varun nodded. "Not much else to do, is there?"

"It'll be a lot of waiting." She patted the taller man on the elbow, which was just about the highest part of him she could reach. "Alright, fine, you've persuaded me. I, Iona, devotee of Aurethen, shall accompany you on your quest!"

Mara tried her best to catch Varun's eye, shaking her head in tiny rapid motions from side to side, but he was grinning. "We would be honored," he said, clasping the cleric's hand in his.

Mara stared at the two of them, disbelieving. *Oh, for hells' sake, I'm getting an adventuring party.*

CHAPTER 9

After Iona had taken a few minutes to grab "the bare essentials," which turned out to include a great jagged-headed hammer whose shaft was longer than she was tall, the three of them headed back out into Nox Valar. Varun whistled all the way down the road, high and obnoxious.

"There can't be a domain of whistling," Mara groaned.

"There might be," said Varun between tuneless puffs. "There's definitely a domain of irritatingness, so it's still worth trying."

Mara turned to Iona, finding herself genuinely eager to talk to the excitable cleric if it meant a distraction from the noises issuing from Varun's pursed lips. "So, the Keepers are…?"

"Of the Eternal Sands," Iona supplied. "They track time." She pointed to the monolithic hourglass Mara had seen on the way in, where aureate sand trickled down behind the smooth glass window. "Most importantly, for your purposes, that includes things like how long it'll be before a soul has no more prospect of being resurrected. Plus what time of day it is, since you might've noticed we don't exactly have sunrises here." She flashed Mara a great wide smile, bright enough to rival any sunrise in any world.

It hadn't occurred to Mara that she'd have no real way of telling how much time had passed, or whether it was supposed to be daytime or nighttime. She'd had more pressing concerns, she supposed.

Iona wiggled her finger up and down, indicating the falling sand. "That gets reset at the start of each day. When it's all fallen, that's the end of the day."

The sand was perhaps two-thirds fallen, Mara thought. Early evening, if she had to guess—not that it made much of a difference.

"So here's what we do," said Iona as they drew nearer to the grand temple that housed the Keepers of the Eternal Sands, and then she frowned. "Hear that?"

Mara strained her ears. She did indeed hear something, a faint wail.

I know what people screaming in fear for their lives sounds like.

"Something's wrong," Iona declared, her face suddenly set with fiery determination. She strode toward the sound; Mara and Varun followed. Most of the people around them didn't seem to have noticed, but those who did were glancing with concern in the direction of the noise, not acting themselves.

Do we really have to get involved? Mara grumbled internally. *Everyone's got their own thing going on—why the need to inter-vene?* But the only two people who represented any prospect of helping her achieve her ends were heading decisively for the disturbance, so she didn't have much of a choice in the matter.

The crowd thinned, everyone moving with varying degrees of hurry away from whatever was happening.

"What's going on?" Iona asked, grabbing the arm of a woman who was running in the other direction with a look of terror on her face.

"Soul stitched," she gasped.

Varun's expression darkened. "Attacking?"

The woman nodded. Iona released her, gesturing her on her way.

"What's a soul stitched?" Mara asked as Iona walked purposefully toward the continued, ever-clearer sounds of fear.

"I'll explain later," Varun said, drawing his swords.

They stood in the shadow—not literally, of course—of a huge sphere, a perfectly round construction of shining black stone. Behind and to the sides, narrow roads led off between one- and two-story buildings, most built of white marble, that might have been residential or commercial or hospitality; it didn't much matter. Before them was a square plaza.

And in the center of the plaza, *something* stood, lurching as if it were finding it difficult to keep its balance.

"Must've been desperate," Iona muttered, hefting her hammer.

Varun held his swords aloft and struck the two blades together, igniting a white flame that flared along the length of both weapons. "Let's put it out of its misery."

Mara looked closer at the creature. It was humanoid, roughly, but a poor imitation of a real person. It looked as if someone had taken gray clay and pressed it into a vague approximation of a human torso, then attached long limbs and a round head. Its skin was dull, the texture of dried mud, and lined with seams that looked as if they were held together with clumsily threaded stitches.

There was only one other person nearby, tall and broad like a heavy barrel. Loose attire in shades of burnt orange hung from their body. Mara couldn't make out much more than that—they were some distance away, off to the side and behind the gray thing from her perspective—but there was nobody else to be seen.

The creature in the middle of the plaza stepped toward Varun and Iona as they approached. Mara had been expecting it to move jerkily, in a lurching, crude imitation of a normal gait—like her newly born wraiths, confusedly struggling to work out which muscles to contract—but it walked smoothly, confidently.

Mara stayed back for the time being. *I want to get an impression of my new assistants' capabilities,* she reasoned. *And besides, I don't want to show off my own combat skills. All Varun knows is that I've got a strong punch, and that thing doesn't look safe to go up against unarmed. Mara, the confused newcomer, wouldn't be brave enough to get into this fight, and that's who they want to help.*

As she drew near to the gray thing, Iona lifted her hammer above her head, the sleeves of her robes falling to reveal impressive, flexed muscles in her arms. Before she could slam her weapon down on the misshapen head, her foe stepped nimbly to the side, thrusting its arm out as it dodged. A sharp hand caught Iona in the midsection; she backstepped, getting out of range. Varun launched himself in, his two flaming swords readying to strike as he flew. The soul stitched took one of the blows on an upraised arm, screeching as the limb was bisected at the elbow; with its other hand, it scratched at Varun's face. He jerked back, barely too slow, and drops of red spattered the stone under his feet at the same time as a gray arm thumped bloodlessly down.

The other person drew near to the fight, raising a hand. A ripple of force emanated from them, pushing the soul stitched to one knee. Iona took the opportunity to throw herself back into the fray, slamming her hammer down on the thing's back. It crashed down into the ground, sandwiched between the enormous hammerhead and the hard stone beneath; rippling, spider-webbing cracks zipped out from the impact.

Iona's shoulders heaved as she panted, lifting her hammer for another blow. The moment the weight lifted from its back, the soul stitched scuttled forward, scurrying along the floor on all fours—two feet, one hand, and one stump of an arm—toward Mara.

Varun threw himself into a dashing blow, but the creature whipped one leg up, catching him in mid-flight. He fell on his back; one of his swords, released from surprised fingers, landed sharp edge down an inch from his face. The soul stitched kept coming toward Mara.

I guess it's on me then, Mara thought, and reached for the aura of death in her ring. She couldn't banish or turn this creature, if her experiences in the Crossing so far were any indication, and she didn't fancy getting her bare hand close enough to its bulbous head to punch it. But she had more up her sleeve. No necromancer worth their salt relied exclusively on pure death spells; any sensible mage developed defenses against simply dropping dead from one magic-woven command to vacate their body.

In the seconds before the creature reached her, she pulled a little of the magic from the ring and cycled it to her feet, letting it taste the stone beneath her. Then she sent some of the power up to stream in quick figures behind her eyes, absorbing some of the half-light that bathed the Sunless Crossing. The stone- and light-infused magic traced simple shapes of power inside her body, and then she let it go.

She lifted her foot and stamped hard, and a fissure cracked from her foot to the soul stitched. It squealed as jagged stone rose from below, stabbing its underside and caging it in sharp-edged fragments. Then she pointed, extending a finger, and a simple beam of light emanated from her hand. The soul stitched screamed, its gray flesh quietly sizzling.

Then Iona was there, dropping her hammer on its head. "Down!" she yelled. "Unnatural! Abomination! Stay! *Down!*"

The soul stitched jerked, then lay still.

Sweat glistening on her face, Iona looked at the stranger, who had traipsed up to the scene while Mara and Iona finished the fight. "Thanks," she said. "I'm Iona."

The stranger's skin was gray, but not the lifeless gray of the soul stitched: it had a rubbery shine to it, and hung loose around the sides of their head and neck. Small tusks peered out from the corners of their mouth, and flat, two-toed feet were visible poking out of the bottom of their clothes. Gleaming black eyes stared intelligently out from a wide face. "Nemmo." The voice was masculine, but a reedy tenor rather than the rumbling bass Mara might have expected from the imposing figure. It reminded her of an old professor she'd once tortured.

"Do you have any magic strong enough to destroy it?"

Nemmo shook his head. "I don't know."

Iona's expression turned exaggeratedly quizzical. "Eh? What kind of spells do you have? Was your magic god-given?"

"I don't think so," said Nemmo serenely.

The cleric gave a confused *tsk* and turned to Mara. "You?"

"Me...?"

"Your spells—anything offensive that could blow this thing up?"

Mara considered what she ought to say, settling on "I'm not offense-focused." It wasn't entirely true, of course; she could absolutely have created a spell that would have destroyed the being before her entirely, but she'd already risked enough exposure with the spells she'd just cast. And besides, she still wasn't exactly sure which of her abilities worked in the Sunless Crossing and which didn't.

"Right." Iona beckoned to Varun, who had pushed himself to his feet and picked up his flaming swords somewhat sheepishly. "You can do it, right?"

"You couldn't?" Varun asked.

"I'm not exactly focused on offensive magic either," Iona pointed out.

Varun snorted. "No need when you've got a hammer like that, I suppose." He glanced down at the soul stitched, which was beginning to twitch again where it lay pressed beneath Iona's enormous weapon. "I think I can do it."

The cleric reached out a hand to the taller man; her fingers glowed a gentle orange-gold. She touched her fingertips to his forearm, and his grip tightened on his sword. His breathing deepened; he stood up straighter.

"Bit of extra power," said Iona, "just in case."

Varun gave her an appreciative nod, then raised an eyebrow. "You couldn't have done that before?"

"We were in a bit of a hurry," she said, shrugging.

He raised his swords, reversing them in his hands so the blades were pointing downward. The white flames rose to wreath his hands in light. With a grunt, he fell to one knee and drove his weapons right into the struggling soul stitched's head. It tried to scream, Mara thought, but all that came out was a stifled yelp.

Varun stood, keeping one hand on the hilt of a sword, and closed his eyes. The index finger of his other hand extended, pointing straight down at the soul stitched. His lips moved silently, with the rhythm of prayer.

A hair-thin line of pure white light shot from his finger, skewering the soul stitched through the back of its neck. The same colorless radiant flames that adorned his sword burst up from the impact, hungrily spreading across the gray flesh, and a few moments later the soul stitched had been devoured, leaving nothing but a smoking pile of ash.

"That could have gone worse," Iona said, swinging her hammer up and over her shoulder with a wide grin.

Varun extinguished the flames on his blades, sheathing them again. Nemmo regarded the annihilated soul stitched contemplatively. Mara, for her part, hid the smile that wanted to creep across her features as she looked at them.

If I can get this newcomer on my side, that's three capable allies, all of whom just want to help. They're perfect. Easily manipulated into doing what I want, as long as I frame it as the right thing to do. Despite her years of practice, it was hard to keep her expression from shifting as a bubble of superior confidence began to form in her stomach.

"Move aside!" a new voice called, deep and authoritative.

Mara turned toward the sound and saw what looked like a gleaming chrome dragonfly zipping through the air toward her, bearing a tiny figure in bone armor on its back. The metallic insect whizzed past, flitting wildly toward each person in turn until they all stepped away from the remains of the soul stitched.

The dragonfly's rider hopped off, nimbly dropping to the ground. They were perhaps eighteen inches tall, including the curling horns that protruded from the top of their full-face helmet, and clad in tiny plates of ivory. The dragonfly hovered in place above its rider.

The little person removed their helmet, revealing large, round ears and a furry head with glistening black eyes and a pink, twitching nose. Their face, soft of hair but hard of expression, had that air of tangibility Varun had pointed out in those who came to the Sunless Crossing while still alive. "Chirripeek of the Nyxian Guard," he said in that low, commanding voice, which caused Varun to do a double-take and Iona to flash an enormous grin. "What happened here?"

"Soul stitched," said Iona, still grinning. "Attacked a coupla people, by the sounds of it, but we managed to, er..." She pointed to the smoking ash. "...obliterate it."

"So I see." Chirripeek smudged the remains of the soul stitched with one bone-booted toe. "Did it manage to do harm to anyone?"

"I don't think so. People were running—it must have done something to scare them away, but once we got here... well, it didn't get another chance."

"Good. We'll investigate, find out exactly what happened." The little Nyxian Guard gestured, and his metal mount descended to allow him to hop back on. Mara looked closer as the rodent-man rose back up into the air. Varun had been right: there was a certain solidity to him that the rest of them lacked, though it was only apparent by comparison. "You know, you ought to wait for the Guard to deal with problems like this."

Iona just stared at him benignly.

"But, of course, most people in the Crossing aren't of the 'wait for someone else to solve the problem' disposition," Chirripeek acknowledged, sliding his helmet back onto his head. He sighed, the sound echoing out from his skull-covered visage. "And, it must be admitted, the Guard ought to have been here sooner, but... well, you took care of the threat. Of course, it would have been preferable if you could have kept it restrained, since we'll just have to find it again when it falls back into the Fields tomorrow, but I suppose Nox Valar is a little safer for now." He cast a critical look over the group. "If you ever want to take a shift defending the Lightless Chasm, we always appreciate good volunteers."

"We'll consider it," said Iona.

Chirripeek nodded, and then he was gone.

Varun turned to Nemmo. "What did you mean, you don't *think* your magic comes from a god? Shouldn't you know?"

Nemmo gave a heavy sigh. His mannerisms were almost slow-motioned, shoulders rising and falling with exaggerated tiredness. When he spoke, though, his voice was intelligent, precise, clipped. "I don't remember," he said. "I've always had my magic—since before I can recall, anyway."

Varun made an expression of what Mara thought was supposed to be sympathy. "You're unraveled?"

"No," said Nemmo, with a great shake of his head. "I checked with the Keepers. I've died twice since coming to the Sunless Crossing."

Iona frowned. "Weird."

"Rather," said Nemmo dryly. "I remember most of what I've done since I arrived, which was … some time ago now, but nothing from before. Yet I've never unraveled. I realized fairly quickly that I do have some access to magical abilities, but I've never quite been able to determine exactly what I can and can't do. It's rather instinctive, I suppose."

"Do you want to know what happened to you?" Mara asked, surprising herself with the interjection.

Nemmo's intelligent black eyes turned to her. "Sometimes," he said. "I can't imagine it's tremendously relevant. The Keepers say I have a very low chance of being resurrected; there must be few left who remember me now." He spread his arms; Mara saw that his hands had seven fingers apiece, each of which was strangely flat, like a small fin. "I spent a while in Respite, just waiting to see whether anything would happen, but I found that if I could know little about myself, I wanted to know more about the Sunless Crossing. So, I came to Nox Valar to meet people, to talk to them. And sometimes to … help them." He glanced at the place where the soul stitched had died. The stone Mara's spell had broken still jutted out raggedly, a cleaner hole in the center where Varun's swords had struck.

He's perfect.

"I think," Mara said, trying to sound tentative, "I could do with some help." She faked a nervous glance away. "You know, probably, but only if you, um…" She trailed off.

Nemmo made a *hrrrm* sound. "Oh?"

Got him.

"I'm new here," she said, turning her face back toward him, "and I don't know exactly how it all ... works..." She gestured in what she thought was a convincingly helpless sort of way. "I need to move on as quickly as I can, and I don't know what that's going to involve yet, but I'm sure I could use as much help as anyone's willing to give."

Varun frowned at her. "It's probably going to be mostly an administrative thing, you know. Are me and Iona not enough? And besides," he said, nodding at the hole where the soul stitched had been, "it looks as if you can take care of yourself even better than I thought."

"I would very much like to accompany you, I think," said Nemmo.

Mara grinned at him, then at Varun. "See? This guy's on board."

"You seem interesting," the gray-skinned man said contemplatively. "There's nothing more worthwhile than being around interesting people doing interesting things."

"Oh, good," said Varun.

"Well then!" Iona chirped, wrapping her arms around Nemmo's wide torso with all the enthusiasm of a puppy licking a child's face. "We're a party!"

Images flashed through Mara's mind: adventuring parties she'd seen, encountered, brutally murdered, or raised from the dead to serve her. Or all four. Some had been genuine threats, powerful bands of so-called heroes with dangerous blends of skills. Some had been easy to wipe out in an instant.

Most of them, though, had seemed to have a genuine friendship, a camaraderie. They had loved each other and laughed with each other. Mara had absolutely hated that.

Oh, hells, what have I just let myself in for?

CHAPTER 10

I t was only a short walk back to the Keepers of the Eternal Sands' majestically intimidating temple. Varun introduced himself in short order to Nemmo, as did Mara; Iona gave him a much lengthier and rather more effervescent welcome as they traveled.

"So," Mara asked Iona when the cleric took a breath from effusively spilling to Nemmo all about the wonders of Aurethen, "what exactly was it we fought back there?"

Iona's face darkened. "Soul stitched are the *worst*," she spat, sticking her tongue out as if she had sand in her mouth. "It's what happens when a... ugh, when a necromancer calls a soul back to the land of the living, and then that soul gets destroyed by divine magic. Not every time, I don't think, but sometimes they just sort of cling to existence and become... well, *that*. I guess the gods' magic and the horrible necromancy magic don't mix well." She shivered, clearly disgusted at the thought. "Can you imagine?" she asked in a low tone. "Corrupting the flow of life and death like that? I can't think of anything more evil."

Mara swallowed. "Nope," she said. "That's the worst."

"And then those things just wander around looking for souls to consume," Iona went on darkly. "They swallow up other people, absorb them. It's horrible."

Wait, so… I mostly just resurrected bodies, no souls, but I did call a few souls back to make stronger undead. And Raskith did it all the time. At least a few of them must've been destroyed with divine magic, which means I was probably responsible for a few of those things.

I don't know why, but I can't help feeling … not good about that.

"Some of them don't eat other souls," Varun said, joining the conversation. "A few of them manage to be pretty close to … whatever passes for normal here."

Iona stared at him until he amended his statement.

"But those ones disappear pretty fast," he admitted with a sigh. "If they don't consume others' souls, they can't survive more than a year."

"Horrible things," Iona pronounced with an air of utter disgust.

They turned a corner and found themselves looking down a street directly to the Keepers' domain. It loomed tall over them, high enough that Mara's neck started to hurt if she tried to look up at the top.

"Right," said Varun, "let's get you in the queue."

He led them down the street to the base of the temple, where several people in monastic robes stood waiting to be approached. Varun picked one, apparently at random, and exchanged a few words with them, then came back, flipping a coin off his thumb and letting it slap into his palm.

"You're in," he said, tossing the coin to Mara.

It was a heavy thing, bigger than most she'd come across in life. On one side was a stern face, old and gender-less. On the other was an emblem that she assumed must represent the Keepers: the hourglass in miniature. And beneath that, a number.

"Fourteen thousand and six," she read.

"Oh," said Nemmo, nodding appreciatively. "That's much lower than the last time I had to join the Keepers' line."

"That still sounds like a really big number," Mara said dubiously. "How long does the line take to get through...?"

Iona tapped a finger to her chin thoughtfully. "They're pretty quick, really," she said. "There are a few of them, and I guess when your entire deal is monitoring the flow of time, you probably get kind of efficient..."

"So...?

"Oh, a few months, maybe."

"A few—" Mara bit back the words that were reflexively leaping up her throat, caging them in her mouth before they could escape and attack someone. "I think it's very unlikely that I have a few months."

"What exactly is it you need to escape?" Nemmo asked.

Mara took a deep breath. "Someone back in my living world hates me. *Really* hates me. But he's powerful, and as soon as he figures out the details, he's going to bring me back with—with necromancy." She glanced at Iona; sure enough, the cleric let out a huge gasp of horror, even putting her hand over her mouth. "He's going to make me his servant, make me do terrible things in his name. And ... I'm either going to suffer through that for I don't know how long, never aging, just watching myself do as he tells me, or ... at some point, I'm going to get killed for him."

She looked at the three of them. Iona looked on the edge of tears; Varun was watching her with a hard expression that she thought might be attempting to mask a deeper sorrow; Nemmo's features, unfamiliar to her, were difficult to read, but his eyes were boring into her.

I've got them hooked.

She swallowed hard for dramatic effect, letting her words come out choked, as if she were fighting back tears. "There are heroes who try to kill him, and a lot of them are blessed by the gods. If he brings me back and I get destroyed by someone wielding divine magic, I'll become..."

"Soul stitched," Iona whispered.

And there's the line and sinker.

Mara nodded, screwing up her eyes tightly. Iona embraced her; Mara took the opportunity to bury her face in the cleric's robes, though she had to bend her knees and lean forward to reach the shorter woman's shoulder.

"Well," said Nemmo, "that's certainly something worth avoiding."

Varun grunted.

"That," said Iona, releasing Mara and holding her at arm's length, staring tearfully into her face, "is one of the most horrible things I've ever heard, and I am *not* going to let that happen." She turned to Varun and Nemmo. "How do we not let that happen?"

"She needs to commune with her god somehow," Varun said, "but with no temple, I don't know how..."

"The Keepers may know," Nemmo said. "The pure measurement of timelines is the primary way in which they share their knowledge, but that knowledge has a source. To calculate how long a soul has until resurrection becomes impossible or inevitable, they need certain information." He shifted thoughtfully, a quiet rumble sounding in his throat. "I have little sense as to whether any of them has direct access to it or whether the magic weaves itself, but in the absence of any better suggestion, knowledge is power."

"I've got nothing else," Varun said. "If she has a while, appealing to another god might work. Or perhaps even some kind of arrangement with the Pale Horsemen to find someone else in her world to resurrect her first, through better means. If time is short…" He cut himself off, glancing at Mara and then away.

"If time is short?" she prompted, suspecting she knew the answer.

He shrugged, not meeting her gaze. "Oblivion," he said. "Utter destruction. It's difficult to remove a soul from existence entirely, but possible."

"No!" Iona protested. "If she doesn't exist, she can't feel anything ever again!"

Varun raised an eyebrow at her, then made a gesture with his head that Mara thought was intended to be an instruction to her: *you answer this one.*

"That would be preferable," she said, "to the alternative."

Iona wailed, pulling at her hair. "That's *terrible!*"

Mara grinned internally, though she kept her expression outwardly schooled. *This one is too easy. Tell her something even mildly sympathy-inducing and she'll go to the ends of the earth to help.*

"Well," said Nemmo over Iona's lament, "it seems the only thing for it is to secure a better coin. One nearer the front of the line."

Mara's eyes narrowed. "How do I go about doing that?"

"The only official way to exchange Crossway Coins, beyond simply persuading someone to give you one for nothing," Nemmo said slowly, as if remembering were laborious, "is through playing Purgatory Poker in certain approved establishments. Quite well regulated."

"Anyone confident they can win a game?" Mara asked, looking at each of her new companions in turn.

"Hells, no," said Varun. "Tried to learn the rules once or twice. Didn't go well."

Iona made the universal wide-eyed expression and exaggerated shrug that meant *beats me*.

"I am … excruciatingly bad at it," Nemmo admitted.

Mara nodded slowly. "And this Purgatory Poker is the only official way of competing for better coins?"

There were nods all around.

Mara let her grin show on her face. "I might know an unofficial way."

"Gront!" Mara called.

They'd trekked back through Nox Valar to the high tunnel that led down to the Ashen Fields, and from there toward Atonement Grove. It had taken longer than Mara had remembered; the first time had been a constant assault of new and astounding sights, she supposed, the ever-whirling barrage of marvel-worthy things making the journey feel shorter.

I have no idea whether Gront and his crew will still be anywhere nearby, Mara thought, *but it's the best lead I've got.*

"You know," said Varun with an air of dry skepticism, "I'm not entirely sure this Gront person is likely to be completely trustworthy."

"He's not," Mara said. "But he's untrustworthy in predictable ways."

"How do you know?"

"I've known people like him," Mara muttered.

"What exactly did you do in your previous life?" Varun asked.

Mara felt her heart leap in her chest. Except it didn't, of course, not really—somewhere beyond this half-lit place, her heart lay still in her cold body, Raskith watching over it like a carrion bird over a little sandmouse choking on its own blood. She'd given some thought to what she would say when the question inevitably arose, but she hadn't settled on an answer that she felt sure would stand up to scrutiny.

"I—"

"Ah!" a deep voice churned. "You're back."

Mara turned toward the voice, whatever answer had been about to come out of her mouth mercifully diving back down her throat. "I'm back," she said.

Gront approached slowly, almost cautiously. His great head turned deliberately, surveying the group. "You've made some friends," he said, sounding almost pleased for her.

"Does the offer still stand?" she asked. "I pick the game?"

He nodded. "You pick the game, you pick the players. The only requirement is that you have enough to wager. I'm not risking my valuable possessions for nothing."

"Right," said Mara, nodding. "Seems like such a good deal."

He inclined his head in what might have been gracious acknowledgment.

"I have," she said, plucking her Crossway Coin out of her pocket, "one Crossway Coin for the Keepers of the Eternal Sands, acquired earlier today."

Gront's fur-swathed face twitched. The muscle that would have been behind an eyebrow in a human face rose. "I think you know," he said, "that that is not sufficient."

Mara turned out her pocket. A dozen more Crossway Coins, each emblazoned with different icons, fell into the grass with a muffled series of clinks. Behind her, Iona, Nemmo, and Varun did the same. Each of them had joined as many queues as possible on the way back through Nox Valar; each coin was worth little on its own, but the accumulated hoard would eventually represent a lot of value to someone like Gront.

"These are all brand-new," Gront said, without even looking at them to check.

"Well, it's an investment," said Mara. "I'm assuming you can't all just go and join every queue multiple times, which means that once you run out of the high-value coins you're holding now, you won't have a lot of inventory in reserve for drawing in … customers."

"There's some truth in that," said Gront amiably, "but the simple fact is that what you have here is, as of now, worth … not very much."

"I thought you might say that," said Mara. "So here's a sweetener: if you play the game, I won't go and tell the Nyxian Guard what you're doing."

Gront's amber eyes narrowed. "And why would you think that would incentivize me?"

Mara shrugged. "Well, as I hear it, the only legal way to gamble Crossway Coins is Purgatory Poker, which this isn't. I'm guessing you approach newcomers because, let's see: anyone who takes you up on the offer and loses can't tell the Guard about you without implicating themselves as a participant; anyone who wins isn't exactly going to go admitting what they've done and have their winnings confiscated; and anyone who doesn't take you up on it at all probably doesn't know enough about how things work to realize you're, let's say, less than above board."

Gront regarded her seriously for a moment. Then he clapped his enormous palms together and chuckled. "That's almost the whole picture," he admitted, "but you can't honestly think you're the first to work it out, can you? Anyone who'd come across me and later found out about Purgatory Poker could easily turn me in. And some have."

"Ah," said Mara. "You don't care about getting caught. Because … it might be illegal, but the Guard doesn't really care?"

"Oh, no," said Gront, flicking an accumulated film of ash out of one claw-like fingernail with the sharp tip of another.

"They do care. Quite seriously—more seriously than you would expect even." His leonine mouth curled into a grin. "But I happen to have a friend or two in convenient places."

Ah. Shit. Mara sighed. *Well, that's unfortunate, but I can't do anything about that now. I wonder how he's convinced a Nyxian Guard to help him—do they need Crossway Coins? Not important right now though.*

She opened her mouth to try her alternative plan of persuasion—namely, offering to loan him her services as a powerful magic-user, although revealing exactly what she could do was something she would prefer to avoid—but Gront was chuckling again.

"I do appreciate the balls it takes to try something like this though," he said, almost fondly. "It happens from time to time, of course—so many of the people here think real highly of themselves. But you..." He let out a long, rumbling sigh. "There's something interesting about you."

Mara didn't let her gaze waver from his face. "Thank you," she said neutrally. "Now, about the cheating."

Gront's eyes widened, and then he let out an enormous, resounding, bellowing laugh. "The cheating!" he bellowed through his laughter, wiping a tear of mirth from his eye with one furry thumb. He controlled himself a moment later, though a low chuckle still intermittently shook his shoulders. "Go on then, tell me."

"You seem to be doing well," said Mara. "But gambling... it can yield great rewards, but it's not often a sustainable career betting against people. Or, even worse, against the house. But if you *are* the house... well, where I come from, at least, gambling houses have managed to make enough money to stay in business for decades. Centuries. There's always an advantage."

Gront pointed one thick, furry finger at her, shaking it in what she thought was approval. "But of course," he said. "Of course." He turned his head from side to side; following his movements, Mara saw that his compatriots were there, surrounding them in a wide circle. "I like her," he said to nobody in particular, then turned his attention back to Mara. "So, what do you propose?"

"If I or any of my … companions detect any interference," she said, gesturing with her head toward Iona, Nemmo, and Varun, "we're free to take action to stop it."

"Entirely fair," said Gront. His wide smile displayed his teeth to their fullest effect: they were long, thick, and curved. Some were sharp, but some were blunted or chipped, and most were stained and yellowing. Rather than diminish the aesthetic, the signs of wear and tear only added to his intimidating presence. "But I don't want to cheat against you. Truly. I can afford to lose a coin or two to someone as interesting as you."

Mara frowned. "There's a catch."

He shrugged. "I might ask for a favor one day."

"Of course." She extended her hand. "Let's play."

He reached out and grasped her hand in his. His palm was warm, rough-skinned, and a little wet; his fingers beneath their thick layers of fur were solid muscle, each closer to the girth of Mara's wrist than her own fingers. "What's it to be then?"

"Me against you," she proposed, keeping his hand gripped in hers a moment longer. "We each take turns to throw a punch. The first person to fall unconscious or yield loses."

Gront's fingers twitched. "Little person," he rumbled, his voice thick with curiosity, "are you sure that's what you want to do?"

She squeezed his hand, then let go and took a step back, eyeing him levelly. "Don't worry. I've thought about it."

He nodded approvingly. "Then let's begin."

CHAPTER II

Mara stood before Gront, close enough that she could reach out and touch him. This close, she had to crane her neck to look up at his head; he snorted and lowered himself gracefully to one knee, putting his face level with hers.

"You hit first," he told her. "One strike, then I take mine."

She nodded. "Of course."

Then she took a deep breath, filling her lungs with the alive deadness that saturated the Sunless Crossing, and reached for her power. She cycled the aura of death around her body, letting it flit through her chest. Her heart flickered for a moment, taking just an instant longer to resume its normal beat; Mara let herself feel the instinctive fear that the momentary arrhythmia sparked in her most primal instincts. She let that fear infuse the power flowing around her as it traced rivers through her limbs, up into her head, where it made her very essence feel cold. Thrills of fright coalesced into icy drips inside her brain, and the drips became streams, and the streams joined the river of magic until a torrent of pure fear raged through her.

Mara released the spell. She felt it washing over Gront, dousing him in terror.

Gront blinked. "Ah," he murmured. "Now, I know that feeling. A lot of the necromancers where I come from liked that trick."

Fuck.

"A spell of fear, if I'm not mistaken?"

Mara could only nod.

"Intended to make me so afraid that I yielded without you ever having to hit me, I imagine." A wry rumble vibrated within Gront's chest. "Not a bad tactic, I suppose. But, you see ... I never did like being afraid. In my world, there's not a lot that can be done to resist the effect for long, but here—well, here there are magics beyond anything I could have dreamed of. One of the first things I bought was an enchantment to protect me from ever feeling afraid again." He tapped his chest; Mara thought she could see a necklace swaying on its chain within his clothing, pushing momentarily against the fabric of his cloak.

"Well," she said, "it was worth a try."

Gront's head bobbed up and down in agreement. "It was," he said. "It was. Now, I have to say, I'm not entirely sure whether that counts as your turn. You said we would take turns to punch, but I don't think you meant to allow a loophole where one of us could kick, bite, bludgeon, for as long as we liked because we never actually *punched*."

"I don't think you'd have agreed to that," said Mara. She was already beginning to cycle her power around her body, reinforcing herself as hard as she could.

"No, I don't think I would," Gront concurred. "My turn then?"

Mara nodded. "Seems only—"

Gront hit her. His enormous hand curled into a fist and slammed into her stomach; Mara felt his knuckles connecting with almost the entirety of her abdomen at once. She fell back, gasping for air. Her magic fluttered desperately around the impact, trying to see what was broken and fix it.

Didn't get the whole protection up in time, she realized ruefully. *Bones all seem to have held up, but that's going to be a hell of a bruise.*

With some difficulty, she steadied her breathing, then gingerly pushed herself back to her feet.

"Ouch," she said.

An impressed twinkle glittered in Gront's black eyes. "Most people wouldn't get up from that," he said.

"I'm not most people," Mara muttered. She'd felt worse at the hands of Raskith's enemies. And at Raskith's hands.

I'm surviving this too—and I'm getting what I want.

She inhaled deeply through her nose, then let the air leave slowly, calmly, through her mouth. Squaring her shoulders, she held herself straight upright, every muscle lengthening.

On the next breath, she closed her eyes and reached for her power again, directing all of it into her right hand.

"Another spell?" Gront said. "An interesting tactic, or a stupid one."

"This," said Mara, eyes still closed, breathing still controlled, "is just me getting ready to hit you."

She pushed everything she had into her hand until her fingers couldn't stand to stay straight; they curled into a fist and squeezed with all their might, trembling from the sheer force coursing through them. Then Mara took some of the aura of death and sent it streaming through her mind, making her keen and focused. Her senses sharpened like a predator's; her heartbeat became loud in her ears. Everything in her strained toward one instinct, stoked by her magic until it was an inferno: *kill.*

When she opened her eyes, every fiber of her being was utterly bent toward the absolute extinction of anyone who dared stand in her way.

Gront's expression shifted. Mara registered only two facts: that he stood before her, and that she was unwilling to permit him the boon of continuing to do so. She drew back her fist, all her strength devoted to the singular goal of obliteration. Power and rage coalesced in her right hand as it prepared to deliver the final blow—

"Alright, alright," said Gront, holding up his hands. "I yield."

Mara blinked, cutting off the flow of magic around her body. For a few moments, her muscles twitched as she redirected the power, sending it harmlessly out into the world or back into her ring. The nerves and tendons in her fingers and forearm ached, burned by the caustic, abrasive strength that had torn through them, that had yearned to burst free but had been forced to retreat unsatisfied. Her senses returned to normal, leaving her feeling as if she hadn't slept for days.

"You yield," she repeated uncertainly.

"Yeah," said Gront. "I've seen that look before. When I died."

Mara wiggled her fingers, trying to shake out the icy needle spikes of cramping pain. "What look?"

Gront tilted his head and raised an eyebrow: *really?* "Little person," he said, "you were absolutely determined to destroy me." He grinned with approval, even perhaps affection. "I might be immune to magical fear, but I can still be sensible enough to recognize when I need to avoid having a comet fall on my head."

"You think I'd have hit you that hard?"

"I've no idea how hard you would've hit," said Gront, "but I think you believed you were about to tear through me like a storm through rice paper. And I don't think you're the type to believe things that aren't true."

Mara held out her hand. "My winnings, then?"

Gront chortled and reached into his cloak. He pulled out a single coin and held it between his great forefinger and thumb for her to see, then placed it delicately in her waiting palm. "If you ever find yourself looking for something to do," he said, "I think we could find some very good uses for you. We're not just gamblers, you know."

Mara grinned. "In another life, I probably would've taken you up on that."

But Gront's got his own agenda, and I've got mine. The ragtag bunch I've got with me are in it to be selfless, or something stupid like that, and that makes them more useful when I'm only here to finish one thing and go.

Gront inclined his head in respect. "I'm sure I'll hear of you again soon," he said. "Or, at least, I'll hear that someone's done something ridiculous and know it's probably you." He stood and beckoned to his crew. "C'mon. We're done here."

The three members of Gront's little party trotted toward him as he turned to leave. They were as Mara remembered: half-orc, goblin, and cetacean-thing. On his way past Mara's group, the goblin sniffed loudly, then glanced up at Iona.

"You're familiar," said the goblin.

"Me?" Iona said, one hand theatrically indicating herself. "Have you ever been to Aurethen's temple on the Road to Eternity?"

"Nah," said the goblin, squinting. "Nah, I reckon I met you once while I was still alive or whatever. Or... hold it, d'you have a brother or something?"

Iona's expression flickered for a moment. Then she schooled it into a look of mild bemusement. "I did," she said. "Or do. Maybe you and I came from the same place."

"Small worlds," said the goblin.

Iona nodded. Her mouth formed a wide smile, but her eyes looked … less than happy to Mara. "Feels that way, doesn't it?"

The goblin cocked his head abruptly, then scoffed and waved his hands dismissively. "Don't matter. Be seeing ya."

"Duznit!" called Gront. "Stop bothering people!"

The goblin scooted away, grumbling to himself, and disappeared into the Ashen Fields with Gront and the rest of his group.

"Well," said Mara, flipping her newly won Crossway Coin, "that went well."

"He hit you hard enough in the stomach that I can see the bruise on your collarbone," said Varun.

"That went reasonably well," Mara corrected.

CHAPTER 12

"If we're going to be a party," said Iona as the group trekked back up the great tunnel that was Ascension Row, "we should probably know more about everyone's capabilities, right?"

Varun shrugged. "Are we a party?"

"Of course we are!" Iona declared, gesticulating wildly. "We're a bunch of heroes brought together to complete a mission—what else are we?"

"A mission to permanently lose one of our members," Varun pointed out.

"Nah," chirped Iona. "Being not obliterated is way better than vanishing from all existence or whatever. She'll realize. And then we can all keep hanging out!"

Varun sighed. "You can't just decide to unilaterally change the mission to something else entirely," he said. "And besides, we're *all* going to have to go to one afterlife or another eventually, so let's try to get Mara into one that suits her. Are we going to have to keep talking about this?"

"No," said Iona, although Mara suspected what she meant was something more along the lines of "yes."

"My capabilities are something of a mystery to me," Nemmo mused. "I seem to have a certain quantity of magic to draw upon, and some things use more than others, but I cast by instinct. I have no defined spells, only the will to do things. Sometimes those things happen, sometimes not." He paused for a second. "In a fistfight, I am completely useless."

Iona patted him on the back. "That's alright," she said, "we'll just make sure you're not the one doing that sort of thing. Do you have a specialty? Offense, healing, empowering or disabling, changing the environment…?"

Nemmo gave the matter immense consideration. Not that he thought for a terribly long time, but the sheer weight of thought conveyed by his heavy sigh and narrowed eyes was astounding. "I seem to be able to change the nature of things somewhat," he said.

Iona frowned at him. "Eh?"

"I can make things believe they are as they might have been, or perhaps as they once were or will be," said Nemmo ponderously. "And simple things like pushing, pulling, some minor restorations. Although I suppose to restore something is simply to make it remember how it used to be."

The group stopped, all looking at Nemmo.

"Huh," said Iona after a moment, since nobody else had anything to say. "Well, we'll … work with that." They resumed their walking; she turned her head to Varun. "You're mostly the flaming swords guy, right?"

He nodded. "My patron saw that I was best suited to hitting things with swords, I guess, and just … made me better at it. I have a couple of basic projectiles and one stronger one that takes a little longer to cast, and that's about it. Almost managed to learn a shield spell, but never quite got it." He scratched his chin with one finger.

"Who is your god, anyway?" Mara asked.

Varun seemed to consider how much to tell her. "Invars," he said. "He's a god of a few things, but mostly change. He saw that I wanted to change things—to make things different—and he offered me the power to make it happen." His fingers clenched into a fist.

I don't want to ask, but … I don't think I can not ask.

Mara took a breath, then let the question fall out of her. "What happened to you?"

His nose twitched. "I died in a… well, a fucking massacre. A pointless one too. My village didn't have anything worth stealing—we weren't in a position worth crushing for strategic value. Some dark lord just waltzed in one day and destroyed the lot of us. My whole family, gone. I've never run into any of them here either. Probably all moved on long ago."

Mara felt a peculiar wrenching somewhere in her torso.

"After I got here," Varun said, looking at the floor ahead of him, "I joined the queue for the Keepers and found out I couldn't be resurrected. At the moment of my death, there was a chance, but … something happened to my body not long after." He grimaced. "I don't even want to know what."

"So you sought out Invars because … you didn't like how your first existence ended and wanted to do something better with this one?" Mara hazarded, suddenly desperate to move the conversation on. She'd known she'd done all sorts of things that the people to whom she'd done them would have considered tragedies; she'd heard all kinds of tragic pleas from people begging her not to kill them; she'd caused immeasurable grief. She knew that. She'd always known that. But something about hearing it directly from one of the people she'd left in her wake…

"Not exactly," said Varun. "There was more after that." He turned toward Iona, walking backward so he could talk to her, nearly tripping in the first few steps but regaining his balance.

"As for your capabilities, you're the one who ... likes hitting things with a hammer?"

"No," said Iona, unconvincingly. Then, almost immediately, "Yeah, alright, fine, hitting stuff with a hammer is pretty great. But I can heal too, or enhance everyone else's abilities. I can do a bit of everything, really." She beamed, evidently pleased with herself, and turned her attention to Mara. "What about you? You're ... a puncher, but you showed off some pretty neat tricks against the soul stitched. Offensive light magic and binding earth magic, right? And I don't know what in all the hells you did to Gront, but I could feel it from where I was standing." She shivered. "It felt like you were crushing all the death in the place into one dense little ball."

"I'm a healer, mostly," said Mara.

Not technically a lie—the most recent academia on necromancy posits that raising the dead and healing the living are two sides of the same branch of magic. So in my world, at least, I'm just a healer who uses their skills a bit differently.

Iona snorted. "You are *not*."

"A weird one," Mara conceded, "but most of what I can do well is internal to the body—my own or others'. I punch hard by making my hand strong, that kind of thing. But yeah, my magic's a bit flexible."

"How does yours work then?" Iona demanded, peering at her. She jerked a thumb over her shoulder toward Nemmo. "His is just shaping a bit of magic at a time from, what, a big reservoir of power? Mine's more rigid—every day, I can cast a set number of spells, and that's it."

Never heard of something like that. Sounds inconvenient.

"So you wake up in the morning and you've got, say, eight spells you can cast any time you like... does it have to be eight different ones?"

"It's kinda complicated," Iona said, running her hand through her hair. "I know a few different spells, and they use different amounts of power. I get a fresh tank each day, or I can do some things to restore it a bit, but in essence, I've got a fixed quantity of magic to play with. I can pump more power into a weak spell to make it stronger, but I can't cast a complex spell with less power... it's a whole thing."

"Hells," said Mara. "I'd get a headache if I had to keep track of that."

"I just sort of know at all times what I've got left, luckily," said Iona. "If I had to write it down or something, I'm not sure I'd ever actually cast any spells. Or I'd use all my magic immediately and then get in trouble when I needed it and didn't have any left." She shook her head, blinking. "What's yours like then?"

"Focuses and rituals, mostly," Mara said. "There's power everywhere—different kinds depending on what's nearby. I can shape some of that easily enough just by telling it what I want it to do, but for more powerful spells, I need to use certain items that help the magic become what I need it to be." A gentle frown pulled at her features as she remembered her teaching. "My master once told me it was like trying to change a cup of water: to make it swirl around, all you have to do is pick it up and move it, but to turn it red, you need to add dye. And then there are the really complicated things, and those need rituals—external items and channels to help shape things in a bigger way than I can manage inside myself."

"Huh," said Iona. "So the stone and light spells...?"

"There was stone under my feet and light all around," said Mara. "Not too hard to persuade it to keep being stone and light in slightly different forms."

Iona nodded, apparently impressed. "Neat."

"You know," Mara began, and then she hesitated.

Iona blinked at her. "Yeah?"

"Well," said Mara, "when I got here, I was … sort of intercepted by someone whose attention I didn't really want."

Iona nodded as if she understood perfectly. "People suck sometimes," she said. "I mean, most are good most of the time. But sometimes they suck. And some people really suck."

"Yeah," said Mara, not sure how to respond to that. "Anyway, I figured that because I was dead, this person must be dead too. When I was alive, I knew some basic magic designed to deter undead things from attacking—you know, you'd hope it wouldn't happen, but occasionally some necromancer would cause trouble—but it didn't work. But my other magic seems to be fine."

"Ah." Nemmo spoke up before Iona could respond. "This is quite a common source of confusion, as I understand it—a lot of magical individuals, particularly those in some sort of holy service, experience a similar disappointment." His gray face wrinkled with what looked like sympathy. "A shame, really, that so many must defend themselves against the dead while they still live."

"The worst," said Mara, perhaps a little too quickly.

"I suspect that most magic of this kind relies on some sort of hierarchy," Nemmo mused. "Some distinction between living and dead; a separation of kind, or perhaps of level. One cannot pull a drowning person from a lake while submerged in the same lake. It must be done from outside."

Mara frowned. Fortunately for her, Iona saved her the trouble of replying.

"What?" said the cleric perfectly flatly.

She's got admirable simplicity, if nothing else, Mara thought with what might have almost been a hint of burgeoning fondness.

"Well," said Nemmo patiently, "when a living person casts such a magic on an undead being, the relationship is clear. One lives, the other does not. The magic knows that its function is to help life command death. When neither party is more alive than the other, there is nothing the magic can see to do, no balance to restore."

"That … actually makes a lot of sense," Mara said.

"Thank you," said Nemmo, inclining his head cheerfully.

The group emerged out of the tunnel into the half-light of Nox Valar, Mara's fingers running ceaselessly across the surface of the coin in her pocket. Meanwhile, Varun had continued to walk backward since turning to talk to Iona, and kept it up even as they headed back toward the temple that housed the Keepers of the Eternal Sands.

"Being a god of backward things and reversals sounds alright really," he said in reply to Mara's questioning frown. "Worse things to be." He almost made it all the way to the Keepers' house without walking into anything.

If we ever have to play a different game with Gront, Mara thought, *I'm getting Varun to race him backward.*

By the time the great glass-sided monolith loomed over them, Mara's coin bore a single digit beneath the emblem of the hourglass. And she was hungry, she realized, and tired; the sands visible through the clear walls of the Keepers' abode had nearly run to the bottom, indicating the end of the day. With no sun to tell her what time it was, she'd almost forgotten that time had even been progressing in the sort of way that could make her need things like food and sleep; it felt more as if things in the Crossing ought to simply happen in sequence, divorced from seconds and hours and days, one after the other because that was their order rather than because the passage of time dictated it.

One of the attendants standing by the base of the temple stepped toward Mara, holding out a hand. "Your sands have fallen," they said.

Mara withdrew the coin from her pocket and held it up, glancing at its face. Sure enough, the number had hit one. She handed it over almost reluctantly: as long as she had held it, it had represented potential, power, value to be spent. Giving it up, even to gain the very thing she had wanted to buy with it in the first place, felt like losing something.

"Come with me," said the attendant.

"Good luck," Iona chirped. Mara strode into the pyramid without so much as a glance back at her companions.

One of Raskith's more extravagant lairs had been a multi-story tower at the corner of several half-crumbled walls. A castle, once, but mostly a ruin by the time he had taken up residence. The tower, however, had somehow been spared whatever ravages had reduced the rest from a seat of power to a dilapidated wreck, and something about the juxtaposition of an ascending stronghold with a fallen pile of stone had attracted Raskith. He'd reinforced the tower and refurbished it, turning it into a veritable grand domain fit for an archmage.

In pride of place in what he called the Room of Meditation on the Nature of Time and Space had been a grand clock, twice as tall as Mara and wider than the span of her arms, a masterpiece of design in spiraling lacquered wood. It was adorned with dozens of great and small contraptions, all powered by the same central clockwork mechanism, all dancing around one another in intricate weaves that began together, diverged in turn to go about their own business elsewhere, then gradually found themselves once more synchronized. Mara had never quite understood the purpose of the Room of Meditation on the Nature of Time and Space, but she had spent longer than she would have liked to admit simply standing or sitting before that clock, admiring it. Once, she opened its doors to see what was inside and found herself lost in its twinkling, orbiting, constant mechanisms, silently tracing what seemed to her like the movement of the entire cosmos within themselves. Their dance was nothing less than the shape of time, of all that was and would be.

Stepping into the Keepers' temple was like falling into that clock, shrinking and disappearing and becoming subsumed within its structures as they turned, endlessly in motion, and then falling again, eternally adrift in a universe composed of labyrinthine components all working separately, indecipherably toward a single purpose. Mara's eyes couldn't decide what to land upon, could barely even orient her in relation to the ground.

The internal structure of the building was composed of four materials: white stone, gleaming metal, clear glass, and sand, sand that could have been white, black, gray, or golden, ever-shifting in the reflected and refracted light. The glass and metal sharpened the Crossing's omnipresent gloom into radiant, focused beams that shone on slopes and funnels and sieves through which the sand fell, constantly fell, and in its falling drove delicate weights and levers and shafts that turned and bloomed and traced almost acrobatic patterns. As far as Mara could tell, none of it actually *did* anything. No engines were visibly powered by the whirring machinery, nor were any hands pushed across a numbered face. Whatever the space was, it felt as if an accurate image of it could never fit within her mind, only fractured glimpses.

"The ornamentum can be quite overwhelming," said the attendant without looking back at Mara.

"What does it do?" she asked in a hushed tone, inexplicably worried that the minuscule vibrations of her voice might break something.

"It does what you see it doing," said the attendant.

"But … what's its purpose?"

Her guide sighed. "Everyone asks that. It's just time. Just time moving things from one state, one position, to another. And then, when the sand runs out, it stops. It resets. It does it again. Nothing is accomplished except that, well, it happens, but isn't that enough?"

Mara looked back at the workings of the hourglass that sat atop the temple, every glance swept away by some new intricacy she hadn't noticed before.

"This is where I leave you," the attendant informed her.

Mara blinked, tearing her gaze from the ever-falling sand. They stood before a plain wooden door; her guide's hand rested upon the handle, ready to turn it. She'd forgotten they'd even been walking.

"I hope you learn something you need," said the attendant, "and not simply something you want."

With that, they turned the handle and pulled the door open, stepping back with a gentle incline of their head.

"Please." They extended a hand formally, gesturing inside.

Mara allowed herself one deep breath. Then she went in.

CHAPTER 13

Paper. Stacks and stacks of paper. Sheets drifting through the air on some undetectable breeze; reams of it littered across the floor in disordered heaps that might once have been neat towers; black ink splattered and splotched across white surfaces, or etched spiderishly across it in a compressed, urgent hand.

Stepping from the impossibly ordered minutiae of the sand-driven workings outside into the utter chaos of flapping white gave Mara an immediate headache.

"With you in a moment," a distracted voice called from somewhere within the cacophony of paper. A few seconds later, a bundle of sheets erupted outward, breaking apart abruptly before gently floating earthward, like droplets from a sneeze. A lined head poked out from the resulting hole in the stacks, cotton-haired and bespectacled. "Hello there," the old man greeted Mara, clambering stiffly through the mountain of paper until he was standing before her, peering up at her through thick lenses.

"He … llo," said Mara, blinking down at him.

"Meachron's the name," he said, adjusting his robes. They hung loosely from his body, the fabric of dappled black and white reminding Mara of Varun's skin; the patterns swirled around each other like an obsidian waterfall throwing up bright foam. "Keeper of the Eternal Sands. You'd be Mara?"

"I would," she said, tentatively shaking his proffered hand. "You're ... *the* Keeper?"

"Oh, heavens, no," declared Meachron, waving his hands with gusto: *absolutely not.* "One of many. I don't know how many. Somebody does. Maybe. Or nobody does! Who knows?" His wrinkled face squashed itself into an expression of deep curiosity. "Somebody. Or not."

Mara stood there, trying to work out what response would get her what she wanted from Meachron as he muttered and fidgeted, seemingly lost in a conversation he was having entirely with himself. "So—" she began.

"You'll want to know something, I expect," Meachron said, turning away from her and running his hands across the tops of several towering sheaves of paper. His fingers skimmed the topmost sheets, deftly flicking several of them onto the floor as if he were digging for something. "Something to do with the timing of something or other, no doubt. Aha!" His left hand suddenly shot out sideways, almost behind him, and tore a handful of sheets out of the middle of a stack, all while his eyes were somewhere else entirely. The dismembered top half of the stack fell neatly down onto the bottom half, balancing improbably. "This'll be it, of course."

"Are all the Keepers ... like you?" Mara asked.

"Oh, I hope not," Meachron muttered, holding his snatched ream of paper in front of his face even as his other hand continued to riffle through the stacks. "Nothing'd ever get done. Or everything'd never get done, or perhaps nothing never—is that everything always? Always never everything and nothing, after all..." He turned, flourishing the sheets in his left hand; all but one fluttered out of his grip and feather-wobbled to the floor. "Here we are then. The Sands tell the truth, you know. Can't help it. They fall, they continue, they tell the truth. Inevitable. Eternal. Quite beautiful."

He's completely lost his mind, Mara thought. *He's not insensible, but he may as well not be part of the real world at all. Then again, maybe that's what existing in a place that's all about time in its purest form does to a person.*

"So," he said, eyes flickering rapidly across the page, "let's see. You are … ah, dead." He glanced up at her. "With me so far?"

"I was aware," she said.

"Excellent, excellent. You'd be surprised how often people manage to skip over that part." He cleared his throat and flipped the page over, then flipped it again and again, horizontally, vertically, and diagonally, then ran it through his fingers as if it were a long scroll. Somehow, despite being only a book-sized sheet, it seemed to keep flowing up and up through his hands. "You may well be resurrected at some point," he said, one eye flicking to her face while the other continued to scan the page. It was awfully off-putting. "Looks as if the true, nice kind of resurrection is somewhat off the table though, I'm afraid."

"I'd guessed as much."

"Ahhhhh*hhhh*." The sound that trilled from Meachron ascended to an intrigued, warbling pitch, like that of an old gossip. "A scandalous life. Still, I see it will be rather a long time until your chance of being restored diminishes to nothing, and rather a short time until it becomes significant."

Mara sighed heavily, causing several nearby sheets of paper to flutter in distress. "What does that mean, exactly?"

"You have perhaps a day or two, in the reckoning of time as it passes here in the Crossing," said Meachron, "before it becomes more likely than not that your resurrection will be, ah, executed."

That's no time at all. I knew he'd move fast, but … by all the damned hells, he must really *want this.*

Oblivious to her thoughts, the Keeper plowed on. "And, if I read this right, which I do, it'll be months or perhaps years before it becomes so unlikely as to be of no concern."

"Right," said Mara. "So … if I want to avoid that happening…?"

"Well, you'd need to get yourself out of the Crossing pretty sharpish, one way or another," said Meachron. "If you're dead and here, you can be made alive and there, or wherever." He dropped the paper unceremoniously.

"I need to leave the Crossing in the next few days or I'm at a high risk of being resurrected," Mara repeated.

"That's the one." Meachron nodded affirmatively. He peered up at her, lifting his glasses to squint with bare eyes. "You've an odd energy, you know. What's death if not time making itself known? But for you, time's never quite run steady, has it?"

I've got everything I could out of him, Mara mused, *and it's been no help at all.*

She thought for only a few seconds about what to do next—less time than the decision merited, she knew, but her only real options were to leave or to act. So she punched him.

He fell back, his glasses soaring merrily from his face, and slammed to the floor with a heavy thump muffled by the carpet of paper sheets. "Not unexpected," he wheezed, "nor blameworthy, but I'd really have preferred it if you hadn't done that."

Mara took a step forward, standing over him. "How do I get out of this?" she demanded. "How do I change things, make it so he can't bring me back?"

"I've told you," Meachron coughed. "And so have others. You need to be away from the Crossing. That's all there is for it."

She scoffed. "What good are you?"

"None, really," he said, propping himself up on one elbow. "That's the thing of it. People always want to know before they know, but they'll know when they know and there's nothing that can be done about it."

Mara turned away, then back again.

I can't let Raskith have me. This system is fucked. She took a shaky breath. *I can't destroy the system, I know that, but… but hells, I feel like I'd feel better if I destroyed the little part of the system in front of me right now.* She paused. Then she drew on the power within her ring.

Meachron raised a hand, instinctively shielding his face from her. Then he froze.

The magic within Mara's body ceased its flow, suddenly cold and inert. She shivered against the spikes of icy pain that needled her from within, as if her blood had frozen in her veins.

"Mara," whispered a voice, a voice that sounded like an icy wind ripping through mountain valleys, like mold growing on an ancient tree, like fire devouring the world. "Mara, Mara, Mara. Were you really about to murder a Keeper of the Eternal Sands?"

"He'd have come back tomorrow," Mara muttered. All her muscles were instinctively flexed, straining against the pain that bit at her from within.

"Murder is still a crime among the half-dead," the voice purred. "He would have gone straight to the Nyxian Guard, and you would have been in rather a lot of trouble."

She swallowed, gritting her teeth. The tendons in her neck stuck out. "Who are you?"

A dark gray shadow detached itself from Meachron's stilled form and stood. Then, like a mist, it spread, dispersing outward, saturating the room. It swirled, and Mara thought she saw tiny flecks of detritus whirling with its currents: soil, ash, bone dust. There were little embers whispering in the air, and the wet smell of freshly dug soil. "You know me," it said.

A fresh torrent of cold surged through Mara. "Rekh."

"Yes."

She tried to drop to one knee, but she was just as paralyzed as Meachron.

"Ah. A moment."

Her muscles released, and she fell abruptly to her knees. "What has this insignificant one done that you would bless her with your presence?" she asked, gaze fixed on the floor.

"Oh, please," said Rekh. "None of that. You and I know each other better than to necessitate all the deference and ceremony, don't we?"

Mara stayed where she was. "You're my god," she whispered.

"I am," said Rekh. "But ... I think of you and I as close colleagues. I'm not so distant. Not so removed."

"Why ... are you here?" Mara breathed.

"As you have found," said Rekh, "I am not venerated in Nox Valar. My philosophy on death, particularly its permeability, is ... unwelcome. There are powers and wills that desire a certain flow, and I represent something of an impediment to that. Other gods of death have their way here, while I myself am a god only of undeath, of false life."

A shock ran through Mara, an even sharper cold on top of the ache she already felt. *I thought I served* the *God of Death... I never did?*

Rekh's swirling form sped up for a moment, as if a miniscule whirlwind had momentarily formed in the room, then returned to its usual lazy revolving. "But here, with the will of death in you and the force of time around you—for the strange little mortal was right: time and death are the closest of brethren indeed—I can make myself known, if only for a while. I will not appear to you again, not until all is done."

"Will you take me to your afterlife?" Mara wasn't sure whether she wanted to hear the answer.

"I will."

She breathed a sigh of relief, her limbs going light and limp. "Thank you."

"I do not want Raskith's plans for you to come to fruition, you know."

Mara dared to raise her head just a little, letting her vision scrape the bottom of the swirling shadow. "But ... is he not a greater servant to you than I am?"

Rekh laughed. Mara thought she might die then and there. When the sound ceased, she gasped for air as if she'd been drowning.

"He is no fool," her god's voice allowed, still suffused with a trace of cold amusement, "but he is dull. Swanning around with his fermented, overripe ambitions of, what, ruling the world? He has no idea why he would want to do such a thing, except that it seems to him what a man of great evil and strength ought to do. If it ever came true, he would lack any sense of what to do with himself."

"Then ... why grant him such power?"

"I do not," said Rekh. "His power comes from himself, not directly from me, though he uses it in my service."

Stupid question. Stupid, stupid question. I knew that already, and now my god thinks I'm an idiot. Stupid, stupid.

"He is useful, in his way," Rekh's voice continued. "He serves me by raising in my holy way, though he does it more for his own glory than for mine. But for you, Mara, I want better. You who revere me by performing my miracles, yet never truly wanted to be part of my family... it makes it pure, guileless, in its way. You deserve a greater fate than to be a mindless servant. So yes, I shall allow you to the final resting place I keep for those who please me."

"Thank you," said Mara. "Thank—"

Rekh cut her off, voice soft. "There is a price."

Mara pressed her forehead to the ground. "Of—of course."

"You must prove to me that you are a deserving servant," said Rekh, and Mara thought the voice took on a new coldness, like the sharp edge of a gravedigger's shovel. "Perform for me the greatest act of undeath."

"Yes, my god," Mara breathed. She raised her head from the floor. The mist and detritus that was Rekh consumed her, wrapping her up in its currents.

"Raise me a god," Rekh whispered in her ear.

Then the god of undeath was gone, simply vanished as if it had never been there. A single sheet of paper fluttered in the air before Mara; she snatched it and read it.

Instructions, she recognized, scanning the list. *What have I just agreed to do…?*

"Can I get up now?" Meachron asked pitifully from the floor.

"Do what you will," said Mara. "It won't matter."

She turned on her heel and left.

CHAPTER 14

Fortunately for Mara, leaving the Keepers' temple was far easier than entering. She opened the door to Meachron's room and found herself immediately emerging into the gloom; when she turned to look back through the open door, she saw that the room on the other side was gone. Even the door whose handle she had been holding only a moment ago was gone, leaving her fist clenched around empty air.

The building behind her was nondescript and could have been anything; she supposed to anyone who'd been looking, it would appear as if she'd walked out of the front door. She had a clear line of sight to the Keepers' hourglass—to its tip, at least, which jutted out above the low buildings between her and it. She cast her gaze down the street, but didn't see anyone.

When she was sure nobody was there to see it, she slumped against the wall, all the strength leaving her. She hadn't openly cried in a long time, and it was a habit she doubted she could break even if she wanted to, but she came close as she drew shaky breaths.

I just came face-to-face with Rekh. I just shared a space with death itself.

Her breathing gradually calmed; she stood, pressing her hands into her face. She gave herself one sharp slap on the cheek, then exhaled firmly and set off.

It only took her a few minutes to make her way back to where she'd been; Iona, Nemmo, and Varun weren't far from where she'd left them, leaning against a wall and eating what looked like sugar-dusted pastries.

"That didn't take long," said Varun, tossing her a pastry. She bit into it and tried unsuccessfully to hide the look of sheer relish that crossed her face as the syrupy flavor of the sweet fruit within blossomed in her mouth.

"It didn't?" she asked around a mouthful of food. "It felt like…" She paused. What *did* it feel like? "Like it could have been a week or ten minutes," she said after a moment of consideration.

"Yeah, that place'll do that," said Varun. "It can be a bit strange."

"A bit strange," Mara echoed, with a wry chuckle that blew a puff of powdered sugar out of her mouth like the breath of a tiny dragon that had just besieged a bakery.

"So," tooted Iona, bouncing on the balls of her feet with excitement, "what did you find out?"

Mara took another bite and swallowed ruefully. "Not a whole lot."

Iona's face fell. "Oh."

"From the Keeper anyway. But … my god, R—" She hesitated, momentarily forgetting that she needed to lie about the name she gave. A chunk of fruit went down her throat the wrong way; she covered her slip with an extravagant coughing fit. "Sorry," she said when she was done, eyes streaming. "Delicious but dangerous." She quickly polished off the rest and stuck each of her fingers in her mouth, giving them a rapid cleaning of any residue. "Anyway, Raskith, he appeared to me."

Iona gasped, clapping her hands over her mouth. Varun frowned. Nemmo leaned forward, his posture curious.

"Your god physically manifested inside the domain of the Keepers of the Eternal Sands?" Varun said.

Mara nodded. "I don't know why or how, but he was there, and he gave me a task."

Iona gave something halfway between a gasp and a squeal. "What was it?"

"If I want him to allow me into his afterlife," Mara said, "I have to perform a ritual. A prayer at the grave of an old god, one of healing and life. An ancestor of Raskith, I think; life gives way to death, and then the whole cycle of rebirth … and so on," she said, trailing off. She'd quickly made up the cover story on her way over; if she'd known she'd only been in the temple a few minutes, she would have spent longer coming up with something that would stand up to scrutiny.

"A ritual," Varun repeated, gazing at her.

"Yep."

"What does the ritual require?" Nemmo asked.

"I need…" Mara had already destroyed the paper bearing the instructions, but they were simple. Even had they been more complex, she would have had a hard time forgetting something so important. "The heart of an infernal beast, a certain book, and … the tears of a god."

The fleshy protrusions that acted as Nemmo's eyebrows rose curiously. His black eyes gleamed. "Well," he said. "Quite a task."

"Heart of an infernal's easy," Iona said, frowning so deeply that Mara thought her round face might fold in on itself. "What was that guard's name, the, um, one with the ears and the dragonfly? Chirripeek—he already said we'd be welcome to help guard the Lightless Chasm, and infernals come through there all the time."

Varun scoffed. "That doesn't make it *easy* to acquire one's heart."

"Tears of a god," Iona continued, ignoring him, "that's trickier. First, you need to find an actual physical manifestation of a god around here somewhere, or summon one, and then you need to persuade it to cry for you somehow."

"I may have an idea," Nemmo said, folding his arms and tapping the thick fingers of one hand against the other forearm. "But I'll need to consider it."

Iona did a double-take at that, then shook her head and fixed Mara with an intense stare. "What's the book?"

Mara sighed heavily. "It's called the *Tome of the Beyond*," she said, "and I *did* know exactly where it is."

"You did know...?" Iona thought for a moment, then stuck her bottom lip out in sympathy as a conclusion came to her. "Ah. You brought it with you and they carted it off to put it in the pile of thrown-away things by the Gilded Hills."

"Yeah."

"Well, that's not so bad," said Iona. "Let's do that one first."

"You should have just told your god that he had a peculiar smell," said Nemmo in his matter-of-fact way.

Everyone turned to him.

"Eh?" said Iona.

"He might have cried," said Nemmo. "One item ticked off."

A moment passed.

The gray-skinned man shrugged. "I thought it was a good joke."

Iona burst out laughing, even clapping her hands together with glee. Varun and Mara exchanged glances; Varun gave one reluctant chuckle, then one genuine one. Mara just rolled her eyes, which only made Iona laugh harder.

These people are idiots.

What she didn't allow herself to think too clearly was that they might well be idiots she was coming to like.

The group had only made it a couple of streets from the temple, heading in what Iona was "optimistic" was the direction of the Gilded Hills, when Mara and Iona suddenly let out synchronized, enormous yawns.

"Ah," said Varun, immediately following it up with one of his own. "The lack of a day and night gets to you, doesn't it?"

"I feel like I should be wide awake and exhausted at the same time," Mara admitted.

Iona, meanwhile, was pointing an accusing finger at Nemmo. "You didn't yawn! You're supposed to yawn when other people yawn!"

He shrugged. "My physiology doesn't include the faculty to yawn."

The cleric lowered her finger, looking almost disappointed. "Oh. Well, that'll be why then."

"I think I need to rest," Mara said. "Do we have time?"

"Oh, yeah," said Iona, nodding. "They probably won't even have got all the stuff from today's newcomers over to the Gilded Hills yet, so we might even be better off checking tomorrow."

"Is anyone likely to … steal it?"

Iona turned to Varun as if expecting him to be the authority on the topic.

"What?" he said.

The cleric raised an eyebrow at him as if to say *don't pretend you don't know what I'm talking about.* "You spent a bit of time with the Chantry, right?"

"A little bit," he said offhandedly. "They're more into stealing memories, really."

Nemmo perked up at that. "In what sense?"

Varun tapped his finger and thumb together as he thought about it. "They want things that mean something. Or, sometimes, they steal actual literal memories. Some of them have ways. They enjoy... I don't know. If you think of any god's afterlife as containing a whole lot of people whose lives consisted of them building up value, getting more experiences and memories and doing things in their god's name, and then bringing all that value to their afterlife, taking something precious is like stealing from a god. It's a thrill."

Iona hummed thoughtfully. "Low risk then."

He nodded. "I'd say so. At any rate, I don't think it'll make a difference whether we go now or after resting. Either way, we've got just as much chance of getting lucky and finding it just as it gets there or missing it entirely."

"Right," said Iona, clapping her hands, "it's decided. Come with me." She turned and started marching back the way they'd come, toward the house of the Keepers.

"Are we really going back on ourselves?" Varun groaned.

"And farther!" Iona cheeped.

"Wait," said Varun. "Are you suggesting we all stay at—"

"My place?" Iona pointed at herself with an enthusiastic thumb. "Absolutely!"

Varun groaned.

"It's got free food and beds," Iona said merrily.

Varun squinted at her. "You're on," he said.

Iona was as good as her word: the temple at which she lived and performed her duties had space and supplies to accommodate their small group. As fortune would have it, Iona was one of only a small number of high-ranking devotees, which gave her sufficient authority to allocate the temple's resources with no questions asked.

"Thank you," said Nemmo as the cleric passed him a plate of bread, cheese, and fruit.

They sat around a small table in a plain room reached by taking a half-hidden flight of stairs a short distance underground from the temple's main foyer. A lot of Nox Valar's buildings, Iona explained rapidly, had basements and lower levels; the city's foundation, as was visible from the Ashen Fields, was a single, enormous slab of hard stone that lent itself well to carving out tunnels and caverns and rooms.

The gray-skinned man peered with what looked to Mara like vague curiosity at the food before him. "I forget when I last ate."

Varun raised an eyebrow. "You don't remember how long it's been since you ate anything?"

"My body doesn't often remember these things," said Nemmo absently, pushing a hunk of bread into his mouth. Mara didn't notice him chew or swallow before it was gone, another portion of food already on its way to his lips. "I don't seem to need much."

"Weird," mumbled Iona, who had somehow managed to finish her entire plate in the space of that one short conversation.

"Not so peculiar," said Nemmo. "Everything in the Sunless Crossing is but a part of the enduring presence of Nyxia, is it not? Even for a god, keeping every tiny detail consistent in a realm made of one's own essence must be something of a tall order."

Mara held up a finger while she quickly swallowed what was in her mouth. "Hang on," she said. "The Crossing is, what, part of a god?"

"So I'm told," said Nemmo, "although people do tell it an awful lot of slightly different ways. Some think of it as the dream of Nyxia, but I think that to be less true than that it *is* her, or what remains of her. Still, from what I hear, many worlds consider their entire existences to have been conjured up by their gods, so I don't imagine that makes the Crossing any less real than anywhere else."

"Huh." Mara chewed a few more bites of food, then tapped her fingers on the table.

I want to ask, but I feel like asking might make them realize they don't know the answer themselves... But I don't think I can help it.

"Are you sure you all want to help me do this?" she asked.

Iona looked as if she'd been asked the most offensive question imaginable. "Why would you even say that?" she demanded.

"Because ... you've all known me for less than a day and you don't stand to gain anything from helping me?"

"Ah, yeah, I guess that's fair," Iona conceded. She took a thoughtful bite, having refilled her plate. "I guess it's probably something all of us have been a bit conditioned to do, right? We're all from worlds where gods intervene and everyone aspires to the heights of great heroes, or whatever. When something comes along that looks like a great and wondrous quest, there's an allure to it."

Mara blinked. "Huh."

"What?"

"I just ... wasn't expecting that," Mara admitted. "I thought you'd say something about it being your divine duty to help those in need."

"That too," said Iona, slurping down a long slice of watery fruit. "This one," she said with a nod toward Varun, "has his savior complex thing—"

"I do *not*," said Varun, almost convincingly.

"—and as for Nemmo... well," said Iona, appraising him, "you said something about wanting to be around interesting people?"

Nemmo nodded benignly. "I'm afraid your initial assessment was accurate too," he said. "I also have some attraction to things that feel like significant opportunities to make a difference in the world. Since I can remember nothing of what I did with my life, and since I will at some point need to move on to one afterlife or another, I find myself worried that I might need to do good deeds to outweigh a lot of forgotten bad ones."

"Why me though?" Mara asked.

"Because what'll happen to you if you can't move on sounds absolutely horrible," said Iona, practically tearing up at the thought.

"Because Nozan knew what she was doing when she introduced us," Varun muttered darkly.

"Because we happened to stumble into one another, I suppose," said Nemmo.

Mara stared at each of them for a moment. Then she found herself chuckling.

"What?" asked Varun.

"I always thought I was unlucky," said Mara.

Iona beamed, leaning across the table to pat Mara affectionately on the arm. "We're in this with you," she said, her expression as radiant as if Aurethen himself had appeared to her and told her she was his favorite.

I am lucky, Mara thought. *Who would have thought the place between life and death would be so full of people willing to just let me use them for whatever I need?*

Her internal voice was usually tinged with malice, even the kind of grand, self-congratulatory darkness she hated so much when she heard it from Raskith. But her latest thoughts had notes of doubt running through them. She didn't much like it.

CHAPTER 15

After a night in small individual rooms with surprisingly comfortable beds, they set off for the Gilded Hills in the morning—"at first light," as Varun had described it, despite the omnipresent twilight of the Sunless Crossing. Mara supposed there were probably all sorts of time-of-day idioms that were still in common use simply because they were so ingrained in language as to not need their original referents.

"How can we all understand each other?" she asked abruptly as they made their way along the great circular way that was the Road to Eternity.

"Because we're all intelligent people with coherent things to say," said Iona cheerily. The cleric had rustled up a heaped-high tray of sweet pastries from somewhere for breakfast and had apparently secreted the leftovers in her voluminous sleeves; she drew one out and munched away as they walked.

"I meant more the actual language," Mara said. "Surely it's not the case that we all speak languages that happen to be identical despite coming from completely different nations in completely different realities?"

"I have given this some thought," said Nemmo.

"Course you have," said Iona fondly.

"I suspect," Nemmo said, plowing on undeterred, "that one property of Nyxia's … dream, or instantiation, or whatever is the true ontology of this realm, is simply the facility of translation. I understand it's easily achieved for individuals or small groups with fairly basic magics, so I imagine it to be a trivial thing for a god to apply at scale."

"So we're all talking in our own languages, but understanding what everyone else says as if they were talking ours too," Mara mused.

"Something along those lines, I think," said Nemmo. "I hear that even those who come from the same world but spoke different languages in life can understand each other here, albeit apparently with something of an audible accent. It seems that the mind hears an accent if it expects to, if it would have heard one from a speaker of that language in the living world."

"That's actually really weird," Iona said.

"I don't think it is, particularly," said Nemmo. "Although I do have a theory that the translation effect encompasses far more than simply converting words in one language to another, if you're interested."

"Go on," said Mara, as Iona scrunched up her face in an exaggerated *yuck* expression.

"Well, idioms cannot often be literally translated," said Nemmo, "since they rely on a mutual understanding of concepts that don't tend to make surface-level sense, or are only intelligible in a shared cultural setting, and so on, but we seem to have no problems understanding figurative speech in the Crossing. This suggests to me that the translation effect must be doing something more complex than a normal spell—perhaps it could even be capable of converting things other than simple words and phrases between residents for the sake of creating a shared understanding. What if, for example, when you hear me say 'blue,' what I understood myself to be saying was closer to something like 'gaseous tentacled light-absorbing smell,' because our worlds are so different that that is a perfectly normal color where I come from?"

Mara and Iona frowned at each other. Varun raised an eyebrow, looking genuinely interested.

"We could not understand a sun's frame of reference, if it could talk," Nemmo continued, appearing not to notice any reaction, "and I imagine neither should we be able to understand each other as easily as we can, given how vastly improbable it is that all our worlds should be fundamentally similar." He took a breath.

"I did not understand ... *any* of that," said Iona.

"Oh, well," said Nemmo.

The Gilded Hills came into view first as a sparkle glimpsed between silhouettes, an indeterminate shining thing somewhere past the buildings and people of Nox Valar. It wasn't long before they stood before what was quite probably the biggest gathering of treasures Mara had ever seen in one place, and it was all just sitting there in a great heap.

A low wall surrounded the pile—or the hill, Mara supposed—but it was scarcely doing its job. Gleaming trinkets toppled over the wall every few seconds, dropping to the ground with rippling clinks; there was simply too much of it to stay neatly piled up. She saw golden goblets, jeweled necklaces, coins upon coins upon coins, and a lot of gold and silver cutlery.

I guess a lot of rich people choke on their food or get poisoned. Either way, you're gonna have a lot of folks showing up here with a fork in their hand.

Iona led the group past the main hill to a lower, duller, more compacted pile that had initially been hidden by the sparkling mass. Papers, cloaks, wooden trinkets, the hole-riddled toes of old socks poking sadly out. It was a lesser hill than the gilded one, but still significant—and, to Mara's eye, entirely disorganized.

"How in the hells am I supposed to find one book in that?" she asked aloud.

"Do you have a spell for locating things?" Iona asked.

"Never learned one," Mara said. Raskith had been meticulous about ensuring that he stored things in places he would never forget and could always easily access—or he'd simply stow them away in an extra-planar space inside his cloak. If he wanted something and didn't know where it was in the first place... well, there was always torture for that. "Not sure I know the book well enough for something like that to work, anyway—I think you usually need to be familiar with the thing you're looking for."

"What's so special about this book, anyway?" Varun asked.

"It's supposed to hold secrets about death," Mara said off-handedly as she scanned the heap of things that had presumably been important to someone once. "And life," she added hastily, "and rebirth, and healing, and everything in between. But I never even read it—I skimmed a couple of pages, but that was it. When I got here, there was hardly anything in it, so I don't know why I need it."

"I imagine," said Nemmo, "that this is the sort of item whose significance is more important than the details of its actual properties."

Iona groaned. "What's that in not-smart talk?"

"Well," said Nemmo patiently, "things here function largely the way people remember they did in life. If something held a particular significance, the memory of that alone—the strength of the belief that it is important—could be sufficiently powerful to use it as something like a ritual focus. Even using a copy that lacks all the things that were distinctive about the original might work, if the mere thought of the item conjures a sense of importance."

"It does the thing we think it does because we think it does it," Varun summarized.

"Or thereabouts," Nemmo said, nodding. "Dreams give things the significance we imagine them to have, I think. I have heard some tales, even though I think them likely to be apocryphal, of people who have become so skilled at directing themselves to truly believe that things are a certain way that the Crossing makes it so for them. I suppose my own magic is a very small manifestation of a similar effect."

Mara folded her arms and tapped her foot, trying not to appear too impatient. "Does that get us any closer to finding the book?" she asked.

Varun stepped toward the pile of lost and abandoned things. "Let me try something," he said, and closed his eyes. One hand dipped into a pocket and pulled out a small dart, which he held delicately between finger and thumb. He raised the dart to the height of his ear, then threw it into a seemingly random point in the pile—or, in fact, into the glittering mound that was the Gilded Hills, his throw going so wide as to simply sail over the intended target.

"Ow," said a muffled voice.

"Oh, shit," said Varun, opening his eyes. "Sorry about that."

The pile of gleaming miscellanea shifted and a white-haired head poked out, followed by the rest of the person's body. A young man emerged, perhaps in his late teens, and tumbled strangely gracefully down the hill before neatly clearing the wall and landing on his feet in front of them. He was outfitted in strange dark gray and black clothing: formal wear, Mara would have thought, if it weren't smudged with soot that looked as if it had been there since he was alive rather than being added by the Sunless Crossing's ashen lands. He had fitted trousers with a pressed crease in the front, shoes that looked to have been polished several times and scuffed several more times, and a buttoned sleeveless garment over a white shirt, a black strip of fabric tied in a knot at his neck before disappearing down into the sleeveless thing.

The man saw Mara assessing his clothing and gestured grandly to himself. "Yeah, I get that look a lot," he said. "Not a lot of worlds have waistcoats and ties and things. Or sewing machines, would probably be the bigger picture there."

"What were you doing in there?" Mara asked.

"Getting myself stuck with some errant projectile or other, by the looks," he said, plucking the offending dart from his shoulder. A little circle of red bloomed on his white shirt, but he didn't seem to mind. "What was that about, then?"

"Sorry," said Varun. "I thought maybe I might become the god of finding things by throwing something and magically hitting the thing I'm looking for."

The man blinked. "Weird. Anyway, no harm done, but be careful what you're doing with those, maybe?"

"Noted."

"I'm Pick," said the man who had been rooting around in the Gilded Hills, pointing one thumb at himself. "You lot just here to admire the view?"

"Something like that," said Varun.

"We're actually looking for something," Iona piped up. "A book."

Pick's stark white eyebrows wiggled. "If it's found its way here, doesn't that mean someone just left it behind? Which probably means they didn't want it no more on account of it being of no use in the Crossing, right?"

"If that's the case," Iona countered, waggling a finger almost in imitation of his brows, "why were *you* in there scrounging for something?"

"I do it every morning," he said, shrugging. "Just have a look around, see if anything's ended up here that's worth more than what people might've realized."

"You're with the Chantry?" Varun asked.

"Might be, might not be."

"Yeah, he's absolutely with the Chantry," Iona said, grinning. "Digging through trash must be the lowest job on their ladder though."

"Gotta pay your dues, I guess," said Pick. "Still, I wish it didn't shine so much. Where I come from, it's pretty much always dark and there's a giant, impassable swirling wall of darkness and terrifying beasts just outside the city." He paused. "So not much different from here, really."

Mara couldn't help an impatient harrumph. "This isn't achieving anything," she muttered in Varun's ear. "What are we planning to do? Just go diving in the pile and hope we come across it?"

"You know," said Pick, who had produced a thick, gleaming coin from somewhere and was rolling it across his knuckles, "I might be able to help."

Mara turned to him. "And how would you do that?"

"Heard you saying something about a book," he said mildly, keeping his gaze casually skyward while his fingers deftly maneuvered the coin. "Might've heard something else about a book lately."

Varun, perhaps sensing irritation boiling within Mara, stepped in. "What do you want in return?" he asked.

Pick opened his mouth, but before he could answer, Iona had dashed in and pressed him up against the wall. Her hands gripped his clothes by his upper chest, which meant she was reaching up over her head, but somehow it didn't hurt the intimidating effect.

"What do you know?" she demanded.

Okay, so I really might like Iona. If nothing else, she gets things done.

"Alright, alright!" Pick protested, his hands flapping around Iona's head and shoulders as if he desperately wanted to push her away but didn't want to be so rude as to actually touch her. "It's only a thing I heard, anyway. Forgotten gods, you're forceful."

Iona released him; he brushed himself down, scowling. "Well?" the cleric pressed.

Pick rolled his eyes, a huge motion that involved his entire head and neck. "So last night, there was word that someone detected some new object showing up, something powerful."

Iona's eyes flicked to Mara, who kept her expression schooled. "Go on," Iona encouraged him.

"One of our people got to it—a mate of mine, Oszcek. Managed to pilfer it off the carrier before it made it over here with the rest of the shiny and not-so-shiny bits. Now, I've not spoken to him, so this is all second-hand, but what I heard is that Oszcek's had to go and lie low because people kept taking a punt at him. Like, the poor bastard's suddenly a magnet for trouble, can't walk two streets without someone just diving for him." Pick grimaced. "He's not the toughest kid, so he's probably just hiding out somewhere. If it's something that shows up in people's senses as a powerful magical item, he'll have had to go somewhere with anti-detection measures."

Mara narrowed her eyes. "You have a sense of where that might be?"

Pick gave her a long stare. Then he sighed. "You're gonna beat me up if I don't help, aren't you?"

Iona beamed.

Pick led them through the streets of Nox Valar, sidling through crowds as if he were a rivulet of water slipping through tiny cracks in a rock. Only the fact that he was taking pains to go far slower than he could have done allowed the rest of them to keep up; it was obvious to Mara that he could have left them behind in an instant, had he wanted to. His sinuous, slippery way of moving among people was evidently a habit he couldn't turn off, because it forced him to keep slowing or even stopping so as not to disappear from their view.

Before long, Mara had no idea where they were; as the streets became narrow and cramped, any landmarks by which she might have oriented herself were concealed by the buildings pressing in on either side. Pick stopped in front of a building that looked the same as all the rest in the row, glanced surreptitiously from left to right and back again, then slipped his hand into a small indentation in the wall. Something clicked, and Pick, beckoning the others to follow, walked straight through what looked like a solid wall and disappeared.

"Huh," said Iona. "That's convincing."

The cleric strode unflinchingly toward the wall and right through it. Varun followed suit, a little more gingerly; Nemmo went through backward, perhaps so he didn't have to look. Mara couldn't help a slight grimace as she approached—from her perspective, after all, it looked very credible that she was about to slam her face directly into a solid wall—but she passed through without issue and found herself looking down an alleyway barely wide enough for two people to walk shoulder-to-shoulder.

"An interesting illusion," Nemmo was saying to Pick. "I take it that what you were doing just before making egress involved some kind of physical contraption that alters the ontology of the barricade?"

Pick glanced back, looking mildly confused.

"He wants to know whether there's an actual switch that turns the illusion on and off," Varun said.

"Yeah, I got that," said Pick. "Just... where I come from, the only people who talk like that are the kind of immorally fancy folk most of us scoundrel types only interact with so we can steal from them. But yeah, there's a hidden switch. It's an actual doodad you can physically flip, but it's enchanted so that only people keyed to it can do it. Changes it from a solid magical wall to, er, a walk-throughable one."

"This is some sort of safe house?" Varun asked as they walked down the alley, which was bordered on both sides by solid walls with no windows. The only way someone could have known it existed was by looking down from above—although Mara, glancing up, noticed a shimmer in the air that suggested there might be an illusion keeping it secret from that angle too—or by measuring the external and internal dimensions of all the neighboring buildings and spotting a discrepancy.

"Off the grid, as it were," Pick muttered.

"I did not understand that figure of speech," Nemmo mused. "Interesting."

"It's supposed to be hard to find, even if you have a rough idea where you're looking," Pick continued, either ignoring or not hearing Nemmo, "and it's got a whole bunch of enchantments designed to neutralize scrying, detection, any kind of magical way of looking for something."

"Sounds useful and not at all like it could be used for nefarious purposes," said Iona.

"Oh," said Pick, "it absolutely can be used for nefarious purposes."

They came to the end of the alleyway, where a single narrow door was set into the marble before them. At least, Mara thought it was a door, but it had no handle, no keyhole, and was, according to all outward appearances, just a featureless flat rectangle. Pick dipped two fingers into a pocket at his chest and pulled out a key, which was secured to the inside of his clothing by a thin chain. He tapped the index finger of his free hand on the door's surface; a gentle glow suffused the area just around the tip of his finger and a keyhole opened up just beneath. He inserted the key and turned it, then grabbed the knob that had appeared, tucked the key back into his pocket, and gave a short but complex series of loud raps on the door with his knuckles.

"In we go then," he said, and turned the handle, whereupon the entire door blackened and disintegrated until a pile of black ash lay at the threshold. "It grows back," he said offhandedly. "More an intimidation thing than anything functional, I think."

With that, he stepped inside, the rest of them just behind him.

"Oi!" he called. "Oszcek!"

Mara surveyed the space into which they had passed: a plain entryway with a door ahead, another to the side, and a flight of stairs on the other side. It was clean; well cared for, if not particularly homey.

I could live somewhere like this, she thought idly.

"Pick!" a raspy voice exclaimed. Mara leaned forward, straining her eyes; that voice had sounded as if it had come from right in front of them, but she saw nothing. A moment later, as if the air had blinked, a pair of floating eyes appeared in the hallway. "Storms and walls, I'm glad it's you."

The rest of the person's body appeared, little splashes of color at a time like ink on blotting paper. A small, pale, humanoid form faded into existence before them. The last thing to appear, as if added as a final touch, was a little bat-like wing attached to one ear, flapping ferociously.

"Course it's me," said Pick. "Anyone else showed up here?"

Oszcek shook his head; the wing fluttered. "Managed to shake them and get here, and since then it's been quiet. But they're gonna keep coming after it, Pick. What do I do?"

Pick raised an eyebrow, turning to Mara and her group.

"Can I take it off your hands?" Mara asked bluntly.

"Oh, endless beasts, of course you can," said Oszcek, and before Mara could so much as nod in thanks he darted into the side room and returned holding the *Tome of the Beyond*, thrusting it out at arm's length as if it pained him to keep it too close to his body.

Mara took it. "Thank you," she said.

Varun cleared his throat. "Is that it?" he asked. "You went to all that trouble to get it here safely and you're just going to hand it over?"

"Yes," said Oszcek very firmly, nodding his head as if he'd never been more certain about anything in his life, or indeed his afterlife. "Look, I picked that thing up and people just started rushing me, trying to kill me to get it. I panicked, I ran, I locked myself away, and as soon as I was in here I realized: *I don't want this thing*! I don't know why everyone else is after it, but I sure as all storms didn't enjoy having them coming after me. If someone had just asked nicely, or at least threatened me politely like an honest thief, I'd probably have turned it over, but no, they were all lunging at me like an owl after a mouse, and that didn't make me feel like doing anything except clinging on to what I had and running off as fast as I could."

"Which is a salient point," said Pick. "You realize that as soon as you leave here, everyone who was after Oszcek is going to be after you?"

"I have a couple of thoughts on how to handle that situation," said Mara darkly. Perhaps a little too darkly; Iona gave her an odd look. She'd only meant to lace her words with a subtle intimation of danger, in the way Raskith used to when he wanted people to feel just a little unsafe without overtly threatening them, but she might have gone too far.

"Oh, good," said Pick with what Mara assumed was an extremely practiced air of false cheeriness. "Well then... Oz, you and I had better go find a few more trinkets so it's not a wasted day, eh?"

Oszcek gave an enormous, relieved smile.

Then the roof collapsed on them.

CHAPTER 16

Mara threw herself back, instinctively raising a shield of solid death aura. She'd been at the front of the group; Iona, Varun, and Nemmo were all behind her, farther from the impact, but Pick and Oszcek had disappeared into the rubble.

A dark, hulking shape rose from the dust like a storm cloud emerging over the horizon. Mara squinted at it.

"Gront?"

"Well, isn't that something?" Gront chuckled. "Somehow, I'm not surprised to see you."

"What are you doing here?" Mara demanded. "*How* are you here?"

"Oh, it's not so strange," Gront replied. "See, I heard—and so did a whole lot of other people—that there was some item or other shining bright as a sun to anyone with the ability to see that kind of thing. Whatever it is, it's either powerful or precious or both, so naturally everyone wants it. I heard this one," he pointed behind himself and Mara saw Oszcek pressed up against a wall, frightened but unharmed, "might be the one everyone was after, and I happened to know there were only a few places he'd be able to go. So when nobody could detect the thing anymore, but it was last seen not too far from this little safe house of the Chantry's, I had a decent idea."

He brushed dust off his cloak, stepped out from the fallen pieces of broken ceiling, and held out a hand to Mara. His massive form took up almost the entirety of the hallway. Behind him, Oszcek let out a squeal and made a run for it, fading back into invisibility as he darted away from the scene.

"I think you should give it to me." He leaned in closer, every trace of his usual congenial air slipping away.

"Why?"

"Because I just went to the trouble of getting levitated over the top of a building and smashing in through the roof for it," he said. "And because, as I imagine little Oz back there can tell you, I am not the worst person that could be coming for it. If you keep hold of that book, you're accepting that people much less pleasant than I am are going to be bothering you extremely rudely until one of them manages to get it off you."

"I need it," said Mara.

"Hm." Gront tilted his head to the left, then the right. Mara heard the cracking of joints, muffled by his heavy fur. Then he hit her.

She was ready for it this time; as soon as he'd appeared, she'd begun preparing her magic to reinforce her body, and he'd had to take a step to put her within his reach. A shield that blended the Sunless Crossing's aura of death with the ambient force left behind in the wake of the roof's destruction materialized a few inches from her in the moment between his fist winding up and the punch landing, absorbing most of the impact.

Some of it still got through, and she felt the drain on her strength as her magic worked to protect her, but she stood firm. Gront recoiled momentarily, but to his credit, he regained his composure before anyone else was likely to have noticed.

"Impressive," said Gront, his lips cracking open in a sharp-toothed grin. He took a step back, flexing his fingers.

Mara raised a hand, shaping her power into visible sparks that flitted and flashed at her fingertips. "Do we have to do this?"

"I'm afraid we do," said Gront.

"What's the plan?" Varun whispered from just behind Mara.

She turned her head toward him without taking her eyes off Gront. "I strike. We all run."

"Where?"

"Just far enough," she muttered. "Nemmo, you said your magic could make things forget things about themselves or something?"

"Ah," came the murmur from her gray-skinned acquaintance. "Yes, I think that ought to work."

"Good," said Mara. "How long do you need?"

"I never know until I try, I'm afraid."

Well, that's not helpful at all.

"We'll make it work," she said, gritting her teeth.

Gront let out an ominous low rumble. "I hate to interrupt," he said, "but I don't believe our business is finished. And, lest anyone forget, my breaking this building will have nullified its protections. There will be others here very soon."

"I can't let anyone else have this," Mara said. "It's ... sacred to me. My god needs it."

Gront raised an eyebrow. "Really now? I would have had you down for the type whose god needs them to, I don't know, knock a few overconfident warriors unconscious or something, not one of a bookish persuasion." He leaned forward. "What is that, anyway? The *Tome of*...?"

Mara quickly held the *Tome of the Beyond* out behind her; someone took it from her hand. "It doesn't matter," she said. "It doesn't even have the text."

Gront raised a thick paw and scratched at the top of his head, looking almost awkward. "I suppose it doesn't matter," he said. "But I still have to take it."

He leaped forth in a sudden burst of speed; Mara reflexively threw up a shield, but Gront's great bulk smashed right through it and crashed into her, sending her flying backward into the others. They landed in a heap in the alleyway, Gront already whirling off them to prepare for a second strike.

Mara pushed herself to her feet and dashed toward Gront, throwing herself into a skid and sliding underneath his next pounce. His massive bulk slammed into Iona as she teetered to her feet, but he'd been aiming for Mara, twisting in the air. The hit wasn't clean; he was turning away from Iona even before he made impact. The cleric dropped onto her rear end, blinking but not badly hurt.

Before Gront could launch his next attack, Varun's hand snapped out and grabbed him by the ankle. The enormous leonid was too strong for one human-sized man to keep him restrained, but it had the desired effect: Gront turned his head back toward Varun and took a mighty whack to the cheek with a white-fire blade for his trouble. He stumbled back, right into a flying knee strike to the back of the neck courtesy of Mara.

Gront dropped to one knee, hands clutching his head.

"Go!" Mara yelled, diving past her fallen foe to grab Nemmo and Varun's hands and usher them toward the alley's exit.

Don't want to lose useful minions now. That's just practical. No other motivation for rescuing them. Nope.

Iona had darted inside the building and hauled Pick out from beneath the debris created by Gront's entrance, but dashed back out again at Mara's call.

"He'll be alright!" Iona yelled as she and Mara—leaving Pick sitting, dazed but out of immediate harm's way, in the rubble—sprinted after Nemmo and Varun. "They're probably safe for now—haven't got the book!"

They caught up to Nemmo almost immediately; he was slow, too slow. Mara pressed her palm to his back and pushed him forward, and Iona wove some sort of arcane gesture with her fingers before flicking her hands in Nemmo's direction. A web of soft light passed from her to him, and he picked up his pace.

"Duznit!" Gront bellowed from behind them, fury reverberating through his voice. "Shoot her!"

Mara threw up a simple bubble of repelling force around them, just in time to catch the crossbow bolt that zipped toward her from the rooftops. She shot a wrathful glance at the source of the projectile; the goblin gave an almost apologetic shrug.

They cleared the alleyway and emerged into the thoroughfare of Nox Valar, sprinting down the streets, taking sharp turns with no real sense of direction. Mara pushed herself, passing Nemmo and coming up beside Varun at the front.

"I have no idea where we're going," she told him, her words punctuated by heavy breaths.

He nodded, his face set. "Neither does anyone else. Lead on."

Mara rocketed around a corner, feet skidding, arms flailing to keep her moving and upright. She had just enough time to wonder what that undulating whispering sound might be before a ten-foot-high wall of water swept into her from the side, picking her up off her feet and slamming her into the side of a building. She fell flat on her front as the water disappeared into nothing, and picked herself up to see a tall, platinum-haired elf woman in spellcasters' robes striding toward her, one hand outstretched in a casting gesture. Mara quickened the flow of her magic, weaving it into self-tracing and reflecting shapes of nullification, of cancellation, and threw out her own spell-interrupting working before the elf could cast whatever she was preparing. The elf finished her arcane gestures and flung her fingers toward Mara.

Ha. How do you like having your spells completely neutralized, you insolent—oh, shit.

A sphere of blue-green energy erupted from the elf's fingertips and whacked into Mara's chest with devastating force. She fell back, gasping for air.

I canceled her spell! Why did it still work? Not the time to wonder, but that's really annoying.

"Give it to me!" the elf commanded, standing over Mara as she got an elbow underneath herself, struggling to sit up.

"Over my dead body," Mara retorted, and hit her assailant with the spell she'd tried against Gront, the one to which he'd just happened to have an inconvenient resistance. The elf's pupils dilated immediately, her mouth opening in a wide gasp of terror, and she turned and fled, her robes flapping behind her.

Over my dead body. Ha. Good one, me.

Varun rushed past, sticking out a hand; Mara grabbed it and let him haul her to her feet even as he continued to run.

"You couldn't have been here two seconds earlier?"

"We had our own problems," he said. Mara glanced back over her shoulder and saw two people lying flat on their backs in the street, though—from her quick look—neither looked mortally wounded.

Iona, just behind Varun, executed a quick running spin so she could fire off two meandering balls of white magic, which bobbed over to the two fallen attackers and sank into their bodies.

"Stop!" a voice called, and Mara looked up to see a small figure, a blurry silhouette against the twilit sky, descending toward them. Even half-seen in motion and pale light, it was obvious who it was. Who else was a foot-and-a-half-tall, bone-armor-clad, iron-dragonfly-riding Nyxian Guard?

"We're under attack!" Mara gasped, plastering a look of harassed exhaustion on her features as she skidded to a halt and raised her hands. "People keep chasing us, trying to hurt us!"

Chirripeek stood casually atop his flying mount, arms crossed, and brought himself level with Mara's face. "It appears to me," he said, "that there is quite a disturbance here, and that you are at the middle of it. Which leads me to think you might be the cause of it." His voice echoed from within his face-concealing bone helmet.

Mara let her eyes widen in innocent fear, though it was frustration that bloomed in her chest at his words. "Not at all!" she protested. "They're all after us, but we didn't do anything to them!" She looked past him: three more figures were striding purposefully down the street toward her. Behind, a good half-dozen more were appearing from the shadows, some with weapons drawn, others clutching glowing items.

"Hm." Chirripeek's dragonfly revolved slowly in a full circle, giving him a clear view in every direction. "It must be said, even if you did do something to wrong someone, this does seem a disproportionately aggressive response from an awful lot of people."

"They want something of mine," Mara whispered to him, trying to sound desperate and helpless. "Something sacred to me. They're trying to kill me so they can take it."

Through the little holes in his helmet, Mara saw Chirripeek's eyes flash.

Shit. I've misjudged. Now he knows I've got something valuable. He's just going to want it for himself. Everybody does. That's how things work, whatever world of the living or dead you're in.

"Well then," he began, and Mara braced herself. "That would be attempted assault, theft, and murder." He held out a hand, palm down in front of him, and a little door on the dragonfly's thorax flipped open. A metal cylinder the length of his arm and twice as thick flew up out of his mount; he slapped it out of the air, his hand sticking to it as if magically adhered, and hefted it over his shoulder like a woodsman carrying a log. "Chirripeek of the Nyxian Guard makes his warning!" the little mouse declared, his voice suddenly amplified. "Leave, or be charged as criminals!"

"Sorry, mouse," a voice called. "We want what she's got, see?"

"That does not entitle you to take it!" Chirripeek said almost scoldingly.

"We're already dead, man," said a different voice. "What does it matter whether we're entitled to shit at this point?"

Chirripeek slapped the cylinder on his shoulder. Mara thought she heard it start humming, low and slow at first, building up to a high whir. "There are laws!"

"What are you gonna do about it?" the first voice challenged.

By way of an answer, Chirripeek pressed a tiny switch on the side of the metal tube. A red-white stream of *something* flared forth, rocketing down the alleyway toward the encroaching thieves, and passed just above their heads before exploding in a shower of sparks.

"That was your last warning!" Chirripeek declared.

The people at the end of the alley had ducked at the shot, but were standing tall once again, giving each other looks as if each wanted to make sure they wouldn't be the only one diving in.

They're committed now, Mara thought, watching their body language. She turned her head to see more potential assailants behind, a couple crouched on rooftops, one hanging out of a window. *This is ... not a good position for us.*

The air felt thick with tension, syrupy, laden with saturating stillness. Mara knew that feeling. The pressure could only build so far before something exploded.

"I tell you, *stay back*!" Chirripeek insisted.

"Sorry, mouse," said one of them. "Think we're sort of set on it at this point."

The bubble of tension popped, the pressure all releasing at once like a world-sinking wave, and everyone sprang into action at once.

CHAPTER 17

Mara fired off two blasts of pure death toward the rooftop assassins before they could loose their own weapons; one shrank back into cover, but the other bellowed in pain and rage.

Not a strong enough hit to kill him, but he'll think twice before coming back out of cover. Plus, his arm'll probably decay and fall off in a few hours, so that's a win.

The group of three at whom Chirripeek had fired his weapon rushed forward wailing battle cries, brandishing curved swords and wicked serrated daggers. The little Nyxian Guard steadied his weapon and calmly fired again, sending a whistling stream of fire toward them. Two threw themselves sideways, but the one in the center took the hit directly to the chest. His war scream turned to an anguished howl as the projectile impacted, throwing out a bloom of flame and smoke. Mara didn't see what happened to him after that, because she'd spun away at the sound of weapons clashing behind her; Varun's blades were crossing with the tripartite staff of a tall, brown-scaled person with six arms, each as long as Mara's whole body; Iona had thrust her hammer upward with both hands, getting its long handle between herself and a heavy blow from an obsidian-headed ax in the hands of a strange creature with birdlike features and a bullish build. Nemmo was nowhere to be seen, though Mara was sure he'd been with them only a moment earlier.

She leaped forward as the ax wielder raised their weapon to strike down upon Iona once more, throwing a magically enhanced punch right in their beady black eye before they had time to make another attack.

Oof. That felt like something cracking. Stupid birds and their hollow bones.

The attacker fell back, clutching at their face. Mara whipped her head around as something grabbed her by the wrist, but it was Iona. A look of uncharacteristically pure focus crossed the cleric's face for a moment, and Mara felt something alien and cold flood through her body. She jerked back, and her hand moved faster than she would have thought possible.

"What did you do to me?" she hissed, unable to stop shaking her limbs as the unfamiliar feeling seeped through her.

Iona gave her a look of confusion. "I made you stronger—pumped you with life magic—behind you!"

Mara threw herself backward and upward, soaring into the air.

Oh, shit. I didn't think I jumped that *hard.*

She tried to reinforce herself with her own magic, but whatever life-suffused power Iona had imbued her with rejected Mara's tinges of death, keeping it away like oil refusing to mix with water. A moment later, she fell on top of a leather-armored orc wielding a mace in one hand and a ball of flame in the other; without thinking about it, without hesitating to remember that she didn't know how to do what she was doing, she flung her legs around the orc's neck so she was sitting behind his head, thrust one knuckle into the muscle between shoulder and neck, rotated smoothly backward and off the orc as he stumbled in pain, and twisted and extended her foot in a vicious kick that sent her heel right into his cheek, all before hitting the ground.

Whaaaaaaaaaaaaaaaaaaat.

The orc crumpled. Mara blinked at Iona, who gave her a wide smile and an enthusiastic thumbs-up.

That's what getting a power-up from a proper cleric feels like? I have to do this more often.

With the smallest of movements, Iona switched from a thumbs-up to a casual point, her finger indicating somewhere just over Mara's shoulder. Mara dropped her hips down and back and kicked down at the ground, sending herself rolling backward; she straightened her arms, rising into a handstand, and dropped her feet right into the face of the cudgel-brandishing gnome who'd been about to rush her. The gnome stumbled; Mara followed up with a punch straight to the face, at which point Iona's infusion ran out.

Mara felt her knuckles fracture with the force as her fist impacted the gnome right under the eye, sending her opponent sprawling. She shook her hand, wincing, and tried to take stock of her situation. Everything suddenly felt slower, her body inelegant.

Chirripeek was fending off two more attackers, then three, then a dozen, with a barrage of bizarre weapons: metal fans that flicked out into butterflies with knife-edged wings, tiny spheres that pulled in everything around them, a vial that shattered and immediately spawned a small tree that speared straight through a shoulder, self-directing flying knives, and more Mara couldn't see from her vantage point. Varun's swords were whirling, leaving trails of burning white in their wake; he wielded them clinically, making precise cuts in the blink of an eye. Iona spun her hammer in wide circles, firing off blasts of magic to keep enemies at bay and whacking them with the heavy head of her weapon when they came too close. Nemmo was still nowhere to be seen. The entire street had devolved into utter chaos, a maelstrom of clashing weapons and bolts of magic and screams.

Mara narrowed her eyes, trying to see clearly. There, at the back of a small crowd pressing toward her group—

Are some of them just shrugging and wandering off?

As she watched, more of the oncoming force appeared to simply decide not to bother, meandering carelessly away. Perhaps it was just that they couldn't be bothered to join the fray, having seen the scale of it, or...

Nemmo appeared behind the lines of those who were still advancing, beckoning urgently.

Nice trick.

She focused her power just beyond the skin of her hand, creating an invisible glove, and forced her way to Iona with punches that landed a moment before they looked like they should have. And she laced the blows with a little death and pain aura for good measure.

"Hey," she called, coming up alongside the cleric as Iona's hammer caved in the side of a feathered head. The stricken fighter's eyes turned white with shock; then the rest of her turned gray-white too, before she abruptly dissolved into a cloud of ashy powder that was lost to the air in an instant. Mara watched it curiously, then sent a blast of force in the direction of an oncoming elf. "Looks like Nemmo's got something."

"We can't just leave Chirripeek!" Iona protested, catching the elf with a sharp jab from the handle of her hammer as he tripped.

"We absolutely can do that," Mara countered. "Besides, I'm not stopping him from coming with us."

Iona huffed and tapped the fallen elf lightly with the business end of her hammer; a spark passed between them, and the elf lay still. "Just knocked out," she said, almost apologetically. "Where's…?" She wheeled around, taking advantage of the momentary space that had opened up around her. "Varun?"

With a swirling stream of white fire, Varun blasted his way out of a scrum of fighters, emerging like a dolphin leaping free from the ocean. The people who'd been surrounding him fell in a heap, all trying to get up at once and falling over each other.

Varun dashed to Iona and Mara. "We have to go!"

A whirring rumble from overhead prompted them all to look up as one: a spellcaster with what looked like metal wings was hovering above, a sphere of energy building between her hands. In the moment before they could loose their attack, Iona tapped Varun and Mara on the shoulder in quick succession; Mara shivered as that sensation of strange power, freezing yet burning, flowed through her, scouring her veins.

Varun threw himself into the air and landed one-footed on the head of Iona's hammer before the cleric let fly with an upward swing, sending the swordsman streaking into the air and leaving a white trail of flame behind him. The airborne mage released her spell before Varun could reach her, missing him in her haste. A moment later, his blades sheared through her wings with precise ease, and she fell screaming. Her ball of power reached the ground before she did, but Iona continued her hammer's wide arc and spun, driving the head of her weapon into the spell like a child playing with a bat and ball. The sphere of power dissipated with a thunderous crack.

Meanwhile, Mara flew forward, one empowered step sending her in an elegant leap, and caught the falling mage with a bone-crushing kick to the ribs. The spellcaster dissolved into ash before she even hit the stones of the street. A second later, Varun landed almost silently, taking the fall of fifteen or twenty feet as if it were six inches.

Iona looked between the two of them, nodding her head and grinning wickedly. "That was *really fucking cool.*"

Mara gave the falsely modest shrug of one who has no intention of actually appearing to be modest. "It was a bit, wasn't it?"

As one, they turned their attention to the group that was still approaching from down the street, Nemmo still waving just beyond. Mara spared a backward glance to see that help had finally come for Chirripeek: a trio of Nyxian Guard, all in that gleaming ivory armor, had appeared from somewhere and set about laying into the crowd. Compared to the little bone-armored rodent, these new members of the Guard were far larger: one was humanoid in shape, but the other two looked more akin to the gargoyles she'd spotted on the roof of the Junction and at the threshold of Nox Valar.

"Just get through this," she murmured, "and hopefully Nemmo knows what he's doing."

"Feels like the entire city's coming for us," said Varun, scowling. "What in all the hells is that book?"

Mara grimaced. "I didn't know it was going to give off this … whatever it is." She turned to each of them, a thought suddenly occurring to her. "Hells, who has it? I handed it to someone..."

Iona patted the front of her robes; a hard *thunk* sounded from within. "Should've passed it off to Nemmo," she muttered, "since he's apparently managed to get out all on his own."

Mara breathed a sigh of relief. *If we'd gone through all this just to realize later that we'd already lost it...* A brief image flashed unbidden through her mind: Varun, Iona, Nemmo, all bound and helpless and ready for her to punish them for their failure. She quickly shook her head, dismissing the notion. *Just because Raskith did that kind of thing to me doesn't mean I have to do it to someone else. Not that I wouldn't. I don't care. Obviously.* Mentally, she rolled her eyes.

"He probably couldn't have escaped if he'd had it on him," she said, partly to distract herself from her thoughts.

The power from Iona ran out; Mara caught Varun's posture sagging just slightly out of the corner of her eye right as she felt herself return to normal levels.

I almost don't want to get powered up, if this is what coming back to normal feels like. I liked normal. Normal was fine.

"I'm tapped out," the cleric muttered, seeing them both suffer the loss of her boost. "Can't do that again today. I've got maybe one more minor spell left in me."

"It was pretty great," Varun said, clapping her on the shoulder. "Thanks."

Mara nodded. "It got us this far, but we can handle this from here."

Varun raised an eyebrow. "We can?"

Mara kneeled, pushing just a little power into her fingertip, and started to burn neat lines into the surface of the street. "I've got a few seconds before that lot arrives, right?"

"Assuming none of them decide to charge," Varun said, "but most of them look like they don't want to be the first one to get here."

"Seeing us cut that mage down and punch her to death probably helped," Mara muttered, finishing her scrawled ritual circle. It was crude and simplistic, given the limited time she had, but any kind of external focus for her power would give her the ability to create grander workings than she could do purely by channeling magic through her own body. "And thanks for that," she said, straightening up and glancing at Iona. The cleric puffed up with pride.

"What does that do?" Varun asked, peering critically down at the lines on the ground.

"Short-range teleport," Mara said. "Would've been about as fast to draw one that blew up that entire crowd, but I don't fancy giving the guards any more of a reason to arrest us. Chirripeek'd go for self-defense, but..." She shot a quick look over her shoulder, spotting that the mouse and his three compatriots had nearly finished mopping up their part of the fight. "Anyway. Ready?"

Without waiting for an answer, she channeled her magic into the burned lines. The world slackened, then snapped taut, pulling itself back into place around them. When it was done, they were standing on the other side of the crowd.

"Ah," said Nemmo, as if praising a sip of tea rather than reacting to the sudden appearance of three people who hadn't been there a moment ago. "How neat."

"No time to hang around!" Iona blurted, already on the move. The group that was now behind them was looking confused for the moment, scanning the alley for their disappeared quarry, but it wouldn't last. The four of them took the first turn they saw, tucking out of sight, but they didn't stop.

"They can still track us," Mara said, not that any of them needed reminding. "We need to end this."

Nemmo somehow managed to give a slow, measured nod even as he moved with long, heavy strides. "I believe I can make that happen. I just need a moment uninterrupted."

"How much more magic do you have?" Mara asked.

"Not much," Nemmo said, his pensive features contorting. "It took a lot to make so many people forget what they were doing there—and of course, to make the light forget to illuminate me."

Varun made a noise of surprise. "That's how your invisibility works?"

"It would be that or make every eye in the area forget to see me," Nemmo said, his breath beginning to come heavier and faster, "and that would depend on me knowing where they all were." He paused, panting. "I do not think I can ... talk any-more," he said apologetically.

"Lead the way," Varun told him.

Nemmo took them in a winding route that seemed designed to keep them on the shortest streets, the ones with the most abrupt turns, the places through which fewer people had any reason to pass. Mara kept shooting glances in every direction, alert to the possibility of any form of assault, but either Nemmo's route was calculated to be difficult to follow or their would-be attackers had given up after the chaos by the safe house.

Or, Mara thought, trying to get a look at Nemmo's expression as they ran, *he's doing something to make people in the area forget where we are... No, if he's running low from affecting a few individuals, I don't think he could do something like that.*

They turned a corner and emerged before a tall tower, gleaming marble jutting straight up into the sky like an arrow pointing to the gods. At its apex hung a huge black bell; at its base was a bridge across a wide stream, and perhaps a hundred yards downstream was the edge of Nox Valar, the place where the city's foundation gave way to vertical cliffs above the Ashen Fields.

"The Belfry?" Varun panted as they came to a halt.

"Needed to be somewhere believably significant," Nemmo managed through exhausted-sounding breaths.

Mara waved, getting their attention and pointing to the tower. "What's...?"

"Exora's Belfry," Iona supplied. "Place of magical learning." She jerked her chin up, indicating the top of the tower. "The bell's only supposed to ring if the entire Sunless Crossing's in danger. Never heard it myself."

Nemmo held out a hand to Iona. "The book."

She dug it out from inside her robes and handed it over.

"I'll need a minute," he said, and closed his eyes, folding his arms over the Tome.

"We can give you a minute," Varun said.

"Well!" called a deep voice.

CHAPTER 18

Mara groaned.

"Whyever would you have come here, I wonder?"

Iona dropped into a fighting stance, her hammer ready to swing; Varun held his arms out to his sides, letting his swords leak white flame into the air. A large, cloaked figure strode slowly toward them.

"Come on, Gront," said Mara wearily. "We're really still doing this?"

Gront took deliberate steps, letting his cloak swish theatrically. "Whatever you have there," he said, pointing to her, "it's worth something. That's clear."

He doesn't know which of us has the book, Mara realized.

"I don't know exactly what it is or what it does," he went on, "but if this many people are willing to chase you down for it, I'd have to be a fool not to be able to turn *some* sort of profit from it."

Mara let her arm move protectively across her abdomen as if she might be keeping something there. Gront's eyes flashed.

"So are you going to give it up?" the great lion-headed man asked. "Or am I going to have to take it?"

"You know," said Mara, "the last person to hold this book would have handed it over with no resistance whatsoever. You're just a bit too late, Gront."

He sighed. "I thought as much."

He stamped his foot. A narrow pole of wood sprouted from the ground beside him—not damaging the stones, just rising as if through nothing but air. A red flag, emblazoned with a yellow sword, appeared at the top of the pole, and a rush of invisible force whooshed outward, pushing Mara back a couple of steps. It didn't feel as if anything had *hit* her, but she found herself raising a hand in front of her head, squinting; she felt suddenly just light-headed enough, just fragile enough, to lose track of the threat for an instant.

Gront took full advantage of that instant, charging forward on all fours and swiping her off her feet with a brutal backhand.

That hurt more than the last one. Which is not good, because the last one hurt like all hells.

Mara groaned, pushing her magic around her body, but it was too late; she'd taken the force of Gront while she was off-balance, not focused on reinforcing herself. She'd need Iona to heal her before she could be much use in a fight, but by then they'd already have lost. She would already have failed.

But he still doesn't know who has the book.

Gront was circling her, steam pouring from his nostrils. She dared to glance at Nemmo; he was still standing there with his eyes closed, the *Tome* thankfully hidden beneath his crossed forearms.

Whatever you're doing, Nemmo, do it quick...

"Ah," said Gront, seeing the movement of her eyes.

Shit.

"Your friends are strengthening you, are they?" He turned and made a dash for Nemmo, but Iona and Varun intercepted him, and he took a step back with two slashes in his cloak and one hand dangling limply at his side; Iona's hammer had struck true, thwacking him in the shoulder. "Well," he said, half-shrugging at Mara as she regained her feet, "it's not enough, at any rate."

"We're not giving it up," Iona told him defiantly. She and Varun had moved so that the two of them and Mara formed a triangle around Gront, neatly surrounding him.

"Of course not." Gront turned his head toward his banner, then stretched out the fingers of his remaining good hand and reached beneath his cloak, pulling out a greatsword that was at least as long as Mara was tall and three times as wide.

Iona held out a hand toward the banner, her fingers dancing in quick contortions. When she thrust her palm outward, Mara felt a strange, numbing sensation whoosh past her, like dipping her face in a cold river.

"Doesn't work like that," Gront said with a grin. Iona's face fell, and then the greatsword hit her in the sternum. She went flying; Gront had hit her with the flat of the blade, not striking to kill. Not straight away, at least.

Varun spun his blades in wide, whirling figure-of-eight patterns, driving the larger fighter back. Gront moved out of the path of the swords rather than putting his greatsword between their edges and his body, ducking and weaving with precise, quick movements. Mara took advantage of the distraction, repeating the same trick she'd used against the soul stitched: she cycled her power to the stone beneath her feet, fabricating a spell of binding, of stability. The ground under Gront cracked open, grasping fingers of rock grabbing at his legs, but he broke free with a simple, powerful step.

"I'm surprised it's just you," Mara shot at him, firing off a few simple magical projectiles. He dodged one and absorbed the rest, recoiling only slightly as they hit. "Where's your crew?"

"Oh, well," said Gront, raising his sword with one hand against the flat of the blade and catching both of Varun's weapons at once. With a powerful heave, he sent Varun skidding backward along the ground. "I thought I'd be noble about it, I suppose, but since you asked, they're just waiting for the signal." He grinned. "Which is this." Then he pursed his lips and let out a high whistle.

Oh, balls, *why did I ask?*

A crossbow bolt thudded into Mara's shoulder; she dropped to one knee, urgently scanning for the source of the missile. The goblin—Duznit—was crouched half-hidden behind a low wall; the half-orc was striding toward her, twin cleavers raised to strike; the whale-like person was advancing, surrounded by what looked like a swarm of buzzing insects. The latter member of Gront's group kept their distance from the other two, perhaps to prevent their cloud of flapping wings and biting mandibles from doing collateral damage.

"Well," said Mara, gritting her teeth, "*this* is a bit of a problem."

"See the half-orc?" Gront said. Even without turning to look back at him, she could hear the grin on his lips. "That's Riddeill. Bit of a hero in his home world, as I hear it. Fended off a hundred of the evil emperor's best swordsmen with nothing but a chef's knife, so I've been told."

"He would tell you that, wouldn't he?" Mara muttered, trying to keep her eyes on all three of Gront's compatriots at once, trusting that the big leonid was having enough fun monologuing that he wouldn't hit her in the back. Yet.

"Ah, it's not him I heard it from," said Gront. "Now the other, I'm not sure you'll have seen one like her before. That's," and he made a noise that sounded to Mara's ears like a driftwood-laden wave crashing against a rough, chalky cliff, and she decided that the closest collection of sounds she could come up with was something like *Vaarschraaff*, "and she, oh, she was *really* something in life. Queen of a whole nation, its borders surrounding forests and seas and all sorts. Slight shame is, her real talents were in working with animals, getting them to do her bidding in all sorts of ways, but you might've noticed there aren't any here in the Crossing. She had half a dozen beasts that never left her side, but none of them could follow. Beasts don't get afterlives, it seems. If tales're to be believed, she wouldn't be the first to spend decades of her life-after-death trying to find some way to reunite with an animal companion that couldn't follow her here. Still, apparently spells for summoning plagues of locusts still work, so... the Crossing works in mysterious ways, eh?" He chuckled. "Oh, and there's Duznit. Duznit shoots things. Hits them sometimes."

"So what now?" Mara asked. "You going to kill us?"

"Well, it wouldn't *really* be killing, would it? You'd come back tomorrow. But no, I don't want to do that. I just want the book."

She turned her back on the three encroaching threats, staring at Gront with as much force of presence as she could manage. "I don't understand you," she said. "Are you a noble gentleman criminal, or are you a disgraceful vagabond?"

He gave the matter a moment's thought. "I'm an opportunist," he said.

A gentle golden flash over Gront's shoulder caught Mara's attention, and she let the widest smile she could muster creep across her face. The great feline face flinched, just slightly. "I think you've missed this opportunity, I'm afraid," she said.

Gront gave her a brief look of confusion. Then he turned, just in time to see Nemmo holding up the *Tome of the Beyond*. With a bestial roar, the huge warrior threw himself forward, but it was as if his strength gave out in midair; he slumped to the ground before making it halfway to his destination. Varun, back on his feet, held the point of one sword to Gront's neck, a pained but satisfied grimace on his face.

"Works like this, though, doesn't it?" Iona called, and Mara saw that the cleric had crawled over to Gront's banner and smashed it to pieces with her hammer.

Well, that's a more straightforward way of getting rid of something.

Nemmo held the book aloft; its covers glowed golden, and as he pulled them open, the pages within fluttered free, turning to sparkling dust that suffused the air. Twinkling gold rose toward the sky or drifted into the stream, where it flowed away, carried by the water from Nox Valar into the Ashen Fields, and from there to whatever lay beyond. In moments, the final remnants of the book were soaked with gold light, and then they were gone.

I really, really *hope he hasn't genuinely just destroyed the* Tome, Mara thought. *That would defeat the point of all this somewhat.*

"Behold," said Nemmo in a smoothly self-important tone, of the sort Raskith used when he was making some great proclamation about how deeply brilliant he was. "Here, beneath the bell that signals the end of the world, I dedicate this ritual to Kontrit."

"What have you done?" Gront growled. Varun let the point of his blade draw just the tiniest speck of vivid red blood.

"I have devoted this sacred item as it was intended to be," said Nemmo. "This book, which in its living world claimed to know the truth of the realms of death, held some true power. But here, between life and death, it was nothing more than a token of regret on behalf of those who knew neither. And so I have consecrated it to the Lord of Regrets, and so our holy duty is done."

Gront scoffed, turning toward Mara. "This was really it? The whole purpose?"

She nodded. "Yep. Holy book. Big credit to be gained with, er, Kontrit for whoever did the ritual thing, but I guess that was us. So … that's it. All done here." She turned to see what Gront's allies were doing: they had halted their advance, staring on in confusion. "Sorry to deprive you of a big fight or whatever, but you can go now."

Gront slapped Varun's blade away and stood, his huge shoulders visibly and rapidly rising and falling. His features were difficult to read, but he looked to Mara as if he were struggling to decide between maintaining his curated image by gracefully accepting defeat and simply flying into a rage and shredding everyone in the vicinity to pieces. Finally, he gave a small nod that Mara thought might have been of respect, and then stalked away.

Duznit, Riddeill, and Vaarschraaff all gave their leader strange looks as he walked toward them, then past them, beckoning irritably as he went. Vaarschraaff dropped her cloud of insects, swiping her hand through the air in apparent irritation.

A couple of Nyxian Guards appeared—far too late, in Mara's view, but she supposed they'd been busy with the chaos left in their wake—saw that the fighting was over before it had begun, and trotted promptly off again.

"What just happened?" Varun muttered.

Mara allowed herself a grin. "We got away with it." She turned to Nemmo. "You didn't actually just destroy the *Tome*, right?"

"Of course not." Nemmo reached into his sleeve and pulled out the book. "I made it forget that it could be detected," he explained, handing it back to Mara. "And then I made the air forget not to look like a book turning to golden dust."

"That's so weird," Iona wheezed, coming up beside them. She was clutching her midsection and leaning on her hammer, and her face was pale, but she was radiating jubilant exhilaration.

"Like it's usually actively remembering not to be that specific—'scuse me—" She burst into a fit of wet coughs.

"That doesn't sound good," Mara said, eyeing the cleric. "Can you heal yourself?"

"No, but ... I'll be alright, just need... need a minute. Catch my—" She hacked up a wad of thick brown phlegm, holding a hand up apologetically.

Varun sheathed his swords, put a hand on Iona's shoulder, and stared intently off into the distance. A white glow passed from his palm to Iona's body, and she sighed with obvious relief, standing a little taller.

"That'll see me through," she said, nodding her appreciation. She turned to Mara. "What about you? You took a hit."

"A bit," Mara admitted. "But it can wait until we're back at the temple. I couldn't have put up much of a fight if it had gone that way, but I can walk."

They started walking in the direction of the temple to Aurethen, each lost in their individual thoughts for a while.

"That didn't go well," Varun eventually said. His tone was serious.

"What do you mean?" Iona asked. "We made it out of there with the thing and none of us died."

Nemmo gave a mild nod of agreement, as if he were too polite to point out that it had been almost entirely because of him that they had all, in fact, not died.

"Only because it didn't come to an actual fight," Varun said. His expression was distant, eyes constantly making quick, tiny motions as if he were playing out an imaginary scenario, or perhaps reliving a real one. "Nemmo got us out of that with a trick—sorry, Nemmo, not to say it wasn't exactly what we needed—but we would've been obliterated if we'd started actual open combat with the four of them. Gront alone was enough to injure you two and … neutralize me. I was no use at all."

Iona patted him on the arm. "Don't beat yourself up," she said. "That big guy's got a real punch on him."

"I'm not beating myself up," Varun protested.

"You absolutely are," said Mara.

Varun shot her a look, saw her completely deadpan expression, and shook his head. "Either way," he said, the slightest smile breaking through his malaised frown, "the next thing we have to do is a fight. A real fight, a big one. And we've just proved we're not ready for that."

"The next thing...?" Iona tapped her chin. "Oh, right, the Lightless Chasm for... what was it again?"

"Heart of an infernal," Mara supplied.

Iona gave one big, affirmative nod. "That's the one."

"Is there an option where we just swoop in after everyone else has finished off the fighting and scavenge a heart?" Mara asked.

Iona turned to Varun, who considered it for a moment before answering. "Probably not. It's mostly earnest volunteers trying to do something noble guarding the Chasm, plus a few Nyxian Guard, but there are already enough people there for the purposes of collecting whatever materials they can use or trade. We'd need to be there right as it went down, get the heart before anyone else was at the scene."

"Which means we probably have to be the one to kill it," Mara said. "Are these things tough?"

Varun just chuckled.

"Well, that's not ominous at all," said Mara.

CHAPTER 19

One good night's sleep, a good meal, and a few strong healing spells later, Mara and the others set out for the Lightless Chasm. The Sunless Crossing was bigger than she'd realized: it took a full two days to walk there, including a bit of a delay fording a river that ran through the Ashen Fields. Fortunately, Iona had prepared a spell that allowed her to dry everyone's feet and clothes—in anticipation of that exact scenario, Mara supposed—and not one of the four of them was any stranger to long journeys.

Finally, they approached the Lightless Chasm. Mara wasn't sure whether optimism or trepidation would be the more appropriate thing to feel, so she tried to convince herself that she was feeling a nice neutral anticipation.

"So," she said, turning to Varun, "do we just ... post up and wait for something to happen, or do we have to register or something, or...?"

He made a show of looking around as if he thought she was talking to someone else, all the while continuing to flip a coin over and over with his thumb in the hopes of securing a long enough string of heads in a row that he would somehow become a god of coins. Or flipping things. Or gambling. He didn't seem fussed about which. "Why're you asking me? Ah—" He tutted as he fumbled the coin and dropped it. "I was at ninety-nine."

"Aren't you the one who knows about all this stuff?" Mara persisted, ignoring his antics. "You had all the answers two days ago, didn't you?"

"I've spoken to people who have done shifts here," Varun said, resuming his flipping, "but I've never actually been. For all I know, there's a ton of paperwork before they'll let you even be near the place."

"Didn't Chirripeek say something about them always looking for volunteers?" Iona piped up.

"He did," Varun confirmed, "but nothing about *how* to volunteer, exactly."

Mara groaned in exasperation. "What even is the Lightless Chasm, anyway?"

They came to a halt.

"That," said Varun, pointing, "is the Lightless Chasm."

A narrow ravine split the Ashen Fields, sundering the grassy plain. It was impossible to tell how deep it went, or how long; Mara could just about make out a layer of soil, a similar deep gray to the grass, quickly giving way to dark stone that disappeared into the depths. From her initial side-on perspective, it could have been as shallow as a dozen feet, but as she drew nearer and the fissure turned longways, she could see deeper, and deeper, and never to the bottom. It simply became darkness, ending somewhere far out of sight—if it ended at all.

Its sides weren't sheer: there were outcroppings, some barely narrow enough to stand on sideways and others wide enough for a small group. On some of the wider rock platforms, there were indeed duos or trios of Nyxian Guards in their white armor, presumably acting as a first line of defense.

"Huh," said Mara.

"There are theories," Nemmo said in the dry tone he always used for explaining topics he found intensely interesting, "that the bottom of the Chasm connects to some other plane of existence. An abyss, or a kind of cosmic ocean."

Mara raised an eyebrow. "Sounds ... esoteric."

"All anyone knows for certain," Nemmo continued, "is that things emerge from the Chasm that ought not to be in the Crossing. Other kinds of dead thing, yes, but also fiends and demons."

"And this happens ... often?"

"Some months pass without an incursion," said Nemmo. "Some days see a dozen unwelcome visitors."

Mara couldn't help a frustrated huff. "I can't rely on that. I have no idea when I might get—get snatched out of this place and shoved into servitude for all eternity. I need to complete this ritual *now*."

"I do understand that," said Nemmo, "but I fear I can do little to speed up the process."

Mara forced herself to breathe, calming the rage that came easily, naturally to her. Years of training had taught her swiftness of wrath, to hone terror-inducing fury as one of the most basic tools in her kit. It couldn't serve her here.

"Well, if we have to wait," she said, turning to Iona, "did I see you trying to cancel out Gront's banner when we fought?"

Iona nodded. "Yeah, it's a simple enough spell. Should've just..." She snapped her fingers. "You know, switched it off. Undone the other magic."

Mara nodded thoughtfully. "I had something similar happen," she said. "Tried to counter a spell back when we were being chased—it should have been trivial to do, but it didn't do a thing."

Nemmo cleared his throat. "I believe I can shed some light on this," he said.

"Go on."

"Well," he said, "as you know, people come to the Crossing from a range of different living worlds. Many of those worlds have their own, let us say, systems of magic. The arcane and the divine function differently depending on the realm from which they come."

"Right," said Mara. "I channel aura in shapes and focuses, and Iona's got her finite set of spells each day, or pool of magic or whatever it is."

"Indeed," said Nemmo. "And, of course, some worlds likely have very little magic, if any, but we are unlikely to meet anyone from such a place here. You can deduce why, I'm certain."

"Because the Crossing is a place to wait for resurrection," Mara answered. "If you're from a world with no magic, no chance of being brought back, you don't have much business here." She felt peculiarly proud of herself, to have solved a problem posed by a teacher who wasn't trying to instruct her in murder and world domination.

"Indeed," he said. "I find that a little sad sometimes." He trailed off, blinking thoughtfully.

"You were talking about different systems of magic," Mara prompted.

"Ah. Yes. Well, I believe that those systems are quite often governed by strict rules. Opaque and obtuse ones sometimes, it must be said, for some are beholden to easily determined mathematical structures while others appear much more vague, but still." He paused for a moment, humming deeply. "As such, while magical workings will generally function as intended within the Crossing—objects or people will be affected as the spell dictates—I believe that magic from one system cannot generally interact with that from another."

"Interesting," Mara mused, and she meant it. "Then, say I were to cast a magic shield, spells cast by people from worlds other than the one I'm from would just go right through it?"

"Most likely," said Nemmo. "Although if someone cast a spell that, say, sent a projectile formed of stone or ice in your direction, a shield would most likely turn that away. I suspect it is only when two magics attempt to engage directly with one another, but the indirect *effect* of a magic becomes an object in its own right, to be affected as usual." He gestured toward Iona. "It may be of interest to you to know that Iona's world appears to be the most, ah, represented? Populous?" His wide gray face crinkled in thought. "The plurality of those in the Sunless Crossing come from her world or a close neighbor, let us say, meaning that she has the best chance of holding the capacity to directly counter offensive spells from any unfriendly forces we might encounter. Peculiarly, her world seems to contain many worlds itself, but all with broadly related magic." He looked around at the group, his glistening eyes almost expectant, like he was hoping for some sort of plaudits for his knowledge.

Varun pursed his lips and puffed. "I mean, this is fascinating and all, but don't we have things to be doing...?"

Nemmo deflated. "Of course. I mean..." He scratched the back of his neck, uncharacteristically tripping over his words. "I mean, *I* thought it was interesting."

"It's very interesting," said Iona reassuringly, patting him on the back. "It's just that we're on a bit of a timer here, is all." She turned to Mara with an endearing, earnest smile. "Are you sure you don't want to reconsider joining Aurethen's followers? He'd probably let you in, and it'd be *way* better than whatever plans you've got."

"Iona," said Varun sharply.

Mara shook her head with a quiet, sad laugh. "I don't think he'd want me," she said truthfully.

At that moment, blessedly, they all turned at the sound of whirring metal wings right behind them. Chirripeek hovered there on his dragonfly, arms folded, chin lifted, appraising them like a sommelier tasting a wine.

"Where in all the dead heavens did *you* come from?" Iona wondered aloud.

Chirripeek simply pointed upward.

"That makes sense," Iona conceded.

"Here to help defend the Sunless Crossing from fiendish invaders?" the mouse asked.

The group exchanged looks, then nodded.

"Yeah," said Mara, "something like that."

"Wonderful," said Chirripeek, removing his helmet and hopping off his dragonfly in one smooth movement; the little creature stayed hovering where it was. "Please, follow me to your induction."

Mara blinked. "There's an *induction*?"

"Well, yes," said Chirripeek over his shoulder, already walking away from them and heading alongside the Chasm. "We expect quality here, you know."

"Right." Mara glanced at the others; Iona gave a cheery thumbs-up, Varun shrugged, and Nemmo just wore his usual look of general pensiveness. She cleared her throat as they followed. "So, er, we're glad you're alright."

"Why would I not be?" the mouse asked haughtily.

Mara tried to find the words for a moment; fortunately for her, Iona jumped in. "Because the last time we saw you was in the middle of a full-on riot in the streets, maybe?"

Chirripeek scoffed, an exaggerated noise of dismissive confidence. "Ha! You underestimate me and the Nyxian Guard if you think one scuffle would be too much for us to handle."

"I was impressed by your capabilities, I must say," said Nemmo. "Quite versatile. Did you enchant those items yourself?"

"I never use anything I didn't make," said Chirripeek, and Mara's estimation of the mouse shot up.

If that's true, he's versatile. I haven't met many tinkerers or enchanters who were battle-ready enough to be the ones wielding their own creations. Raskith did, but creating magical weapons by binding dead souls to them sort of feels like cheating. I wonder whether Chirripeek's from a world with a magic system that lends itself well to creating tools and weapons?

"Impressive indeed," said Nemmo appreciatively.

"Yes," agreed Chirripeek.

Well, I never did like false modesty.

"You've timed it well," said the little Nyxian Guard, turning away from his path parallel to the Lightless Chasm and approaching a long, low building a few hundred yards away—close enough that it would almost certainly be the first place to know of any developments, but not so close that it was liable to fall in at the slightest tremor. "We're expecting a threat in a few hours."

Relief flooded Mara at the thought that she would soon have two of the three items she needed, though the flood was quickly dammed as she remembered that the third item was a god's tears.

I still have absolutely no idea what we're going to do for that, but… well, I need all three things, so I may as well just focus on the one I can actually get here for now.

"What sort of threat?" Varun asked.

"Oh, the usual," said Chirripeek. "Demons from the foulest pits, or perhaps incomprehensible terrors adrift in a cosmos of fear and abominable apathy." He paused. "But probably just a few demons."

Was that a joke?

They reached the building; the door opened for Chirripeek and he beckoned them to follow him in. Inside was a large, open space with a few hard benches oriented toward what looked like a speaker's stage, complete with a lectern and chalkboard. The mouse beckoned to them to sit.

"There is, I believe, one other new group I need to collect," he said, then wandered out again, leaving them to their own devices.

"I like him," Iona said, smiling beatifically after the little Nyxian Guard as the door closed behind him.

"He's ... something," Mara agreed. She glanced over at Varun; the swordsman was staring at the back of the bench in front of him, his knee oscillating rapidly up and down. She sidled over, leaning in. "You alright?"

"Hm?" He blinked, looking up at her. "Oh. Yeah."

She took one long breath while holding his gaze.

He rolled his eyes and relented. "Alright, so maybe not exactly."

Emotional support. I can do this. It's just a trickier and more insidious form of manipulation than, I don't know, threatening to break their knees. And then heal their knees and break them again. Either way, I need to keep him from getting all mopey if I want him to be of any use to me. Just need some sort of insightful question to get him to open up...

"What's up?"

Nice.

He stared back at the floor, biting his lip and wringing his fingers. Mara got the impression that he would talk in his own time, so she stayed silent.

"We would have been absolutely destroyed in that fight," he said eventually.

"We weren't though," Mara said in what she hoped was a reassuring sort of way.

"Only because we were lucky," Varun said in a low voice. "We can't rely on being lucky every time." He let out a sigh that rumbled up his throat and out through his nose. "I need to—to not fail again. And I don't know that I can guarantee that, not the way I am now."

Oh, no. This is bad. Platitudes won't work, but I don't have anything useful to suggest... what would Raskith do?

"What do you mean, not fail *again*?" she asked, resisting the urge to snap her fingers in gleeful celebration when she saw the expression on his face.

Now we're getting somewhere.

Varun stared at his own feet for a few moments longer. Then he took a deep breath. "Not long after I got here," he said, "I met a... a girl."

Mara forced herself not to raise an eyebrow suggestively.

"Not like that," he said, apparently detecting her would-be reaction. "She was ... twelve, maybe thirteen, and she didn't have anyone here. Didn't know anybody in the Crossing. I was trying out being an Ashen Shepherd at the time—didn't last long, but she was one of the few I met as they arrived. She, er..." He swallowed. "Her parents didn't send her here, exactly, but they may as well have. They had these plans for her, see, expected her to be a powerful mage, but she wasn't developing as quickly as they wanted. They'd pinned all their hopes of getting out of their shitty lives on exploiting their kid, I guess. So, they sent her to this... this wizard, and his methods were ... unforgiving."

Mara's eyes suddenly felt hot and prickly. Parts of the story sounded just a little too familiar; she wasn't the girl in the story, she knew that, but a short biography of each of them as children might not have read too dissimilarly.

"Anyway," said Varun, "she didn't make it through whatever training they were inflicting on her. But she knew they were going to want her back."

An unpleasantly warm, thick lump was beginning to form in Mara's chest. "What do you mean, they were going to want her back?"

"Well, she was their meal ticket," Varun said bitterly. "And they'd paraded her around, promised all sorts of people all sorts of things when she came into her power and made them rich and influential. They couldn't have her just … gone. They were going to be looking for ways to make sure they could still get what they wanted out of her." He paused, blinking heavily. "I promised her I'd do everything I could to help her move on. We pledged her soul to the Marquis of the Final End."

"One of the gods of death, right?"

He nodded. "Yeah. In a place full of death and gods of death, the Marquis is … one of the most palatable ones to most people. His thing isn't so much about venerating the state of death itself, or the act of killing, as it is about accepting that life and death are just the names we give two joined parts of a single journey. Death isn't really a thing you do, you know? It's just a marked-off section we've decided to give its own name."

Mara gave a quiet laugh. "You're starting to sound like Nemmo," she said. "All wise, or whatever."

"Hardly," said Varun, though a small smile pulled briefly at his lips. "Anyway, it… it didn't work out. They called her back before we could finish it and get her somewhere safe where she could rest." He closed his eyes for a moment, then opened them wide and shook his head as if trying to wake himself up. "At least, I assume that's what happened. She went somewhere, and I didn't see her again."

"I'm sorry," said Mara. She reached out, intending to put a hand on his arm, but stopped just short and withdrew. "So that's why Nozan brought us together? So you'd have a chance to … redeem yourself?"

He laughed ruefully. "Perhaps," he said. "But there's no guarantee of success. I think she probably thought less about the prospect of me making up for the past and more about the fact that I wouldn't be able to resist at least trying to help. Got me out of her hair, anyway. I don't know whether you noticed, but I didn't really fit in at the Cavalcade."

Mara thought briefly back to the image of the many-colored convoy dancing and singing and blaring its way through the Ashen Fields, and the monochrome man traipsing along beside it. "Could've fooled me."

"Anyway," he said, his knee beginning to jiggle again. "I'm not enough. I couldn't help her and if it weren't for Nemmo, I wouldn't have been able to help you either."

"Well, that's the thing," said Mara. "If it weren't for Nemmo, we would probably have been stomped by Gront and his gang, and if not for Iona, we might well have been eaten by the soul stitched, and if not for you, I might still be wandering around the Ashen Fields with no idea what was going on."

Varun was still for a moment. Then he smiled at her. "Thanks," he said. "I weirdly feel better."

"You're welcome," said Mara.

I mean, that was all just practical, true stuff. But hey, if he wants to take it as emotional support, that's fine by me.

"Anyway," said Varun, sitting up a little straighter, "it's obvious we're going to need to get ourselves a little more, ah, coordinated in battle. And I need to step it up a bit on the becoming-a-god thing; can't let that slip."

"No," said Mara, as earnestly as she could muster, "mustn't forget the whole ascending-to-divinity scheme."

"What we need to be thinking about," said Iona, suddenly leaning over the back of their bench and putting her face right between the two of them, "is the party dynamic."

"Have you been sitting right behind us the whole time?" Varun asked.

"See," said Iona, ignoring him entirely, "we've got, let's see, one punchy person who's also an enviably versatile spellcaster, one swordsy person with a few offensive magic bits, one hammery person with a decent chunk of divine power, and … whatever Nemmo is. It's not a great balance."

"I would describe myself as a variable utility mage," Nemmo contributed; Mara whipped around to see him sitting right next to her.

Must've made me forget he was there… better not say anything I wouldn't want him to hear, even if I thought it was said in private. Or he was just quiet, and I was just unobservant.

"Right, well," said Iona, "that's not the most well-defined function as far as it relates to, you know, combat potential." She huffed through pursed lips, turning it into an accidental whistle. "What we need," she said thoughtfully, "is something like—"

The door opened again and Chirripeek entered, flanked by what Mara could only have described as a party of adventurers.

"Aha," said Iona.

CHAPTER 20

The newcomers stopped just inside the building; the door swung shut behind them. Mara sized them up, uncertain whether she ought to look earnestly curious, dismissive, or intimidating. There were two gnomes, one in his middle years and the other barely an adult. The older of the two had a lute and some sort of wind instrument slung across his body; brown hair, white at the tips, poked out from beneath a smart felt hat. The younger had eyes brighter even than Iona's, which were staring at Mara's group with undisguised awe. He was practically bouncing on his toes, which was causing the sheathed rapier at his side to clack against the floor.

Behind the gnomes, nearly twice their height, stood an elf woman with flowing brown hair and a full quiver of arrows peeking out over her shoulder. Some sort of circlet adorned her head—carved wood with bone detailing, Mara thought—and her leather armor was scuffed with use. Next to her was a half-elf, eyes and tightly curled hair a rich brown. He wore a plain brown cloak, belted with plaited rope. Mara couldn't see any weapons on him—a spellcaster, perhaps.

Standing just behind and to the side of the rest of the group, as if protecting them from the threat of a flanking attack, was a horned person with night-black skin. Twin curved swords hung at their sides; though they stood casually, there was something about their stance that suggested a readiness to draw and slice before anyone could so much as blink.

There were a few moments of tension as the two groups surveyed each other. Then the young gnome clapped his hands, chuckling gleefully. "Hello!" he chirped, waving enthusiastically as he practically skipped over to them. "I'm Jumper, and this is—well, and that's—I mean, they can tell you who they are." He stared straight into Mara's face, then blinked and flashed a twinkling smile. "You look frightening!" he told her merrily.

"Thanks," she said with no inflection whatsoever.

"Ha. Anyway, we're the Rainbow Rangers. We're dead."

"Oh, us too," said Iona, nodding in understanding.

"How'd it happen?" the gnome asked, but the older gnome gave one loud clap.

"Jumper," he admonished, "it's impolite to ask people how they died."

"Is it?" Jumper's face contorted in deep thought. "I mean, we got here by dying, so I suppose it's like asking a living person how they were born. Which would be..." He trailed off.

"Impolite," the older gnome supplied.

"Right."

The gnome with the white-tipped hair sighed, though his expression betrayed his amusement. "Forgive my nephew," he said. "He's immensely enthusiastic about just about every-thing. It's refreshing a lot of the time, but it's got him into his fair share of trouble." He headed over and extended a hand to Nemmo, who was sitting nearest him. Nemmo shook it. "I'm Wrenn," he said, then pointed to the rest of the group. "Arhiel, Oren, Void," he said, indicating the elf, the half-elf, and the horned person respectively, as they all took seats nearby.

"What brings you here?" Varun asked.

"Oh, just doing what we can to be of service," said Wrenn. "Before we came here, we were trying to make a difference in our homeland. Help people, save villages from roaming giants, that sort of thing."

"That's how we died," said Jumper cheerily. "A bunch of fire giants pillaged this town, so we stopped them!"

"Did you stop them though?" Mara asked. "If you died in the process?"

Wrenn nodded. "Took all of us to put ourselves in the way of a final attack from a giant fire demon thing. We absorbed it so it didn't hit the village, but we didn't make it."

This doesn't make sense, Mara thought, looking at Jumper's eager face. *These people* died *trying to be heroes, but they're here trying to do the same thing together again. How has getting killed not put them off?*

"Tell me about your combat capabilities," Iona said, leaning in.

Wrenn glanced at the others. "No reason to conceal anything, I think."

"Void here runs in and does a lot of damage before anyone notices them," explained the elf—Arhiel. "I cover them with ranged attacks and a few basic offensive spells—they hit hard, then they get out of the way if they can."

Right. One of those dish-it-out-but-can't-take-it fragile big hitters.

"Once they're clear," Arhiel continued, "Jumper gets in close and starts picking things apart with his rapier. He gets underestimated a lot."

"People don't often get a chance to revise their opinions," said Jumper matter-of-factly, "because what usually changes their mind is me poking them full of holes."

"Meanwhile," said Oren, the half-elf, "I look at the situation and work out what would be most useful—I can get in close with Jumper to eliminate a target, or I can try to control a crowd. Plus, I've got a bit of healing capability if someone's in trouble."

"And while all that's going on," said Wrenn, "I'm doing what I can to put everyone in the best fighting shape possible. Making them stronger, maybe lowering some of our enemies' defenses, healing if needed."

"And I jump back in and hit things when they're not looking," Void supplied.

Iona gave one loud clap, pointing excitedly at the Rainbow Rangers. "See? See? *That's* a party dynamic! They've all got defined roles to maximize the effectiveness of the whole thing. What do we do? We just sword! Hammer! Punch! And then panic when it's not really working."

"I am also there," Nemmo contributed.

"And Nemmo's also there," Iona said without missing a beat.

Mara groaned. "We've been in, like, two fights. Do you usually just settle into a role with a new group straight away?"

Iona, Varun, and the Rainbow Rangers all nodded.

"Oh," said Mara.

"Oh, and we also have Stripsey, of course," said Jumper. "He's a badger."

Oren tilted his head from side to side in an *eh, not quite* gesture. "More of a demi-fey in the shape of a badger."

Right on cue, a black-and-white face poked out from the collar of Oren's cloak, its ears tickling his chin.

It's like a triple-size rat, Mara thought with some small degree of admiration; whatever a badger was, she didn't think there were any in the world she'd lived in.

"We don't think he died when we did," said Oren, scratching the badger's neck. "He just showed up a few days later. Has a way of being wherever he feels like being. We're actually not sure what he *technically* is, just that he's probably not a regular animal."

"He's a shenanigans badger," said Arhiel fondly.

"That's about it," Oren agreed.

Mara blinked, looking from Stripsey to Oren to Arhiel and the rest of them, and then back again. *Oh, no,* she thought. *Actual combat capability mixed with bizarre levity... yep, this is an honest-to-goodness adventuring party alright. I've killed enough of them to know one when I see it.*

A not-insignificant part of her was recoiling at the thought of working together with a group like the Rainbow Rangers. She'd always hated so-called heroes: with how often they paused to make stupid quips, half of them shouldn't have been anywhere near as powerful as they were. And yet ... another part of her, whether she was willing to acknowledge it or not, was starting to just about understand the appeal of having a tight-knit party of companions to fight and laugh with. Nope, she wasn't acknowledging that just yet. But there was something both warmly and off-puttingly familiar about the obvious chemistry between the group.

Shit, she tried not to let herself think, looking first at the Rangers and then at her own group. *I'm turning into one of them, aren't I? Oh, Rekh, consign me to an oblivion of agony before I start giving out high-fives or whatever adventurers do.*

Up on the stage area, Chirripeek clapped his hands twice. The assembled volunteers fell silent, all turning toward him.

"Welcome," said the mouse, standing on top of the lectern. He gestured to the chalkboard and words appeared in white, dusty lettering despite the lack of any visible chalk:

LIGHTLESS CHASM VOLUNTEER GUARD INDUCTION.

"On behalf of the Nyxian Guard, I extend our thanks to you for your willingness to shoulder the noble duty of protecting the Sunless Crossing from the dreadful creatures that crawl from the Lightless Chasm." He cleared his throat. "You will follow my instructions and do all in your power to destroy anything that emerges. Understood?"

Nods all around.

"Does anybody require loaned equipment? Weapons, armor? It's all extremely basic, of course, but if anyone doesn't have their own...?"

Heads shook.

"Excellent," said Chirripeek. "That concludes the induction." He hopped down from the lectern and strode toward the door.

"Wait," said Iona, raising her hand. "That's it?"

The mouse shrugged without looking back. "It's a formality. Follow me. We have positions to take up."

The two groups shuffled out of their seats and after the Nyxian Guard with varying degrees of enthusiasm. Jumper was at the front, bouncing merrily along; Mara held up the rear, Varun and Void just ahead of her. The black-skinned horned warrior was eyeing Varun's black-and-white marbled face with surreptitious curiosity as they left the building and headed back toward the opening in the earth.

"You're a part-human too?" they asked after a moment in a half-whisper.

Varun shrugged. "Something like that. It's not all that uncommon where I'm from. My father liked to say we had ancestry going back to people of stone and fire, and the two lines mixed to make obsidian somewhere along the way, but I think it's probably just different kinds of people. I can't do anything different from regular humans, anyway—not because of my ancestry, at least."

Void nodded. "I'm probably at least a quarter demon or something. Never got a straight answer out of my mom. There are a lot of us on my world—don't think many others have a name for us though. Usually, people just call me a half-devil or something. Can't be bothered to correct them most of the time, especially since it tends to make them scared of me."

"You like having people be scared of you?" Varun asked.

Void shrugged. "Wouldn't say I *like* it, but it's come in handy."

Iona appeared beside Mara, having worked her way to the back of the group. "Here's what I'm thinking," she said very seriously. "Varun attacks first, with a bit of a buff from me. You work crowd control and punch anything that gets too close. Nemmo makes our enemies forget not to die. We win. Happy times." She peered up at Mara as if eager for her approval. "Thoughts?"

Mara shook her head, then blew out a long stream of air. "I have no idea," she said. "Never really thought about it. Always been more of the..."

She paused. *I can't very well say "the sit-back-and-watch-while-my-army-of-undead-slaves-destroys-everything type," can I?*

"More of the lone warrior type, I guess," she said. "But it sounds like what you've done there is taken the format the Rangers used and tried to slap us onto it. A hard hitter, a supporter, crowd control, and... er, Nemmo. We might not fit that paradigm, you know? Probably need to find our own."

Iona huffed in frustration, but she was nodding. "You're right," she said. "It'd be too easy if we could just copy what they were doing. Still, maybe we can learn something from this."

"Maybe we can." Mara slipped across the group to Nemmo, who was strolling along and staring vaguely upward, apparently deep in thought. "What are you thinking?" she asked, finding that she was genuinely interested in the answer. Varun and Iona had, apparently, both taken the same lesson—that their little party was less than adequate when it came to combat situations—deeply to heart. Nemmo, she suspected, would have a different take.

"I was considering the nature of unraveling," said Nemmo, his expression not changing. "I understand there is something of a limit on how long a soul may remain in the Crossing before it is, ah, forcibly moved on by one means or another, but it seems to me that a soul might do an awful lot of unraveling in that time. Or, indeed, that if the moving on relies on the correct administration of the process, there are almost certainly untold souls who have stayed past their allotted time thanks to something as mundane as the imperfections of manual logistics."

Mara couldn't help but laugh at that. Nemmo broke whatever gazing moment he was sharing with the sky and turned his head toward her.

"Did I say something amusing?"

"I'm sorry," she said, shaking her head. "It's just—talking to you is an experience."

He cracked a wry smile. "So I've been told."

"So... what, you're saying there are probably ancient souls still hanging around that have unraveled way more times than any soul should?"

"Something like that," said Nemmo. "It seems impossible that there aren't. And who knows what might happen at those sorts of extremes?" He lowered his voice almost conspiratorially, as if sharing forbidden knowledge; Mara thought he was probably just excited that someone actually wanted to hear what he had to say. "And who is to say that only the souls of people are subject to unraveling? Many worlds consider places and certain objects to have a soul of a kind, even if not one that can usually die and enter the Crossing. A pet theory of mine is that, given the sheer length of time this place has existed, it would be almost astounding if there did not exist here one example or another of a location that has itself unraveled and become a sort of ghost. A threadbare place, partly existing and partly not." A satisfied hum sounded in his throat.

"You..." Mara paused, not sure what it was she wanted to ask. "You said you've died twice in the Crossing, right? So ... one more and you start unraveling?"

"That is the conventional wisdom," said Nemmo with a sigh, "although I never quite seem to adhere to conventional wisdom. I suppose there must always be exceptions to prove rules."

"What sort of thing can happen, exactly?" she asked. "Varun said you start to—to lose parts of yourself, or something."

"It is not the most uniform process," Nemmo said. "Most lose memories. Some become less attached to the physical confines of the Sunless Crossing—to the degree that it exists physically at all, of course. Some become more sensitive to certain stimuli. A few gain the ability to see in the dark, I think."

Mara turned the information over in her mind. "Not all of those sound ... bad."

"I don't think it is," said Nemmo. "It is like death, perhaps. Differences in the dreams each of us experience as uninterrupted, singular existences, which cannot in themselves be inherently good or bad."

"Some gods would disagree, wouldn't they?"

Nemmo gave a quiet chuckle. "Most likely, yes. But in few worlds do all the gods agree on what constitutes an unambiguous good. I think if there were some entity that gave such things absolute definitions, someone would most likely have tried to kill it. And besides, it clearly holds little power to compel."

"It's not done much to raise awareness, if it is there," Mara agreed.

"Quite," said Nemmo.

"How did you die?" Mara asked after a brief pause. "Here, I mean. I know you don't remember before."

"Ah," said Nemmo, sounding almost amused. "Nothing interesting, I'm afraid. I've been here just about long enough that it was inevitable I'd have an accident. The first time, I fell off the side of Nox Valar. Silly, I know, but a surprising number of people do it. The second was a misunderstanding that ended with me getting stabbed."

"Huh."

"It happens to all of us eventually," he said, sounding less interested in the topic of his own abrupt stabbing than in anything else he'd spoken about.

"You're not exactly interested in fighting, are you?"

"I am not," Nemmo confirmed. "I think many of those who inhabit the Crossing see combat as the primary way of demonstrating their personal value, but I find it difficult to share the sentiment. I understand the purpose, of course, but there seems to be a high proportion of, let us say, heroic types who see battle as an end in itself rather than an unfortunate but necessary means to a greater goal."

The group came to a sudden halt; Mara nearly walked into Oren's back. She'd barely noticed where they were going, but this was apparently it. They had reached a stretch of the Chasm that was, as far as she could tell, indistinguishable from the rest of the huge cloven wound in the earth.

"Forecasts suggest an incursion here," Chirripeek announced, buzzing overhead on his dragonfly. "We should have a few hours to prepare, but make no mistake: even a single one of these beasts is a threat that should not be underestimated. Use this time wisely."

He pointed down into the Chasm at the little groups of Nyxian Guards who waited in its shallower platforms. "Those are the first defenders, there to assess any threat and deal with small encroachments. You new volunteers will wait here to clear up any stragglers that make it past them. I doubt there will be many, but one should always prepare for a harder fight than anticipated." He paused for a moment. "That said, if two groups of fighters can't deal with a few demons, whatever *are* you good for?" With that, he flitted a hundred yards or so down the Chasm and alighted, retrieving an impressive array of tools and weapons from within his metal mount and inspecting them.

Varun stuck his tongue out in the direction of the mouse. "Rude."

"Well, then," said Iona, plonking the head of her hammer down on the ground and folding her hands atop the end of the handle. "Preparations, eh?"

The Rainbow Rangers set about cleaning their weapons, casting spells Mara guessed were empowering enchantments, and holding quiet discussions about the battle to come; Mara, Iona, Varun, and Nemmo looked at each other for slightly too long until Iona finally shrugged.

"I don't really know what I can do to prepare," she said. "Most of my spells only last a few minutes, so there's no point casting them ahead of time."

"I shall contemplate the nature of the Chasm," Nemmo announced, then sat down cross-legged and closed his eyes.

Iona raised an eyebrow at him, then made a *pff* sound. "That'll help." She turned to Varun. "Hey, you can do the whole attempt-to-ascend-to-godhood thing."

"That is a good point," Varun murmured, and promptly pulled out a crumpled sheet of paper, which he started folding in intricate patterns. "Nope, not quite like that—start again— that's not it—maybe this could be a tree?" He gave up and tossed the sheet in the air, then cut it in half as it fell. "God of paper slicing, maybe."

Mara wandered off, heading for Chirripeek. The mouse was examining his tools with a keen, shining eye, manipulating them expertly in his tiny fingers.

"Are you the *only* Nyxian Guard or something?" she said, not bothering to make her interruption polite.

Chirripeek looked up at her with a squeak of what might have been irritation. "Absolutely not," he said. "We number in the… I'm not sure exactly how many of us there are, actually, but it's a lot. Something like eight in ten are gargoyles, and there are plenty of those around."

"Right," said Mara, nodding. "How come you're the only one we ever seem to run into?"

Chirripeek's head tilted to the side curiously, then he chuckled and went back to inspecting his gear. "If you must know," he said, "I admit I may have taken something of an interest in you."

"In the group," Mara asked, "or in *me*?"

"A little of both, but primarily the latter." Chirripeek sighed and put his things down, jumping casually onto his dragonfly and rising until he was level with Mara's face. "That first time we encountered one another, when you contained the soul stitched, I thought I felt something."

Mara folded her arms, letting her face take on an unimpressed scowl. "You felt something."

"I have enough experience with magic from different realms to understand a little of what I see when someone casts a spell," said Chirripeek. "I was curious: the effect of your magic was to shape light and stone, but it began as energy affiliated with death. I found that peculiar."

Mara met his gaze. "How so?"

One of his round ears twitched. "Well, to have a command of death magic sufficient to shape it into other elements and purposes is quite something. It suggests a level of, ah, expertise.

Highly sought after in the Sunless Crossing, since death energy is everywhere here." He gave a half-smile of amusement at Mara's expression. "You thought there would be more ... disdain for those who wield the magic of death, didn't you?"

"I never heard of a place where it wasn't regarded unfavorably," said Mara. "At best."

"Few living worlds tolerate practitioners of death magic," Chirripeek acknowledged, "but... well, being dead, and among the dead, invites a rather more sophisticated view."

"Life and death as two parts of the same journey," Mara murmured, thinking of what Varun had said about the Marquis of the Final End.

"Quite. There are, of course, uses to which death can be put that are violations of the natural way of things, but not all applications of death are as unsubtle and distasteful as ... let's say, necromancy."

Mara tried very hard not to let anything show on her face.

"To shape an end for something can be a noble thing," the Nyxian Guard continued, apparently unaware that he had said anything to cause a reaction in her. "Pain can be made to die, thereby healing a soul. That which has lingered for too long can be allowed to go, thus making space for new life. And so on." He paused for a moment. "Really, death is only the name we give to the idea of the quietest part of a cycle: the space between end and beginning. Those who command it with sensitivity, with imagination, can do incredible things."

Mara kept her face very still. Needles of heat pricked unpleasantly at her cheeks. *I could have been the kind of person he's talking about? I didn't have to be what Raskith made me?*

"At any rate," Chirripeek went on more slowly, perhaps sensing her discomfort, "you will most likely find that embracing the fullness of what you can do is a better direction for you than trying to shape it into something else. If you had drawn on all that aura of death and released it in a pure form, it would have been far stronger than the inefficiently squashed, disguised version you ended up with."

I can't though. Mara glanced back at her group, her eyes lingering on Varun's face. *I can never reveal what I can do to him. What I* did *to him.*

"If someone thinks less of you for who you are," said Chirripeek, apparently following her gaze, "that is not your fault."

Mara turned back to the mouse, readying herself to say something scornful. Instead, she just groaned in frustration. "Why is everyone irritatingly wise and empathetic?!"

"Years of training," said the mouse flatly.

Mara couldn't help cracking a smile at that. "Are you..." She hesitated, then plowed on. "Are you not worried about dying here? Us already-dead folk just come back, but don't you just ... disappear?"

Chirripeek shivered, one ear flicking a few times as though dispelling a chill. "I try very hard not to die," he said simply. Then he dropped back to the ground and started working on his tools with even more fervor than before. "We should all do the same."

Mara kneeled beside him. "You know... you probably don't need to be here. There are, what, nine of us not including you? We can handle it."

The mouse's hands paused in their work. He swallowed, then took a deep breath. After a moment, his glistening eyes fixed Mara with an intense stare. "Where I come from, the existence of worlds beyond death is largely unknown," he said, taking his time to consider each word before speaking. "Most people go their whole lives assuming that there will be nothing for them when they die, that they only have one life. For some, that can be difficult. For many, it motivates them to make that life as meaningful and purposeful as possible. It's quite a beautiful thing, I think." He gave a strange smile, one that looked genuine and sad at the same time. "I stumbled upon a way to leave my world and visit others, and I learned that death need not be the end. But I spent much of my life accepting that it would be, and I don't intend to let go of that acceptance. I will not shirk my duties as a guardian of the Sunless Crossing for fear of disappearing. I will rejoice in spending a singular, finite existence doing the best I can."

With that, he turned back to his work.

CHAPTER 21

Mara walked slowly back toward her group and the Rainbow Rangers, her mind churning through thoughts like an oar through a weed-choked river.

Death didn't need to be solely an object of fear, or a tool for creating it.

Death could be just a part of the journey that began with life.

People could deeply believe that death was truly, irreversibly final and in spite of that—no, almost because of it—live the most fulfilling lives they could. They could learn not to fear it.

None of it made sense. Raskith had spent years teaching her that death was something everyone feared, that—despite the many gods who offered bounteous and wonderful afterlives—it was almost impossible for a living person to conceive of dying as anything except a terrible and unwelcome end. He had shown her how to wield the fear of death, holding it over people. He had taught her to subvert death, to inspire the greatest of terrors by creating a broken, dead facsimile of life.

And what she had done in life hadn't only affected the living. No: by raising bodies from the dead, she had removed their chances of being fully restored to life, if that were a path they desired. She'd probably screwed up a lot of hopes for going to certain afterlives that required particular rites to be performed on one's body. And, though she had only ever raised mindless corpses, had her work with Raskith continued, she would have become stronger and learned to pull back unwilling souls. Souls that, if destroyed by divine magic, would become soul stitched: hungry, afraid, and monstrous.

Raskith would never have thought to do something so radical as *accept* death, least of all his own. She'd thought that it was a strength of his, doing everything he could to master death so as to conquer the living and extend his own life—and he had safeguards, she knew, plans upon plans to prevent himself from ever truly dying and facing whatever lay in wait for him beyond—but … perhaps it wasn't. Why go to so much effort to control something, to keep it beneath you and subject to your command rather than the other way around, if you didn't fear it?

"You look like someone just told you your pet fish died," Iona said, snapping her out of her thoughts.

"What?"

Varun's brow creased as he took in Mara's face. "What in all the hells did you and the mouse talk about?"

"Oh," she said. "Just…" *Think of something, think of something, think of something.* "Death." *You idiot.*

"It's a big topic!" Jumper chimed in.

Mara groaned internally. "Yup. Lots to think about." She kneeled and stared at the ground for a few moments, visualizing lines and angles. "We haven't really been in a fight we knew was coming before," she said, beginning to trace rough circles in the ash with the tip of a finger. "But magic with preparation is what I do best, not improvising on the fly."

Iona plonked down beside her. "I mean, your *on-the-fly* spellcasting is still pretty impressive."

"Thanks," Mara said absently. She was sketching a draft, an initial outline; the details were left deliberately undone. She'd need to make changes to the overall structure once she'd finalized the purpose and function of the circle, but to do that, she found it was easiest to create the suggestion of the shape first. "It's a trade-off. Flexibility or power. If I prepare something like this, it's pretty rigid—I can't change how it works once it's in place, but when it's triggered, it'll do whatever it's designed to do much more powerfully than if I just make up a spell in the moment."

"What's this one going to do?" Iona asked.

"Not entirely sure yet," Mara muttered. She finished her scribbles and stood, beckoning Varun and Nemmo over. "We don't really know what's going to come out of there, right?"

"Just ... infernal beasts of some description," said Varun, frowning at her circle. "I feel like I've seen something like that before."

"We're from worlds with similar magic systems," Mara said, perhaps a little too quickly. "Makes sense that you'd have come across something similar."

Varun didn't press the point. "Could be one big one, could be a few little ones. Flying, digging, walking... we need to be ready for anything."

"You've not heard anything about the kind of things that usually show up?"

"It's not consistent, from what I know," said Varun. "There are some Nyxian Guard with the ability to forecast when something's expected to come out, not completely confidently, but enough to be useful. Not sure how it works. Similar to what the Keepers do, maybe? Anyway, I've never heard that it gives any useful information about the nature of the event, just the timing."

Mara bobbed her head from side to side for a few seconds, thinking about it. "Right," she said. "Iona's got support covered, so I don't need to make something to strengthen the rest of us. Varun and I can hit single targets pretty effectively, so … something to contain and do large damage to a big area at once? If we can get a good hit in quickly, even if there are multiple enemies, that'd be a good start."

"I meant to talk to you about the support thing, actually," Iona said. "It was … more difficult than usual to give you a boost, back in that street. Like your body was resisting it."

"Just wasn't used to it," said Mara, remembering how Iona's life magic had felt so foreign as it worked its way through her. It hadn't been the most unpleasant thing, but it had been … a shock, perhaps. Like tasting fruit after a lifetime of plain bread. She'd already had her own death magic reinforcing her limbs, but Iona's power had driven it away, a bright light scaring shadows into cracks and hidden corners. She supposed what she said was true: she just wasn't used to feeling… well, life. Maybe there was something to the notion that life and death weren't as fundamentally opposed as she'd thought, but she couldn't reconcile that notion in herself just yet.

"Right," said Iona. "Well, hopefully, it'll be easier this time. I know you can power yourself up a bit anyway, but it looked like you were having a good time once the spell did stick."

"It's good stuff," she admitted, to which Varun nodded appreciatively.

"What might we do to best support you in your preparations?" Nemmo asked. "Depending on the usual duration of your castings, it seems advisable to begin promptly."

Mara considered her half-made circle. "I need something for containment," she said, "something for destruction, and … something for chaos."

Iona reached into her robes and pulled out a small, clear gem with neatly cut sides. "That's for keeping things in," she said, tossing it on the ground.

"Keeping things in?"

The cleric clicked her tongue with distaste. "It's a soul gem," she said. "Living people in my world use them to contain the souls of… well, animals, usually. Trapping human souls is considered a bit, er, less than ethical. And very illegal." She scowled deeply, then brightened and continued her explanation more cheerily. "Anyway, they can be used to power certain kinds of magic. It's more common than you'd probably like to think."

"Why do you have one?"

Iona shrugged. "I died with one on me and I didn't want to give it up, so I kept it hidden. Not because I thought I'd ever use it or anything. Just because it seemed in bad taste to have something like that at all, so I didn't want anyone else finding out about it. Or using it." She shuddered. "Can you imagine if someone found a way to put that thing to use here? It could be … horrible."

I'm already thinking of ways I would've tried to use something like that, Mara realized. *If Raskith were here, he'd already have a plan for trapping some appallingly powerful dead soul and using it to cause untold levels of destruction.*

"There's no soul in it now, I take it?" Nemmo inquired, peering down at the plain, unassuming gem.

"Nope." Iona shook her head. "Empty, but … it's a pretty good representation of the concept of containment, right?"

Mara nodded. "It should work perfectly. Thanks."

"I might have an idea for destruction," said Varun, and he jogged over to Chirripeek. Even looking at the tiny Nyxian

Guard from a distance, Mara could feel the exasperation coming off him at being interrupted again, but the conversation seemed to go well; the mouse nodded and reached into his dragonfly, then handed something to Varun. "This should do," Varun said as he rejoined them, passing Mara a minuscule … something.

"What is this?" she asked, holding it up to her eye.

"Remember how he had that metal tube thing back in the alley yesterday?"

"The one that was firing some kind of explosive projectile?"

Varun nodded at the thing held between her fingers. "That's one of the projectiles. Doesn't look like much, but it's doubly dangerous: packed with explosive powder and enchanted to blow up as if it were much bigger."

Iona whistled appreciatively. "Nice. Just need something for chaos then?"

Nemmo cleared his throat. "I believe I have something that should serve the purpose." He held up a rectangular box about the size of his palm. "I must suggest that nobody inspect this too closely."

Iona, naturally, was immediately peering in as closely as she possibly could, getting her face within a few inches of the item in Nemmo's hand. "Why? What is it? Does it explode? Is it magic? Can I kill a god with it? Does it make *me* a god if I have it? Is it gonna—"

"It is a deck of cards," said Nemmo, "but not an ordinary one. To draw a card from the deck is to ask fate to wreak havoc upon you and the world around you. Once a card is drawn, its effect cannot be negated."

"What kind of effects are there?" Iona asked, her lips forming a curious O.

"I have only the vaguest of notions," said Nemmo. "The person who explained it to me described a few she had heard could happen: the destruction of all items on one's person, a permanent boon to one's skills, a mystical assistant to serve any whims for a time, a powerful demon becoming eternally determined to kill the one who had drawn the card... She decided that it would be a good idea to illustrate the power of the deck by drawing a card herself. She simply vanished, and I have not seen her since." He shook his head as if he would prefer not to remember. "She did mention that one of the cards—the worst one, as she described it—could pull a soul from a person's body. I suppose that a person who is only a soul with no body was simply pulled... well, who knows?"

"That," said Iona, "is *really* cool."

"It is not to be trifled with," said Nemmo very seriously— even more seriously than usual, somehow.

"Does your ritual use up the items involved?" Varun asked Mara. "Will all of these things disappear?"

She shook her head. "Some kinds of spell destroy their components," she said, "but in this case, I'm just using them as a way to shape the magic into having the effect I want. Everything should be left behind." She thought about it for a second. "Except possibly the explosive, just because that sounds kind of volatile, anyway."

"Fun." Varun cracked a toothy grin.

Mara turned the spell over in her head, visualizing the connections between the items. There were standard forms for achieving most basic ends, but the individual nature of the ritual pieces always demanded a level of flexibility: the lines and glyphs needed to account for what was there or the whole thing would fall apart. It would be like building multiple perfect floors of a building in isolation, then realizing that each was a different size and material; it just wouldn't fit.

But this would work. A sense of excitement bloomed in Mara at having the chance to do what she was best at, to create a real working rather than spinning something up in haste. She could already see the completed circle in her mind, and the effect it would have when activated.

Without saying anything further, she kneeled and began to burn shallow lines into the ground, copying the design in her head across to reality. The others watched for a few minutes, then turned away to prepare themselves. At least, Mara assumed that was what they were doing. She didn't look up.

By the time the Lightless Chasm vomited up the demonic contents of its infernal stomach, Mara was ready.

"Are there usually this many?" Varun muttered as the scale of the incursion became clear. Red arms, black wings, gray-furred hooves—and other limbs Mara couldn't put names to—all were reaching over the side of the abyss and pulling themselves up into the Sunless Crossing.

Two Nyxian Guards, stony-skinned gargoyles wielding heavy weapons, flew out ahead of the horde and soared over the heads of the waiting defenders.

"Major breach!" one called, its voice rasping as if its vocal cords were slabs of jagged slate sliding against each other. "More than expected—hold them! We'll rally!"

"Be ready!" Chirripeek cried, soaring overhead.

Iona clapped her hands together with performative enthusiasm, but worry was creasing her features. "Should we ... get more people or something?"

"Those Guards will fetch support!" Chirripeek answered. "Others will see. More will come to help." He zoomed off to circle over the Chasm, but Mara could still make out a quiet, "I hope."

"We can do it!" an enthusiastic voice called; a little way to the side of Mara's group, Jumper was waving and bouncing on the balls of his feet. The Rainbow Rangers had taken up a diamond position: Void at the front, Wrenn at the rear, Jumper and Arhiel at the sides. Oren stood apart from the rest, a little way back.

"We should probably have worked out a formation," Varun muttered. He, Mara, Iona, and Nemmo were farther back from the Chasm, Mara's spell circle between them and the infernal fissure. The Rainbow Rangers were more than keen to dive in headfirst and let Mara and her group clean up what remained, and that suited everyone fine.

Mara shook her head. "We were never going to devise and implement an entire strategy in the time we had," she said. "Watch them. See if you can learn anything. Get behind them if you have to. Use their formation as cover."

Iona tilted her head, her big eyes filled with innocent confusion. "That sounds ... slightly callous."

"Do what it takes to survive," Mara said through gritted teeth.

"Bit late for that," Varun said, then grimaced at the twin glares Iona and Mara shot at him.

The first creature ascended from the bowels of the Chasm into the half-light of the Crossing: a green-skinned figure walking on two spindly legs, grasping with long, multi-jointed fingers on the ends of six ungainly arms so thin they might as well have been exposed bones. In an instant, Void was upon it, dashing forward from the Rangers' formation and whirling across its torso with twin curved blades. The creature screeched and fell apart, but its bisected top half continued to crawl with those spiky fingers, gnashing its teeth. It was hard to make out, but Mara thought it had a second mouth inside the first, independently smashing its blunt teeth together.

Void cut the top of its head off, at which point it stopped gnashing and lay still.

The first invader was dead within a few seconds, but in that time, a dozen more had emerged from the Chasm.

Jumper leaped into action, throwing himself into the fray. A slim blade gleamed in his hand, flicking once, twice, three times, faster than Mara could see. An instant later, dark blood misted the air around him. He stepped back with a quick, efficient movement of his feet, avoiding a clumsy blow from a hammer-handed creature with a mishmash of spines and fins sticking out of its angular head, then lunged and speared it right through its single eyeball.

Meanwhile, Arhiel dashed around the group of demons, loosing arrows and the occasional spell into the midst of the battle. Wrenn was in constant motion, keeping himself as the third point of a triangle between himself, Jumper, and Arhiel; the older gnome glowed with a gentle blue light that flowed in ethereal trails between himself and the other two. Void kept disappearing from Mara's sight somewhere in the chaos, then reappearing somewhere else entirely to deal a devastating blow before vanishing again.

A whole group of creatures fell at once, and Jumper darted away, putting some distance between himself and the rest of the crowd. "Oren!" he called.

A moment later, a shaggy brown blur loped across the fields and flung itself into battle, knocking down a dozen demons at once. As it slowed, Mara saw what it was: a great wolf that must have been nine feet from head to tail, its enormous jaws slathered with dark-stained spittle.

"They've got a guy who can turn into a wolf," Varun muttered. "Can one of us learn to turn into a wolf?"

"Shh," Mara hissed, watching the fight as it progressed. The Rainbow Rangers were more competent than she'd expected from their general demeanor, but then she should've remembered that that was par for the course when it came to adventuring parties. All quips and jokes when they weren't in a fight, then surprisingly capable when the situation called for it.

They knew each other well, that much was clear; they relied on strengths and compensated for vulnerabilities. Arhiel's precise arrows constantly disrupted potential threats to Jumper; the little gnome flitted about like an arrow himself, his rapier downing enemies with every slash, but he was too eager to put himself in harm's way. Even as he needed protecting himself, Jumper protected Oren's wolf form, throwing himself at anything that might blindside the druid. Void danced through the battle, striking wherever there was an opening, taking advantage when one of their allies had the attention of a creature, and Wrenn strengthened them all, occasionally tossing projectiles at errant monsters. If a demon turned its attention toward Wrenn or Arhiel, one of the others would be on them in an instant, keeping the elder gnome free to manage the battle and the elf to toss ranged attacks at the crowd. And, amidst the chaos of everything else going on, Mara caught the occasional glimpse of a small, furry, black-and-white shape throwing itself with reckless abandon at any demon the rest of the Rangers missed.

"They're … smooth," Iona said, sounding almost awestruck.

"But they're not winning," Mara realized. There were just too many demons, and more were climbing out of the Chasm.

I only need one heart, she thought. *I could just take one—there are enough corpses already—and then just … leave. I'd have what I needed.*

She sighed.

But I'm not going to do that, am I? And not just because I still need my allies and they wouldn't be happy about it. Oh, gods, now I'm thinking of them as allies instead of minions. Being dead's making you soft, Mara.

"Prepare yourselves!" Chirripeek called, soaring over Mara's head. The mouse zipped into the Rangers' fight; almost immediately, things started exploding. "Rangers, fall back and reform!" he commanded. "You've done well!"

The Rainbow Rangers heeded the instruction, disengaging from the fight and retreating behind Mara's group to catch their breath and heal. Which meant that Mara was up.

"You're sure this'll work?" Varun muttered.

"Don't ask that now," Mara shot back, dropping to one knee. The jumbled horde of demons must have been a hundred strong, their bodies lining the side of the Chasm, spilling thickly out into the Crossing like poisonous tar. She focused her will on the long line that extended away from her and joined the ritual circle ahead, a magical fuse scratched into the earth. The power of death surged through her, and she touched her finger to the end of the fuse line. She only needed a spark to ignite the process, and the spell would do the rest of the work.

Magic zipped into the spell circle, setting the runes and lines alight. It was a more focused version of the concept Mara applied when she shaped spells within her own body, but the difference was like throwing paint at a wall compared to a fine-headed brush. She could only press and mold things into rough forms, but the ritual circle could carve it into far more specific functions. And it could call more magic from the world around it, shaping the aura into power within itself, rather than needing Mara to supply it with all the energy it would use.

The magic connected with the three items placed within the circle. It flowed around the shapes and glyphs, circulating thousands of times in a second and becoming ever more sharply defined with every pass. It learned what it was there to do. It took on the aspects, the significance, of the components it touched.

The spell waited, building and building as it did, for enough of the infernal creatures to come within its radius of effect.

Then it exploded.

"Ha!" Iona whooped.

The effect was like one of Chirripeek's projectile bombs, magnified and exaggerated. Flames in shades of green and purple and black and orange erupted from the circle, billowing, almost solid—less like licking flames, more like expanding magma—and engulfed everything in its range. The fire expanded, and then, as if hitting the inside of an invisible sphere, it stopped. It swallowed itself, imploding with all the force of a collapsing mountain, condensing into a single tiny point before regurgitating itself. It spat out sparks and charred bodies, and those that were anything less than completely destroyed wandered only a few confused steps before realizing how utterly dead they were. Little red glimmers dispersed from the disintegrating corpses, floating almost peacefully away before detonating and filling the entire area with a pyrotechnic cloud.

"Holy fucking *shit*," Varun said.

"Yep," Iona agreed.

"Quite potent," said Nemmo. Then he chuckled. "Holy fucking shit indeed."

Black smoke briefly covered their view, but it quickly cleared to reveal a field strewn with demonic corpses. Or parts of them, at least. And, to Mara's dismay, what was left of them was rapidly decaying.

I'm not gonna get a usable heart out of any of those.

"Fight's not over yet," Varun said darkly, raising his weapons. "That was a hell of an attack, though."

"I'll be honest," said Iona, "I thought you were exaggerating when you were saying your prepared spells were way stronger than your improvised ones, but remind me never to doubt you again."

Mara grinned. "I'll hold you to that."

"Greater demons emerging!" Chirripeek called, flying in a wide arc around the space occupied by Mara's group and the Rainbow Rangers.

Mara turned to the Rangers; they looked in good condition, with only a few scratches. A lot of blood covered Jumper and Void, and Oren's fur was matted and dirty, but none of them seemed badly hurt. "Ready for more?" she asked.

Arhiel nocked an arrow to her bow, pulled back the string, and shot one of the frontmost demons right in the heart. "Naturally," she said.

CHAPTER 22

Looking back on it later, Mara would barely remember the next few minutes. She would recall how they'd felt like years at the time, but she'd be damned if she could recount much of the detail of what actually happened beyond a vague impression of chaotic red, of surging claws, of pain and rage.

Any semblance of a formation, of a plan, was in tatters. She had access to nearly limitless quantities of death aura from the general ambiance of the Crossing, but she could shape it only so quickly. And forcing so much magic through her so rapidly took a toll: her internal channels were exhausted, scoured to the point of agony, as were her muscles.

Varun was still swinging his swords, but he was visibly slowing. Iona had lost her hammer somewhere along the way; she was focusing on lending as much strength as she could to the others, but it couldn't keep them going forever. No matter how much magical power she imbued into them, their bodies could only be tricked for so long into thinking they had strength left when they simply had none. And, judging from the increasingly desperate look on her face each time she renewed her casting, she was rapidly running out of spells.

Nemmo had proved far more useful than Mara had expected, laying down some sort of wide-area magic that seemed to distract or stun any demon within reach. Most managed to shake off the effect within a few seconds, but a few seconds were all that was needed to do a lot of damage. That done, Nemmo had flitted around the field, doing what he could to alleviate tiredness and pain, and occasionally simply touching a demon and causing its head to explode. Mara assumed that one wasn't the sort of thing that could be done a lot of times in quick succession, or she'd have been irritated both that Nemmo hadn't already won the battle single-handedly and that he was bordering on obscenely powerful.

The Rainbow Rangers, too, were in bad shape. All were still on their feet and fighting, for now, but not one of them had got to this point without sustaining some sort of nasty visible wound. Oren had dropped his wolf form; his brown cloak was soaked red around his shoulder, but he was smacking at the foes around him with a polished staff.

Chirripeek was darting around on his dragonfly, launching all kinds of ranged assaults wherever he could, but he too was slowing. His steed was meandering rather than zipping, his attacks spluttering rather than emphatic. When he dipped down to ground level to pick up Iona's fallen hammer, it looked more as if he were doing it to give himself a break from attacking than because it was the most important objective. The heavy weapon dangled, disproportionately huge, from his struggling mount until he managed to drop it to Iona and return to firing off whatever he could muster at their foes.

The group was indisputably faltering. But the crawl of demons from the Chasm had ceased. There were only a dozen or so smaller enemies left, surrounding one greater foe that stood fifteen feet tall and brandished a brutal double-headed greataxe. Not so long ago, that would have seemed easy to deal with: when they were all fresh, cutting down twenty lesser enemies would have been trivial. Now, though, it was taking every ounce of strength they had just to keep themselves alive.

We're so close to finishing this, Mara thought, deflecting a demon's clawed strike with a heavy, clumsy swing of her arm. *If I could just find space to cast even a basic ritual, we could turn the tide and end it.*

"Why in the hells don't we have reinforcements?" Varun cried, catching a scything arm on one blade and lopping it clean off with the other.

Chirripeek descended into the battle, panting as he raised and fired a tiny device that looked like a crossbow without a string. "Something must be happening elsewhere." There was doubt in his tone now though. A lot of doubt. Chirripeek had no more faith that anyone was coming to help, Mara realized.

"Can you make space for me?" she called. "Give me one minute, uninterrupted, and I'll end this."

The mouse fixed her with a hard stare, but just for a moment—a nimble, bat-like form shot toward him, forcing him to execute a tight rolling dodge in midair. Then he nodded. "Protect the ritual caster!" he bellowed, the instruction carrying to all in the area.

Does he not know my name? Mara briefly wondered, then put all thoughts out of her head except creating her working. She kicked out hard, sending an arachnoid creature with crimson and black skin scuttling backward—its legs cracked and leaked at the joints under the sudden pressure—then disengaged, forcing her exhausted legs to carry her just far enough from the main fray that she could collapse to her knees and start scrawling a new circle right next to the first. She grabbed for the little emblem of destruction that had been a key focus of that explosive ritual, placing it in the center of her new lines even as she drew them with her other hand. Beside it, she placed what she thought was the cleaved-off hand of a demon.

The eight-legged fiend rocketed toward her, leaving half its limbs behind as the force of its movement shattered its flaky carapace. Varun was there before it could reach her, slicing off the remaining legs and following up with a spinning slash that carved the creature's head in half. Its momentum sent it sprawling toward Mara, the sharp edges of its broken shell carving deep gouges in the field beneath, but it slid to a halt before it could reach her. She barely noticed it at all.

The greater demon turned its attention to Mara, its enormous horned head swiveling in her direction on a neck thick with corded muscle. It stepped toward her, trembling the grass around its footsteps.

Void whirled forward in a low dash, spinning and slashing at the creature's ankles. Their swords bit through tough gray fur to reddish-blue skin, but the demon was too hardy and Void's arms too weak. It swiped one arm casually down, smacking Void into the grass with an irritable flick of its fingers. Then Jumper was upon it, his rapier flicking and flashing, drawing heavy drops of blood from its meaty fingers. The demon barely adjusted its step to launch the gnome into the air with an unceremonious kick. When Arhiel's arrows pierced its chest, it simply broke off the shafts and kept moving, undaunted; clinging, thorny vines that wrapped around it courtesy of Oren frayed and snapped as it flexed. Iona and Varun hit it in the lower abdomen from both sides at once, hammer and swords—the blades only faintly sputtering with holy light now—crashing into its body. The demon stumbled at that one, but an ear-shattering roar and two powerful swipes later, the cleric and the swordsman were on their backs in the grass.

"No more!" Wrenn cried, his fingers weaving intricate patterns across the strings of his lute. The music spluttered and stammered in staccato stutters—if a bard had played such a tune in a tavern, they would have been asked to leave in short order, but it was no song of merriment or revelry. Wrenn's was a complex, entangling song, precise in its apparent chaos.

The demon slowed. Not just in that it decelerated its stride, but that its entire being became lugubriously unable to keep up with the normal flow of time. A frown slid gradually across its face.

Nemmo stood beside Wrenn, his hands upraised. A colorless haze emanated from him, pressing toward the demon. In slow motion, the creature shook its head and fell to one knee. As its shin hit the earth with a thump muffled by languorousness and thick grass, a flash of silver shot through the air.

"Begone!" Chirripeek bellowed, throwing himself from his dragonfly and slamming into the demon's skull between its horns. He raised something that looked like a chisel with an enormous, blocky handle, then thrust it downward. The thing oscillated wildly, driving down into the demon's head faster than any eye could keep up with. A shower of flesh and bone gushed forth, drenching Chirripeek in gore.

The enormous creature cried out, its voice distorted by its detachment from the flow of time. Even warped as it was, it was plain to all who heard it that it was a scream of utter agony, the wailings of a beast that had dragged itself up from the pits of some vile hell only to learn that there were greater torments in the world.

Wrenn clapped his hands over his ears, his song washed away by the demon's cry like scraps of driftwood in a tidal wave. Nemmo fell back too, clutching at his own head.

"Uncle Wrenn!" Jumper screamed, crawling through the grass, one hand desperately extending toward the older gnome—and then the greater demon, freed from the effects of Wrenn and Nemmo's magic, slammed its palm down on him at full speed and with full force.

Jumper groaned. His eyes fluttered. Then his skin darkened and flaked, and a moment later, he was ash in the breeze.

The demon reached up and grabbed Chirripeek in a fist that completely engulfed him, hurling the mouse off its head. The Nyxian Guard fell, sprawling at its feet.

In the few moments that had passed since the greater demon began its slow approach toward Mara, the lesser creatures had not been idle. The Sunless Crossing's defenders were barely weathering an onslaught of grabs, slashes, rips, clubs, blows, pain. Mara only registered the scene in the very backmost part of her mind. To allow it any further in was to fail in her task, and she could not allow that to happen. She had to … trust that her allies would keep her safe. That was a strange feeling. Not an entirely comfortable one, but not an entirely unpleasant one either.

One of the smaller creatures broke from the entangled mass and made a beeline for Mara, but Iona came out of nowhere. The cleric missed wildly with a swing of her hammer but kept her momentum going, throwing her own body right in front of the lupine beast. She took a hard blow to the torso, but she stayed firm: her arms wrapped around the thing's forelimbs, grappling it, keeping it from Mara.

Mara finished the circle.

A wave of nearly invisible flame whooshed forth, passing harmlessly through Iona. The demon in her grasp was less fortunate: it screeched like a tearing sheet of metal as the power engulfed it, disintegrating it. The fire kept going, drawing its destructive aptitude from Chirripeek's weapon, selecting only those targets whose blood was pure hell-born infernal, like that of the severed hand in the spell circle. In moments, the flock of lesser demons had evaporated, leaving the Chasm's guardians to fall exhausted into the grass as their enemies vanished.

The greater demon planted its feet and stood firm against the spell. The fire washed over it, scouring its skin, peeling off chunks of its flesh. Blood still spilled freely from the hole in its head.

But it did not die.

Mara fell to her knees, every scrap of energy gone from her. She idly realized that the soul gem and Nemmo's mysterious deck of cards were gone from the first ritual circle, most likely blasted into the Chasm by her hasty spell.

That was everything I had. That's everything any of us has. And there's still one standing. We've lost.

A tiny form twitched in the grass before the great vile demon, and Chirripeek of the Nyxian Guard clambered waveringly to his feet. His fingers reached for some hidden clasp, and his blood-smeared bone armor fell from him, leaving him clad in a simple black tunic.

"I will not allow you to remain in this land for one more moment, foul beast," the mouse spat. "This is the hallowed land of Nyxia, and you have no place in it."

The demon's toothy maw split in a twisted smile. It raised one hand, opening its fingers, then brought its palm down upon Chirripeek like an avalanche. The mouse disappeared.

Except for one hand, which rose defiantly from the earth just long enough to make a beckoning gesture before falling still.

With a whizzing chirrup and a gore-marred gleam, Chirripeek's dragonfly shot through the air, dove into the hole its rider had made in the enormous skull, and buried itself in the greater demon's brain.

The beast's head trembled. It grasped confusedly at its exposed cerebrum. Then, as blood began to flow from its eyes and soak the grass beneath, turning the dusty coating of ash into a dirty reddish paste, it gave one halting groan. It fell to the side, rolling onto its back; its hand lifted from where it had slammed down upon the Nyxian Guard who had killed it. It lay still.

Mara crawled to the demon's corpse even as it began to gray and decompose, thrusting her hand into its chest and ripping out a heart as big as her head. With the very final bit of will she could muster, she nudged the flow of death around the heart, keeping it preserved from decay.

Then she turned to Chirripeek, who lay in a hand-shaped imprint pressed into the surrounding grass and dirt. The mouse was smiling.

"A noble way to go," he said.

"You can't die here," Mara told him.

"I can," said Chirripeek. His shining black eyes fixed on her. "Something is wrong. This incursion... no Guards to help... it's..." He took a final, shuddering breath, and the gleam in his eyes faded.

Mara watched the life leave him, as she had watched it leave many before. There were a few moments, she knew, when life was gone but death had not yet come in its fullness, when dying was still something that was happening to a person. Some spent those moments fearful. Chirripeek's were dignified. Next should have come the peace, the finality, the painlessness, and relief, of being entirely gone.

Not for Chirripeek.

Just as his final rest should have come, the mouse's body twisted and withered. The flesh became desiccated; the eyes deflated and sank; the fur lost its sheen, dried up, and fell out. A fibrous string of faint light floated free from his chest, then frayed and scattered into nothingness. Chirripeek's corpse crumbled, and then only a shirt the size of Mara's hand remained.

They had won a hard-fought victory, Mara knew. Those who remained were gradually finding their feet, smears of blood mixing with ash from the grass on their skin. Every one of them looked more than ready to collapse from sheer exhaustion.

I brought us here. Because I had to. And we won. Didn't we?

CHAPTER 23

Mara opened her eyes to the morning, such as it was. The perpetual twilight of the Sunless Crossing waited for her outside, she knew, and her room in the basement of Iona's temple was constantly suffused with a dim magical light. She'd never thought she would miss the sun. Perhaps it wasn't the sun she missed at all but the unignorable marker of where the world sat in the cycle of time. Raskith had always hated both aspects of the sun: its brightness and its perpetual motion. He would never have openly admitted it, but Mara knew him better than he thought; Raskith was nothing if not afraid of the passing of time. Every rising and falling of the sun reminded him that more of his life was gone forever, unrecoverable, and that there were fewer days left to enjoy his ultimate domination once it was achieved.

This day, though, Mara felt that the unchanging tedium felt fitting. Her body felt drained, her mind a tangle of fuzzy strings. Something in her knew that, after the long trek back from the Lightless Chasm, she'd slept for eight hours, give or take. From her perspective, though, she'd closed her eyes and opened them again to see that nothing had changed whatsoever.

She rotated with as little effort as possible, moving her feet to the edge of the bed and letting them dangle down to the floor. That done, she allowed her body to fall out of bed and balance upright more than she actually stood up, then trudged to the door and pulled it open.

Iona was standing outside.

"Oh," said Mara blearily. "Morning."

Iona looked Mara up and down, sighed heavily, then wrapped her in a warm hug. Mara stiffened momentarily, then let herself relax into it. It was too much effort not to.

Maybe I don't actually mind the whole hugging thing as much as I thought I did.

"How are you doing?" Iona asked without letting go.

"Not sure," said Mara truthfully. "You?"

Iona pulled back slightly, keeping her hands firmly on Mara's arms. "Yesterday was absolutely horrible, and I hated it, and I never want to do anything like that ever again, ever," she said in a tone that was somehow both matter-of-fact and deeply pained. Mara was almost envious of the cleric's openness to her own feelings, if it meant she could express herself with that kind of honesty without sinking into vulnerable embarrassment.

"Yeah," said Mara, nodding. "That ... about sums it up."

Iona led her by the hand to the common room with its small table, upon which a breakfast of oats and honey had been set. Varun and Nemmo were already there, each clasping a mug of something steaming.

Mara slid into the chair next to Varun, accepting another mug from him gratefully. "I'm the last one awake?"

"You did a lot," said Varun, who was staring at nothing in particular. Even as he'd slid the mug toward Mara, he hadn't looked at her.

Nemmo nodded, exhaling heavily. "If not for you, I suspect we would all have met with a terrible fate," he said.

"We'd have come back, though," said Mara, taking a sip. Whatever was in the mug, it was refreshing, almost a little spicy. "Jumper should've returned this morning, right?"

After the battle was over, the Rainbow Rangers had said their farewells with what still seemed like genuine friendliness despite the thick layers of physical and emotional fatigue that weighed all of them down. When Mara, Iona, Nemmo, and Varun were far enough from the battlefield that it was touching the horizon, only then did a bone-clad flock of Nyxian Guard— far too late and far too few in number to have helped with the battle—appear to clean up the mess. They had at least had one of their number help shorten the journey back from the Chasm with a nauseating but effective teleportation spell, for which Mara supposed she had to be grateful.

"He should have fallen back to the Ashen Fields just as he did the first time," Nemmo agreed. "Still, I imagine he would have preferred not to have suffered a painful death in the first place."

Mara took a long draught. "Probably not. He was just trying to save his friends—he put himself in harm's way for them." She glanced up at Iona, who was preparing something bready and sweet-smelling. "You all put yourself in harm's way for me."

"Course we did," said Iona, shoving a thick hunk of airy bread into her mouth. "That's what we all do for each other. Just how it is."

Mara tried not to let her reaction show, but her face burned and prickled unpleasantly. Partly to provide an alternative reason for her emotions, and partly because it was the only image she could think of, she swallowed and spoke quietly. "And ... Chirripeek..."

Silence smothered the group like a heavy blanket.

"He understood what might await him," Nemmo said. "Better than most, I suspect."

"It's horrible." Iona's lip began to tremble. "To just disappear like that, no chance of an afterlife or a resurrection…" She took another hefty bite and chewed, breathing loudly through what was evidently a runny nose. "All souls deserve to go to their rightful place of final rest. It's just… I don't even like thinking about it." She screwed up her face, tears squeezing themselves from her eyes and streaking down her cheeks. "But I have to feel it, but it hurts, but it's…" She descended into huge, whole-body-wracking sobs.

"Total oblivion doesn't sound like the worst thing," Varun said, raising an eyebrow without breaking his thousand-yard stare.

"He said something," Mara muttered. "Something about things not being right. That shouldn't have been as big of a group as it was, and the Nyxian Guard should've been there sooner. A lot sooner."

"That sounds like a way bigger problem than we're equipped to deal with," Iona said forlornly, sniffling and wiping her face. "That's, like, Arbiter and Sovereign territory."

"And besides," said Nemmo, peering curiously at Mara, "I shouldn't think we have the time to concern ourselves with such grand matters. Not to mention that, should we succeed in the mission that brought us together, the affairs of the Sunless Crossing will hardly be relevant to you."

"I guess not," said Mara. Her body felt as if it were shrinking into itself. There was something in her, some conflict of feeling, that she couldn't quite identify. A sense of being pulled in one direction and torn in another.

After a few minutes of silent eating, all the faces around the table downturned and gloomy, Varun gave a loud sigh and slapped the table. "Things didn't go well. No arguing with that. But we only have one thing left to collect, so ... shall we just focus on that for a bit?"

There were nods all around. Then another period of silence, this one consisting mostly of the four of them all glancing thoughtfully at each other. Mara suspected none of them wanted to speak first, and all were waiting for someone else to say something.

"Tears of a god," she said when the awkwardness became too much to bear.

Iona nodded slowly, eyes wide and gleaming. "That is ... what we need, yeah."

"Any suggestions?"

Varun made a noise of non-committal helplessness: *pffffft*.

"It's not as if there are gods just walking around," Iona pondered, bopping the remains of her bread along the table as if to demonstrate the notion of *walking around*. "Or, well, there probably are, but they don't make themselves known. Technically, this whole place was made by a god—all the souls here are only here because of Nyxia, after all—so maybe there's an argument to be made that any tears here are the tears of a god, but somehow I feel like the ritual isn't going to be persuaded by that kind of technicality."

"I've never successfully argued a spell into changing its mind," Mara agreed. She turned to Varun. "Any chance you can ascend to divinity ... ideally today, and then give me some of your tears?"

"Working on it," he said, back to staring at nothing in particular.

Mara frowned. "Are you?"

"I'm going to be the god of achieving nothing and putting off ever even trying to do anything," he said flatly.

"That would not be a good god to be," Iona said in a tone that suggested she thought she was giving extremely helpful advice.

Nemmo lifted a hand from the table, gesturing as if he were about to speak, then put it down again. Mara blinked at him expectantly.

"I mean, we all saw that and it kind of feels like you want us to ask you what you were going to say, and at this point, we're just going to wonder what it was until you say it," she told him.

"I have been in the Crossing for some time," said Nemmo. "I cannot even say with certainty how long. It may be far longer than I remember. In that time, I have come across many people and heard many strange things—some of which might be true, others of which are most likely as far from the truth as anything could be, with few reliable means of knowing the difference—"

"Oh, get to the *point*," Iona groaned, rolling her eyes so hard that her irises practically disappeared. "I like you, man, but you don't half take your time saying things."

Nemmo blinked ponderously, then his face cracked into a grin of amusement. It was a peculiar sight on his characteristically stoic face, but Mara had to admit, it suited him. When his broad gray brow softened, his eyes shone with a twinkling wit.

"There are those gods that exist beyond our ability to access them, yes?" He waited for everyone to nod. "Then there are those who are dead and whose temples are in the Storm of Broken Worlds. Also inaccessible."

Mara tried not to squirm in her chair.

"As Iona says, there are tales of the occasional deity deciding to take physical form and walking among us, but those are few and far between and unreliable," Nemmo continued. "And then there are—or so I have heard—those that are physically incarnated in the Sunless Crossing in perpetuity."

Iona spat out a wet mush of bread in disbelief. "There are *not*," she said.

"I did say I could not be certain whether such a thing is true," said Nemmo. "Some accounts certainly are not. I have heard many a fanciful story of gods choosing to exist within the Crossing for various reasons, most of which have to do with the teller of the story achieving some sort of astounding personal glory. But there is a whisper louder than most of a sect that reveres bound gods."

Iona's eyebrows twitched at that. "What do you mean, *bound*?"

Nemmo leaned forward, apparently enjoying the fact that the one who had complained about his storytelling method was now enraptured. "Many faiths have more than one god," he said in a low voice. "Often, one or more members of a given pantheon finds itself opposed to the rest. They disagree with some teaching, or rebel against the hierarchy. Perhaps they become labeled a demon or a creature of evil, or perhaps the other gods destroy them entirely." He paused. "But gods are difficult to destroy. So—as I hear it—there come to be those fallen gods who have been confined by the rest of their kind. Imprisoned, kept away from the world they once ruled, stripped of most of their power."

Varun's fingers were tapping a slow rhythm on the surface of the table. "You're saying that when gods banish one of their own from their world, they lock them away in the Sunless Crossing?"

Nemmo spread his hands wide, disclaiming responsibility for whether any of what he'd said was true. "So they say. It makes a certain amount of sense, I think. Troublesome gods who cannot be entirely annihilated are sent somewhere they can do little to interfere with the workings of the remaining deities. Of course, they still manage to snatch a few souls from their intended afterlives, but I imagine a god would think that a relatively small price to pay to have such an adversary removed from their world."

"And there's a group of people that worship these gods that the other gods didn't want around?" Mara asked.

There were other gods in my world, and some stories say they tried to cast Rekh out more than once. I guess they just ... couldn't.

"That seems to be the gist of it, yes," said Nemmo. "There are other interesting factions in the Sunless Crossing too, you know. One disparate group simply spends their time in pursuit of grand truths about the nature of all things, since the Crossing is something of a nexus point and therefore, in their view, closer to the universal and the absolute. Whether there exists such a thing as pure morality, for example."

"Domain of the good," Varun said, apparently for the sake of argument.

"Not immune to interpretation and dispute," said Nemmo, casting a quick, knowing look in Mara's direction. "There are vanishingly few gods claiming to represent pure goodness as their aspect, and those who do tend not to, ah, *do* very much." He cleared his throat. "Whether domains exist unaltered across all worlds equally is another interesting question, given that some worlds lack knowledge of entire concepts well known to others. And questions such as what it means to be *real*, and if such a thing is even a meaningful concept when multiple things that appear to be mutually exclusive are in fact all existent at once. A faction of philosophers, in short. I rather like them." He took a bite of his food. "And then, of course, there is the rumored group whose purpose is to take care of the temples and graves of dead gods in the Storm of Broken Worlds, although I understand that tends not to go well. It's not a place conducive to... well, doing anything, really."

Mara swallowed her food a little too hastily, launching into a spluttering cough. "There are people revering dead gods? For what purpose?"

Nemmo tilted his head one way, then the other. "Who can say?" he said. "There are many people, and many kinds of god a person might want to follow. Paying some sort of service to even the sort of god whose place of worship lies within the Storm could prove beneficial. Some think none would be so brave or so foolish, but I have no hesitation in assuming that it does, in fact, happen, or at least has happened at one time or another. The Crossing has existed for long enough that it seems unlikely that there is anything left to do here that at least one person has not already tried."

"So," said Varun, his face set and serious, "how do we find this … cult of imprisoned gods?"

Nemmo made what was probably supposed to be an emphatic sort of gesture with his spoon, but a glob of porridgey food slopped onto the table and rather ruined the effect. "I think," he said, "these are the kinds of things that tend to stay in secret, dark places. So, I suggest we talk to someone who knows those places well."

"Who do we know who fits that bill?" Varun asked.

Nemmo just stared at him.

"Oh," said Varun. "Right."

Following Varun's—admittedly uncertain—directions through Nox Valar, the group was soon standing at the intersection between two wide streets.

"I think there's one around here somewhere," Varun muttered, turning in circles. "I can't remember what direction we came from now. Am I the god of getting lost?" He shook his head, reorienting. "Nope, it was that way. Another domain missed. Well, almost had it."

Iona groaned and wandered off to the other corner of the intersection, putting her hand over her eyes to theatrically scan the area. Nemmo followed her at a slow trot, just tilting his head slowly from side to side as if humming to himself, seemingly unbothered by anything that was going on.

Mara frowned. "You probably shouldn't beat yourself up every time it turns out you're not the god of every single concept," she said. "Doesn't seem like a realistic expectation."

"It doesn't matter if I'm not the god of every single concept there ever is or was, as long as there's one exception. But I need to find that exception."

Mara wanted to shake him, to tell him that Iona and Nemmo were perfectly fine doing everything they could to help her without feeling they had to achieve divinity to do it, but she let him stew in his feelings. He was motivated to become stronger, and she wasn't about to get in the way of that.

"Is it really just so you can help me that you want to become a god?" she needled, hoping to strike some nerve that would get him even more worked up.

He stopped and gazed at her, then huffed and looked down at his feet. "I couldn't help Liarna. The girl I told you about. That was the first thing I'd cared about since coming here, and I failed. That fucked me up a bit. I don't mind admitting that. I'm not failing again, not if I can help it, but it's not just that."

"What, then?"

"It'd be pretty difficult for me to get out of here," he said, "what with my body having been... whatever happened to it after I died. But I want to get out of here. I want to go back to the world I came from."

That caught Mara off guard. "Why?"

"Because I want to find the bastard who killed me and my whole village," said Varun, practically snarling at his toes. "And his apprentice too." Mara's heart would have stopped if she hadn't already been dead. "And I'm going to kill them both."

He stared at the ground for a few moments longer, then glanced up at Mara as if he'd been expecting some sort of response.

"Right," she managed to choke out. "Makes sense." She coughed, then swallowed, then coughed again. "I don't think you mentioned he had an apprentice."

"Can't be completely sure it's the same one," Varun said, "but there were these stories about some ... necromancer or dark wizard or something who'd started taking territory in the area. People mostly thought of him one of two ways: either he was this terrifying boogeyman, or he was just some jumped-up idiot with a god complex who'd been lucky not to have been killed already." He took a wrathful breath. "Most of the stories were in agreement about one thing though. He wasn't working alone. Had a younger sidekick, so naturally, you assume he's training them up to be a necromancer too. Or to kill them and steal their life force at some point. I don't know how these things work."

Both of those theories are actually correct, as it turns out.

"There was talk that it was a woman. Young, attractive. People wondered whether she'd been forced into it or whether she was ... you know, some kind of evil-worshiper who was infatuated with him or something." He ran a hand through his hair, grimacing. "Lot of rumors that they were ... you know. Either with her consent or without."

Mara felt a strange twist of rage in her throat. Nothing like that had ever happened, but she felt sick at the notion that people had even thought it might have. *But of course people thought that kind of thing,* she reasoned. *People* always *imagine the most lurid things they can think of when they don't actually know. I must have looked like some kind of little girl all doey-eyed at my evil, powerful master.* She barely suppressed a shiver. *Gross.*

"Anyway," said Varun, mercifully distracting Mara from the mental image she was really, *really* trying not to conjure, "that's the plan. Ascension, then murderous vengeance."

"What's not to love?" Mara said, forcing herself to grin at him.

"Ideally, I'd actually be the god of murderous vengeance," said Varun idly, turning in circles again, "but I think that spot's already filled. Several times over, even. Also, it'd be useful for accomplishing that one thing, but I don't know whether I want to live up to the ideal of that for eternity." He pointed. "Aha."

Mara peered down his finger, seeing nothing but a plain wall. "What?"

"There's a little pattern of holes in the stone," he said, wandering over. "Almost missed it, but it's there."

Iona and Nemmo noticed and rejoined them; Varun ran the tips of his index and middle fingers over the wall, which looked perfectly smooth to Mara's eyes until she leaned in closer and squinted. There were indeed neat rows of tiny holes, each barely thicker than a hair, smoothly drilled into the marble.

"How in all the hells did you notice that?" she demanded.

"I'm extremely perceptive," Varun murmured as he peered in close, entirely failing to notice when Mara gave him an extremely obvious open-handed whack on the back of the head. "Ow."

Iona stuck her head underneath Varun's armpit to get a closer look. "So this is, what, another Chantry safe house?"

"Something like that," he said, contorting his fingers to cover what looked like a deliberate arrangement of the holes. "They're all hidden in different ways—some are under full illusions like the one where Oszcek was holed up, some just look like regular buildings with complex locks, some are underground. I heard of one that was in a pocket dimension, but I think that was probably just a rumor—probably one the Chantry started to make themselves sound impressive. Not the easiest thing to create a separate universe in a place like the Sunless Crossing. Already weird enough, time-and-place-wise." He pursed his lips and blew into the topmost hole; a high, wavering pitch whistled back through the ones his fingers hadn't covered.

A thin column of dust puffed out from within a seam in the wall that hadn't been there before. With a muffled scraping sound, a square section of the wall slid aside, creating an opening just wide enough for a person to fit through. On the other side was total darkness—magically created darkness, Mara felt certain, since the exterior light of the Sunless Crossing simply stopped, creating a straight-lined border between light and dark.

"Right," said Varun. "I don't know who'll be in here, so bear in mind it might be someone who likes me or someone who really doesn't."

He stepped inside, disappearing into the darkness. Mara followed; the moment she crossed the threshold, light and dark flipped, revealing the interior space in golden lantern-light and concealing the outside from her view.

"Neat trick," Varun murmured. "There's probably some sort of proximity-based illusion that keeps the open door hidden from anyone not already standing right next to it too."

"That's pretty much it, yeah," said a familiar voice. A figure in sharp clothing was descending a half-hidden staircase, emerging into view; their shock of white hair was the last thing to become visible.

Varun visibly tensed, drawing in a sharp breath and holding it. "Pick."

"Last time I ran into you lot, it didn't go too well for me," said Pick, folding his arms. He glanced at Iona as she appeared in the room. "Thanks for hauling us out of the debris back at the other place, but..." His gaze flicked back to Mara, then Varun. "I'm sure you'll all understand if I'm not keen to repeat the experience."

"That didn't go well," Varun admitted. "Are you alright? Is Oszcek?"

"We both got ourselves healed up," said Pick, casually digging non-existent dirt out from under a nail with the thumb of the same hand. "Still would've *reeeaaally* preferred not to have needed it, though. Plus, the Chantry wasn't super impressed with us. Nick one thing not even knowing its value, end up giving it away so as not to get killed, wind up damn near getting killed anyway. It's not the best of outcomes." He rolled his eyes theatrically. "Still, they saw fit to put us both under separate house arrest, which just means we get to lounge around in what is, frankly, a pretty cushy set-up. I've got all kinds of fruit upstairs—some real animal meat, even. That ain't easy to come by. Would offer you some, but you got my last house dropped on me, so I dunno whether I'm feeling the most hospitable."

"That's fair," said Varun.

"Yup," said Pick.

"I mean, Gront would've jumped on your house whether we were there or not," Iona muttered, but everyone opted to ignore her.

"We just want some information," Mara tried.

Pick raised a white eyebrow. "Oh, right. Information. What sort of information?"

"Maybe try being more subtle," Iona hissed at Mara's side, but she was already plowing ahead.

"We need to find a member of the cult of bound gods," she said flatly.

The eyebrow rose higher. "Right. What makes you think I'd know anything about that?"

"If you didn't," Mara said, "you'd have asked what cult I was on about."

Pick opened his mouth, then shut it again and clicked his tongue. "Yeah, that's a fair point." He raised his chin, staring down his nose at her. "Next question, then, is what you're gonna give me in return."

"I won't drop another house on you," said Mara with a saccharine smile.

Pick's confident expression faltered for a moment. He glanced at her companions. "She's bluffing, right?"

Iona spread her arms wide and shrugged exaggeratedly. "I genuinely don't know," said the cleric in a cheerful tone. "Wouldn't risk it, personally."

Pick sagged. "Look," he said, "I realize I'm not the most intimidating person, or the most powerful or whatever. But I've got some dignity, right? I can't just go giving out things for free."

His expression was beginning to remind Mara of a hilldog she'd once seen begging for a scrap of meat that was barely on the right side of rotting. She sighed and shook her head at the ceiling, as if saying *I know he's useless, just bear with him* to some unseen god.

"What would you value enough to give me what I want in return?" she asked.

His face lit up, snapping from sad and sagging to audaciously cheerful in an instant. "Well, now," he said. "There are few things the Chantry values more than the opportunity to steal something from a god, or an afterlife. Memories are a good one—lives are almost like an investment to a lot of gods.

They make a person, let that person live a life and collect experiences over time, and then they die and their soul's whisked away to the afterlife, all its memories and qualities hoarded forever. So those always attract a high value, if you've got any you're willing to give away."

Mara glanced at Nemmo. "Could that be what happened to yours?" she asked.

He shook his head. "I did wonder, but I had a mnemosymancer—a memory mage—take a look at my mind, and apparently nothing was removed in the way the Chantry would achieve such a thing. It was rather more as if nothing had been there in the first place, a complete obliteration of existence. Sometimes I wonder whether I simply came into being as I am, and—"

"What in the lamp-lit shadows are you two going on about?" Pick interrupted.

"Oh," said Mara, pointing a thumb at Nemmo, "he's an amnesiac, but not unraveled."

"Weird," said Pick, almost appreciatively.

"You know," said Iona, "we're actually hoping to take something from a god. But we need your information to be able to do that, so … can't pay you now, but I'll take whatever magicked oath you like, promising to give you part of what we get."

Pick hummed, evidently considering it. "No deal," he said. "I'm not a speculative buyer."

"I don't like you much," said Iona earnestly.

"Eh."

Varun spoke up. "The memories with the most significance are the most valuable, right? The ones we … feel the most?"

Pick nodded. "That's about it, yeah."

Varun stepped forward. "I have one."

Mara grabbed his shoulder, turning him toward her. "What are you doing?" she hissed.

"Paying the bill," said Varun. "We need his information, so I'm doing what it takes to get it."

Mara shook her head firmly. "I can't let you do that."

"Why not?"

"Because—because it doesn't make *sense*! Why would you give up something precious for me? We barely know each other!"

Varun fixed her with a hard stare. "We've been over this," he said. "Why won't you let people help you because they just want to?"

"Because I don't deserve it," she shot back.

There was a brief moment of deeply uncomfortable silence.

"Er," said Pick, "this feels like a private thing—"

"You think any of us feel like we do?" Varun demanded. "I keep getting *so close* and failing. When I was alive, I got most of the way to building a house, then it burned down. I had a farm nearly prepared to begin work, then I changed my mind and went to train as a guard in one of the big cities instead. Gave up on that too, of course. I was *this* close," he held up a finger and thumb a smidgen apart, "to opening a store, and then I got murdered for no reason. Tried to save Liarna, didn't manage it. Can't become a god. I've never succeeded at any-thing. *Anything*." He paused for breath. Mara briefly thought about interrupting, saying anything to distract him from his furious self-loathing, but something told her to let him finish. "You don't deserve help. I don't deserve the satisfaction of man-aging to finally succeed at something by helping you, whatever. But for fuck's sake, can we just let each other have it anyway?"

Mara scanned his face as he stood there, breathing heavily. "What are you going to give up?" she asked after a moment.

"Liarna," he said, and then turned to Pick. "Do it."

Pick nodded, then tapped Varun smartly on the forehead with two fingers. A thread of glowing white *something*, almost congealed in texture, passed from Varun to Pick. The swordsman's eyes rolled back in his head.

Mara turned to Iona and Nemmo. "Just so we're clear," she said, "the man made his own choice, but I think it was deeply stupid of him to give up his memory of someone that important to him, even if it hurt. Especially if it hurt."

Iona was scowling in disapproval. "How's anyone supposed to feel the things they need to feel if they don't remember the most important bits of their lives?" she muttered. "Can we just tell him about it, fill in the blanks?"

"I wouldn't do that," said Nemmo, shaking his head. "The act of excising a memory is precise in the cuts it makes, but deeply brutal in the wound it leaves. Such things are best left untouched, never to heal."

Iona harrumphed. "So I can't even tell him off."

"He'll remember that he lost something," said Nemmo, "just not precisely what. Feel free to berate him all you like for having given it up."

"Oh, good." The cleric turned her attention to Mara. "So if you think it's stupid not to feel what you need to feel, have you reconsidered pledging your eternal devotion to Aurethen? Or, you know, just switching to any god with a nicer afterlife where you'll get to keep having emotions?"

"You've really gotta stop trying to convert me," Mara said, shaking her head. "I don't have time to get in a whole new god's good graces." She took a shaky breath, a wave of cold nausea suddenly hitting her. "It's been long enough now that I could get plucked out of here and shoved into a fresh corpse at any moment."

"Well," said Iona, "let's hope that doesn't happen, eh?" She gave a double thumbs-up, flashing a toothy smirk.

"All done," said Pick. Mara turned back to see him clutching a fist-sized ball of the same glowing substance he'd pulled from

Varun's head, which he tucked inside a pocket. It created no visible bulge, suggesting that it had either shrunk to fit neatly within or that Pick's pockets were deeper than they looked. Varun himself was standing still, blinking as if waking up from a deep sleep. "Much obliged. This'll work, I think."

"Do different memories have different values?" Mara asked, curious. It was the sort of currency in which Raskith might have invested had he known how: valuable for sale, certainly, but also deeply personal, the kind of thing that could be used to gain more than just money.

"This one's glowing pretty vividly," said Pick, "which generally means there's a lot of intense feeling associated with it. I can't actually look and see what it is though. Takes a whole different set of skills to do that."

"Wait," said Iona, "I'm feeling everything all the time. I should've just given you a memory of what I had for breakfast last week." She smiled brightly to herself, practically radiating warmth and delight at the mere thought of whatever last week's breakfast had been.

Pick shrugged. "You still could if you want. Don't think I've got much else to offer in return right now, of course."

Varun blinked and shook his head as if waking up, then turned to the others with a bemused expression. "Did I just give something up?"

"You did," said Iona, huffing at him and scrunching her face up in absolute disapproval.

"Huh," said Varun. "That's weird. I remember deciding to give up a memory, and I remember that I had that memory, and it was important, but I have no idea what it was. It's like looking at a painting with a bit cut out of it—I can see there should be something filling the gap, but not what."

"Good for you," said Pick. "See? He doesn't even know what he's missing out on. What a favorable transaction for all involved."

"Just keep up your side of the bargain," Iona practically growled.

Pick raised his hands in mock surrender. "Course. What do I have if not my word and my reputation?" He puffed his cheeks out, then frowned. "What did I say I'd do for you again?"

"Cult of bound gods," Mara said through gritted teeth.

"Ah, that's the one." Pick adjusted his clothing with a neat motion. "Well, I can't exactly *introduce* you to 'em, since they're very much underground and secretive and that, but—"

Iona dashed forward and gripped the thief by the throat, which for her meant reaching up above her head. She pushed him back against a wall, her robe slipping down her arm to show the muscles in her forearm bulging. "We gave you what you asked for," the cleric hissed, simmering with rage. "We didn't do that for nothing. You *give us* what we bought from you."

Pick's face was rapidly turning purple; he patted Iona's wrist desperately, signaling submission. "Alright!" he choked as she released him. "I might know where one of the groups meets. That enough?"

Iona glanced back at Mara.

It's all we're gonna get.

Mara nodded; Iona backed away from Pick, staring daggers at the white-haired Chantry member. He rubbed his throat, spluttering intermittently. "I'll draw you a map?" he said, voice hoarse and scratchy.

"Hells, no," said Mara. "Varun gave you—" She stopped herself, glanced at the swordsman, and set her jaw. "He gave you something important," she said. "For that price, you're taking us there."

"I'm not supposed to leave the safe house," Pick moaned in a tone Mara would have expected from a child who was upset that their parents hadn't bought them a sugared peach: *but I waaaant oooooone.*

Iona flexed her fingers menacingly.

Pick sighed and gestured for them to follow.

CHAPTER 24

Pick led them out of Nox Valar and down the vast tunnel that was Ascension Row. As they reached the bottom, where the corridor of stone opened out into the Ashen Fields, Pick turned sharply and strode alongside the base of the vertical cliff upon which the marble city sat.

"What are the odds he's leading us into some kind of ambush so he can just steal our stuff and get back in the Chantry's good graces?" Mara muttered to Varun as they followed.

"I don't think so," Varun said. "The Chantry can be a lot of things, including outright robbers and murderers when it suits them, but they're rarely dishonest in a situation like this. He named a price, we paid it. If that breaks down, business stops getting done."

"Would they lie about what they had to offer if they thought it'd get them a better price?"

"Oh absolutely."

Mara sighed. "I'm not holding my breath that this is going to give us what we need," she said. "But I have no idea what we do if it doesn't."

"We make a new plan and try again," said Varun.

Mara narrowed her eyes at him. He seemed lighter, more optimistic. She hated it. Not just because she found cheerful people immensely irritating in general, but because Varun shouldn't have felt that way. He had suffered. To lose that was to lose what drove him to make things better in the future.

"I don't think I have time for a second plan," she said in the end, turning her gaze back toward Pick.

The thief stopped beside what looked like any other part of the cliff. "Reckon this is it about here," he said, nodding toward the wall.

Mara waited for him to do something. He just stood there, looking between them and the blank stretch of sheer rock.

"How do we get in?" she asked.

"Buggered if I know," he said. "I just heard this is where they meet. A mate wondered if it might be worth breaking in to steal whatever dark relics they've probably got in there, but I guess nobody ever did. Or someone did and died doing it. Who knows?"

"You," said Iona, who'd been staying close to Pick as if making sure he wasn't about to run off, "are infuriatingly unhelpful."

"Nah," said Pick. "I'm exactly as helpful as any given situation deserves, I reckon."

Iona punched him in the stomach.

"Probably deserved that," Pick wheezed.

"You did," Mara confirmed. She turned to the rock and ran her hands over it. Nothing but smooth stone. "Anyone got any kind of spell for dispelling illusions or anything?"

Iona flicked a finger toward the wall, then shrugged. "Didn't do anything," she said, "but then it wouldn't if this is a spell from a different... what'd you call them, Nemmo, *system*? Spells that interact with other spells only work on magic from the same world or whatever, right?"

Mara clicked her tongue, thinking. *Raskith had a ritual spell for revealing hidden things*, she remembered. *Never taught it to me, but I think I remember what it looks like. Maybe this isn't a spell at all, but some other kind of hidden place… Worth a try.*

"I'm gonna try something," she declared, kneeling. "I don't have the right components, so this might not work, but I can at least shape the spell." She drew a few lines from memory and a general understanding of which shapes and angles ought to create the effect she was looking for. The ritual circle looked sloppy, but she pushed her magic through it anyway.

The faintest sliver of golden light traced a ten-foot square in the stone.

"Well, look at that," said Iona. She nodded appreciatively. "Er, what *am* I looking at?"

"There's something hidden here," Mara murmured, following the line of light with her finger. There was no seam she could feel, no obvious mechanism, and the stone on both sides of the square felt perfectly real and material—not an illusion, as far as she could detect. "Either a door with some kind of concealed method to open it, or a spell that's not just making an image of stone but projecting an actual physical stone wall, which would be impressive."

"I have heard of such things," Nemmo declared, clearing his throat and standing before the wall. He uttered a series of noises that Mara thought might have been words in various languages, holding his hands aloft as if pushing against an invisible wall a few feet from the real one. Nothing happened.

"How come I didn't understand that?" Iona asked.

"Ah," said Nemmo, looking a little frustrated. "I think there are some quirks to the Crossing's translation effect—it seems to rely on one's own perception of speech, both the speaker's and the listener's, which I think explains the approach to idioms we discussed before. I am now speaking in what I assume was my native language in life, so this feels to me like a natural tongue that can be comprehended without effort. Thus, you hear it in the language to which you have the same relation of ease and fluency. If I choose to speak in a language in which I myself am not entirely versed, then you hear an equivalent tongue other than your own. I am given to understand that cants and ciphers are similarly indecipherable except to those the writer or speaker believes ought to be able to understand them, or perhaps to those who believe they themselves ought to be able to understand, which is somewhat useful for less-than-legal activities."

"Weeeeeird," said Iona.

Nemmo nodded. "Quite." He paused. "Also, it permits one to adopt an accent for the purposes of humor."

Iona clapped her hands in delight, immediately rattling off a rapid-fire sequence of tongue-twisting phrases in various accents that sounded to Mara's ears very much like ones native to countries bordering her own.

I guess if it's to do with perceptual equivalence, I'm hearing the accents of places that mean similar things to me as the ones Iona's imitating do to her. If she's putting on a voice from a place that was a neighboring ally to her home, I'll hear something like the accent of a place my country saw as a neighboring ally.

Iona finished her oration and beamed expectantly, as if waiting for applause. Nemmo simply sighed, folding his arms and regarding the stubborn cliff. "I had rather hoped this might be the sort of hidden door that requires a password."

Iona stuck her tongue out. "Just 'cause you said a bunch of things to it in another language, how d'you know any of it was the password?"

"Well," said Nemmo amiably, "I suppose that is the relevant question."

Iona turned and hit the wall with her hammer. Other than a resounding metal-on-stone smashing sound that reverberated through Mara's teeth, it had no effect. The cleric huffed and pointed the still-ringing head of her hammer in Pick's direction; the thief quavered. "You're *sure* you don't know how to get in?" she demanded.

"Very sure," Pick said, nodding rapidly. "Only thing I know about the place, other than there's apparently a cult in there, is it's been here a long time. Like, really long. Before almost anyone who's still here would remember, that kinda long."

Nemmo tapped his fingers to his chin thoughtfully. "But it was not always this?"

"How would I know?" Pick said. "But nah, probably not. Someone made a hidden place in the foundation of the city at some point, seems the most likeliest scenario."

Nemmo hummed deeply, then folded his fingers together and closed his eyes. The hum vibrated through his body to the ashen grass beneath, and through that to Mara. She felt the deep, resonant harmonics stirring things in her memory, bringing back images and sounds and smells of a life she'd left behind so long ago that she no longer felt it had ever been hers. She closed her eyes and allowed the sound to tremble through her, a constant, comforting low sonority with shifting overtones that washed new colors, new memories, through her more quickly than she could keep up with.

The sound ended, fading away like the last red leaf of autumn. Mara kept her eyes closed for a moment, trying to savor the memories for as long as she could, that impossible sweetness achievable only by things that have long disappeared into the past. When she couldn't deny that the image was gone, she opened her eyes, blinking away—no, that mustn't be a tear, surely, just dust from standing amidst swaying ash-coated blades for so long. Varun was blinking too, surreptitiously dabbing his fingers to his cheek. Pick was staring at the ground, swallowing hard. Iona, of course, had burst into a full-throated wail that reminded Mara of the time she'd disturbed two foxpuffins that were trying to mate on the crenellations of Raskith's tower.

Nemmo stepped toward the wall and touched it delicately with one fingertip. The stone disappeared, whisked away into nonexistence. Dividing the previously unbroken stretch of rock from itself, a square tunnel led downward into darkness; the orange glow of torches bloomed at the place where the route turned and disappeared from view.

"What did you do?" Mara asked, doing her best to keep her voice level despite the thickness of her throat.

"I made the world remember being other than as it is," said Nemmo quietly, almost reverently. "Or, perhaps, I made this part forget where it sits in time, relative to the rest of the place." He turned and regarded the others with an air of mild confusion. "Apologies," he said, "but I think perhaps I may have briefly made the rest of you forget when and where we are too."

Mara gave a dismissive don't-worry-about-it wave. "It's fine," she said, flashing the briefest of smiles to emphasize just how fine it was.

Varun walked up beside Nemmo, admiring the clean lines of the hole that had appeared in the stone. "So ... the wall thinks it's in a past time when there was no concealing effect?"

"Possibly quite a narrow moment," Nemmo said, "between the creation of the entrance and the placing of the door, or spell, or whatever it was that has kept things out for so long."

"That's ridiculous," said Varun, staring at Nemmo with new appreciation.

"Everything used to be so beautiful!" Iona wailed, tears and snot coating the lower half of her face. "The children were so pure and—and the trees were all big, and the air smelled of sugar and the rivers were clear and—"

Mara slapped her.

"Thanks," said Iona, working her jaw and wiping her face with her sleeve. "Needed that, probably." She gave Nemmo her most angular scowl, which on her soft-featured round face was less a predatorial lion and more a mildly grumpy housecat. "Don't do that again!" she commanded, brandishing an irate finger. "I mean, maybe tomorrow or something, because it was actually really nice, but not while we're in the middle of something!"

"Understood," said Nemmo, inclining his head graciously. "I believe I will be unable to repeat the effect for at least a day or two, in any case."

"Can I go now?" Pick asked.

"Oh," said Mara, who had almost entirely forgotten that he was there. "Er, yeah. I guess."

"If this turns out not to be what you say it is," snapped Iona, whirling to direct her berating finger at Pick, "I will find you and crush your bones with a brick."

The thief swallowed. "Noted." He gave a brief, abrupt wave, then darted off into the grass and vanished like a whisper in an earthquake.

Mara stepped up beside her companions, standing shoulder-to-shoulder at the threshold. "We don't know what we're going to find down here," she said. "You're all sure you want to come?"

"Course," said Iona, giving Mara a reassuring pat on the arm.

"We're in this," said Varun.

Nemmo simply nodded.

Mara took a deep breath, then stepped from the Ashen Fields into the hidden tunnel in the foundations of Nox Valar.

CHAPTER 25

The tunnel wound on for what felt like an impossibly long time—longer even than Ascension Row, albeit mercifully trending downward. Still, even without an unfavorable incline, Mara had to pump renewed strength into her legs more than once. Her knees and ankles ached with every step down the uneven, pebble-littered tilt.

Intermittent torches burning with real flame—not the magical rainbow spectra of the torches that heralded arrival into Nox Valar—washed the wide space in a faint orange glow that turned ragged and frayed when it touched the roughly carved walls; thin threads of light and shadow wove themselves together, making the tunnel feel darker than it was.

"Someone's been here recently," Varun observed. "Those aren't enchanted torches—that's actual fuel burning."

"We must be nearly at the end," Iona moaned. "Nobody could keep walking for this long just to do cult things. Most *gods* wouldn't want to walk for this long!" She threw up her hands, then clapped them to her cheeks as if shocked at her own words. "I mean," she rattled off, "of course gods are very good at walking, sorry if you're a god and you're listening, I was just exaggerating, it's just that it's very long, very sorry."

Mara pondered that. "Where do you think we are?"

The cleric shrugged. "Not a clue. We've not gone in a straight line, so for all I know, we're just spiraling down and down and down beneath Nox Valar. We didn't pop out over the Ashen Fields on our way down through the plateau the city's built on, but we could well be below ground level by now…"

"If I had to hazard a guess," said Nemmo, "I might suspect us to be somewhere beneath the region of the Road to Eternity." He gestured vaguely behind them. "A short time ago, there was a slightly steeper turn in our path, followed by a more consistent arc. Pure speculation, of course, but I cannot help but be reminded of turning onto that circular road."

"It'd make sense," Iona said darkly. "Above is where we pay tribute to those gods who give us miracles and beauty. Below is where those who were cast out of the light dwell."

Mara suppressed a shiver, thinking of how Rekh's name had been omitted from the list of deities in Aurethen's temple.

Do I really want to give my eternal afterlife to a god that openly acts as an agent of pain and perversion of the natural way of things? She shook her head, giving herself a mental slap on the cheek. *Too late to change your mind now, Mara. It's Rekh's afterlife or servitude under Raskith, forced to wreak havoc on the living.*

They came to an abrupt halt as a low sound, muffled and dampened by distance, swam up the tunnel: voices, thick with the natural reverberation of the enclosed space. Slowly, cautiously, they continued down the tunnel until the voices grew louder, brighter, nearer. Light shone more clearly, more radiantly, from around one final corner.

"I guess this is it," Iona whispered.

Without pausing to think, Mara stepped around the last turn.

She groaned. "Oh, for hells' sakes."

"And what," said Gront, "might you be doing here?"

"I could ask you the same question!" Mara retorted, throwing her hands up in exasperation.

Gront had been kneeling in front of a low stone altar, a robe the color of dark wine draped around his shoulders, but he stood and turned calmly, his posture warm like a reverend welcoming his congregation. His group—Duznit, Vaarschraaff, Riddeill—stood around the edges of the wide space, looking far less hospitable than their leader. The area between them had been carved into a rounded space that resembled nothing so much as an underground church, complete with stone pews that, judging from the lack of any visible seam between them and the floor beneath, had been hewn into shape when the cavern was built. Icons and sigils Mara didn't recognize littered the nooks and niches of the curved wall, carved in wood or painted on canvas or sculpted in clay.

"This is a place of worship," said Gront.

"I can see that," said Mara. Behind her, she heard Iona, Varun, and Nemmo emerging cautiously into the space.

"You are not worshippers here," said Gront. His voice, always deep like the darkest parts of the ocean, carried a sharpness, a warning of danger. "This place is not yours."

"I need something," said Mara. "It doesn't have to concern you."

"Well, now," said Gront. He made a tiny beckoning motion without lifting his hand from his side, and in an instant, his three compatriots had slipped behind him and formed a diamond with Gront as the frontmost point. "That rather depends on precisely what it is you need, I should think."

Iona stepped forward, raising her hammer in both hands. "What do you do in this place?" she hissed.

Gront turned his head from one side to the other, casting a performative look around the whole space. "Worship," he said.

"Of whom?" Iona demanded.

Gront's broad shoulders rose, then fell. Steam puffed from his nostrils. "Where I come from," he said eventually, "there are many gods for the world's people to revere. But my people... well, most of my people dislike the notion of worship. Admiration of strength, perhaps, but I come from a culture of people who, on the whole, would prefer to fight a being as powerful as a god to prove their strength than ever bow before one." His nose twitched. "After I came here, I discovered that there were many more gods than I had known. I heard a tale..." He turned to Vaarschraaff, who gave him a slight nod. "A tale of a god who fell from their power for the crime of wanting to empower the people over whom the other gods desired to rule. There are many such tales in different cultures, in fact."

He paused for a moment. Mara waited.

"But this particular god," he continued, "desired not just to empower mortals, but to end the power of the other gods. To take away their weapons and bring a final close to the games they played with one another, games that destroyed whole countries in a single turn." He raised his head, golden eyes boring into Mara. "Personally, I can't help but feel ... sympathetic. My own world was always ravaged by war, but by the time I left it, there was almost nothing else. Gods directing their pawns for purposes too many people were happy to accept as mysterious, unknowable, divine. People threw their lives away, and ended others, for the sake of a master plan they believed existed beyond their sight."

"I think a lot of people in a lot of worlds have probably seen the same thing," Varun said from behind Mara.

"True," said Gront. "Still, I found myself gravitating toward this god who would remove mortals from the game tables of the divine. Put us in charge of our own fates." He gestured around. "So, I come here to pray, for that god is not well-liked among the Crossing's powers that be. You might have noticed it's something of a pro-divine-power establishment." He shifted, for the first time looking slightly uncomfortable. "And one of the things my god would do," he continued, rubbing the back of his neck, "is do away with a place such as this entirely. It serves no purpose but to return us to the game, reusing our pieces on the same boards."

"Are you saying you want the Crossing … gone?" Mara asked.

Gront turned his palms up in a neither-here-nor-there gesture, smiling faintly. "Personally, I'm in no rush to enact that part of the plan, but … I can't say I disagree." He fixed Mara with his warm amber eyes. She felt as if she might be absorbed into them, crystalizing into a solid piece of resin like a fossilized bug. "I do not actively work to subvert the order here. I do not harm anyone. I simply come here to reflect upon the will of the god I follow. I differ only from those on the Road to Eternity above us in that I cannot do so openly."

"How do you know this anyway," Mara asked, "if it's all so secretive? Has your god spoken to you, told you its teachings, or have you learned them from somewhere else?"

Gront's great brow furrowed. "I … heard whispers on the wind. I listened, and I looked closer, and I followed the trail. And then…" He spread his hands wide. "Then, when one's god is hidden, faith takes over. Not everyone is so lucky as to have a god who makes everything direct and clear."

Mara scoffed. *Rekh might not be a good god, but he does at least pass on his instructions directly. I don't think a god who spells out their teachings in whispers on the wind is for me.*

"What about the rest of you?" Iona asked, directing the question to the three standing behind Gront's hulking frame. "Do you worship the same god?"

Duznit shrugged. "Not particularly a fan of the worship thing in general, to be honest with ya." He squinted at Iona in the torchlight. "You really do look familiar."

"Got one of those faces," Iona said.

"I follow another," rasped Vaarschraaff. Her voice was like coral scraping over an ossified ribcage buried in grains of red stone beneath foaming waves. "But I come when my friend worships. Moral support."

Riddeill just held up his hand and shook it in the universal sign for *a little yes, a little no*.

"How do you get down here, anyway?" Varun asked, the mundane question slipping through the mist of unresolved tension like a firefly. "Under normal circumstances, I mean."

Gront frowned. "You turn the handle and the door opens."

Iona groaned at the ceiling. "There was a *handle*," she lamented.

The cloaked leonid cleared his throat with a sound like a boulder falling into a mossy valley. "What do you want here?" he asked.

"I need the tears of a god," Mara said bluntly. *No point lying about it.* "Know of any that spend a lot of time crying?"

Gront's eyes widened for a moment before he controlled his expression. "An interesting requirement," he said. "You couldn't have asked around the Road to Eternity?"

"Those gods aren't *here*," Mara said. "I need one that's physically in the Crossing."

Gront regarded her for a moment, then shook his head and let out a short growl of laughter. "You are one of the strangest people I've met here, and that's saying something."

"Do you know of any crying gods?" Mara repeated.

"What makes you think I would know what's down here?" Gront asked. "My god isn't one of the imprisoned ones, just not one whose worshippers are looked on kindly."

"Wait," said Iona, "yours isn't even down here?"

Gront shook his head. "There are the bound, and then there are ... the ones whose prayers are said in secret. Some overlap. But no, I haven't heard of a crying god—not that what I've heard of counts for much. There is no single church of the bound gods, at least not to my knowledge—"

"Albtraum's trying to start one," Duznit piped up.

"There is no church accepted as the definite church by anyone except its own devotees," Gront said smoothly, "so I don't exactly make a point of knowing everything that's ever been locked up. I haven't been into the deep reaches of this place."

"I did once," said Duznit.

Gront turned to the goblin, not bothering to hide the surprise on his face this time. "Why'd you do that?"

Duznit shrugged. "You were praying for ages. Got bored. Had a wander."

"Did you find anything?" Mara asked.

"Got spooked, turned back, but ... I heard sobbing," said Duznit, his eyes glazing slightly. "Terrible, terrible sobbing. Like someone had suffered more than anyone could possibly suffer in a hundred lifetimes, and they couldn't die until they'd cried enough to wash away all of that."

"Perfect," said Mara.

"That's *horrible*," said Iona at the same time.

"Yeah," said Duznit, blinking, "was a bit."

"Which way?" Mara asked.

The goblin pointed to the only other tunnel leading out of the cavern of worship. "There're a bunch of smaller tunnels leading off that one. Think it was the fourth or fifth left. You'll hear it, probably."

"What do you plan to do?" asked Gront. "Find a crying god and ask it nicely if you can take some of its tears?"

"Something like that," said Mara. "Or punch it until it gives them to me. They're bound, right? Depowered?"

Vaarschraaff gave a sharp, rasping chuckle.

"Bound they might be, little person," said Gront, "but still gods. Stuffing a divine power into a prison of flesh and chains makes it smaller, yes, but denser. They are what they are by their nature. That might be suppressed, but it can't be taken away."

Mara drew her shoulders back, standing tall and straight. "This is probably my only chance," she said. "Even if it's stupid, I can't turn back now."

"Very well," said Gront, and he stepped aside.

Mara walked straight past him and down the next tunnel. She didn't look back, but after a few moments' hesitation, she heard her companions follow.

"Oh!" yapped Duznit as Mara's group passed him, snapping his fingers. The next word out of his mouth sounded like a name, but not one Mara knew.

"Nope," said Iona. "Nope, nope, nope."

Mara kept walking.

Like the one before, this tunnel was lit with wall-mounted torches. Unlike before, the flames that spilled and sloshed in the black iron bowls were clearly anything but natural. It burned a bizarre silver-flecked black, constantly in motion, each torch a tiny crashing ocean of fire. Its light cast the tunnel in an imitation of moonlit shadow: most of Mara's vision was occupied by a pure, deep, rich darkness, but the occasional ridge and bump in the wall stood out in pale white flashes. Once they were out of sight of the church room, she turned to look at the others; their faces reflected gentle silver light, looming out of the blackness that surrounded them.

Mara felt strangely at home.

The feeling evidently wasn't shared by the others though. Varun was trying to hide the fact that his teeth were chattering;

Nemmo's eyes were wide, in constant fearful motion; Iona had her arms wrapped around her torso as if trying to embrace herself.

"You don't have to come," Mara said.

Varun's eyes flicked to her, a little sliver of knife-like gleaming motion. "It's a bit late for that now," he observed.

"I am with you," said Nemmo, "but … be careful. More than careful. Something bites at me about this place. It does not want us here."

Mara nodded. "I don't want it to come to this," she said, "but be ready for a fight."

Varun unsheathed his swords and held them in front of him, visibly concentrating on the blades. Nothing happened.

"What's…?" He tried again. Nothing.

"Some kind of anti-magic effect?" Mara hazarded. "One that covers all magics, if this place has gods from all across the worlds?" To test the hypothesis, she held up a finger and drew on the light that surrounded them, condensing a little aura into a tiny ball. A moment later, a mote of gray luminescence floated above her fingertip.

"I can't feel my power," Varun whispered. "It's like my connection to Invars is … gone."

"Maybe this place doesn't tolerate gods at all," Mara muttered.

Iona, her face still downcast and shadowed, waved a hand. A stone on the ground lifted a few inches, then fell back down with a quiet crack. "It feels harder," she said quietly. "Like pulling the magic out of a swamp. But it's there. Aurethen's with me."

Varun's face went even whiter in the silver dusk. "Then … Invars has left me?"

Iona shrugged without looking at him. "You gave up the part of your history that most motivated you to effect change in the world," she said tonelessly. "He made you his champion for a reason, and you let that reason go."

Varun's eyes widened. Mara took a step closer to Iona and put a hand on the cleric's shoulder. "Hey," she said. "What's going on with you?"

Iona lifted her chin to look at Mara, then turned her face away. "I'll be alright," she said. "Just... I didn't think I'd ever hear that name again. All the worlds, all the realities, and the Crossing won't let me forget that one."

"We need to get ourselves together," Mara insisted, looking at the three of them. Varun looked like someone had just killed his dog; Nemmo was visibly twitching, as if being constantly jabbed in the ribs; Iona looked determined not to express anything at all, which would generally have been fine by Mara, but was so out of character for Iona that it was perhaps the most concerning thing of all. "We're about to confront a god. We have to be ready."

"I do not know that it is possible to be ready for such a thing," said Nemmo, his voice wavering.

"Gods and hells!" Mara snapped. "I'll go by myself!"

"We can't let you do that," said Iona, glancing at Mara. Her voice was still muted, but she at least looked less as if she might simply stop moving and stay there for the rest of her afterlife. "We're a party, remember?"

"Right," Mara said, nodding enthusiastically. *There we go. Get them in that hero mindset. Heroes wouldn't abandon a friend. Classic.* "Like the Rainbow Rangers, or whatever. Working together, getting things done. Right?"

Varun nodded, taking a deep breath. "I hit things with non-divine swords before, and I can do it again." He gave a hesitant half-smile.

"I shall do what I can," said Nemmo simply. He stood a little taller, his body tensing for a moment as he controlled his shivering.

"That's all I can ask," said Mara.

She turned and led them down the corridor. Faintly visible shadows within shadows, holes even blacker than the omnipresent blackness, suggested forks and new paths on either side.

"Duznit said it was the fourth or fifth left," she muttered. "And we'd know it because we'd hear it."

She had no idea how many turnings they passed. It might have been dozens, or it might have been only one or two; the darker patches that implied new tunnels could just as easily have been nothing more than rock a little more or less smooth than its immediate surroundings.

Then she heard it.

It was no cry a living being ought to be able to make, nor one any mortal ears should have to hear. It bounced off the walls of the tunnel, hitting its own vibrations midair, growing and looping and feeding off itself like an unbroken ring of swollen leeches all endlessly sucking the blood from one to the next, around and around in a nauseating circle. It jabbed boiling and freezing needles into the most sensitive parts of Mara's brain; it cut off slices of her soul, hammered them into a flat, mushy paste, then jammed them back in again; it bit at her with scraping, rough-edged teeth and sanded the wounds with a gritted tongue.

Mara blinked, realizing she was lying on the cold stone floor of the tunnel. The sound faded, though an ambient reverberation continued to saturate the air around her. The others were all similarly afflicted: prone, or in the process of getting up, hands pressed to ears and temples.

"What in the name of all that murders and despairs was that?" Varun whispered.

"I think that might have been a god," Mara murmured. She shook her head, trying to clear the sensation that it had been filled with a sludge of stone dust and thick slime.

"We can't—" Iona gasped, her terrified eyes more white than iris or pupil. "We can't go to that—that thing, we can't."

"We have to," Mara said grimly, using the wall as support to push herself upright. "We've come this far."

She realized then that Nemmo had been letting out a high-pitched, distressed whine since the appalling cry had retreated. He was sitting and holding his knees, staring at nothing.

"Hey," she said, leaning down and putting a hand on his shoulder. His eyes whipped across to hers, staring at her with an intensity she'd never seen from him. "Look, if you need to turn back, I can do this by myself. If I die, I just come back tomorrow."

The whimper died in Nemmo's throat. He shook his head decisively. "No," he said, his voice scratchy and pained. "I said I would aid you however I could. That has not changed."

He held out a trembling hand; she took it and pulled him to his feet. Iona and Varun, though their faces looked as if they'd seen death itself—in a way, she supposed, they all had—met her eyes and nodded.

"Then this is the way," said Mara quietly, and headed down the tunnel the sound had come from.

There were no more torches, but there was a sourceless light that gave her better visibility than she'd had for some time. Empty cells lined the sides of this new tunnel, cells whose bars were of a thick metal that was blacker than black.

At the end of the tunnel was a door of richly lacquered wood, a simple iron handle set in its center.

"Ready?" Mara asked.

"No," said Iona.

"Gods, no," said Varun.

"Absolutely not," said Nemmo.

Mara almost laughed. "Me neither."

She opened the door.

CHAPTER 26

On the gleaming, polished black-and-white stone floor of the circular room lay a woman. Her hair and skin glowed rich and golden; she wore a simple white dress that radiated a comforting light. She was sprawled face-down, hands up near her head. An aureate thread extended from her ankle across the floor, winding in spirals until it disappeared into a shadowed alcove within the high wall.

Mara took a cautious step inside the room. The others followed. The door closed behind them with a thud; when Mara glanced back, it was gone. There was nothing but a smooth stone wall.

"Is this…?" she whispered as quietly as she could.

"I don't know," someone whispered back. She wasn't sure who.

The woman on the floor gave a great sob that wracked her body. Mara stiffened, but she felt no pain: it was, she thought, the same voice, the same tone, but without the terrible effects of the cry they had heard before.

"Are you alright?" came Varun's voice from behind her.

The golden woman quieted and lay still for a moment. Then she pressed her palms into the floor beside her head and pushed herself to a kneeling position, facing them. Her hair covered her face, but Mara could see the perfectly smooth skin of her jaw and ear poking out.

"Why have you come?" the woman asked in a voice like a bell ringing out across a silver field beneath a clear blue sky.

Um. Mara froze, thinking. *Something tells me it's not a good idea to tell her I came to take something from her.*

"I … am in pain," she said after a moment. "Like you."

The woman shook her head, a faint, regretful smile just about visible as her hair swished in front of her lips. "Nobody is in pain like me."

Mara took one more tentative step forward. "Would it help you ease your pain if you could … take away a little pain from someone else?"

"Oh," she said. "You come to ask for something."

Her voice hardened, the sound turning calcified and rusted. Mara heard Nemmo begin to mutter something under his breath behind her.

"Not to ask," Mara said. "I want to understand. I want to help take away some of what you feel."

I have absolutely no idea whether this is the right approach, but it's all I can think to say right now.

"Really?" A warm tinge of hope entered her voice again.

"What's your name?" Mara asked, extending a hand.

Why am I reaching out to her? This is a very bad idea. Very, very bad idea—

A golden hand shot up, fingers snapping closed around Mara's wrist. The woman tilted her head, letting her hair fall away from her face. She turned her eyes on Mara, and they were abyssal pits of red and black. "Rhúnn," she said, opening her mouth in a wide smile.

Mara couldn't look away. Dimly, as if through a thickly pouring curtain of blood, she heard a gasp from behind her, followed by a wail of despair. But that didn't matter. No, what mattered was the face that dominated her vision: golden skin cracking, terrible eyes widening in ever-deeper pools, that smile that grew and grew until Mara felt as if she'd already been swallowed and just hadn't yet realized she was dead and digested. She was disappearing, devoured and torn into infinitesimal shreds by something so much greater than herself that she couldn't begin to understand it.

Hands grabbed her from behind and tore her away, ripping her out of the unending descent that was the god before her. Varun put his body protectively between Mara and Rhúnn; Iona held Mara's face, staring desperately into her eyes.

"Are you alright?" the cleric demanded.

Mara nodded, blinking, trying to dispel the feeling that she'd been shredded and imperfectly woven back together.

"We have to go!" Iona pleaded. "We can't be here!"

"But you only just got here," said the voice of Rhúnn.

Mara turned toward the golden woman. She stood there, her face broken in half by that consuming smile.

"I'm sorry if I disturbed you," Mara managed to gasp.

"Oh, not at all," said Rhúnn, the gaping mouth continuing to open independently of the words her voice was speaking. "Guests are always welcome."

The thread at the golden woman's ankle went taut. Her body fell limp, ragdoll-yanked into the obscured alcove on the other side of the room.

"We can't be here," Iona muttered. "We can't, we can't, we can't be here."

A single cry, devoid of echo or distortion, rang out around the room. Mara stumbled back, feeling the cold stabs of pain in the deep parts of her mind. Immense fingers the color of ash-flecked obsidian extended lazily from the shadows, bracing themselves against the threshold. A hard-muscled forearm followed, trailing clanking chains of mingled onyx and gold; the thick links didn't just wrap or tie around the limb, but buried themselves in the flesh, pulling and tearing at old wounds with every movement.

Then came Rhúnn in its fullness, pulling itself free from the shadows. Its arms were many and as varied in form as the denizens of the Crossing, and all but one were wrapped, held pressed to its torso by an encircling wreath of chains of different thicknesses, all fastened to the god's body by links that hungrily delved into its flesh and embedded themselves beneath muscle and bone. Beneath the swaddle of enfolding limbs and metal, its torso was that of a giant human. The legs of Rhúnn were bullish and powerful, black-furred at the knees and chitinous at the ankles, and its skin writhed and squirmed like the crawling things beneath the earth. Its head was long and equine, possessed of an elegant brutality, garlanded with a mane of black fire. Steam billowed from flared nostrils. Its eyes were infinite atrocities.

What looked like an empty sack of some dull yellow cloth trailed behind it by a thread. The golden woman, Mara realized, her skin emptied of its contents, whatever flesh or power had animated her returned to the true body of Rhúnn.

"Oh, no," wailed Iona. "No, no..."

Mara put a hand on her shoulder. "We're here together," she said, though her voice wavered and shattered any illusion of bravery. "Just ... lend me whatever strength you can, and I'll protect you."

She turned to the others: Nemmo had his eyes closed, still muttering something under his breath. Varun was staring at Rhúnn, frozen.

"Hey," she hissed. "We have to be in this together."

"Why," Varun murmured, "did we ever think we could do this?"

"We can!" Mara insisted. "We're already here—we have no choice now! It's fight or die."

Iona let out a sob. "Rhúnn the Choked," she whispered. She held out one finger and touched Mara limply on the arm; Mara felt a weak infusion of strength flowing through her, a trickle rather than a torrent. The death magic that usually inhabited her body still fled from Iona's bright power, but instead of scouring her clean and filling her with energy, all Mara felt was a vague, listless bump of refreshment, as if she'd drunk a strong tea.

We're here now. Nothing else for it.

Mara let out a furious scream and charged, firing off hasty beams of power from her fingers. As she reached the bound god, she launched herself into the air and slammed a palm into its jaw, striking as hard as she could at the underside of that horse-like head.

Taking her lead, Varun leaped in with a vicious whirl of his blades, carving patterns in the air before slicing at Rhúnn's flesh. His swords, dull and unlit, bounced off harmlessly; the cracking sound of metal on stone rang through the chamber.

"No!" came the distraught cry from Iona, and then the cleric was beside them, swinging her hammer with all the strength she could muster.

Rhúnn stood and absorbed their best efforts. Strike after strike crashed off its body, moving it no more than a single falling leaf could move the ground by landing on it. Varun screamed and slammed both his blades into Rhúnn's abdomen with vicious, sawing cuts. For a moment, Mara thought the skin might break. But when Varun could cut no more, panting and sweating and gripping his weapons desperately, it was as if he'd never touched the god.

"Disappointing," said a voice that had no source, no sound, no limit, but was instantly and inescapably everywhere at once.

It's barely even noticed we've been hitting it, Mara thought, an oceans-deep despair flooding her. *It just hasn't taken its turn to hit back yet.*

"Get away!" she cried, grabbing Iona and Varun and practically throwing them as far as she could from Rhúnn, pumping her legs and dashing away from the god. Nemmo hadn't moved; his face was troubled, deep in thought, but he was doing something.

Whatever he's trying to do, Mara thought, *it's probably the only hope we have now.*

"Protect Nemmo!" she ordered; the three of them stood between Rhúnn and their friend, even as mucus dripped from Iona's chin at her trembling sobs and Mara's legs quivered with hopeless fear.

"Useless," said the all-invading voice of Rhúnn, and the god reached forth with its single free hand.

The shadow of Rhúnn's palm violated Mara's sight, filling her vision with a violent, insistent black. In the darkness, Mara vanished, and fragments of the person she had been drifted before her, torn and scattered. She was a child again, filled with that innocent delight that only children ever truly know and adults spend their lives failing to recapture. Then that was torn away and Raskith loomed over her, the size of a tower, spreading the rich fabric of his cloak wide and covering whole continents with his shadow. His eyes, sparkling like the fermented dew on a rotting fruit, peered down at her, crushing her under the force of his gaze. She turned her face downward to hide from him and saw that there was another her on the ground at her feet, as small compared to her as she was compared to the giant vision of Raskith.

Mara kneeled and reached for the tiny image of herself, but her fingers slipped. The little Mara popped, mosquito-fashion, leaving only a tiny red splatter that spread and took on a mirrored sheen until she could see her face in it. Her skin sagged; her eyes dulled; her muscles wasted away until she was looking at herself as a ghoul, a half-dead thing. A chain yanked roughly at the ghoul-Mara's neck, and she saw Raskith's long fingers holding the other end.

Then she watched her family die in all the ways she had thought about since Raskith had taken her from them. Every moment she had spent during her apprenticeship fearing what he might do to them if she disobeyed, every unbidden intrusive nightmare scenario she had seen in her mind over and over until she had finally become truly numb to it, all of them played out in front of her now.

Mara screamed. She cried. She held herself and was silent. She swore in great tirading floods. She scraped at every surface she could touch until her fingers were worn down to nubs of white bone poking through abraded red flesh. But she could not escape.

When she thought she could no longer bear it, that her soul would surely fade away and die forever from the sheer torment, white chains erupted from the ground and enveloped her in their cold embrace. Imprisoning metal links tightened around her body and burrowed into her head, wrapping around her mind and squeezing. A lock clicked shut.

All the feelings disappeared. All the rage, all the pain, all the fear. Swallowed, chained, locked up, suppressed, choked. Mara found herself begging for the anguish to come back.

She blinked. Cold stone pressed against her cheek.

There was still something constricting her heart, she knew. Not the heart that beat in her imagined body, but the thing that made her who she was. She hadn't thought such a thing truly existed, but she could feel it now. Like so many parts of the body, it was only noticeable when something was wrong with it. She'd just been subjected to a torrent of the most intense emotions she'd ever felt, then wrung dry and strangled.

Iona's eyes were staring into hers from where the cleric lay. Her round face was devoid of expression, her gaze unfocused. Varun, too, was still motionless, just beginning to blink gormlessly as if drunker than drunk.

"What...?" Mara stood unsteadily, turning to face Rhúnn. The god stood there, its one free arm wrapped across its chest in a single-handed folding of the arms. Mara knew she ought to be terrified still, but everything felt dull. Cauterized.

"That," said Rhúnn, "is what I feel for every moment of my existence. I told you. Nobody is in pain like me."

"I'm sorry," said Mara. What else was she to say?

"We must leave," a clear voice interjected from behind. Mara turned: Nemmo stood there, a door of plain oak set into the stone behind him. "Now," he said, gesturing beseechingly toward the door.

"These chains," Rhúnn spat, its voice carrying the weary anger of one who has suffered for lifetimes on end, the targets of their ire long since lost to time. "To be able to affect only three... Pitiful."

Mara and Nemmo put their arms under Iona and Varun's shoulders, helping them to their feet.

"But," said Rhúnn, and then it paused. "I am ... still a god."

Rhúnn raised its hand. Black flame spilled from its fingers, a star-bright mote of light forming above its open palm. Tiny chains wound around the little ball, and the god scoffed.

"I can only be bound so far," it muttered, and then it closed its fingers around the light.

Power pulsed out from Rhúnn's hand, blowing Mara back like a storm wind. The god drew back its arm.

I don't need to wait and see what that spell will do—it'll obliterate whoever it hits. Mara reached past Nemmo to the handle of the door, yanked it open, and pushed Iona toward the opening.

"Go *now*!" she screamed.

Beside her, Nemmo encouraged Varun through the door. Iona turned as he pushed her past the threshold, extending a hand to pull Mara through. A thunderous boom and a flash of light from behind made Mara turn, and she saw Rhúnn hurl its spell at her. She had perhaps a second before it hit.

Mara took a deep breath and prepared herself to die again.

"Finish your mission," said Nemmo. His body was suddenly between Mara and Rhúnn, blocking her view of the incoming projectile that would kill her.

But she still knew when it reached them, because Nemmo's face—calm, almost serene—contorted for just a moment in pain. Then his skin turned black and flaky, and a moment later he was dust falling gently down to smear on the clean stone floor.

Mara stood there, frozen. She stared down at what had been Nemmo, then up at Rhúnn. The god's inhuman face dripped with unnatural flame and hungry drool.

Hands wrapped around Mara from behind and pulled her backward.

The door closed.

CHAPTER 27

Mara turned her head rapidly from one side to the other, her neck protesting at the movement. Her lower back ached; she had fallen as she was pulled back, landing hard on her tailbone. The door had vanished the moment it closed, replaced by plain stone walls. She still felt dulled, her edges sanded smooth, like a clockwork mechanism whose cogs had worn down until they slipped out of alignment, rotating uselessly, exhausting themselves and achieving nothing.

"We're in…"

"Aurethen's temple," Iona said quietly. Her voice was very close to Mara's ear; Mara, feeling warm breath on her neck, realized that the cleric's arms were still wrapped around her. "Our rooms under the Road to Eternity."

"How did Nemmo…?"

Iona released her. Mara turned but stayed seated. Iona and Varun were sitting on the floor too, both staring off as if unable to tear themselves away from whatever image Rhúnn had burned into their minds.

"No idea," said Varun. "He must've … made the door forget it was gone, then made it forget where it led to."

"We'd all be dead if not for him," Iona said matter-of-factly.

"He's..." Mara swallowed. "You saw what happened, right?"

They nodded. "It's his third death in the Crossing," Varun said grimly. "He'll start unraveling."

"He'll still be himself," Mara said. "Right? One unraveling shouldn't be too bad... isn't that how it works?"

Varun shrugged. "There's no science to it. He might forget things, or he might be different in some other way. If he comes back at all. Who knows what happens to people who get disintegrated by gods? Nobody knows where they end up between dying and coming back—I mean, Nemmo would've been the person to ask for theories on that, but..." He trailed off.

Mara bit the inside of her cheek until she thought she would make herself bleed. "He saved me," she said eventually. "He put himself in the way of the spell that killed him. It would've been me."

"That's what friends do for each other," said Iona. Her round eyes met Mara's, and she gave a sad smile.

Mara took a few breaths, trying to suppress the feeling that she was about to burst into tears. *At least it feels like I'm getting my emotions back after what Rhúnn did*, she realized. *Never thought I'd be glad of that. I thought Raskith had burned them out of me, but ... that was nothing compared to the way Rhúnn locked everything inside me.*

"Iona," she said, "did you ... know Rhúnn?"

A sound that might have been a muffled sob bubbled from the cleric, and she stared at her feet. "Rhúnn the Choked," she said after several moments, "was bound by Aurethen."

"Wait," said Varun, "what?"

"It's in the teachings of Aurethen's early divinity," she said, a tear streaming from her eye. "He gave us all the richness, all the variety of feelings, and he shared them with us, and it gave him pure joy. But Rhúnn was jealous of the... the vibrancy of people, and Rhúnn tried to take it away. Not by making us sad—no, sadness and fear and anger are Aurethen's too, they're part of existing—but by making us dull and empty, devoid of feelings." She shook her head. "Aurethen chained Rhúnn to keep us safe. It never fully worked—Rhúnn was still a god, and its power still lingered in quiet, dark places. But Rhúnn was cast away, so it couldn't take away what made us children of Aurethen."

Mara and Varun digested this.

"Are you saying," said Varun, "we just met the most evil figure in your entire religion?"

Iona nodded and drew her legs in close to herself, wrapping her arms tightly around them. "Rhúnn is the darkness that tries to squash the light in all of us."

"That must be—" Mara began, but she couldn't find the next word. Difficult? Strange? Horrendous? Nothing seemed to capture it. "I'm sorry," she settled on. "You were there because of me."

"I don't regret it," Iona said. "Honestly." She pulled her knees in a little tighter. "It sucked, yeah. But ... I was there because I wanted to help. That wasn't wrong."

"Same," said Varun, still staring off. "Apparently Invars isn't happy about it, but, well, who cares?"

Mara looked between the two of them, taking in their despondency. *Look at them. They're both broken because of me, but because they care about me for some stupid reason, they don't even feel like that's a bad thing. A few days ago, I would have thought that meant there was something seriously wrong with them, but ... I don't think I believe that now. What the fuck have these people done to me?*

"Varun," she said, "are you... what are you going to do now?"

"Seems obvious enough," he said, shrugging without looking at her. "Just gotta stick with the becoming-a-god thing.

I don't need to be a chosen champion of a divine being if I'm a divine being myself, right?"

"It's really that simple for you?"

He nodded. "Yeah, pretty much."

"But ... you gave up the memory of—" She stopped herself before she could give away the details. "You gave up the memory of the thing that motivated you to do that in the first place," she corrected.

"But I remember it was important enough to me that I needed to do it," he said, as if it were simple. "I don't think it's completely gone. The event, whatever it was, that's been pulled out of me, but the feeling's still there. And I've got you to motivate me now, anyway. I had some other reason before, but if ascending helps you achieve what you need to do, that's enough for now."

How can he talk like it's so straightforward? Like caring about me is just self-evidently enough to give him a purpose?

Varun shook his head and stood, stretching. He reached out a hand to Iona, who unfurled herself and took it.

"Hey," he said. "Are you alright? Not just about Rhúnn, but ... there was something else."

Iona nodded, wiped her eyes, and took a deep breath. "It just caught me off guard," she said. "Hearing that name."

"Was it..." Mara hesitated, unsure whether to press, but if she knew anything about Iona, it was that she wasn't afraid to share her inner thoughts and feelings, even negative ones. "Didn't Duznit say something about a brother before?"

Iona half-laughed, shaking her head. "Yeah. He did."

Varun leaned in, looking as if what she said next could be enough to prompt him to go straight out to find Duznit and kill him. "Did that goblin kill your brother?"

"Oh, gods, no," said Iona. "Nothing like that. No, I... I knew Duznit when we were both alive. I ran a store, just a little one.

Supplies for travelers, that kind of thing. He came through a few times, bought and sold some things." She smiled faintly. "The first time, I had this instinctive fear that he was going to ransack the place, but he was actually a really friendly customer. The town I lived in was small, I'd never really been anywhere else, so I guess there were still these old notions and stories about goblins all being evil or something, but... well, I don't know what it's like in the worlds you all come from, but they're just people the same as everyone else."

"I never actually met a goblin before," Varun said. "Maybe my world had them at some point—they were in a lot of children's stories, but either they went elsewhere or died out."

"Anyway," said Iona, shrugging almost apologetically, "I don't know if I'd say Duznit and I were friends, exactly, but I think we liked each other."

Mara frowned. "But it wasn't your name he said, and it wasn't you he thought he knew. Right?"

"Yes and no," said Iona. "When I was alive, the name most people called me was—um." She swallowed. "The name Duznit said. And most people saw me as... well, as a man."

"Oh," said Mara. Then, "*Oh*."

"Yeah. I was never a man, but that's what the world and the people around me kept telling me I was. But when I died and woke up here..." She gestured to herself. "I was who I'd always known I was."

"The Crossing allows us to be who we really are," Varun said, nodding.

"I've met a few other people who went through the same thing," Iona said almost absently. "Some of them had completely different bodies, others just changed a little bit. Or not at all. Not all of them cared about looking like what other people thought they should look like." She took a deep breath.

"For me, though… this is me. Much more than I was when I was alive."

"I'm sorry," Mara said. "Not—not that you got to be you, but that … um. It just must have been a shock, hearing that name."

Iona's eyes glazed slightly for a moment. "Yeah. I never felt like it was mine, so … when I got here, I decided that I didn't owe it to anyone to pretend to be someone I wasn't anymore. I found Aurethen and realized I could finally feel everything, be every part of myself at once rather than having to—to not feel it, to hide it. I told myself: *I owe no one*. And then … those words became a name. *Iona*. A name that fit me."

She paused for a moment. Mara waited for her to continue.

"It's not as if my name is who I *am*," she said. "It didn't change *me*, but it felt like a word I could call myself. That's who I've been ever since—who I was all along. So, um, someone calling me a name I thought I'd left behind was … not pleasant." She shuddered. "No, not just not pleasant, it was *absolutely horrible*."

Mara realized that she wanted nothing more than to wrap Iona in her arms and tell the other woman that it would be alright. She'd wished for the same comfort herself a hundred times over the years before finally succeeding in making herself believe such things were weak and foolish. In the moments it took her mind to register what she was feeling, Iona had turned away.

"I should go and pray," the cleric said quietly. "I don't… I don't know what we're supposed to do now. Or how I'm supposed to feel whatever I'm feeling about any of it." She scoffed ruefully. "Emoting is supposed to be what I'm good at, but … I don't even know how to start understanding what I'm feeling right now."

"It's not your responsibility to know that," said Mara.

"What do I do if I can't even *feel* right?" Iona murmured as she left the room, trudging up the steps to the main part of the temple. When she was gone, Mara groaned and put her head in her hands.

I should have just done this whole thing on my own. People are too messy. I don't have the time to be getting all—all worked up about emotions and stupid shit like that. I've got an undeath to avoid. I can't afford to be caring about how people feel, for rot's sake.

"It's not going as well as you might have liked," Varun said dryly.

"It's not even that," said Mara, face still pressed into her palms. "It's you lot being all ... you."

"Come again?"

"I'd have been happy spending my afterlife alone, but then you three come along and now I have to worry about you!" she ranted, taking her hands away from her face so she could point at Varun. "Other people are a liability! Look what's happened now, Nemmo's been vaporized—yeah, he'll probably come back, but I'm still *worried* about him and that's a distraction— and Iona's so upset she's not even emoting it properly, and you gave away one of the most important things to you and pissed off your patron god and you're actually fine with it!" She took a deep breath.

Varun gave her a moment. "Are you done?"

"No!" she declared, then hesitated. *Actually, I'm not sure I have anything else to get off my chest right now. Ruins the effect a bit. Ugh.* She folded her arms and huffed. "Yeah, I'm done."

"I really am fine with it," he said.

She blinked at him. "Huh?"

"I lost Invars's support, I guess." He rolled his eyes, shrugging. "I still feel like I want to make a change in the world. I gave up what I gave up because I thought it would help me change at least one thing for the better. If Invars thinks that's reason enough to abandon me... I don't think I want to be the champion of a god like that." He gave Mara a half-smile. "I made a decision that doing what I could to help you was more important than Invars's bigger picture. I'm happy with that decision."

Mara stood there, torn between embracing him and slapping him in the face.

"Could have gone better, of course," he said ruefully, saving her the trouble of deciding. "I mean, we've got no reason to think Nemmo won't come back the way everyone else does, but ... it's not what any of us would've wanted. We still haven't exactly worked out how to be an effective party in battle, or whatever words Iona would use for it."

"I just don't think we're exactly a good match-up for it," Mara said.

"Oh, well." Varun thought for a moment. "Maybe we're not the most natural fit for a team of heroes or adventurers, but ... we're friends, right? I'd rather have that."

Mara had nothing to say to that.

"Anyway," said Varun after a moment, "I'm sorry. I don't know what we do now, how we get you what you need."

"Me neither," said Mara, "but... hey, at least we get to not know together. Or something."

"I'll drink to that," said Varun. "Or I would if I had a drink." He glanced toward the stairs. A faint, mournful voice drifted down from above. "I might not be a fan of Aurethen, exactly, but I think I'm going to go and pray with Iona. Can't hurt. I think."

Mara nodded. There was nothing else she could think to do.

They ascended the short set of steps together and emerged into the main room of the temple, where most of the worshiping was done. Iona kneeled before an altar in the mishmashed space of a dozen different decorating sensibilities, her forehead pressed to the floor. Her body was shaking with visible sobs.

Varun and Mara sat beside her, letting her know they were there with gentle touches. She acknowledged their presence by squeezing their hands, but stayed where she was. Mara couldn't make out what she was saying, but the whispered words were spilling from her like a baby bird tumbling out of its nest, uncontrolled and free-falling.

How long do I have to sit with her? Mara wondered. The answer came to her almost immediately: *As long as she needs.*

"I'm sorry," Iona said, those words clearer among the surrounding stream of mumbled prayer. "We've failed."

"We haven't," said Mara, patting her back. "I mean, maybe we failed at that one thing, but that doesn't mean we're failures. I don't think, anyway." *Raskith would've said we were. If I didn't pour his wine to exactly the right level, that made me a failure. But he was wrong about a lot of things.*

"Rhúnn was too much for me, Aurethen," Iona lamented. "It made me feel and then not feel, and it made me want to not be here anymore, and that's not what you taught me. You taught me to be who I am and feel what I feel and be in the place I inhabit. I wasn't strong enough, and I—"

She broke off with an abrupt gasp, sitting bolt upright.

"What?" Mara asked.

"I felt—" Iona touched a hand to her heart. "I thought I felt—"

Golden light swelled before the altar, washing them all in a saturating warmth. Something took shape in the glow, solidifying and condensing. Arms, legs, hands, a head, close to human proportions but not quite the same, all pulled themselves together from pure illuminance.

Then a new, rich voice formed words, words that emerged into existence like molten gold flowing through the channels of a mold and settling into intricate and wonderful shapes, beautiful and gleaming.

"You are strong enough."

Mara felt hot tears begin to flow down her face the moment that voice embraced her. It was the very antithesis of Rhúnn's cold, appalling tone: it warmed her from inside, like hot cocoa, from her deepest core to the tips of her fingers and toes. She felt something she hadn't felt in years as that voice wrapped her in its luxurious comfort: she felt safe.

"I don't—" Iona blinked, holding out a hand to the shape in the light. "Aurethen?"

The god nodded its head as its form solidified and settled. Aurethen's shape was that of a wise ape, golden-haired and merry-cheeked. "Rhúnn is all that is terrible," it said. "All that is unfeeling and empty. To know horror before Rhúnn is to affirm yourself as its opposite. That is the way it should be."

Iona stared at her god, its ardent radiance reflected in her glistening eyes. "I was not... not equal to it," she said, her tone breathless with reverence.

"Nobody is," said Aurethen. "Nobody ever is. It is the terrible task before all people to feel Rhúnn's brand of despair at times in their lives. It demands great strength to continue in the face of such a thing, but impossible strength to defeat it entirely. There is no shame in struggling when all feels hopeless. That is the existence of mortals—and of many gods."

"I failed," Iona said, her face screwing up as fresh tears spilled.

"You could not defeat a force as old and strong as many worlds," said Aurethen. "To consider such a thing a failure is to reject the possibility of success."

Iona nodded. "But it hurts," she whispered.

"As it must," said Aurethen. "I cannot take it away, nor would I if I could, for even the feelings that bring us pain are bright against the darkness of Rhúnn. But I can share in your hurt." And he bent his great head forward and shed a sparkling tear, weeping with his cleric.

A god is ... crying with one of his people. Suffering with her. Sharing what she feels. Being in the same moment, the same experience, as her. Mara could hardly digest what she was seeing. *Rekh would never. Hells, Raskith would never. They spend so much of their existence appearing to be on some other level, separate from us lower people. But Aurethen... right now, Aurethen's just another person in pain, the same as Iona.*

She barely registered that the tear that had fallen from Aurethen's chin was still gleaming silver-blue on the stone, still in its droplet shape.

The god wept with Iona for a few minutes more, and then he put a glowing hand on her shoulder.

"Do not be afraid to fail," he said. "Nor to suffer. Reject hopelessness and despair where you can. You are a brightness."

With that, he faded and was gone.

Iona stared into the space where he had been for a minute or more, and then she wiped her face and sniffled. "Did that really happen?" she asked in an awestruck whisper, looking between Varun and Mara as if terrified they might tell her they hadn't seen anything.

"Yeah," said Mara. "I think so."

Iona reached down and gently picked up the shining tear of Aurethen, holding it up reverently. "It's beautiful," she said. "Do you think... do you think he knew we needed a god's tear?"

If he knew what it was for, he sure as all rot wouldn't have given it to us, Mara thought with a twinge of something she thought might have been guilt.

"Maybe," Mara said aloud. "I think he just wanted to ... be with you. To feel what you felt, and to let you know he was there, going through the same thing."

A dreamy smile spread across Iona's tear-streaked, red-dened face. "Well, anyway," she said, holding the tear out to Mara, "this is it, right? The last thing you need for your... what was it again? A prayer or a ritual or something?"

Mara froze for a moment, forgetting what she'd told them. "Yeah," she said, blinking rapidly. "Yeah, I don't know exactly what it does, if anything, just that it's glorifying Raskith by celebrating rebirth or something. A ceremony of devotion at an old god's grave."

"And if you do that, he'll let you into his afterlife?" Iona pushed the tear toward Mara again.

She took it, nodding. "That's what he said."

"So," said Varun grimly, "we need to find that grave. And there's only one place to find dead gods."

"The Storm of Broken Worlds," Iona murmured. "Do we have to go ... you know, *in?*"

"I have no idea," Mara said. *I really don't. I hadn't thought through what I would do if we ever got this far—all I know is I have to cast the spell according to his instructions somewhere in or near the Storm. I guess I was hoping he might show up and be a bit clearer about it.* "I think we can start on the edge and ... see what happens?"

Iona strode abruptly toward the stairs. "Right," she said over her shoulder. "Well, we'd better get going—no idea how long we've got, so we should probably get this done quickly." Before she even reached the stairs, she turned and burst into tears again. "I don't want you to go though! Not so soon!" She ran to Mara and wrapped her in the kind of hug a baby bear might give its mother if it were afraid of falling off her back.

Mara tensed for a moment, then relaxed and hugged Iona back. "I know," she said. "It's all happened so fast, but ... this is what I've been trying to do since I got here."

"I thought you might change your mind," Iona said into Mara's leather-armored chest. "You'd decide to stay with us, maybe worship Aurethen—no, I'm over trying to convert you, but you could be happy just staying here for a while, right?"

"I could," Mara admitted. Saying it aloud lifted something in her, opened a door, and let light shine in where it had been dark for a long, long time. "I could be happy with you all. But I can't risk it. The longer I stay, the more I risk being resurrected and turned to … horrible purposes."

"We could find some way of protecting you," Iona's muffled voice said. "Some spell or something that would shield you."

Mara glanced at Varun. "Do you think such a thing exists?"

"Maybe," he said, "but I've tried to find it and I never could. It's beyond me, or I'd have tried it already. As far as I know, the only way to protect yourself from resurrection is not to be in the Crossing."

Mara nodded seriously, then cracked a smile. "Are you not going to get all teary and emotional about me leaving too?"

He snorted, then squeezed his eyes closed and shook his head as if telling himself not to cry. "Believe it or not, I'll miss you," he said. "But I can wait to be sad about it until we've finished what we need to finish for you."

Mara nodded. "Thank you," she said. "You've been … probably the best friends I've ever had, alive or dead."

Iona finally released her and stepped back, holding her at arm's length and looking her up and down as if making sure she was dressed appropriately for the occasion. "Well, then," the cleric said, smiling through her tears, "we'd better get you out of here."

Iona held out a hand, and Mara reached out to take it.

Her fingers passed right through Iona's. Or—no—when she held up her hand, her fingers weren't there at all. Her palm, then her wrist, evaporated into intertwined strings of light, dust, and blood.

"Oh, fuck," said Mara.

Varun's eyes widened. "It's happening," he said. "She's getting called back."

"No!" Iona reached for Mara's arms, trying to grab hold of her, but Mara was unspooling, fracturing. "We have to stop it!"

"We can't," Varun said, his voice laden with weary despair. "It's too late. I failed again."

I am never going back to Raskith, Mara thought desperately. *Never.* Her arms and legs were gone. In moments, her torso would be lost, and then her head would fall apart into threaded filaments and unwind itself, and her soul would be sucked from the Crossing and into the world of the living. *I would rather die for good. I would rather—*

A memory flashed through her mind, an almost forgotten spell. It had been one of the first Raskith had taught her, a failsafe of sorts to ensure that she could never be turned against him. If she thought she was in danger of being ensorcelled to betray her master, she was to reach into the depths of her own being and cut the thread that tied her to life, killing herself in an instant.

The only way to avoid being resurrected is ... not to be in the Crossing. Nobody knows where you go between dying here and coming back the next day.

It was barely even a spell, requiring no magic and no ritual; she simply had to find a particular part of her soul and sever it, which, for someone as well-versed as she was in manipulating the channels of power within herself, was trivial.

Raskith had taught her that such a thing was a last resort, but he had made it very clear to her that she was to remove his game piece—herself—from the field rather than allow it to be wielded by another hand.

I will not be wielded by anyone's hand. Especially not yours.

As her shoulders and neck began to disappear, her vision swimming with iridescent flecks, Mara took one last look at the faces of Iona and Varun. Then she dove into her soul, found the thread of her existence, and snipped it cleanly in half.

CHAPTER 28

Gray stalks flecked with gold. Movement in a non-existent breeze. A swirling sky above a half-lit field that could have gone on forever.

And a bright droplet falling from the heavens, descending, arriving.

Mara opened her eyes.

It worked.

She held her hands in front of her face, turning them over to inspect her palms and fingers. She clutched at her shoulders and torso, cupped her face in her hands, squeezed her calves.

I'm all here. Raskith didn't get me back.

The air filled with her laughter, a disbelieving sound of utter relief. Her legs lost their strength, and she fell on her face in the grass, laughing until she cried. The all-coating ash dusted her clothes and mixed with her tears, streaking her face with black, but she didn't care.

I've won.

She flipped onto her back, staring up at the twisting vortex that was the sky of the Sunless Crossing.

No, she realized, the jubilation fading. *I haven't beaten him yet. I might have stopped him from achieving his goal this time, but he'll try again. And again. I can't repeat that trick or I'll start unraveling, and before long I'll probably unravel to the point that I forget how to do it. Or lose something else I don't want to give up.*

Mara sighed heavily. The grass shifted and rustled beneath her.

No. This isn't a solution. But it's still a victory for now.

She stood, brushing the ash off herself.

Wait. I'm back in my old clothes?

The green clothes and brown leather armor she'd acquired from the Junction—the homey lodge where Irasca had taken her shortly after her arrival—were gone. In their place was the outfit she'd been wearing when she died: black leather over black robes. The clothes of a necromancer.

I can't let the others see me like this, she thought, spinning in place and looking for any sort of landmark on the horizon. *Got to get to the Junction, and soon...*

"Welcome back," said a familiar voice.

Mara whipped around. Nemmo stood before her, arms folded in his sleeves. He cast a quick, curious glance over her clothing, then exhaled and fixed her with his black eyes.

"Where did you come from?" Mara asked.

"I walked up behind you," Nemmo answered. "You were turning all around, but never this way."

Mara's eyebrows furrowed. "I thought I was turning in circles."

"It's a disorienting place," said Nemmo with a slight shrug-like tilt of the head.

He seems ... different, Mara thought, watching him as he regarded her with what felt like an unfamiliar sort of interest. Nemmo had always been perceptive, always intelligent, but he had given the impression of one whose mind was always half somewhere else entirely—not distracted, exactly, but abstracted from his immediate surroundings. That air was gone now: the Nemmo before her was sharp, present.

"I think perhaps we both have some explaining to do," said Nemmo.

In the rich glow of a hearth-warming fire, Mara and Nemmo sat opposite each other in comfortable chairs, holding warm bowls of food.

"I remembered who I am," Nemmo said. His voice was ... not deeper exactly, but smoother, stronger, more present in the low ranges. "Or who I was."

Mara nodded, not yet sure how to behave around this new version of her friend. "That's ... good?"

"It is," he agreed, "since most who unravel lose things rather than gain them. Although that is sort of what I've done. I've found and lost, all at once." He blinked, shaking his head. "Sorry. I must've been infuriating to be around, all the drawn-out cryptic talk. Truth is, I felt like I didn't know anything at all, but if I said it in a way that sounded intelligent, I thought maybe I would somehow ... become that person."

"I think you were asking the right questions," Mara said cautiously. "You didn't get to the answers a lot of the time, but I don't think that would've been the most important thing."

He inclined his head almost gratefully. "I appreciate that," he said. Then he sighed. "My name is—or used to be—Mnemoch. And I was a god."

Mara blinked.

"Or... well, in some ways, I was a god. In other ways, you'd probably associate with divinity, not so much." He clicked his tongue. It was almost entrancing to see a familiar face moving in completely different mannerisms. "I started as a mortal who was exceptionally good at forgetting. Or bad at remembering, depending on your perspective. Eventually, the domain of forgetting noticed me. I'm not even sure there *is* a domain of forgetting, if I'm honest—how would I remember?—but at the very least there's some subset of the domain of memory, or something that functions along those lines. I was blessed with power over my memories and those of others, but I didn't know how to use that power. Still, people started praying to me, and some of those requests I fulfilled."

Mara bit her lip to stop herself from jumping in with a hundred questions.

"People need to forget sometimes," he said. "I heard a story once of a man who could forget not the smallest detail of anything he had ever seen. Before long, his entire existence was nothing but remembrance; his mind could not stop remembering, and so there was no room for the present. He simply kept reliving his entire life, and then I imagine when he got to the point at which he had started remembering, he was forced to go back through the memory of remembering, and on and on."

"That's one of the worst things I think I've ever heard," Mara said.

Nemmo gave a quiet chuckle. "Yeah. For my part, I helped some to heal, and probably made it impossible for others to properly process things they should never have given up." His eyes sharpened. "Speaking of which..." He made a quick gesture with his fingers, then sighed with what Mara thought was disappointment. "That was supposed to give Varun his memory of Liarna back—I still have some of my abilities, and remembering is just undoing a forgetting. I suspect I can't do things like that from a distance anymore though. Ah, well."

He fell silent for a moment; Mara leaned forward. "You said you *were* a god," she prompted.

"Right." He nodded. "Well, a god of forgetting can't exactly remember much. Memory isn't really part of such an existence. So I never knew what I was. At some point, I imagine someone killed me—you know, most gods have people try to kill them at some point, but for me, it wouldn't have been all that difficult. And because my soul never recognized itself as divine, never spent time building a place to dwell in the cosmos, I came here as other souls do."

Nemmo—Mnemoch—took a deep breath. On the exhale, his shoulders slumped, leaving him deflated like a half-empty sack.

"I suppose I was still a god, or at least most of one, while I was here. But unraveling has claimed something of mine. I no longer forget who I was."

Mara hurried to swallow a mouthful of stew. "Isn't that … good?"

"I told you," said Nemmo. "A god of forgetting shouldn't remember what it is. Instead of losing a memory on my unraveling, I've lost my inability to remember. And with it comes knowledge clearer than any I have had in a long time: I can no longer lay claim to the domain of forgetting."

"Oh, shit," said Mara, unable to think of anything else to say.

"Quite," said Nemmo, sounding almost amused. "It's not the worst thing, if I'm honest. I know a lot more now than I did, and I still have a few of my old tricks—and now I actually know what I have and how to use it, so if anything, I'm more powerful than before." The corner of his lip quirked up. "I should go and find the new god of forgetting and kill them with my superior strength, don't you think?"

Mara narrowed her eyes at him.

"I'm joking," he said, shaking his head. "I have nothing to gain from such a thing." He ate a few spoonfuls of his food, then gestured to her with his spoon. "Well, that's my story. Care to fill me in on yours?"

A tremor of cold anticipation sparked through Mara. *What do I do here? I wanted to keep my past secret from all three of them, but it's obvious to him now that I've been hiding something. If I tell him, the other two will know, and then they'll want nothing to do with me.*

Which you should be fine with, a small, dark part of her whispered. *They were just pawns. Disposable. They've served their purpose, and now you can finish things without them. Throw them away like you meant to from the beginning.*

But the rest of her squashed it. *No. That's not me. Not anymore.*

She took a deep breath. "I'll tell you when we find Iona and Varun," she said. "You should all hear it."

Nemmo nodded, apparently satisfied.

"Tell us what?"

Mara turned in her chair as Iona and Varun came through the wooden double doors. A pang of terror squeezed her throat; she whipped back around and pressed herself into her seat.

"Welcome back," said Varun; Nemmo gave him a nod.

"What happened, anyway?" Iona asked. She and Varun were both still concealed from Mara's view by the back of her chair. "That didn't look like you just died, Mara. It looked like you were about to be resurrected, and then... and then... did you *kill yourself*?"

"Something like that," Mara murmured.

"I mean, why do you even know how to do that?" Iona's voice was growing closer, right behind Mara now. "I'm glad it means you just came back, but ... that was really kind of scary, you know."

"I'm curious about that too," said Varun, his tone cautious, "but, well, glad you're both ... here."

Mara heard him step up beside her chair, felt him emerge into view even as she tried desperately to pretend he wasn't there, it wasn't happening, she wouldn't see him, and he wouldn't see her. But he was there. It was happening. He saw her.

"What are you … wearing?" he asked slowly, putting a cloth bag down on the floor.

"Huh?" Iona practically bounced up next to him, beaming at Nemmo as she came. She turned her smile upon Mara, and her expression froze into something confused and complicated.

"Mara," said Varun, his voice choked.

"Yeah," she whispered, holding herself and staring at anything that wasn't him.

"Why do you look familiar?"

She glanced at Nemmo. "You can show him, right?"

Nemmo tilted his head. "Are you sure?"

"Do it."

Nemmo made a small gesture with his fingers. Varun gasped; his eyes widened, his fingers twitched, and the tendons in his neck bulged. Only a second later, his head drooped, shoulders hunching. He stood there, arms hanging limp at his sides, looking almost as if he'd died again where he stood. "I remember," he said listlessly. "I remember Liarna, and before. It was you."

Mara's mouth trembled. She tried to form words, but none would come.

"Um," said Iona, looking between them with concern. "What's going on?"

"Mara killed me," said Varun. "She and her master tore through my town, killed everyone I love, killed me. Burned it all down."

Mara cleared her throat. "Can you show him what happened after?" she asked. She wasn't looking at anyone or directing her words in any direction, but Nemmo understood they were meant for him.

"I believe I can," he said solemnly. His hands contorted in another, more complex gesture.

Varun lifted his head, blinking. His face twisted into an expression halfway between agonized rage and utter sorrow. "You're the one who raised my body."

Iona put her hands out between the two of them, shaking her head. "What are you talking about?!" she demanded, the beginnings of anguish soaking her voice. "It's Mara! Our friend!"

"She was the apprentice," Varun said. "The master necromancer's servant. They killed me, and then she ... turned me into some walking corpse for—for *training*. Had me shamble ten paces and then fall flat on my face, as if murdering me and abusing my body wasn't humiliation enough."

Iona stared at Mara, great globule tears swimming in her eyes. "Is it true?"

Mara nodded.

"Why did you... why..." Varun put both hands on his temples and scraped his fingers down his face as if trying to pull his skin off. "Why did you find me? Make me feel like you were my friend?"

"I didn't look for you on purpose," Mara said quietly. "We just ... stumbled across each other."

Iona's face was turning redder and redder. "You lied to us," she seethed. "What was that ritual going to be for, really? You hid who you were before, so you sure as death couldn't have told us the truth about everything else. Do you even really need to move on?"

"Most of it was true," Mara said helplessly. "I really do have someone—someone with very, very bad intentions—looking to bring me back. The man who took me from my family when I was a child, trained me in his ways, laughed at how much I hated him. He made me just barely strong enough that I could be a weapon in his arsenal, and then he killed me so he could call me back and take my free will from me."

Iona stamped her foot hard on the wooden floor of the Junction. "Well, that's still absolutely horrible!" she practically screeched. "But—but—but you're not a good person, Mara!"

Mara slumped even deeper into her chair. "I know."

"The ritual," Varun pressed. "What is it really?"

"It's what I said," Mara said. She felt more exhausted than she ever had in her life—or her afterlife—but not quite so exhausted that it hadn't occurred to her that she could still avoid revealing *everything*. "It's a prayer, or, or something like one, and if I do it, then my god will let me move on from the Crossing so I can never be brought back."

Varun and Iona looked at each other for a moment. Then Varun picked up the bag he'd placed on the floor and tossed it to Mara. It landed heavily in her lap; she felt three things inside, one large and book-shaped, another small and round, and one unpleasantly squishy.

"Finish what you have to do," Varun muttered, not looking at her. "Then you'll be gone from here."

He turned to Nemmo, who was sitting on his own chair with a contemplative look on his face.

"Was that you restoring my memories?" Varun demanded.

Nemmo nodded. "It turns out I'm, ah, somewhat divine."

"Great," said Varun, gesturing as if to say, *of course you are*. "Glad to hear it. You coming?"

Nemmo's eyes flicked to Mara. "I think I might stay here for a few moments," he said.

"Right," said Varun, nodding. His neck tensed; his cheeks tightened. "Well then." With that, he strode away without a further glance.

Mara looked toward Iona's feet, unable to make herself look any more clearly than that. The cleric stood unmoving in the middle of the room, her down-turned face hidden by her hair.

"I told you," said Iona. "I owe no one. And certainly not you."

She strode after Varun. Her footsteps quickly faded into silence, and Mara was left curled around herself, fighting the sensation that the chair supporting her body was the only thing preventing her from falling through the entire world and disappearing.

"Well," said Nemmo quietly, "I imagine that went about as badly as you were expecting."

"Something like that," said Mara, the smallest possible amount of air passing through her lips. Her lungs, her throat, her mouth, all felt apathetic, too tired to form words correctly.

Nemmo let out a long breath, then patted the arms of his chair percussively. "What now then?" he asked.

"Why are you still here?" she said as if it were an answer.

He folded his legs and leaned back pensively. "I suppose there's something about being so intertwined with the ... malleable nature of memory and the past that makes it easier for me to see you as who you are now, not who you were."

"Who I am *is* who I was," Mara said, pressing the side of her face deeper into the cushioned backrest of her chair. "I'm still that person."

Nemmo sighed and stood. "I can see you believe that," he said, "so I don't think there's much to be gained from trying to convince you otherwise, but..." He walked past her chair, laying a hand gently on her shoulder. "Well, identity is somewhat malleable too. Or, of course, if twisted by force from its natural shape, most things will gradually return to the form they're supposed to have when that force is removed."

She turned her head to look up at him. "What?"

He gave an apologetic half-shrug. "I'm still not particularly good at speaking directly, apparently. But I think a lot has happened to you. It's changed you, but it's pushed you down two different roads at once. This might be a chance to decide which you follow. Not everyone gets that chance."

With that, he exited the Junction. But for the quiet crackling of the fire in the hearth, all was silent.

Mara was alone.

CHAPTER 29

She stayed in that chair for longer than she meant to. *I should stand up*, she kept thinking. Then the weight of everything soaked her bones and drained the vitality from her muscles, and she found herself simply ... not moving. *I just need to stay here a minute longer. Then I'll get up. Yeah.*

She thought that same thing a dozen times or more, each time genuinely believing that the next time would be the one where she would finally manage to get up. But it never was.

Hey, she thought idly. *Gront's god. The one that wants to destroy the Crossing, if he was right about you. Go ahead. Wipe the whole thing out right now. I'd be grateful.*

"Look who 'tis," said a familiar gruff voice. "Went'n' got yourself in a scrap, did ya?"

Mara sat bolt upright.

Oh, look at that. I could have sat up all along.

Irasca floated before her, his opalescent wings shimmering as they oscillated. "You look like shit," he said, by way of friendly greeting.

"No," said Mara in mock affront. "Really?"

"Sure as death," the old fey said, nodding almost cheerfully. "You been 'ere, what, two days? Three? Lotta people get 'emselves killed quicker'n that, but it ain't exactly a long streak neither."

"Did it to myself, if you can believe it," said Mara wryly. "Remember how I told you I needed to avoid getting resurrected?"

He nodded, stroking his impressive beard.

"Nearly got caught," she said. "Decided to try dying and coming back instead."

Irasca let out a great resounding laugh. "That *worked*?" He shook his head, sighing with mirth. "Gods, that's a hell of a thing to've done."

"For one definition of *worked*, sure." Mara stretched out, feeling her body waking up from too long squashed into an inactive ball. "It's not over. Just ... managed to put it off this time."

"Hrmm." Irasca narrowed his eyes, peering at her sharply. She folded her arms and started to sink back into her chair again, reflexively making herself small at the feeling of being examined, but caught herself and shook her head, sitting up straight. "Well, seems obvious you've been through a fair bit since last I saw ya, eh?"

She took a heavy breath, nodding. "You can say that again."

"So," he said, hovering down to sit on the armrest of the chair Nemmo had vacated, "what's the plan now, hrm?"

Mara spread her hands in a helpless motion. "I don't see any option except to finish what I've started," she said quietly. "It's either wait for ... *him* to bring me back and be tortured forever, bound to his command, or... or head to the afterlife of the one god who'll have me, even though I can almost guarantee that afterlife is going to be absolutely fucking horrible."

"That ain't the most appealing buncha options," Irasca said, eyes wide in a contemplative stare.

"Nope," Mara agreed.

He frowned at her, then scratched at his chin. "You seem different, ya know. Like you ain't the same as you was."

"That's what different usually means, yeah."

They stared at each other for a moment, then Irasca's lined face cracked into a grin. "True enough," he said. "But ... you sure you ain't missing a third option here?"

An unpleasant wave of warmth shimmered up Mara's body, passing right over the back of her neck and to the top of her head. "It's too late for me," she said. "I don't *deserve* a way out of this. I am who I am, and I put myself here." And she believed it, because to allow herself to doubt it would be to accept that she had never truly been the person Raskith had tried to make her, and that would be admitting that she had done things that a better person should never be able to live with.

Irasca cast his eyes downward, nodding slowly. "Well," he said. "If that's truly the way you're feelin', I prob'ly can't say nothin' to change it. Just, ah... be careful. Somethin' ain't right—Nyxian Guard ain't been where they oughtta be. 'S like they've all been called somewhere else, but damned gods know what'd need that much of a force to handle." He paused, giving her an almost hopeful glance. "You'll be on your way, then?"

"I'll be on my way," Mara agreed. She stood, swallowed, and forced her tone to become cold, controlled, level, even around the uncomfortable sensation that her throat was beginning to close in on itself. "I don't imagine we'll see each other again."

"Shame, that," said Irasca. He sat there on the arm of the chair, gazing heavily into the fire. He didn't acknowledge her as she left.

After the warmth of the Junction, the Ashen Fields felt positively chilly. There was no cold breeze, of course, no bite upon the wind in that airless place where the grass swayed because it knew that was what it ought to do, not because any zephyr susurrated it. But Mara still felt cold.

Where do I go now? she wondered, even as she strode through the ashy grass, her legs pretending to have a purpose in the hopes that one would somehow manifest, or at least that it might make her feel better in the meantime. *Rekh's instructions said the Storm of Broken Worlds, where the dead gods are, but … the Storm surrounds the Crossing in all directions. Do I need to raise a particular god, or just any?*

"You there!" called a voice, strangled as if recently punched in the throat, but doing its best to sound grandiose neverthe-less. "Have you thought about converting to the Sisterhood of the Great Orgrumm?"

Mara stopped. She turned. A hooded figure stood there, clearly doing its best to make its shoulders look broad and confident, but ruining the effect by fidgeting with its fingers.

A choked squeal slipped out from beneath the hood as Mara's gaze found Orgrumm's face. "Oh, *shit*," said the pig-duck-man-thing. "Please don't hit me."

Mara very seriously considered killing Orgrumm then and there. She imagined it a few different ways: beating him with her fists, stuffing grass into his mouth until he suffo-cated, simply reaching in and severing his life-thread as she had her own.

If I visualize it hard enough, maybe that'll be enough to make me the evil necromancer Rekh wants … Or I could just do it.

She stepped forward.

Faces flashed into her mind: Varun, Nemmo, Iona. She heard the things they would say if they saw her doing the things she was imagining doing.

She sighed and turned away. "Piss off, Orgrumm," she said.

"With pleasure!" he squeaked, hoofing it off to somewhere else—anywhere away from her, most likely.

She watched his retreating form for a moment, then surprised herself. "Wait," she said.

Orgrumm froze, then turned around very, very slowly, as if expecting her to obliterate him at any moment.

"What's your deal?" she asked him.

"My...?"

"Why do you do the—you know, the thing? Trying to convert people? What's in it for you?"

The beaked face contorted in surprise and thought, as if nobody had ever asked him that question before. "I *think* I was powerful once," he said, his voice becoming less squeaky as he dropped the proclaiming tone. "I don't know how to be powerful again, but I thought maybe having followers would help."

"Why do you want to be powerful?"

Orgrumm shrugged. "Haven't really thought about it," he said. "Just feels like the thing to do, maybe."

Mara tilted her head in a half-nod. "Fair enough. Is there an end goal for what you'll do when you get powerful?"

"I suppose ... leave," Orgrumm said, melancholy but earnest.

"Leave?"

"I died a long time ago," the porcine would-be-god said, his nose twitching. "Don't think anyone wants to take me on to whatever's meant to be next. Think the Shepherds might've forgotten to push me on, or else nobody wanted to bother with me."

Mara waited, sensing he wasn't finished.

"I think I'd like it to just end, you know," he said. "Sort of going through the motions now, really. Things only felt worth doing when I knew they'd be over before long, but now... well. You know. You go on for a while and then you don't anymore. Only way it all works."

Mara stared at him for a long moment. "Good luck with that," she said.

Orgrumm sniffed, a sound like a boulder being dropped into a swamp. "Thank … you?"

Mara turned and resumed her trudging through the grass, heading nowhere in particular. A straight line outward from the Junction must eventually carry her to the Storm of Broken Worlds that ringed the Sunless Crossing, she reasoned—and her logic held. It took her almost two days of solid walking, carrying her up the length of the world-breaking fissure that was Lightless Chasm, but the vast calamity at the edge of the world finally emerged into view.

"What do I do now?" she muttered.

Finish it, the voice of Rekh said, as clearly as if her god's dead and death-despising lips had appeared an inch from her ear. *Raise me a god, and be welcomed into my eternal palace.*

"What happens when a dead god comes back to life?" Mara asked.

The voice was silent, lost to the fluttering grass like water dispersing in soil.

Without allowing herself to think about it, Mara strode for the Storm of Broken Worlds.

CHAPTER 30

At the edge of the Storm was chaos. Where cataclysm met grassland, the fringes of both the Crossing and the Broken Worlds disappeared into one another with all the violence of oil thrown into a flame.

Mara kneeled before the boundary between ashen grass and whirling, maddening, all-encompassing disorder, and she began to draw. There had been instructions on that piece of paper Rekh had bestowed upon her in Meachron's room, but she barely thought about them: she touched her hand to the earth, and as surely as if Rekh itself were there holding her wrist, she drew patterns she knew to be correct without consciously knowing what it was she was drawing.

Was it really only a few days ago that Rekh gave me this mission? she wondered, the automatic movements of her fingers giving her brain time to wander elsewhere. *I feel like I've lived more since then than I did in the whole last decade of my life.*

Her spell circle closed. There were no items to focus the magic's purpose, no repositories from which it could draw power. None of that was necessary for this first casting, for Rekh itself supplied the purpose and the power.

This is just the key to open the front gate, Mara mused, watching as her ritual lines lit up. A white glow hissed from within, then darkened until a fog of black unlight spilled forth toward the Storm of Broken Worlds. Where the darkness touched the maelstrom, the force and presence of the storm retreated, opening a path for Mara to enter. *The work here isn't done.*

She stepped into the storm. The way closed behind her, leaving her standing inside a small bubble of clear space surrounded by utter devastation. Hesitation was pointless, consideration no better than procrastination. Every direction was the same vortex of terrible pandemonium. So she simply walked forward, whatever *forward* meant in a place such as the storm.

Whispers flitted into her ears, telling her things. Promising her things. She ignored them.

Sharp tongues of lightning lashed at her bubble of protection, bouncing off harmlessly with ear-splitting cracks, their bright flashing light briefly illuminating the chaos outside with every strike. Mara ignored them.

Faces pressed at the invisible border that sheltered Mara from the destruction outside. Perhaps they were truly there and visible to any reckless enough to put themselves in the Storm to see them, or perhaps they were mere specters clutching at the power of death in Mara, manifesting and being lost again.

They cried. They screamed. They batted eyelashes. They vomited. Mara ignored them too.

The ground beneath her feet was dry and cracked, not at all like the long grass of the Ashen Fields. One step landed on something flat and hard and cold; she looked down to see her foot resting upon a white slab of stone, upon which was carved something in letters she didn't recognize. But she knew their kind. She'd seen enough gravestones in her life.

And there were ruins too: ruins of what must once have been ornate temples of black stone or red brick or simple wood. Once tended, perhaps, but forgotten, lost, worn down as fewer and fewer people cared to remember or venerate the god in whose honor the structures had been built.

I'm walking over one huge temple in honor of the death of godhood.

For some reason, the thought didn't disturb her much. She briefly wondered whether she ought to be disturbed that she wasn't disturbed, then shook the notion from her mind.

Stop.

It wasn't a word she heard so much as a command she felt. Her legs ceased their striding. Her breath stilled. She almost thought her heart might hear the order and decide it ought to stop beating.

Here.

Mara unslung the satchel containing the *Tome*, the tear, and the heart, dropping it unceremoniously on the ground. All around her, the phantoms of divine and wrathful things long since turned to angry dust hammered at her little bubble.

She took a second to gather herself, but no longer. The fingers of her right hand wrapped around the vial that hung from her neck; her left hand reached toward the earth. Then she dove into herself and extended her consciousness at the same time, tracing the lines of power in her soul even as she felt everything that lay beyond her.

The Storm of Broken Worlds was death in a way she had never felt before. She'd known *dying*. She'd known *dead things*. But this... this was as if the domain of death itself had taken physical form, coalescing into a wild flood. She reached out to siphon the tiniest drop of its power.

Pure emptiness seized at her heart with vicious, squeezing claws. She let out a scream that ripped at her throat, toppled onto her side, and lay there gasping for air.

I've died again, she thought. *I'm more-than-dead. I'm gone. I never was.*

It took her a few minutes to remember who she was and where she was, the sense of brutal despair gradually fading into her periphery—withdrawn, but far from gone, like the Storm itself as it continued to batter at her protective shell.

"Hells and deaths," Mara whispered, pushing herself upright on shaking arms. She took several deep breaths, then slowly reached for her vial once more. This time, she drew upon the latent aura of death in her soul first, channeling it through herself, sending it to flow through her necromantic focus until it was imbued with a sharpness of will, a resolve to direct the world to Mara's purposes. Then, when her very being was saturated with power, she pulled once more upon the thread of power within the Storm of Broken Worlds, as carefully as she possibly could.

Death suffused her. It pounded on the inside of her skin until she thought she would tear open and all the power inside would leak out like a bursting cyst. It wrapped itself around her mind, her heart. It froze her. It burned her. It emptied her of everything and filled her back up with nothing whatsoever, then took that away too.

When the deluge of power settled, calming from an icy torrent to a steady stream, Mara kneeled. She took a moment to *feel*, to reach within herself and absorb all the sensations that there were. Within the channels of power that circled her entire being, there was a fullness and an emptiness, a notion that something unsolid had been stuffed into her until no more would fit. Her muscles felt at once vibrant and listless, as if all the physical fibers had been snapped and replaced with

... something else. As if she no longer possessed any strength of her own, but a force from beyond her continued to animate her body.

Is this what it feels like to be a ghoul? she wondered. *Did all the bodies I raised from the earth feel the way I feel now, all hollowed out and stuffed full of someone else's will?*

Nausea twisted her stomach. For a moment, she remembered what it had felt like to be jolted with Iona's life magic. It had burned, yes, abrading and searing, but it had also felt cleansing. Affirming. At the time, her body and her soul had reflexively tried to reject it, but now she thought she understood the appeal. She had spent so long soaked in the ichor of death that it was part of who she was. She would never be able to scour it away, not completely. But then, perhaps she wouldn't want to even if she could. Death, life ... all but parts of the same journey. That suddenly seemed so clear, so obvious.

But the kind of death that filled her now was no natural end. It was hungry, perverse. It didn't want to share the journey, to be part of something bigger. It wanted to devour, to undo the finality of a peaceful end. The Storm of Broken Worlds was the collected rage and despair and intent and regret of hundreds upon hundreds of dead gods, and gods did not like to be dead. When gods didn't like something, they tended to remake things to better suit their tastes, and that process rarely left worlds undamaged.

Only now, only when she had finally become saturated with the thing she had sought for most of her life, did it become appallingly, viscerally clear: *I don't want this. This is not who I am.*

But I've made my choice now.

Mara's finger trembled, but she could no longer do anything to stop it. The power within her channeled itself into her fingertip, and her hand moved across the earth, tracing the largest and most powerful spell circle she had ever drawn.

Death poured itself into the lines, imbuing them with its will, its force. The heart, the *Tome*, and the tear hovered into place within the ritual symbols, settling in and lending their meaning to the casting like words dropped into gaps in a sentence.

While her finger moved almost independently of her, Mara's mind expanded outward. Connected as she was to the Storm of Broken Worlds, she found that she could dive into its currents and let them carry her, washing her awareness through the expanse of chaos. Most of it was wide nothing, featureless and desolate, the ground eroded smooth by the constant force of the swirling storm. Here and there, shapes that might have been ruined skeletons jutted out of the ground or flew along with the cutting winds.

The Storm never ended. Mara tried to find its outer edge, but the horizon never grew any closer. She let herself skim around the ring that was the Storm's inner boundary, where it circled the Ashen Fields—a whole world within, and yet that circle felt so tiny in comparison to the fullness of the Storm.

Somewhere within that neverendingness, her mind stumbled across something unexpected. People, dozens of them—hundreds, even. The material cladding their bodies felt familiar to the Storm, because it was dead: bone, Mara realized. Somewhere inside the Storm, protected by some working of the powers that oversaw the Sunless Crossing, a massed force of the Nyxian Guard were ... pushing against something?

What are they doing? Mara wondered, half aware as she watched that her hand was still in motion, the spell two-thirds complete. *Is this where they've all been this whole time? Chirripeek said something was wrong, that the Nyxian Guard weren't where they should have been... is this what he meant?*

The amassed Guards were arranged in a half-circle several people deep, weapons aimed and spells focused on a point somewhere in the center. Mara let her drifting consciousness float toward the space the Guards had collected around.

Her mind lurched instinctively away, jolted back as if stung. The eddies of the Storm flowed around the Guards' area of focus, unwilling to pass through it. There was something familiar about the aura that leaked from that spot, a cloying, oversweet sensation.

The Storm contracted as if preparing to give birth, squeezing tight around that focal point before relaxing back into its constant flow. Mara concentrated on the spot, trying to see what was happening. She could feel something like a tearing, a hand reaching into a wound and pulling it open, a forced entry.

She could dimly hear—not *hear*, not really, but the awareness granted to her by the connection to the Storm—the cries of the assembled Nyxian Guard as the flow of the Storm clenched once more. Something about *coming through*, or *can't hold him*, or *fall back*.

The wound in the fabric of the Storm tore a little wider, and Mara recognized the power that flowed into the winds from beyond. She would know that fermented richness anywhere.

He's ... here.

Raskith was coming.

With a supreme effort of will, Mara forced her muscles to obey her. She screamed against the indomitable pull that moved her, but she had already given up control. To Rekh, to the Storm, to the undying power of undeath. And before that, to Raskith, to the promise of power, to the fear of what she would be reduced to if she rejected the sole path life had placed before her.

No. No, I gave up my whole life already. I am not *giving up another one.*

Mara threw herself against her own power until something broke, and then she dove into the sheer, enormous lake of death aura suffusing her, found the stream that linked her to the Storm, and dammed it.

The power from the Storm of Broken Worlds drained from her in an instant, pouring out of her as the connection to its source dried up. She fell hard to the earth, her muscles limp and slow to follow her commands.

Am I too late?

Slowly, like a baby horse taking its first steps, she raised her body and stared at what she had done. Her spell circle looked complete. Until she moved her hand from where it rested on the ground and saw one unfinished line, one broken connection.

It's not finished.

Relief flooded her as surely as the power of the Storm. Wet tears splattered across the burning lines of power as they faded.

I am not who Raskith tried to make me. Not who Rekh wanted me to be. I'm probably going to be completely obliterated by the Storm of Broken Worlds now, but that's fine. My soul will be ripped apart and, I don't know, scattered on the winds or something.

A small smile crossed her face as she sighed with satisfaction.

Outside the little bubble of stillness that continued to protect her, the scything gusts of the Storm accelerated. They whipped and sliced and howled. Mara closed her eyes, expecting the protection of Rekh's spell to fade at any moment and the devastation to devour her.

But it didn't come. The noises of the Storm shifted and faded, the cries of the dead gods carried away like a fog dispelled in the emerging sunlight. Mara opened her eyes.

The Storm of Broken Worlds was ... retreating? No—it was still there, its raging vortices visible if she looked closely. But something was suppressing it, imposing upon it, stifling it like a half-opaque blanket. She could see back to the Ashen Fields, even spot the gleaming heights of Nox Valar in the distance.

And, just around the circle of the Storm, she could see a scurrying swarm of bone armor, all hastening outward from some central spot. As the horde of Nyxian Guard scattered, leaving behind a red-and-white mound of shapes that quickly decomposed and turned to heaped mulch and an unmoving army of bone-wearing warriors—*Guards dying*, she thought, *the way Chirripeek did, and the gargoyle Guards dying and turning into statues*—Mara saw the thing from which they were fleeing.

Hovering atop the slaughter pile, arms outstretched, was an excruciatingly familiar figure in dark wine robes.

CHAPTER 31

She couldn't make out his expression at such a distance, but her imagination easily filled in the gaps. Raskith would be floating there above his butchery, a rich smile upon his lips, a dead glow in his eyes. The false, uncannily youthful black of his hair and beard, the almost sickly sheen to his skin—he would be there presenting himself, displaying himself in all his power, daring anyone to come and disagree that all of this was now his to rule.

He beckoned, and Mara saw something else emerge from the tear in space through which Raskith had come. A floating figure, shoulders hunched. It was difficult to tell, but she thought those fluttering trails were the remnants of torn robes.

Is that ... Daroc?

Raskith pointed in a smooth, singular, commanding gesture, and the thing that had come with him flew forward and extended its arms, though she thought its face stayed turned down toward the ground. Rows of rust-streaked metal spikes shot out of the earth, instantly impaling a dozen or more of the fleeing Nyxian Guard, even changing their trajectories to strike up at Guards who could fly with magic or on gargoyle wings.

"I have come," said Raskith, and his voice reached Mara's ears as clear and loud as if he were speaking right beside her. She knew that spell, and she knew its reach: even as far away as Nox Valar, he would be audible. "I have come to claim something that belongs to me. But now that I see what lies before me... well, I may just claim all of it. For I am Lord Raskith, master of death."

He thinks he can just walk into the afterlife and take it for himself? Mara thought, momentarily bewildered. Then she shook her head. *No, actually, that tracks.*

Raskith's head turned toward her.

Oh. Fuck.

"I see the item I had misplaced," said Raskith's voice, as smooth as hot wine, and in only a few moments he had closed the distance between them.

Mara turned her face up toward him, kneeling on the dry ground. He hovered above her, staring down impassively at his apprentice.

Then his mouth curled into a shape that might, from a distance, have been mistaken for a smile of that pitying kind of relief and joy a parent feels on finding a lost child. From where Mara was looking, though, she saw it for what it was: a sneer of disgusted satisfaction.

"You made this harder than it needed to be," said Raskith. "I thought I taught you better than that." He inspected his nails, supremely arrogant. "It took me longer than I expected to break through to this realm, you know. And more effort. I started the process almost as soon as you so tragically left me, just in case my efforts to raise you somehow failed. Which, of course, has turned out to have been prudent."

Mara met his gaze, weighing whether the satisfaction of spitting in his face would outweigh the punishment it would doubtless incur.

One dark eyebrow curved upward. "Your refusal to return was *deeply* frustrating, by the way. As has been the continued effort of this place's defenders to keep me out, although…" He gave a short, sickly chuckle. "Well, you can see how well that's ended for them."

"Fuck yourself in every dead world and then do it again," said Mara.

He shook his head in what looked like genuine amusement. "As enjoyable as that sounds, I have better things to do. If you had just cooperated with your raising, we could have taken over half our own world by now. This one has his uses, but really, Mara, he would be *nothing* compared to the power you and I would wield." He gestured toward the wraith of Daroc as he spoke. The old wizard hovered beside his master, head bent forward, gently shaking as if sobbing.

"You would never have been satisfied with only taking over one world," Mara said.

"Of course not." Raskith gave a sweeping, all-encompassing gesture with one hand that flicked his cloak back grandly. "I would always have come here eventually, but I had hoped it would be with you at my side rather than because I needed to drag back a disobedient child."

Mara scoffed. "Do you really think you can take this place? There are *gods* here. Gargoyles, monarchs. People who keep the ledgers of eternity, who see all of time at once. And beings who've existed far longer than you will, who've accumulated more power than you'll ever have."

Raskith swooped down with all the speed of a diving eagle, grabbing her chin in his long fingers. "I will *never* stop existing," he hissed. "I am the master of all existence—of life, of death. All the power that is worth wielding will be mine. Do you hear me?"

Mara laughed. She couldn't help it. "You've seen *one* world," she told him, relishing in every little twitch of his expression, every slip of his composure. "You think that just because you can call yourself powerful in one place, you'll go unchallenged in the countless realities? There are so many worlds, the odds of ours having even a single person half as strong as the weakest person from another place are tiny—and that's before you even start to consider the kind of power people have beyond life." She shook her head, putting all the scornful pity she could into the motion. "You don't even know how pathetic you are. You don't have a clue."

Raskith's neck tensed. The muscles in his face fought to maintain calm stillness, and utterly failed. He drew back his hand and whipped it across her face; she sprawled on the dirt, her cheek stinging as if sliced with a blade.

The master necromancer turned away from his fallen once-apprentice, sighing with the air of one forced to do things they consider far beneath them. "And yet," he murmured. "And yet." His face turned back toward her, and his eyes landed on the spell circle in the dirt. "Now, now, dear Mara, whatever have you done here?"

He descended into a kneeling position, though no part of his body or clothing ever touched the ground, and peered at the ritual lines.

"Fascinating," he whispered. "And far beyond you, unless you have had an awful lot more time here than I would have guessed. No, some other master had a hand in this... but no matter. Evidently, you failed at the last moment, as I would expect from one as pitiable as you."

"I rejected the power of *gods* to keep that spell from completing," Mara spat. "I denied forces far greater than you."

Raskith burst into dry, fruity, sour laughter. "And for nothing at all," he said, wiping an imaginary tear of mirth from the corner of his eye. "Although, I must say… if I read the purpose correctly, it shows a certain lack of ambition to only raise *one* god from the dead, do you not think? And to let them keep all the power for themselves? Dear me."

He pointed, and a thin beam of purple light emanated from his fingertip to the circle in the earth. Mara threw herself at the ground, ready to claw away the dirt upon which it was drawn with her bare fingers, but the phantom Daroc flicked at her with one hand, like shooing away a bothersome fly, and the air whooshed from her lungs as his will threw her onto her back. With elegant, efficient motions, Raskith cut through lines that had specified limitations to the magic, and he redrew their specifications to permit *more*. All but the final line complete, he sighed in satisfaction and took one more long look at Mara.

"You know," he said, "you really are a tremendous disappointment. Fit only for obliteration, in the end. But this is a rather good gift, so perhaps I will permit you to stand at my side for eternity after all."

"I'll spit in all your wine and bleed all over all your fine carpets," Mara told him.

He gave a genuine smile at that, flashing white teeth. His eyes sparkled with ruthless mirth.

"Well," he said, "let's see if you survive this first, shall we?"

Raskith completed the circle.

All across the expansive prairie of the Ashen Fields, up in the eternal heights of Nox Valar, throughout the entirety of the divinely dreamed dominion that was the Sunless Crossing, the omnipresent half-light *shifted*.

Already on edge as the Crossing's residents were from the bizarre voice that had declared its supremacy over them, some failed to heed the change in their distraction. Some noticed it straight away, hairs on arms and the backs of necks rising instinctively at the slight brightening, the richer hue of the world around them. There were glances up toward the sky, that lightless miasmic swirl, then in the direction of the outer limits of the Crossing, where the Storm of Broken Worlds ringed the entire universe in impassable devastation.

Shouts went up as the denizens of the Sunless Crossing became increasingly, undeniably aware that two things were happening.

First, that the Storm of Broken Worlds had become translucent. It was still *there*, but it should have been a raging, incontrovertible cascade of force and fury. Instead, it was like a clear river flowing almost serenely in circles.

And secondly, that there was someone—multiple someones, in fact—*inside* the Storm of Broken Worlds. Nyxian Guards, for one thing, most of them fleeing from the Storm. A person lying in the dirt, a floating figure above them.

And then, above again, another figure, dark-robed limbs outstretched as they floated upward. A line of crackling indigo-black sparked between them and a glowing circle in the ground beneath, and a colorless whirlwind of power surged into them from the surrounding winds of the Storm. And as it did, everything lit up just a little, as if light that had been long contained within the rushing tempest were leaking out into the Sunless Crossing. Saturations deepened; hues solidified; brightnesses pulsed; shadows evanesced.

Something, the more perceptive among the watchers realized very quickly, was very, very Not Right.

Mara could only stand there on unsteady legs and watch as her master ascended, power pouring into him from the spell circle she had made beneath him and the very Storm itself around him. The rage and strength of gods long dead, funneled by the will and working of Rekh's design, flowed into him. His hands glowed midnight blue; his hair and clothes thrashed around him, giving him an air of grandeur that Mara knew he would have found deeply satisfying; his eyes shone brightest black.

He rose and rose, and then he stopped. The rush of power calmed. Raskith turned his face skyward and took one long, anticipatory breath. Then he pointed down at the finished spell circle beneath him, and the lines fulminated with indigo lightning. Smooth arcs and elegant shapes became jagged, rude openings in the ground, from which dark red mists and bright white flashes of light and flowing viridian currents erupted forth and saturated the space around them.

Mara grabbed the vial that still hung around her neck and pulled desperately at the aura of death that still hung thick and heavy around them. No longer was it a violent, violating cascade; whatever Raskith had done had reduced it to a calm, almost confusedly docile stream, and Mara took as much of it as she could into herself, cycling the power of death through her focusing vial and around her body as she had done hundreds of times.

Even with her body reinforced as staunchly as she could muster, the weight of the magic that poured from the spell circle—the one she herself had begun, had spent her entire afterlife pursuing—nearly crushed her. She staggered back, reflexively trying to cast a basic pushing shield that would keep the pressure off her, but it was as futile as holding an umbrella overhead in the depths of the ocean. She cried out, for all the good that could do.

The specter of Daroc floated toward her, his head still bowed as if in prayer or utter regret.

Of course his head's down, Mara realized dimly, even as she screamed wordlessly against the force pushing in on her from all sides. *I punched him so hard his neck snapped.*

He raised a hand, and Mara prepared herself to die again.

Only fitting, I suppose. I killed him, he kills me. Can't really complain too much about that one.

The pressure faded. Not enough that Mara could let go of her reinforcing magic for even a moment, but enough that she was no longer paralyzed by the agony. She gazed wide-eyed at the undead old wizard, then glanced up at Raskith. The master necromancer hung in the air in glorious contemplation, beholding what he had wrought, paying no attention at all to the two of them.

"Thank you," she said.

Daroc pointed toward the edge of the Storm of Broken Worlds. Mara took the hint and ran.

CHAPTER 32

She emerged into clearness, into still air, and gasped at the shock of her first pure breath. The relief of no longer feeling that crush across every inch of skin, the sensation of full lungs after straining for breath, was almost painful.

"What the fucking shit is going on?" an extremely familiar voice demanded.

Iona stood there, hammer in hand, positively glaring at Mara with all the force of a hundred suns in a world with none of its own.

"There's a master necromancer in there," Mara said as quickly as she could, "and yes, it's the one who—the one I knew, and I know you have no reason to believe me or help me, not anymore, but he has to be stopped and I can't do it alone, I need your—"

The fields shook. The grass trembled in the real motion, the first it had felt in a long, long time. A distant rumble sounded from the foundations of Nox Valar.

Out in the Storm, Raskith floated with outstretched arms, his palms upturned, fingers curled into wicked gnarls. And the earth beneath him broke apart.

Deep darklight bubbled up from the spell circle. The fissures in the ground thundered outward, turning hundreds of yards of dirt into a spiderweb of deep, wide cracks with the circle Mara had drawn at its center. And from those jagged cracks, fingers reached up and seized the terrain of the Sunless Crossing, emerging from some long-hidden depths.

Fingers of bone, fingers of red flesh, black flesh, flaking gray flesh; wings of steel, wings of stone; other limbs whose nature was too alien to name.

Mara recognized the magic for what it was: not the resurrection of actual corpses, not really. Gods didn't leave bodies to bury. No, Raskith was summoning nightmarish forms from other realms, and having them emerge from the ground as if breaking out of their interment was pure theater.

But … she knew the purpose of the spell Rekh had had her make, and she could just make out threads of light of all colors weaving terrible aurorae across the Storm, emanating from the old ruined temples and tying themselves in complex patterns to the nearest form. Whatever remained of the forgotten gods whose temples littered the Storm of Broken Worlds, whatever intention or spirit or consciousness drifted through the chaos beyond the border of the Sunless Crossing or waited dormant in their old abandoned houses, those beings were tethering themselves to the bodies Raskith had brought. He was taking the power of dead divinities and shackling it to terrible bones and rotten flesh. All of them dead, all of them divine, and at the same time as far from both dead and divine as could be imagined.

Dry, bitter laughter soured the air. Long-forgotten, long-dead gods were crawling into the Sunless Crossing, and Raskith was laughing at what he had wrought.

Iona clicked her tongue. "Yeaaaaah, so… I feel like that's a pretty decent reason to team up, right?"

Mara hugged her as tightly as she possibly could.

"Alright, alright," said the cleric, pushing Mara away—but gently, purposefully, rather than in rejection. "Look, you've obviously done some shit. Been through some shit. I don't know. You manipulated me, and Varun and Nemmo, and that's not forgotten or forgiven."

Mara bowed her head. "Of course."

"But *that*," said Iona, pointing with the non-business end of her hammer in the direction of the wraith-gods assembling outside the Ashen Fields, "is a way bigger problem right now, and… and I believe that fucker right there is a whole lot more evil than you are—and it looks like—is he raising *gods* in there?!"

Mara nodded wearily.

Iona threw her hands up, hammer and all. "That bastard—dead *gods*?! That's just *the worst*!—and I believe you're not on his side, so… so… so let's *fight* him!" she exclaimed, then stood there panting from the effort of blurting it all out.

"It's going to take more than just the two of us," Mara mused. "No offense. He's still finishing the spell, binding them all to him, and that'll take a minute before he's ready to do anything, but we can't just go up against him by ourselves."

"Eh," said Iona, still breathing heavily. "Lucky for us, I feel like this whole situation's kind of hard to miss."

As if on cue, swathes of people came striding toward them from the long grass of the Ashen Fields. Varun, Nemmo, the five members of the Rainbow Rangers (and one badger poking out from within Oren's cloak), Pick, Gront and his crew, even Irasca and Orgrumm, and dozens more: Nyxian Guards and huge warriors and quick-footed rogues and robed spellcasters. And all were gathering around Mara and Iona.

"Um," said Mara. "Why's everyone looking at me right now?"

"Because you just came out of there," said Varun, staring hard at her. She blinked, reflexively wanting to break his gaze, but forced herself to hold it. "And... well, don't think this settles things, because there's still a lot between us, but you're obviously not on his side. This is the one you've spent every moment since coming here trying to get away from, right?"

She nodded.

Varun sighed. "Your methods might have been... well... But you must have been desperate. And you must know him better than anyone else here."

Mara took a deep breath, squaring her shoulders and standing tall. "Yeah. I do."

"So," said Varun, "how do we beat him?"

Mara turned her attention back to the Storm of Broken Worlds. The land beyond the ash-dusted grass was positively crawling now with undead things, all beginning to bow to their new master. "I have no idea," she muttered. "But I do know one thing." She looked between Varun, Iona, and Nemmo. "We never quite worked out how we were supposed to work as a team, but... well, when I was alive, I wasn't ever a member of a party like all the heroes are. I was watching. Overseeing. Directing one large force against another. And occasionally punching things."

She raised her head, taking in the assembled forces of the Crossing. As she looked over the group, a cacophony of sound and color rushed up and joined the crowd: Nozan and the Cavalcade of Strays, complete with their carts and all the exploding and fizzing and quacking and burning and dancing things that came with them.

"Sorry we're late!" called Nozan, raising a hand. "Had to go back a couple of times—the beer kegs kept rolling off the wagons!"

A few cheerful acknowledgments came up from the crowd.

"You were saying," Varun prompted.

Mara allowed herself a grim smile. "Let's rally the forces."

Where an expansive field of swaying, ash-covered grass met a featureless dirt plain, an army of the dead gathered.

On the dry side of the line, where the frenetic chaos of the Storm of Broken Worlds was barely visible, like a heat haze in the air, Raskith floated above a line of raised gods. He raised his arms regally and the sky above darkened, the whirling vortex and its dancing lights suddenly muted. Forked lightning ripped through the air around him, casting jagged shadows and illuminating his forces. There were gods that walked and gods that flew and gods that looked as if they were only deigning to take a physical form because Raskith had demanded it rather than because it was what they truly *were*, and the great wizard Daroc somewhere among them, and hulking skeletal gods and fishlike ones and ones that looked as if they were trying to transcend color and—

It's for show, Mara told herself. *They look more terrible than they really are.*

I think.

I hope.

She stood on a platform of raised stone behind her own army: an army of the once-living and the living who served the world of the dead. Nearest to her were those who specialized in raining down destruction from afar: the rangers, the spellcasters. Then came the bulk of the force, the warriors. There were distinctions in how they fought, of course, but Mara didn't have time to learn the intricacies of every fighter's skills. Dotted among them were clerics and bards: those with the power to heal, to augment, to strengthen. Iona was in there somewhere. And on the fringes and at the forefront, those who could leap in and hit hard and fast before retreating to find another vulnerability. Varun, Void, Pick—Mara had assumed the thief wouldn't have any real use in combat, but he claimed to have seen more than his share of scraps and he was willing to throw himself into battle, so she let him.

The Cavalcade had brought the kind of toys that could do a lot of damage if they could be placed or thrown in a vulnerable spot; those were distributed among the fighters, with a small stash kept separate at the rear of the force. And, though they had been secretive about it, Mara knew that more than a few of the gathered defenders were initiates of the Chantry of Endless Acquisition, and that they had distributed a small number of items with interesting histories among their allies.

"None of them are real gods," said Mara flatly. "Not in the way they used to be. Don't be too impressed."

Nemmo stood beside her, hands folded behind his back. "I see that," he said.

"We fought a *real* god," said Mara, shuddering at the memory. "These are pale imitations of that. For now, anyway."

"Could they become divine again, if given time?"

"No idea." Mara folded her arms, musing on the question. "When we raise a person, the body gets imbued with our will— it's still dead, just animated by little workers pushing on the right anatomical levers to make it do what we want. The spirit never comes back. But this…"

She tilted her head at the display in the Storm. *Raskith thinks that what he has is a powerful weapon, and … I hate to admit it, but he's more likely to be right about that than I am to be right about doubting him.*

"I don't know how it works with gods," she admitted. "Do they ever properly die? Most of them, if not all, don't really have physical forms, right? And I don't think any of those are their true forms. I think Raskith's just forced a bunch of immaterial beings into bodies that don't really fit them." She paused, contemplating. "Still, I wouldn't be surprised if even false bones of gods can do things I wouldn't be able to predict. Gain new powers, ascend to some imitation of divinity. Who knows?"

"Quite," said Nemmo. He narrowed his eyes, humming softly. "I do not imagine these corpses will become true gods any time soon. But they do not need to if they can destroy our force. And that is something I am very confident they *can* do."

Mara nodded. "Anyone who dies will come back tomorrow, but … if everyone gets taken out for a day, who knows what kind of Crossing will be here to come back to?"

"I think the time for speculation may be over," said Nemmo gently.

On the other side of the expanse that lay between them, Raskith held out his hand, pointing accusingly at Mara.

"You," he said. Mara could feel every head wanting to turn toward her as the voice boomed as clear as glass in their ears, but her forces kept their focus on the enemy before them. "You are nothing more than a disappointing child. I raised you. I gave you everything. And you repay me by becoming *mediocre*. By lowering yourself to ally with your lessers rather than dominating them to your will. By daring to stand against me. Against *me*?!"

He roared the last word, and the grass of the Ashen Fields all swayed away from him with the whooshing force of the sound. Ashen dust drifted up, powdering Mara's little army in charcoal gray.

"You also murdered me," said Mara, amplifying her voice as her master had. "So there's that."

"I don't need you," Raskith said. Mara could almost taste the acidic scorn dripping from his words.

His mask's slipping. He doesn't need to present himself as the refined Lord of Death anymore. Now he's just the ruthless destroyer.

"You never did," she said, "but you ruined my life anyway."

"*Ruined!*" he practically screeched. "I *made* you! You would be *nothing* without me! I committed myself to *charity* for you, denigrating myself by teaching *my* glorious works to one so base and filthy as you!"

"So why do it at all?" Mara shot back. It was a question she had wondered about since he had first taken her, and he had never really answered. Her best guess had been that he could detect some latent potential in her, some untapped affinity for death magic, and had decided to invest in the resource she might offer. It certainly wasn't that he'd ever truly cared for her.

He didn't respond for a moment. When he did, his voice was slick with calm cruelty. "I wanted to see how much pain I could cause," he said softly. "Destroying whole towns, marching dead armies across the continent, murdering entire governments at once... all those things were satisfying, yes, but impersonal. Sometimes I would permit myself the pleasure of being present at the moment of death or suffering, and I would relish in it, but it was such an impermanent joy. I wanted to keep something close to me, something I could come to know intimately. Something that would feel a different kind of suffering, a deeper, more personal tragedy. And..." He took a long, shaking breath, like that of a man taking his first drink in years. It made Mara's skin crawl and her veins turn cold. "It was *glorious*," he pronounced. "The difference between a goblet of week-old blood and drinking fresh from the vein of the cow."

"Hey, Mara!" Varun called from the front of her force. "This guy fucking *sucks!*"

There were grunts of assent throughout: *Yeah, he does,* and *What a horrible man,* and *I don't like him at all.*

"Can we just kill him now?" Varun asked.

"About time, I think," Mara agreed.

"I look forward to walking over your corpse," Raskith's voice said in Mara's ear.

He doesn't know how death works here, she realized. *Not that it helps, since he can still obliterate me—hells, he's learned things from the* Tome of the Beyond, *maybe even spells to take us not-quite-dead out permanently. But ... still, he doesn't know the rules of the Crossing like we do. There's got to be something in that.*

"It's starting," she said aloud.

With a flexing of her will, Mara sent threads of power to the sigils she'd quickly instructed a few of her fighters to draw at regular intervals across the field. She couldn't see them through the throng, but she knew they would just have flashed yellow. The sign to everyone to prepare themselves for the battle to begin.

A frisson of nervous tension visibly swept through her forces, then settled as they readied weapons, nocked arrows, and began to weave spells.

The dead gods across from them finished obsecrating to the master who had raised them and bound their allegiances to him. They turned, their attention landing on the massed defenders of the Sunless Crossing. It occurred to Mara that her army must look like little more than scattered grains of spice and seasoning to some of the more enormous beasts that beheld them.

"You think we can do this?" she said quietly.

"Oh, probably not," said Nemmo. "But I don't think we can *not* do it."

"Helpful."

"I try."

"No, you don't."

"No, I don't."

Raskith swept his arms slowly upward, palms forward, in the most dramatic gesture he could muster. He didn't need to gesture at all, Mara knew, but it wouldn't be Raskith if he didn't make it more theatrical than was necessary. The necromancer's body glowed a menacing indigo. Green beams of light shone upward from behind the undead divinities, making it look as if they were walking away from a peculiar sunrise—the first sunrise in the land of the dead, if its name were anything to go by, and perhaps some of those dead gods had been at first sunrises before.

The divine undead advanced.

Mara flicked the signal runes to red.

And her force strode forth to meet them.

CHAPTER 33

Chaos erupted as the two forces clashed. Almost immediately, Mara saw that Raskith had no concern for formation. Why would he need something so mundane, when his meanest footsoldiers were grand divinities?

Raskith's undead gods peeled off in all directions—left, right, above, below, loping on foot or soaring on great wings or burrowing with powerful claws or effervescing from one place to another without visibly passing through the space in between. Mara's force lost its cohesion as they were assaulted from all directions, slammed and battered by enormous bones and half-rotten flesh. The gods were becoming more and more real at an alarming rate, Mara realized: those that had been entirely skeletal only moments ago were beginning to regrow muscles and skin, and those with less traditional physicalities were solidifying, colors deepening. Whether it would make any difference to their strength, she couldn't say for sure, but she was fairly convinced it wasn't going to make them any *less* formidable.

"*Shell,*" she commanded, sending the word directly to the minds of a dozen individuals scattered among her army. Each of them bellowed the word and those around them called it out in turn, spreading the order to every person on the field in moments. Her fighters tightened up, pressing in closer together. Several mages raised their hands as one, and a protective domed shield sparked into existence around the whole force. "*Bite.*"

Quick, lone warriors, small and erratic like jumping gnats from Mara's vantage point, darted out from within the shield. Void would be among them. Varun. Each of them leaped into action, throwing themselves at the nearest of Raskith's raised gods for one solid strike before darting back within the protection of the shield.

Good. They can follow directions, at least. Mara shook her head. *I was stupid. Trying to be part of a party of adventurers is the least* me *thing I could possibly have been doing. But commanding a force, understanding all its strengths and how to use them… now* that *I do know how to do, thanks to the man I need to defeat now.*

"*Needle*," she ordered, and a curtain of flying projectiles emanated from within the shield. Arrows, bolts, javelins, daggers—and spells in every color, hissing and sparking across the space, burning the ever-falling ash.

Most of the attacks her army had launched found their targets, sinking into the bones and bodies of the undead gods that were by now beginning to surround their dome of protection. But if any of it was having an effect at all, it was so insignificant as to be invisible.

"We didn't expect a few arrows and a hard whack or two to actually take out even a single god," Nemmo reminded her. She jumped, having all but forgotten he was still with her as she focused single-mindedly on the scene below.

"I know," she muttered, waving him off. "Go do your thing?"

"Of course," he said, disappearing toward the throng.

Might've been a bit rude to him there, Mara acknowledged briefly, then shook the thought away. *No time to be polite. He knows that.*

A peculiar half-satisfaction brewed warmly in her stomach at the thought that she was actually bothered about how she'd treated someone who Raskith, if he were in her position, would have considered a lesser, a subordinate, unworthy of anything beyond the bluntest orders. But she shook that away too. No time to dwell on that either.

A titanic piscine skeleton, soaring on fins of thin gray skin that looked as if it had been stretched to the point of tearing, nipped at the shield around Mara's forces with rows of thorny teeth in a long-snouted maw. It was only a passing, glancing blow, really; the revived god had put no effort into it, casually opening and closing its mouth as it went past, but the place where its teeth crashed against the boundary of the shield fizzed with tiny white flames and trembled. Mara held her breath, watching the quiver in the shield trying to spread outward, but it steadied and held.

That's the best protection we've got, and it won't stand one solid hit.

She turned her attention up from the battle, gazing over the top of the two armies to where Raskith floated above the dry plain of the Storm of Broken Worlds. Even at such a distance, she knew his eyes were boring into hers.

He looks so lonely, there in the sky all by himself. Then again, I must look the same... Wait, he's alone? Where's Daroc...?

Below her, Mara's little force was all but swarmed by Raskith's revenants. Forms of bone and flesh and other things converged upon the shield's bubble from every direction, almost hiding it from Mara's vision.

As long as they're all bothering to stop and focus on this fight, they're not heading off to the Crossing to cause untold chaos, Mara reminded herself. *This isn't a loss yet.*

"Ready," said Nemmo's voice in her mind.

Mara nodded, even though nobody was there to see it. "*Hatch,*" she said.

The mages maintaining the shield changed their focus as one, breaking the dome into pieces and throwing it outward as hard as they could. The shards of shield battered the gods that had pressed up against the spell, pushing them back, leaving dents and cuts in the bones and flesh. From within the broken half-sphere, taking advantage of the momentary space between defenders and attackers, another slew of missiles rocketed out and bombarded the ring of gods. Most stayed solidly in place, but some drew back, creating gaps in the wall of divine undead.

"*Scatter.*"

Fighters darted from the pressed-in mass, creating streaming lines like marching ants before breaking into smaller groups, each forming up around a single opponent. At the same time, a white glow pulsed from a figure striding away from Mara and toward the battle.

She felt the wash of Nemmo's spell as it passed over her, soaking into her. Its only effect on her was a gentle warming, like dipping into a fresh bath—in the short time they had had to plan, she and Nemmo had been careful to stipulate that his casting would need to be targeted. She wasn't sure what it would do to a resident of the Sunless Crossing if it were allowed to affect them as it did its intended targets, but it seemed safest not to find out.

The emeritus Lord of Forgetting held a hand high, walking purposefully toward the center of the fray, and the white light whooshed out from him once more. It carried a rich tinge, like a misting of liquid gold, but also veins of dark ink.

As Nemmo's magic passed over the undead gods, several froze. One went careening off before smashing headfirst into the ground, putting a huge jagged crack in its own skull; two or three shook themselves as if trying to loosen something stuck within their bodies; one simply screeched and dissolved into wisps of smoke that danced through the falling ash and mingled with it and were gone.

Mara absorbed this information, but her focus was on Raskith. His reaction was the one she wanted to see. His face was impassive at the scene of his confused army on the plain below, giving nothing away at the sight of the first true blow struck against his force. But as the third wave of Nemmo's spell reached the master necromancer himself, Raskith's face twitched. There was no mistaking it, even from her vantage point over the top of the battle beneath them.

Mara allowed herself a small smirk of satisfaction.

Nemmo's spell was designed with one effect in mind: to make those it touched forget that they had returned from death. To believe that they were still dead, if only for an instant. They'd had no idea how well it would work, but Nemmo had speculated that, assuming it could take hold at all on such a target as a thralled god, the most likely result would be a kind of dread. What god would dare even to imagine that they were capable of dying? If, even for a moment, they could be made to *feel* what it was like to be dead, it could be the closest thing a god could know to true terror.

And, as an additional benefit, it looked as if it had made Raskith feel as if he were capable of dying too. Though he alone of his forces had never been killed and raised again, Nemmo's power was still enough to make the necromancer forget that he had no knowledge of the taste of death. For someone like

Raskith, who had spent his existence trying to lord over death, to control it, to wield it over others and keep it from himself, the feeling must have been excruciating. The thought of her former master feeling the cold fingers of death finally reaching for him, after so long pointed at everyone else around him, gave Mara no small gratification.

I have to defeat him, Mara reminded herself. *While he's still here, his forces will keep fighting for him. But I'll never get close while he has this many pieces on the field between us.*

Amidst the swaying blades of grass that were the Ashen Fields, her forces were rallying against Raskith's undead servants. Most of those who had come to join the battle were already in some kind of team or party, so Mara had had them stick to their strengths. Existing groups were reuniting on the field, some with a new addition or two to fill roles that had been open—Mara had ensured that every small squad would have a heavy hitter, a healer, someone to empower their teammates, someone who could cast supporting spells to slow, weaken, or deter their foes, and someone to distract or absorb damage.

It seemed, as each of Raskith's undead minions found itself set upon by a cohesive team of fighters, that the strategy was working. Mara saw Varun slashing at the limbs of a frog-like, screaming beast as Iona poured revitalizing energy into him; beside Iona, Irasca pulled iridescent threads from the air and wove them into a net; then his tiny fey form zipped over the batrachian head and dropped the net before welding its edges to the ground below with a thin beam of burning energy. Orgrumm, to Mara's surprise, hopped up and socked the enmeshed toad in the eye with a solid jab before darting away again, drawing its ire and streams of acidic spit so Varun was free to duck back in and slash at its neck.

On the other side of the field, Gront had raised multiple of his banners, and it was readily apparent that they were having an invigorating effect on those all around him. Warriors sliced with more force; rogues darted with greater agility; archers loosed arrows faster, more precisely. As Gront swung his greatsword at a slithering beast with a dozen bird-like legs and a gaping, fishy mouth, Duznit clung onto his shoulders with one hand and loosed close-range bolts from his crossbow with the other. The great leonid put his whole body into every swing of his weapon—with a blade as large and heavy as that, it was probably necessary, but it gave him an air of extraordinary deliberateness in how he wielded his strength. How Duznit was managing to hold on was anyone's guess, but the little goblin managed to adjust his position to compensate for every movement Gront made. Meanwhile, Vaarschraaff had taken up position next to one of Gront's waving banners and raised her hands, sending out swarms of biting insects and summoning thrashing tendrils of plant matter from the ground; Riddeill had disappeared from sight, only to burst out of the earth directly beneath their god-foe, carving two great wounds in its rancid flesh with his serrated cleavers.

And then there were the Rainbow Rangers, acting as a single unit as they had done at the Lightless Chasm. Void whirled, struck, and whirled away again; Jumper leaped into the gap and stuck whatever was in front of him full of holes; Arhiel's hands were a blur as she fired off arrows and offensive magics; the giant wolf that was Oren tore at his prey with great jagged teeth; Wren switched between tunes that dismayed their enemies and ones that lifted their own spirits; darting between all of them like a little whirlwind, Stripsey the demi-fey maybe-badger tossed himself enthusiastically but with complete ineffectiveness at any enemy he could reach.

Iona struck the first real blow for Mara's forces. The toadish colossus her team was fighting slumped under the simultaneous weight of a flying kick from Irasca and a descending punch from Orgrumm, just as Varun hacked through two of its knees. It dropped heavily, sending clouds of ash into the air as its fall shook the grass. Before it had a chance to recover, Iona flew in and crushed its skull with her hammer, smashing the blunt head right into the weakened spot where Orgrumm and Irasca had hit it. The frog gave a pathetic croak, its limbs twitching; without hesitation, Iona extended a finger and drilled a beam of divine light right through its eye. The once-god trembled, then moved no more.

A momentary flash of instinctive concern scratched the back of Mara's mind, some sense that something about that scene should be giving her cause for alarm, but she pushed it away. There were too many immediate threats to start worrying about implications.

Scattered cheers rose as the first of Raskith's unholy minions was dispatched, but the morale boost didn't last. Two of the nearest wraith-gods let out screams of rage at another of their kind being defeated; a charging bullish form flailed around, goring a Nyxian Guard on each of its three horns; a half-opaque thing like the hellish spawn of a dragon and a mole burst out from the earth and swallowed up a whole party of Mara's defenders in its abyssal jaws.

Mara allowed herself a brief moment of grief as the impaled Nyxian Guards breathed their last and turned to dust, never to be seen again in this world or any other, or froze in statue form to fall still and lifeless to the ground. Then she pushed it away.

Everyone here knew the risks. Especially the Nyxian Guards. Honor their choice by making it worthwhile.

Varun, Irasca, Orgrumm, and Iona turned their attention to the gods that had bitten holes out of the Crossing's army of defenders; the Rainbow Rangers joined them, having managed to subdue the two smaller fiends that had occupied their focus by pinning one atop the other and hammering the upper skeleton's bones a good three feet into the ground, locking them both in place. Elsewhere, the undead and the already-dead appeared from Mara's perspective to be locked in equilibrium, most of the small battles raging with no clear victor.

That's bad. These are new raisings, as weak as they'll ever be. If we can't defeat them quickly, we're going to get exhausted and they're only going to get stronger.

She turned her gaze once more to Raskith.

I have to end this. My allies are keeping the gods occupied, so I should be able to pass through. Not that I expect to be able to beat him in a direct battle, but … I don't see what else I can do.

Mara stepped off the edge of her raised platform and drifted down to the battlefield.

Somehow, this still feels like the right thing to do. Making a stand against him, even if it's hopeless. Even if it's the end of me, or not the end of me in a much worse way. It feels … worth it.

She drew upon the power in her ring and the death-suffused space around her. It circled her body as it always had, filling her with strength … but it didn't feel complete.

I think I get it now, she mused as her feet touched the grass. *I don't think I ever would've while I was alive, but … death, life, they go together. They complete each other. And they're both worth defending.*

Ahead and above, the silhouette of Raskith loomed against the sky.

He will never *understand that.*

She clenched her fist.

Time to finish this.

Mara strode across the field, finding a clear path through the motion, the noise, the devastation. All around her, blades clashed with bone, spells sank into skin, and fire ate at rotten flesh. But she only had eyes for the man who would declare himself lord of all death.

Until another figure appeared in front of her, blocking her vision. She raised a hand without bothering to look closely, trying to push the offending obstacle aside. When the person didn't move, she almost walked right into them.

"Move," she grunted.

With a hoarse growl, the wraith that had been the grand mage Daroc grabbed her and threw her halfway across the battlefield.

CHAPTER 34

Mara twisted in the air, managing to get her feet under her. She skidded to a halt, gritting her teeth. *You are* not *getting between me and him*, she swore.

Daroc's torn, half-rotted robes fluttered as he floated dispassionately across the field toward her. On either side of them, battles raged: Jumper zipped past Mara and buried his rapier in the bulging eye of an eel-like creature with four heads and a whipping tail that must have been fifteen feet long; a flash of radiant light and gleaming metal prefigured a resounding crash as Iona's hammer arced over her head and pulverized the prehensile wing bones of a looming bat-thing; a cry of pain soaked the air above the plains and Pick, blood blooming at the shoulder of his white shirt, fell back so two spear-wielding Nyxian Guards could put themselves between him and the atrociously wide maw of something that looked like a toadstool with the head of a cat. The constant dusting of gray flakes of ash was still settling on recently exhumed ivory, staining it: these bones were at once old and new, ancient things now newborn again, fresh from the earth yet coated in dust.

"I'm sorry I killed you," said Mara. "And that I have to do it again."

The undead face of the great wizard lolled to the side, his head still slumping on the neck Mara had broken. His eyes, shadowed beneath his lowered brow, rolled up toward her.

"Actually, not so much," said Mara. "If I were in your position, I'd be pretty grateful if someone killed me."

She almost thought she saw the ghost of a smile on the old specter's face. Then Daroc, bound to obey Raskith's command, reached out a hand.

Here it comes.

Mara steeled herself, reinforcing her body with the power of death. Daroc's casual gesture still blew her off her feet.

She flew ten feet backward, landing on her back and skidding half as far again before throwing her feet up over her head and rolling upright.

I never faced him directly the first time, she remembered, tasting blood in her mouth. She spat a glob of mingled clear and red into the ashen grass; it ran down a leaf, turning black as it went, leaving a trail of green that was soon repainted gray. *Raskith handled that. I just punched him when he was already beaten.*

"It was me that brought you back, remember?" Mara tried, less because she thought it might work than to give herself a moment to recover. "I feel like you should be serving *me* right now, not..." She made a rude gesture at her former master, lording it over the battlefield from on high. "Yeah, I know he made sure the actual working tied you to him, but surely the spirit of the law—"

She crossed her arms in front of herself, throwing out a shield of unrefined force as Daroc loosed a barrage of white-green missiles in her direction. Most of the projectiles bounced off her protective wall, but some made it through; she winced as she took hits to her ribs, her thigh, her shoulder.

If I weren't reinforcing my body as hard as I can right now, any one of those could've taken me out. And that's Daroc on back-from-the-dead power, from a raising done with the most basic look at the Tome... *this guy must've been a* monster *when he was alive.* She grunted, eyes involuntarily flicking back up to the silhouette floating above the action. *Now he's had time to perfect the* Tome's *enhanced raisings, who knows how strong the next version could be? And if he was powerful enough to stand up to a full-power Daroc before, how in any of the damned hells am I supposed to stop him now?*

Mara cycled power through her body as quickly as she could while Daroc regarded her, apparently in no major hurry to continue his attack. When his next assault came, she flicked her hands, redirecting his spells so the energy dispersed around her rather than requiring her to absorb it directly—a slightly more refined defense, possible with a quick shaping of magic, but not one she could keep up if he decided to go all-out.

I need to do something to change the direction things are going.

"*Display,*" she muttered, sending the command to the tiny army that clashed with gods all around her.

Daroc raised both hands. His shoulders rose and fell as if sighing regretfully. His fingers curled; wisps of white, tinged with poisoned green, traced draconic loops in his palms.

Mara readied herself for whatever power was about to strike her.

Daroc's hands drew back, ready to thrust forth and release the spell—and a *boom* shook the air. Another, and another, and again, deep thunderous claps and rapid-fire clusters of clicks. Color threw itself across the sky, color like the Ashen Fields never saw, stars of red and blue and yellow exploding and sparkling; trails of incandescent white zipped in obscure polygons; whirling galaxies of many-armed, many-ringed flares wheeled overhead. Light and sound swallowed the battle, a Cavalcade-invoked force like a god of revelry summoned to drown all the others in its chaotic merriment.

Daroc paused. Mara took the opportunity to throw herself forward, low and quick, and barrelled into his undead form shoulder-first. He was powerful, but his bones were fragile; she felt him crack as she tackled him to the earth.

But, even with his body brittle and shattered and rotting, Daroc's magic was very much alive. A fingertip pressed into Mara's ribs; her limbs all involuntarily pushed her off the old wraith as her muscles were wracked with electric jolts of sheer agony.

"Mara!" a familiar voice screamed, and from her helplessly tormented position on the ground she registered the rapid passing of a shadow overhead, a leaping figure flying over her body, before Varun descended upon Daroc and thrust both his swords through the mage's skull with an appalling, thick *crack*.

The pain faded; Mara scrambled to her knees to see Daroc, the twin blades still embedded in his head and Varun still holding them in trembling fingers, rising slowly upright again.

"What does it *take*?" Varun cried. He yanked his swords back and swung them in a clean arc, cutting more chips of bone from Daroc's dead head. Fragments of skull fell to the grass; the undead wizard floated, undeterred. "I can't even kill—a ghoul—whose head—I'm fucking dismantling?"

The edges of his swords were becoming ragged, jagged, nicked from constant slamming into bone. His strikes slowed, arms tiring. His blades were dull and blunted. What had been the head of the grand wizard Daroc was a little white spine with thin, limp folds of skin hanging from it.

But Daroc was not defeated.

With a flex of his palm, he drove Varun to his knees. The swordsman cried out in rage or pain or both, his arms hanging uselessly at his sides.

"Why?" Varun demanded of the headless wraith, of the necromancer in the sky, of the sky itself, of nobody in particular, of all the gods ever to live or die. "Why am I cursed? Why is it that every time I get close to something, I fail? I *almost* saved Liarna. *Almost* helped Mara complete her quest—gave up my most precious memories to do it—and then failed at that, or maybe at knowing whether I should've been trying to help her in the first place, I don't know. Almost caught the falling branch that knocked my uncle unconscious and he never woke up. Almost caught a big fish to help feed the village when times were bad, but instead, the innkeeper's kid had to settle for a minnow." He was ranting, furious, his gaze somewhere else. Mara suspected he'd forgotten where he was. Daroc loomed over him and let him rave. "Almost broke down the door in time to save the blacksmith's dog from a fire, almost baked a good loaf of bread but ended up making my niece vomit, almost-almost-almost, almost found a god to follow before he abandoned me... almost killed an archmage's ghoul, except somehow that didn't work out either." He stared wrathfully, self-loathingly, down at the swords in his hands. "It's always *almost*," he muttered. "Every time."

A tiny spark of blue flame licked at the edges of one blade. Mara almost thought she'd imagined it.

Daroc's shoulders quirked in a gesture that, had he still had a head, might have looked as if he were wordlessly asking Varun whether he was done.

"I guess I almost survived a grand battle for the fate of the world too," Varun said, sighing. "Well. It fits." He closed his eyes, waiting for Daroc to finish him.

Mara reached out a hand, desperately assembling whatever spell she could that might push the old wizard away even for a moment.

Then Varun disappeared in a towering column of blue fire.

CHAPTER 35

ot air blasted outward from the pillar of flame, an angry wave of dry heat that withered the grass and reddened skin. But it didn't burn. Not quite.

Almost.

Mara held her forearms in front of her face until the rolling calefaction had passed, gritting her teeth. It was forceful enough to keep her in place, protecting herself against it, but not painful. There was almost something familiar about the sensation, some intent to it she couldn't quite place.

The blue fire twisted up into the sky and disappeared. Mara uncovered her face, steeling herself for the inevitable sight of Varun's scorched corpse.

Within a blackened circle of flat grass, Varun kneeled. His swords burned a ferocious blue. The black and white marbling of his skin reflected the flame, the dancing of the fires making it look as if the patterns on his face were nimbly weaving around one another.

"Ahhhh," said an appreciative voice beside Mara. She looked up from where she was still kneeling in the grass: Nemmo stood there, hands clasped behind his back, a wide smile on his pachydermatous face. "I think our friend might have finally managed to achieve a goal."

Varun stood slowly. His eyes darted back and forth, his expression incredulous. He raised one sword and pointed it at the beheaded, floating ghoul that was Daroc.

"I think I'm a god now," he said. "So ... you should maybe just surrender."

Mara almost burst out laughing. She glanced at Nemmo. "Is this for real? He's actually ascended?"

Nemmo shrugged. "Why not?" he said, sounding more amused than anything else.

Around them, the god-corpses had ceased their assault. Each of them, from hulking behemoths to narrow-limbed insectoid things to little skittering avians, turned to face the man standing in the center of the field. Mara's forces took the opportunity to hammer away at the undead deities, forgoing any sense of turn-taking in favor of dealing whatever damage they could to their opponents while they had an opening. Some of the dead gods were slain in those moments, crushed to bone dust or torn into tiny scraps of rotted skin or otherwise violently persuaded to give up their tenuous hold on existence. But most remained.

"I'm finally strong enough to finish something," Varun declared, brandishing both swords in curving patterns that left trails of blue in the air. "This ends now."

"Does being a god automatically make you, like, extremely theatrical?" Mara whispered.

"In most cases," Nemmo said.

The hovering body of Daroc drew back both hands, then thrust them forward in a rapid palms-out motion; a beam of black energy leaped from him to Varun. The swordsman whipped around and sliced at the incoming projectile, the edge of one blazing blade rising to catch the tip of the beam before it could hit—

And missing by a hair.

Varun's sword cut the air a fraction of an inch ahead of the surging spell, which sailed right through his attempted defense and struck him full in the chest, sending him spinning through the air to land ungracefully on his side.

"Ow," said Varun.

"Um," said Mara.

"I thought as much," said Nemmo, with what Mara thought was an air of distinct smugness.

Varun pushed himself back to his feet. If Daroc had still had a face, Mara was certain it would have looked utterly bewildered. "That hurt," said Varun, gesturing scoldingly with the tip of a sword. "But I think I might have learned something."

He dashed forward and raised both blades to one side, bringing them down together in a single sailing sweep just as he reached Daroc. The cut met the wizard's collarbone and cleaved through flesh, muscle, and bone, opening a neat gash spanning from beside his neck, down through his chest, all the way to the other side of his body. Except—not quite. The arc of Varun's swing carried his swords right through Daroc's body until they emerged half an inch before completely bisecting the old mage: the thinnest slice of tissue still connected one half of his body to the other.

Varun rested his swords on his shoulder, apparently unbothered by the flames whooshing from the weapons, and regarded his handiwork. "Oh, that's irritating."

"What are you *doing*?!" Mara screamed at him.

He glanced back. The specter of Daroc took advantage of the distraction to raise its hands and weave a rapid, complex series of signs; a net of purple gossamer threads appeared surrounding the new ascendant's head, loosely woven together at first before tightening and shrinking, vanishing into Varun's face and scalp. Mara couldn't help but remember once seeing a fishmonger loop a wire around the thick neck of a heavy cod, then pulling it tight, severing the head neatly from the body in a single easy motion.

Varun cried out, pressing his hands to his head. His swords fell from his fingers; he dropped to his knees.

"We have to help him," said a new voice from behind Mara.

She turned to see Iona, staring at the battle between the new god and the old wizard with an expression of deep worry hardening her usually soft face.

"I don't know what just happened to Varun, but he's still going to get killed unless we do something." The cleric shook her head. "Can you take the wizard?"

"Not on my own," Mara said.

Iona met her gaze with her round eyes, then smiled—a small, reflexive smile, as if she couldn't help it. "That's alright, then," she said.

"Do you have enough left to give me a boost?" Mara asked.

Iona held out a hand. "Course."

Mara took it.

The clean, visceral, torrential, pure, chaotic, burning, star-tling sensation of Iona's infusing life magic poured into her, flowing through the internal channels that stored and shaped her power. Her death magic, the aura that had filled her with a familiar, constant sense of emptiness and strength at once, instinctively tried to flee as it had before, a shadow desperate to outrun the white light that threatened to scrub it out.

But Mara held it.

She exhaled, and she thought of all the things Raskith had taught her. Everything he had ever claimed as part of his belief system—the opposition of life and death, the right of the living to subjugate the dead, the superiority of the one over the other, the sheer insistence on dividing the two, on defining them as separate—she rejected. She held the flow of death within her, forcing it to stand its ground rather than run from Iona's brightness. As the two powers met, she exerted her will upon them, reminding them that they were not contradictions, not mutual destructors, but two sides of a single coin.

Where life met death, where the liquid light began to mingle with the flowing dark, a reaction sparked. Incandescent black and white fireworks fizzed and flared within Mara's body and spirit, little magnesium fires scouring her soul.

And then the resistance ceased. The barrier broke. The two magics, life and death, flowed freely within one another, separate and together. And a new strength filled her.

Mara opened her eyes and beheld the Sunless Crossing, a space between life and death, made of both and neither. She saw its gray shades not as the dull compromise between white and black but as the recognition that both belonged. And there were other colors, new ones: where souls walked, they left trails of light in their wake, kaleidoscopic testaments to their liminal existences. A ten-foot-tall silhouette of blue surrounded Varun, mimicking his movements like a shadow; a warm orange glow followed Iona's every motion; purples and pinks twisted around Nemmo's head as if tracing the pattern of his thoughts. From the surrounding dead gods emanated colors Mara couldn't name, more like absences or subtractions. And from her forces rose steam-like clouds of vibrant hues, puffing and streaming like powdered paint. It was all a vivid proof of the *existence* the Crossing held, a prismatic affirmation that those who inhabited this place were, in every way but one, just as alive as anyone else.

"What just happened?" Iona asked warily. "You look … worryingly delighted."

Mara stretched her arms, grinning. "Raskith doesn't get it," she said. "He thinks death is a thing to be dominated. To keep at arm's length, to fear and do all he can to turn away from himself. But life, death … they go together."

"Right," said Iona, sounding uncertain. "And this, er, philosophical epiphany is relevant here because…?"

"It's not just philosophical," Mara said. "We—all of us here—we're alive and dead at the same time. This whole place is between the two—or both at once." She cracked her knuckles. "I've been thinking death was where I belonged, or that it was the only power I could wield. But I've *always* been in between. And now I've got magic from both at the same time… well, how could I possibly be better suited to defend this place? Me and the Crossing, we're made of the same stuff right now. And that has power."

"You're the all-powerful champion of the Sunless Crossing," Iona breathed, awestruck and radiant.

Mara snorted. "Gods, no." She took a step toward where Daroc still loomed over Varun—though the old wight had turned toward her, perhaps sensing the blooming of a new power. "I'm a necromancer."

She bent her knees, just slightly. Then she *jumped*.

The new energy coursing through her body followed her motion, complimenting it like a dancer trailing a ribbon. Strength lashed through her heels, pounding into the ground below her, and she took off. She flew across the grass, a low-swooping predator skimming the tops of the leaves, sending little clouds of ash specks into the air. She covered the distance to Daroc in a second, rotating at the last instant to slam into his chest with the ball of one foot and landing delicately on the other.

The ruined body of the wizard drifted backward, bereft of its head, one half of the rest of its body cleaved from the other.

His broken parts floating, only joined together by the vague suggestion that they used to be a single body, gave the impression of a loose sack of disparate butchered animal chunks drifting in water, waiting to be devoured by blood-sniffing creatures.

Varun stood, raising an eyebrow. "What happened to you?"

"Epiphany," said Mara, frowning in the direction of the recovering corpse of Daroc.

"Ah, right." Varun nodded. "Welcome to the club."

"Not quite the same club."

Varun gave a small smile that suggested he didn't quite know what to say to the person who had just witnessed him ascend to divinity. He cleared his throat and raised his swords, turning his attention to Daroc too, as the old wizard came floating back toward them. "Shall we finish him off together then?"

"I think we should," Mara said.

Varun went low, his swords scything through the grass. Shorn leaves flew up in little dark, dusty clouds. Mara went high, arching her back and pulling her arms in to rotate in the air. As Daroc advanced, the two of them met him in a single, concerted, devastating blow: flaming swords hewed at his legs; a fist trailing black and white sparks, with rapid-spin momentum behind it, hammered into his brittle ribcage.

The magic that had held Daroc's body aloft failed him. He fell, little more than a heap of shattered bones and sliced-up hunks of rotting meat.

One hand, the tender flesh falling off the skeleton in snakeskin slivers, rose and formed an arcane gesture. Mara stamped on it before it could do anything, crushing it into white dust in the gray grass.

She kneeled beside the fallen wizard. "I'm sorry for what he did to you," she said quietly. "And what I did to you. I hope you can rest now."

Her fingertips brushed the corpse; she extended her awareness into the body, feeling for the fragile weaves that tied Daroc to Raskith. As broken as he was, the connection was weak, the threads stretched too thin. She followed the tapestry of puppeteer's strings through Daroc's body to the point where a single thread reached out from him to his master, and took hold of it. Quietly, respectfully, she snapped it. The whole intertwined network of controlling strings went slack and fell apart, slipping away like scraps of cloud blown apart in the wind.

The mound of dissected tissue that had once been the great mage Daroc shuddered, then lay still.

Mara stood and took a breath. Then she turned her attention to the rest of the battle.

And realized that she was surrounded by dead gods.

The undead divinities had formed a ring with her and Varun in the center, a wide circle sixty or seventy feet in diameter. Her allies were still taking every opportunity to hammer at the gods with everything they had; though some had fallen, those who still stood showed no signs of succumbing to the onslaught from the Crossing's defenders. Though they had their attention fixed on Mara and Varun, the dead gods were still lashing out almost uncaringly at their attackers. The hulking shape that was Oren's wolf form lay bloodied; Wrenn was screaming something over a body Mara couldn't quite make out; the white hair of Pick, stained red, flashed from within the swaying grass; Irasca, visibly exhausted, clung to the shoulders of a panting Orgrumm; Gront's banners were disappearing faster than he could create them, and Vaarschraaff was holding her hands over the wound that had once been Riddeill's left arm.

The Crossing's forces were losing.

"We can't just destroy the ones that are left with force," Varun muttered, standing with his back to Mara. "They're too strong now. We have to end this."

"Only one thing for it," Mara said, turning her gaze to Raskith. "Hey!" she called, projecting her voice so that everyone on the battlefield could hear her. "You! Why don't you come down here and face me? I'm the one you want!"

"You *were*," said Raskith lazily. "I'm not sure I care about you anymore. Although I do congratulate you on dispatching Daroc, again. If somebody wouldn't mind collecting the pieces of him, I can feed them to some hellhound or other later."

"You don't get it," Mara said. "This isn't your place to take. This is where the dead live, where the living die. It is the land of the dead, and we, the dead, claim it." She paused. "Except for the Nyxian Guard and, er, other living people who come here for decent reasons." Her finger jabbed at him with all the force she could muster. "But not you! Our deaths belong to all of us, and we will *not* let you rule them."

Raskith chuckled, deep and rich and sour. "You've really had such a change of heart? After everything *you've* done, Mara?"

She swallowed. "I'm not who you tried to make me."

"I see that. Disappointing. Still, I was *trying* to make you someone who could wield even a fraction of the power I do, and it seems you've fallen short. So I fail to see what you can do to stop me." He spread his arms wide, descending until he hovered ten feet above the ashen grass. The gods ringing Mara and Varun parted to give them a clear view as he flashed his white teeth and gestured grandly. "I wield the power of the beyond. I command the long-dead gods. I am he who shapes death to my will."

"You're just afraid of death," Mara told him. "That's all it is. You're a coward."

Raskith paused, for just a moment. "I am not," he said.

Mara took a step toward him. "You can't bear the thought of your life ending, the way it should," she said. "And that's what's going to ruin you."

Raskith's eyes widened. Then he laughed, a loud, sickly, fermented guffaw. "Ruin *me*?" He mimed wiping a tear of mirth from his eye. "It is *impossible* to defeat me now," he said.

Mara glanced at Varun. "What about *almost* defeating him?" she said quietly. "Reckon you could pull that off?"

The swordsman grinned. "I think I can give it a good shot."

"No more talk," said Raskith. "But I do look forward to continuing the conversation when this is over." He swept one hand forward, and the reverie of his god-pawns was broken.

Mara threw herself down as the fastest and first of the nightmarish beings swiped for her with crooked claws, skidding on one knee beneath the blow. She straightened her leg and popped up into the air, spinning and driving the other knee into the beast's serpentine head. It fell back, trailing warped streams of uncolor in Mara's new sight. Before she hit the ground, a wide parachute-like wing swept up at her from beneath, catching her and attempting to fold spindly limbs around her. She stabbed straight fingers down at the thin skin that stretched between wing-digits, tearing a hole right through and tumbling out of its grasp.

Streams of blue flame streaked past Mara and severed the great wing, which slumped loosely to the ground with a muffled thump. Varun whirled across an oncoming wall of clawing, reaching, grasping god-things, both blades slicing in tandem, opening cuts, sparking off bones. Mara dashed in his wake, hurling fists and feet at anything in striking distance, targeting weak points his swords had exposed, snapping skeletons. The head of a huge slithering locust-nematode creature slammed down helpless on broken vertebrae; a roc-thing with spindly many-jointed mandibles fell back as its legs departed its body, leaking clouds of yellow-black blood; Mara thrust her fingers into a wound Varun's swords had just torn in the flesh of a being like a tentacled pyramid and tore out whatever innards she could grab, filling the air and the grass below with spurting, pulsing viscera. A bristling man-shaped tree bore down on her before bursting into a cloud of tiny wooden birds that flapped and pecked at her; she simply reached out and severed each of their little tethers to the unliving world, made small and vulnerable by their division across so many smaller bodies.

A firework in the shape of a bird swooped toward Mara; she leaped up and cleared it, throwing a bolt of heavy force down and crushing it into the ground. Landing on the swinging arm of a skeletal man-bull, she flipped off, lashing out on the way down with a kick that sheared humerus from radius.

Across from her, Varun raised both swords overhead and slammed them down on the furiously snapping jaws of a rabbit-headed cylinder of gleaming light and metal, then spun and slashed at a wriggling storm cloud that had lunged at him from behind. Through the gap his blades opened in the cacophony of dead gods, Mara saw Raskith.

She took the opening, rocketing across the Ashen Fields and sailing between looming walls of wrathful gods. Fingers and teeth and wings and spines and tendrils stretched out toward her, but she burst through and emerged on the other side of the circle of gods that had surrounded her and Varun.

Momentum carried her well beyond the battlefield; as she landed in the long grass, she spared a glance backward to see the remainder of her forces outside the pressed-in throng of corpses still indomitably doing all they could to keep heaping damage on the shambling raised gods. Some of the Chantry's toys were in play now: Void ran in circles with an outstretched dagger, twinkling doubles of the weapon appearing in its wake and homing in on their enemies' vulnerable spots; a trio of Nyxian Guards hefted a sword that swelled from a one-handed weapon into a huge shimmering blade that must have been fifteen feet long and brought it hammering down; Arhiel sprinted around the perimeter of the fight, loosing glittering arrows of some sparking bluish metal that burst into corrosive splinters as they landed; a series of smoking explosions went off from an array of narrow tubes half-buried in the earth, launching wailing projectiles into the fray.

But the Crossing's forces were still thinning. Fewer and fewer were still standing, and the situation only looked to worsen as, having lost their positional advantage over Mara, the mass of gods began to turn their attention outward to the army at large.

She turned her gaze forward once more, pushing the fight behind to the back of her mind.

If I can finish this here, all that ends too.

"Sorry about the wait," said Varun, sliding to a halt beside her. He was stained with the dust of crushed bones and a blooming array of bodily fluids in a dozen colors. Something viscous dripped from the tips of his blades, hissing as it landed in the grass.

"I'm here!" called another voice, and Iona tumbled ungracefully past before coming to a halt in a heap a few feet ahead of Mara. "Stopping is hard," she complained, popping up and dusting herself off.

"Well," said Nemmo, and Mara glanced to her side to see him already standing there with his hands behind his back as if he'd been there the whole time, "this feels appropriate."

Raskith spread his arms wide, his mouth beaming, his eyes full of rage. "Very well," he said, his voice laced with poisonous confidence. "This is what you choose? To defy the man who gave you everything you have?"

"No more talking," said Mara, and leaped into battle.

CHAPTER 36

Raskith raised a hand as Mara flew toward him, and a blunt battering force whacked into her torso. She sailed sideways, gasping momentarily for breath before cycling the mingled powers of life and death freshly around her body, reveling in the purity and speed of the refreshing wave of energy.

Varun launched himself toward the master necromancer, that enormous blue double following him in Mara's new vision. Raskith squared up to meet him, and Mara saw a great indigo-black shadow rearing up behind her former master, spreading pointed wings wide, extending deadly claws.

Raskith himself barely moved as Varun reached him. The swordsman's blades slashed the air an inch from the necromancer's face, arms, and torso, but with the slightest motions, Raskith evaded ever being struck. Mara narrowed her eyes at the scene, at the bizarre sight of Raskith—who spent battles commanding from the back or slinging spells, not directly engaged with close-quarters fighters—staying within Varun's reach, weaving easily out of the path of his strikes.

That shadow behind him, the one she instinctively knew was part of her new life-and-death sight rather than something everyone else could see... what was the significance of that? Every living and undead being was leaving trails in her vision, as if the Crossing were remembering each instant of life that passed through it. Behind Varun was the fiery blue giant that she could only assume he had just gained with his ascension, some kind of manifestation of his power—or perhaps a connection between his mortal, finite body, tethered to one place and time, and wherever the source of his newly acquired divinity resided, somewhere transcending normal realities.

That's not his strength, Mara realized as Raskith ducked neatly under a cut that should have decapitated him. Iona had caught up now, following Varun's blows with hammer-swings of her own, but the would-be lord of the dead gave no indication that it was any more difficult for him to evade two warriors than one. Nemmo had stayed back, frowning at the scene, glancing occasionally over at Mara as if curious about what she might be thinking. *He's enhancing himself. Some spell of strength manifesting as that shadow, or maybe the shadow itself is some infernal dead thing he's bound to himself with the knowledge in the* Tome of the Beyond. *But if I can sever it...*

She swiped her hand through the grass, allowing a thin sliver of energy to extend from her fingers and slice through the blades near the base. Thin fronds of gray-gold drifted away, leaving a circular patch of grass short enough to see the ground beneath. Into the earth, she started scratching lines.

Raskith noticed, turning toward her. His body continued to nimbly slide itself out of the way of any harm, even as his feet carried him in calm strides in her direction.

"Keep him busy!" Mara called.

"I'm *trying*!" Varun yelled back, raining a barrage of omnidirectional strikes upon Raskith. The necromancer didn't even seem to notice, simply not being wherever Varun's swords were.

"A suggestion?" Nemmo piped up, standing in a posture of calm consideration.

"Please!"

"Why don't you try *almost missing*?"

Varun paused for a moment, an expression of utter perplexity crossing his face. Then a wicked grin slid into place. "Aha," he said.

His blades danced through the air; Mara glanced up and saw the colossus that doubled his movements behind him suddenly shrink, pull in closer, match him more precisely, as if the two were becoming better synchronized. Raskith moved to dodge out of the way of a whipping, whirling, shearing slash—and stopped in his tracks as the blue-fire blade sliced through the sleeve of his robe and opened a neat line of a wound in his upper arm.

"Impossible," Raskith murmured, sounding somewhere between disbelieving and thrilled. He turned slowly to face Varun, catching the head of Iona's hammer in his palm as she swung it at his shoulder. "How?"

"Turns out I can *almost* do anything." Varun's voice was chipper, a grin of infuriating smugness on his face. "Even impossible things. So ... prepare to be almost defeated, I guess."

Raskith snarled and thrust his hand upward, sending Iona's weapon curving away from him and dropping heavily into the grass. She slumped, her hands still gripping the handle; in the moments she was occupied hefting her hammer back up, Raskith pointed a sharp finger at Varun. A burst of purple magic erupted between them, bolting for Varun's chest.

It bounced harmlessly off his sword.

"Huh," said Varun. "If I think of it as almost getting hit, that seems to work."

Raskith let out a roar of frustration, possibly the most genuine emotion Mara had ever seen him show, and slung a sequence of screaming-skull fireballs at Varun. The swordsman stood and closed his eyes; the wailing, infernal faces engulfed him in black fire. The flames died as quickly as if a blanket had smothered them, and Varun stood there with what Mara knew Raskith would consider a deeply irritating smile on his face.

"Almost took all of those hits too," said Varun cheerily. Raskith's face contorted, all his attention now on the infuriating obstacle that was Varun, and at that moment, Iona's hammer thwacked him squarely in the back of the head.

He stumbled forward, right into a web of graceful strikes from Varun. His body twitched, trying to evade the blows as it had before, but each of them caught him. Just glancing blows, but enough to send him rapidly back-stepping away with parts of his robes shredded.

Mara finished scratching the pattern in the grass and immediately slammed her hand down in the center of her hastily drawn spell circle, flooding it with the power of life and death. The lines in the earth shaped her will into a purpose, and that purpose flew for the connection between Raskith and the great shadow at his back, biting into the narrow line that tethered them together. It was a basic spell, one that in lesser hands should have stood no chance at untying the working of a master like Raskith, but Mara wielded it like a scalpel.

Raskith felt it, his gaze turning once more toward Mara as his will poured into the connection at which she was cutting, thickening it against her assault. He screamed in rage and extended both hands; a wall of force surged out over the field, knocking both Varun and Iona prone on its route to Mara. She braced herself as best she could, most of her attention still invested in gnawing away at the link between Raskith and his umbral benefactor.

It's going to hit, she thought. *It's going to knock me back, and I'll lose the link to the spell circle, and we'll have no chance of cutting off his strength.*

She waited for the blow to come, to be blasted off her precious position. But it never came.

Mara raised her head, even as most of her mind continued working to divorce Raskith and his shadow. Nemmo stood before her, his arms outstretched.

"Took a lot to make that forget to hit you," the erstwhile god muttered. "It was ... very intent." He collapsed to one knee, panting.

Raskith's eyes widened, his face oscillating between furious and stunned. It was all the opening Mara needed. Her spell seized the binding between Raskith and the power with which he had invested himself. As neatly as scissor blades through sewing thread, Mara's will severed the connection.

The necromancer reeled at the shock; the great shadow behind him, visible only to Mara, contorted in apparent agony before disintegrating, scraps of its flesh tearing off piece by piece and drifting away into nothingness.

"What have you *done*?!" Raskith bellowed, his body twitching as if trying to remember how it had moved with such grace before.

"You really shouldn't have come here," Mara said, striding closer to him. "You're still not getting it."

"You think you understand better than I?" he screamed at her. Spittle flew from his purple-red lips; his pale skin was reddened with angry blotches. "I, who have dedicated my *life* to mastering death?"

"That's the thing," she said. "Your *life*. You're on the outside. It's not yours."

"It *is* mine," he spat. "I control it. I control you."

Mara sighed. "Honestly. I know you always liked a monologue, but you're getting really repetitive."

Raskith's eyes bulged in fury. "No matter," he said, shaking out his fingers and stretching his neck. "I am still a master mage, far older, far wiser, far stronger and more experienced than any of you." Punctuating his words, he flicked a finger casually in the direction of Nemmo, who immediately doubled over and vomited blood into the grass. "Defeating me," he pronounced, then pointed at Iona and shot a beam of green light at her, which she barely caught on the head of her hammer but went flying anyway from the force of it, "is *impossible* for the likes of you."

Varun sighed. "We went over this already," he said, and without giving Raskith a chance to say anything more, he whipped both swords up in a cross-shaped slash that caught the necromancer under the ribs on both sides at once. Raskith gasped and staggered backward, raising his hands just in time to conjure solid plates of purple light that caught Varun's next blow.

"I have survived worse than you," Raskith hissed. One hand flashed inside his robe and came out holding something that looked like a dark blue pebble.

Passenger sparrow egg, Mara knew. Raskith had something of a fascination with the creatures: little birds who, as soon as they were mature, found a larger and stronger bird and stuck their beaks right into the back of the bigger bird's neck. The brain matter from the passenger sparrow's body passed right through a tube in the beak and occupied the skull of the host, leaving what was in essence an undead body piloted by a little bird whose original form, devoid of life, still clung to the base of its neck. Raskith had seen them as a wonderful reflection of how death could be mastered and wielded; Mara had always seen his interest as peculiar, given that the bird had to give up its original body to survive, which Raskith most certainly would not be willing to do. That egg would contain a little sparrow who had died before hatching, making it an even more powerful and complex representation of death and, therefore, a potent focus for spells.

"Look out!" she yelled at Varun, who had the good sense to throw himself to the ground as Raskith's finger moved impossibly quickly, tracing a series of glyphs that converged on the egg. A winged form trailing black fire screeched out from Raskith's hand, leaving a neat haze in the air behind it.

Varun popped up again and sliced for Raskith's hand, but the purple-robed mage summoned a ghostly chain that encircled the flaming swords and held them fast, forcing Varun to let go so he could dodge a shining green scythe that appeared in the air and swung for his neck. Mara launched herself into the fray, firing simple blasts of energy at her former master.

I don't think I can get anything to land on him, but if I can at least distract him for a moment, maybe I can create an opening...

Raskith barely bothered to glance in her direction, waving a hand vaguely toward her missiles. They dissipated pathetically.

He can just counter my spells, Mara thought, throwing a quick punch that Raskith deflected with the chain in which Varun's swords were still bound, forcing her to slide back to avoid being cut by her ally's weapons. *He knows my capabilities, and he knows he's strong enough that he can just use a basic dispelling trick...*

Wait.

"Stay at range!" she yelled over her shoulder to Iona and Nemmo. "Throw whatever you can at him!"

Raskith actually chuckled, even as he twisted and slapped Mara in the face with a palm laced with conjured black spines that tore into her flesh. "I taught you better, didn't I? You really think their spells can harm me?" He whipped the chain around toward Varun's chest; the new god barely slid out of the way, reclaiming his swords.

"Actually," said Mara, as blood dripped from her chin, "I do."

Power surged through her as she pushed her new life-death strength to its limit, channeling energy to her fingers and toes, her joints, every little muscle that could contribute anything to this one motion, and she thrust her arm forward in the fastest strike she could muster. Raskith's nose broke under her palm; she felt the sick crunch and saw the thick red begin to spray. He lurched back, hands going to his face, and Iona and Nemmo loosed their spells.

A great pink-white dolphin-shaped working sailed from Nemmo's hands, lithely undulating through the air. From Iona's hammer, a golden ape leaped forth, pulling its hands back to swipe or crush. Mara wasn't sure whether those were the shapes their spells had taken or whether her new vision was manifesting icons of her friends' power, but it didn't matter: the two shapes converged on Raskith, diving in toward him. He snarl-sneered and raised a hand, lackadaisically dismissing the spells.

But the magic persisted.

In the instant between Raskith's attempted dispelling and the magic slamming into him with all the force Nemmo and Iona could muster, Mara just about managed to find a moment to relish the look of shock and fear on his face. Then gold and white sparks exploded as the magic hit, blowing him off his feet.

Varun dashed after him, not giving him a moment to react or recuperate; his swords traced elegant, complex spirals as he dealt blow after blow, Raskith unable to do anything but hold up his hands and summon the most basic of impact-dampening shields. The twin blades rose and fell in one great cleave, and Raskith fell gasping to his knees, leaking blood from a hundred wounds.

"Told you," said Mara. "You could never understand death as well as the dead."

Raskith stared ahead, a glazed look of stunned confusion on his face. Blood dripped thick and dark from his neat beard. Varun held the point of one sword to his chin.

"Want me to finish it?" Varun asked quietly.

In the instant Varun turned his head toward Mara, Raskith let out a primal roar and grabbed the front of his own tattered robes, tearing them apart to reveal his pale, gaunt chest. And the spell circle engraved in pink-white scars on his skin.

Mara had a second to take in the design. She recognized those shapes, though their complexity and the power required to make them function would have been far beyond anything she could ever have produced as a necromancer. Embedded in various nodes in the design were little sparkling gems: she remembered him once boasting of a new method he was developing to crystalize little slivers of the corpses he'd raised or the enemies he'd dispatched, turning their remains into death-affinity jewels that could fuel his magic. Evidently, he'd succeeded. She wondered, in that flickering moment, whether Daroc's flesh was in there. Whether hers was.

Then Raskith's spell activated, channeling obscene power through the lines carved into his own body, gathering focus and sharpness from the mineralized scraps of the departed, sucking magic from the reservoirs the master necromancer had cultivated for decades. Varun turned back, his eyes widening, and then he was engulfed in a cataclysm of light and sound and darkness and silence.

The spell Raskith had woven was like nothing Mara had ever seen. Even the dead gods over whom he claimed command were an order of magnitude less terrifying than the true sheer offensive capabilities of a mage of his power. Varun disappeared in an appalling onslaught of iron spikes and purple thorns and bellowing monsters and descending fires, all collapsing in upon him at once.

It only took an instant, and then the spell was gone, imploding into Varun with all the force of a dying star. The new god fell hard on his back and lay still.

As one, Iona and Nemmo loosed needle-thin beams of light in retaliation: gold and white lines intersected somewhere in Raskith's body and kept going through him, forming a cross with him at the center. He fell.

Mara dashed over to Varun, skidding on her knees beside his fallen form. In her new sight, the great blue-fire warrior that had accompanied him had vanished; the life was gone from him.

Except ... don't people who die here turn to ash?

A tiny blue flame flickered over his chest.

"Almost got me," he wheezed.

She grinned. "Almost?"

"No more talking," said Varun, and went limp. But he was breathing.

Mara stood and turned to face Raskith. He looked so old. So frail. So pitiful, panting on all fours with his robes ripped to pieces to reveal emaciated, jaundiced limbs and his carefully cultivated hair and beard all out of place. He was a cellar of fine wine with all the bottles smashed. All the strength was gone from him, exhausted by his final gambit.

His usually clear and piercing eyes, now unfocused within sunken sockets, rotated up toward Mara. "How ... the dispel...?"

"I told you," she said. "This place isn't yours. If you'd belonged here for even a day, you'd know different magics can't interact."

"I'm not defeated yet," Raskith rasped. "I told you. It's impossible. Even... even that one couldn't do it." His chin jerked in the direction of the fallen Varun.

"But he almost did it," said Mara. "So ... all that's left is for me to finish it off."

She stood over the man who had defined her entire life and sighed.

"I knew you were never really going to teach me to become as powerful as you," she said. "I knew I would just be a pawn, a tool. But just outright killing me to become another walking skin-sack ... that stung."

"Fine," Raskith spat. "Kill me. I know how it works here—I've read the *Tome*. I'll die, and I'll return to the Sunless Crossing tomorrow and begin again. You can't win."

Mara's eyes widened. She chuckled. Then she threw back her head and laughed like she hadn't laughed in years, until she was doubled over and hiccuping and gasping for breath.

"What?" Raskith snapped.

"Oh, hells," Mara muttered, wiping away a tear. "You *really* don't know how it works here, Lord of the Dead. Did the *Tome* say what happens to *living* people who die in the Crossing?"

A muscle under Raskith's eye twitched. "I—the distinction was not—"

Mara leaned in close. "Annihilation," she whispered. "No resurrection. No afterlife. Just ... *gone*. Eternally."

He swallowed. "Lies."

"It's not pretty, I'm afraid," said Mara.

Raskith bellowed with fear and rage and surged to his feet, but she caught him with a simple, lazy kick to the chest. He fell on his rear, then scrabbled to his knees, staining his fingers with ash and dirt. His eyes met hers.

"Goodbye, Master," said Mara.

Then she punched him.

Raskith's head snapped to the side. The bones that connected it to the rest of his body shattered; muscles tore; tendons popped.

He dropped like a sack of butchered meat, staring at Mara with still-open eyes. She watched impassively as the end took him.

Skin stretched and stained and dried out; muscles wasted; inside his body, organs turned desiccated and powdery. Red-gray fluid dripped from his eyes and nose and mouth; his so-insistently-black hair went white, wiry, thin, and fell out.

"Little servant," said a familiar voice that sounded from the air itself. It vibrated through the ground beneath her feet and echoed between her ears.

Rekh's here.

A black shadow rose out of the grass, a human-shaped darkness that kneeled by Raskith's side and cradled his head.

"You had your uses," said Rekh flatly. "And you did many foul things in my name. You have at least a modicum of gratitude for that."

"I ... served you," Raskith said, the words coming out as the hoarsest hisses from disintegrating lungs.

"No," said Rekh. "You served yourself. Nevertheless, I would have gladly taken you into my afterlife. Where you would have suffered for eternity, but still. I suspect you would have preferred that to ... cessation of existence."

Raskith's eyes, dried and shrunken, gave the most pleading look they could. "Take ... me."

"Oh, no," said Rekh. "I cannot." The shadow stood. "May your memory inspire depravity and injustice."

Raskith's skin flaked and turned black. Mara thought she heard the ghost of a scream, a pathetic fluttering of air through decomposing vocal cords. Then it was over. Nothing remained.

The shadow that was Rekh turned to face Mara. "It seems I can no longer take you either," it said with a trace of disappointment. "Impressive. Irritating, but impressive."

Mara's breath caught in her throat. "What do you mean?"

"I had such plans," Rekh said. Its humanoid form lost its solidity and warped into a series of ever-shifting shadows: a headstone, a skull, a dagger. "You would have felt such sweet agony for all eternity." A wisp of smoke crept toward Mara; a sharp scent of rot and poisoned sweetness cut at her nostrils. "You did what I asked, yes, but we both know your heart was never in it."

Mara swallowed as the inchoate darkness that was Rekh lingered around her.

"If the Marquis ever gives up his rule," Rekh whispered, "ever throws you from his halls... I'll be waiting."

The god of all that could be made wrong and perverse about death faded and was gone.

Mara turned back toward the battle for the Sunless Crossing. The great skeletons were falling into heaps of disordered bones, thudding and clacking against each other. Long-dead skin putrefied and decayed and mingled with the ash in the grass. Colors faded; motion ceased. With Raskith's death, the god-wraiths relinquished their hold on half-life.

She fell to her knees in the grass, suddenly more exhausted than she had ever been in her life, or since.

It was over.

CHAPTER 37

"**W**ell," said Mara's reflection, "I have to say, I didn't expect this."

She sat cross-legged on the edge of the pool in Atonement Grove, elbows on knees, chin in palms. "Me neither."

"I know. I really thought we were past the point of … whatever we were past the point of." The Mara in the water shrugged. "We've done bad things. A lot of bad things. Those don't go away."

"Of course not," said Mara. "But maybe knowing that—knowing the wrong we've done is still there, accepting it, doing what we can to make things better from here—maybe that's all anyone can do."

"I'm still not convinced we're a *good person*," said the reflection, who could be nothing but entirely honest. "But then I'm not convinced there's such a thing, really."

Mara nodded thoughtfully. "We might have to ask Nemmo about that one."

Her reflection put on a slow, ponderous voice. "*The distinction between* being *good and* doing *good is widely considered a matter of perspective*," she said in a truly terrible impression of Nemmo.

The two chuckled, then glanced at each other, then laughed again. They lapsed into a few moments of quiet reflection, and indeed of reflecting.

"You know," said Mara eventually.

"Of course I do," her reflection interrupted.

"You know," Mara pressed on, "if we hadn't been so certain we were irredeemable at the start, if we hadn't been so sure no other gods would ever take us, that Rekh was our only hope of escaping Raskith, we could have avoided a lot of hurt."

"We could have," said the Mara in the water. "But I think we had to see it to understand."

Mara swallowed. "It shouldn't have taken that," she whispered.

"No, it shouldn't," her reflection agreed. "But it did, and here we are."

Mara stood, brushing leaves off her new coat: black and fitted, tapering in at the waist and then out in white-accented pleats to her knees. More white flashed from within the lining and details at the lapel, the cuffs, and the collar. Pick had helped her have it made; her old necromancers' robes no longer felt as if they fit her. No longer matched who she was.

Two days had passed since the great battle at the edge of the Sunless Crossing, where the liminal fields of alive-death met the devastation of the Storm of Broken Worlds. There had been deaths, of course, some that were undone and some that weren't. The Nyxian Guard had lost no small number of its bone-armored warriors forever. Stripsey the badger had been swallowed by some whale-mole hybrid but emerged unharmed and chipper when it was all over. Oren, Void, and Wrenn had all died and returned; Jumper was still inconsolable about what he saw as his failure to protect them, particularly his uncle. None of them had yet unraveled, though—the same couldn't be said for Pick, who had come back with a peculiar penchant for simply passing through solid surfaces every so often. He hadn't yet worked out how to apply it deliberately, but it would doubtless aid the Chantry of Endless Acquisition when he did.

All of Gront's crew but the hulking lion-man himself had met their ends and returned. Mara hadn't seen much of them since; they'd kept to themselves, but she'd heard they were occupied trying to solve some schism between the various worshippers of bound gods. The rising of a significant number of long-dead gods had had some sort of theological implication for many of their beliefs, Mara assumed.

Orgrumm had improbably survived, which was—according to Irasca himself—the serendipitous result of the duck-pig taking a fey dropkick meant for a god behind him, which flung him out of the way of a penetrating drill of magical energy that would have eviscerated him. Iona had lived. Nemmo too.

Varun had almost died. But not quite.

She hadn't spoken to them yet. There had been too much to do in the immediate aftermath, too many questions from important people—she'd been dragged in front of the Godless Monarchy to answer for her part in the whole thing, which had gone better than expected when half the people she'd met since arriving in the Crossing had turned up to vouch that the battle would never have been won without her. And, if she were honest with herself, she'd been putting it off.

But the time for putting things off was over.

"What do we do now, then?" her reflection asked.

Mara sighed. "We go and bring an end to it, I think. A final end." She turned her gaze toward Nox Valar. "To all of it," she murmured.

"You're afraid," said her reflection with, as ever, absolute truth.

"Of course I am," she said. Then she strode away from the pool, out of the fruit-scented grove, and toward the marble heights of the great city before her.

"You're leaving," said Iona the moment she saw Mara arriving in the temple of Aurethen.

Mara nodded.

"To...?"

"The Marquis," said Mara, then shivered. "At least, I hope so."

Iona's soft face broke into a wide smile. "You managed to change your allegiance?"

Mara shrugged. "Apparently. Rekh said something... I think I've just changed, you know? Enough that my soul's not meant for Rekh anymore, but for the one who sees life and death as parts of the same journey."

Iona nodded appreciatively, her hands gently clapping together. "That's not easy," she cooed, her eyes widening as if sharing salacious gossip. "You must have had a real ... change of heart."

Mara nodded. "I did."

Iona's expression became more serious. "I'm sorry—" she started.

Mara held up a hand. "You were right," she said, and left it there.

Nemmo emerged from the door that led down into the underground parts of the temple. "I thought I heard you," he said. "You're not staying, then?"

She shook her head. "I can't. Or—maybe I could, but I shouldn't. I don't want to. I'm done." The image of Raskith's last moments flashed into her mind. "I'm not going to cling onto living. Or, you know, unliving. He couldn't let go, and I won't be like him." She met Nemmo's eyes. "My time's come. It's past."

Nemmo nodded sagely. "Too few are capable of recognizing that, I think," he said.

"Are you sure?" Iona needled. "There's more to see, more to do—more to feel!" She took Mara's hands and squeezed. "You could have a whole new existence."

Mara squeezed back, then—kindly, but firmly—released Iona's hands. "No, I couldn't," she said, smiling faintly at the cleric. "But thank you."

Iona pouted. "Figured. Had to ask, but ... I do get it." She suddenly lurched forward and wrapped Mara in a tight hug. "I'll miss you."

Mara froze, then relaxed into the embrace.

"You hug better now," said Iona's muffled voice from somewhere around Mara's abdomen.

"What are you two going to get up to when I'm gone?" Mara asked.

Iona let go and drew back, wiping a tear from her eye. "I'll just stay here, I think," she said. "Keep doing what I've been doing. Maybe try to find people who think it's too late for them to have a happy ending and ... show them it's not." Mara raised an eyebrow. "I don't *just* mean converting them to following Aurethen," she clarified. "But I'll be mentioning it as an option."

"I think I have some traveling to do," Nemmo mused. "I hear the old band of philosophical souls has been speculating recently on the nature of place in the Sunless Crossing: given that the Ashen Fields can grow and shrink to accommodate any number of arrivals, where does it go when it is not here?"

Mara blinked. "What?"

"I think there might be some rather interesting places that exist in ways other than the ones to which we're accustomed," said Nemmo, a beatific smile on his face, his black eyes twinkling. "I would rather like to see what that's like."

"Well," said Mara, "you enjoy … that."

"I fully intend to," he said. She didn't doubt it.

"Have you seen Varun, by the way?"

Iona waved generally around. "He's wandering somewhere. If he wants to find you, he will."

Mara nodded, then took a deep breath. "I'm sorry," she said. "For lying to you. For using you. And, er, for being so bad at knowing what to do without you that I nearly let Raskith take over the whole Sunless Crossing."

"I don't think you knew you had a choice," Iona said. Nemmo nodded. Nothing more needed to be said.

Mara took a step back toward the door and paused. Something swelled up in her throat.

How did I end up feeling this way about these two?

She shook her head and smiled to herself.

If I hadn't, who knows where I'd be?

Mara opened her arms and ran to them, wrapping both of them up.

"Take care," she said, then released them and turned before anyone could possibly say anything to make her stay longer.

"Leaving without saying goodbye?" a familiar voice asked.

She stopped in the middle of the Road to Eternity and turned. Varun stood leaning against the half-constructed frame of a temple at the side of the road, arms folded, one eyebrow raised.

"Evidently not," she said. "Is this *your* temple?"

He sighed. "I really, sincerely asked them not to build it," he said. "Not really my thing. You know what they're calling me?"

"Varun the Proximate," Mara said, a sly grin quirking the corner of her mouth.

He groaned and rubbed the back of his head. "It's the *worst*. God of being near, but not quite there? I mean, come on." He let out a loud huff through his nostrils. "Thing about it is, all the people who've suddenly decided to worship me in this full-on way are doing it completely wrong. There's this one guy who lives at the Junction who almost worships me but doesn't really, and he's the most pious follower I've got."

Mara couldn't help bursting into laughter at the exasperated look on his black-and-white face.

"What?"

"You did it," she said. "You *became a god*, and all you can do is complain about it."

He snorted. "Fair point." Then he took a few steps toward her. "You know," he said, his tone suddenly sharp, eyes suddenly set, "after what you did... I thought maybe I'd just rage and seethe and curse your name and hate you and never speak to you again. Then the whole battle happened. We won it together. When I recovered, I was still thinking I'd probably go with the whole hate-you-forever thing. Almost got there too. I was close. Really close."

"But not quite?" Mara said quietly.

Varun took a deep breath, and then his features relaxed into a gentle half-smile. "Not quite," he said. "Almost though."

"You could probably condemn me to some hell or other now," Mara said. "I wouldn't hold it against you."

"I know you wouldn't," he said. "That's why I'm not gonna do it. Where'd be the satisfaction in that?" He raised his chin, indicating another building farther up the Road to Eternity. "Say hello to the Marquis for me."

She nodded, then pressed her palms together in mock prayer. "Thank you for the blessing, O Varun the Proximate."

He mimed kicking at her. "On your way," he said fondly.

"Really, though," she said. "Thank you for everything. Especially the bits I didn't deserve."

"Which was all of it," he said, though he was still grinning.

"Exactly," she said. "Thanks."

She turned away and took a few steps. When she heard a sharp intake of breath behind her, she stopped and glanced back.

A girl stood before Varun, perhaps thirteen years old.

"It's you," he said, his eyes wide with wonder.

"It's me," she said.

"I thought—they took you back...?"

"Almost managed to keep me too," she said.

Varun's face split into a smile to rival Iona's widest. "Almost, eh?"

Mara gave them their privacy and continued down the Road to Eternity.

The temple in honor of the Marquis of the Final End was a morbidly gray building that looked more like a mausoleum than a house of worship, but one in better condition than was usual: its stones were clean, its lines and angles sharp. Its door gleamed golden from within the gloom, and windows of yellow and pink shone in the walls.

Nobody was inside when Mara entered. The interior was almost gaudy compared to most spaces she'd seen since coming to the Sunless Crossing: books whose spines were every hue and shade lined the walls, and vibrant carpets streaked through the space. She took the door immediately opposite the entrance and emerged into a circular atrium; long pews ringed the space, and in the center was an empty throne. A face was etched into its back.

Mara descended the steps to the throne and kneeled before it.

"I don't know how this works," she muttered under her breath. "But ... well, I think I get it. I think your teachings and the things I believe are the same. I think I'm yours to take to whatever comes next. Or doesn't. If you'll have me."

She waited. A moment passed.

"Please," she said. "I don't have anything else now."

A low hum sounded, as if a deep old voice were echoing through the wood of the throne. And she felt it, felt the Marquis's presence asserting itself. It was impossibly ancient, and it was infinite—and yet it was not, for its boundaries were sharp, defined, inalienable. It went on forever, and it terminated cleanly, both at once.

Mara closed her eyes and let the arrival of her new god wash over her. Her bones felt warm. Something like peace, long overdue, saturated her soul.

Then it was whisked away like a scarf on the wind. Something new took its place, something questing and curious, something all-encompassing and ever-shifting.

Mara opened her eyes. A purple sheen crawled across the visage of the Marquis carved into the throne, asserted itself over the face, formed new features.

"Hello, Mara," said a new voice. Shining black eyes peered down at her from within a dark blue face, neither male nor female, smooth and symmetrical. The features were undeniably beautiful, but it seemed to Mara as if they were bizarrely altered with the slightest change in perspective—though they remained attractive, they never seemed to stay quite the same from one moment to the next.

"You're not the Marquis," she said.

"No," said the newcomer. "I'm not. But you know me. You called for me, in fact, when all seemed lost."

"I..." Mara frowned. "You're Gront's god? The one that wants to destroy the Sunless Crossing?"

"Misunderstanding," said the face, grinning widely. "I want change, yes. I want things to be *better*. Don't you think things could be better?"

"Of course, but—"

"And all I need," said the blue person who had somehow taken the place of the god that was coming to collect Mara for her eternal end, "is your help."

She blinked. "What?"

"You see, I've been taking notice of you. And I think someone with your very particular set of skills could be perfectly suited to helping me with something. A beautiful boon I've been working on, something to spread to all the living and the dead in all the worlds, to bring wonder and delight." The face tilted forward; curved horns and white teeth gleamed. "I think I'm going to call it the Scarlet Joy."

END OF BOOK ONE

BOOK CLUB QUESTIONS

1. Would you want to exist forever in an afterlife, or do you think it might be better to come to a final end?

2. Mara is willing to manipulate and deceive in order to avoid an undesirable fate. Do you think her actions—for the purpose of trying to escape being eternally bound in servitude to Raskith—can be condoned?

3. Do you think it's possible for a truly evil person to become good, given the opportunity? Or would that simply suggest they were never fully evil in the first place? ("There's no such thing as a truly evil person" may be your answer, and that's okay!)

4. What (or whom) do you think is the biggest factor in Mara's shift from manipulating people for her own gain to genuinely caring about others?

5. Do you think Gront is an immoral person who can appear polite, even charming, or a good person who sometimes

does immoral things? How does that compare to your view of Mara at the start of the book? What about at the end?

6.   If Mara—as she is at the end of the story—could go back to the moment Rekh gave her the mission to raise a god, what do you think she might do differently?

7.   Do you think the act of manipulating death through magic is inherently evil, immoral, or unnatural?

8.   As a much more typical adventuring party than most of the characters in this book, the Rainbow Rangers are some of the most earnest do-gooders Mara meets. What do you think she learns from them?

9.   Do you think Mara deserves forgiveness from Varun for being an accessory to his murder and raising his corpse?

10. Iona considers Rhúnn, who takes all feelings away and leaves people empty, just about the worst thing she can imagine. Is it worse to feel overwhelming negative emotions, or no emotions at all?

AUTHOR BIO

From England's beautiful Westcountry, Chris Durston balances a full-time day job with running around after a toddler and trying to squeeze in time to write books and music. Fortunately, his wife is ludicrously supportive.

He's spent pretty much his whole life knowing he wants to write stories, but only got around to actually doing anything about it in 2020. (Well, there was that 200,000-word novel he wrote aged 13 or so, but that was legitimately very bad.) Since then, he's had three independently published novels, a collection of articles on video games, and a dozen or so short stories included in anthologies. The kindness of strangers he met on the internet has somehow seen him become involved with Cthulhu Dreamt, a multimedia storytelling project from Fable Factory and Action Fiction, and from there to Black Ballad.

He and Reed Reimer of Fable Factory occasionally create ambient-ish music under the name Cedarstone, which you can find on most streaming platforms.

Visit chrisdurston.com to learn more.